Chapter One

Since childhood, Arden had heard the whispered tales of hidden realms beyond mortal reach, where ancient beings ruled kingdoms and bargains could buy anything. They said the fae could grant miracles, but she knew that only fools still believed in miracles anymore.

They were nothing more than bedtime stories, told to children who went to bed with hungry stomachs and worn blankets that neglected to keep them warm. She knew the reality of surviving in Hallow's Reach; there were only locked doors, empty hands, and a city that turned its back when you needed it most.

Her brother, Callen, had stood by her through every hardship life had thrown their way. They had learned how to raise each other, long before the world had turned its back on them. Arden had never given up home for a better life, even when Callen got too sick to take jobs down at the dock. She doubled down, bringing in every coin she could as she watched the sickness steal a little more of him each day.

She pushed open the door to the tavern, the scent of damp wood and cheap ale enveloping her as she stepped inside. The dim candles scattered around the room did nothing but illuminate the dirt that clung to every surface of the bar as their smoke danced in lazy ribbons above the few scattered patrons hunched over their drinks.

She looked around briefly before she spotted Luthan in the back booth, exactly as expected. He watched the room with an air of indifference, danger coiled beneath the relaxed posture of a man too confident to care. He didn't acknowledge her as she approached; he simply nudged out the opposite seat with his boot. Arden sat in the offered chair, her cloak dripping steadily onto the warped floorboards.

"This better be worth it," she muttered.

Luthan smiled but said nothing as he slid a folded scrap of paper across the table. The candlelight danced across his skin, illuminating the inked dagger that curled up his forearm menacingly.

She took the paper, eyeing it warily. "Where is everyone else tonight?"

Luthan waved at the woman behind the bar, signalling he wanted another drink. "Heist up in Aeridor, big haul coming off the docks."

"You're not with them?"

"It's a simple job, they don't need me."

Arden fiddled with the paper, nervous that he had stayed around just to ensure she wouldn't get herself into trouble. "You just wanted to keep an eye on me." She felt like a child, almost pouting under the weight of his gaze.

"Listen, we've got scores to settle here and if you don't want the money..." he trailed off, attempting to snatch the paper back from her.

She clutched it tighter, before unfolding it and holding it up to the light. She read over the words a few times, certain she must be missing something. "Dyer's Wares" her brow furrowed and she leaned in, trying not to be overheard. "That's the third time this month, shouldn't we cut the old man a little slack?"

Luthan looked at her, one brow raised in mock amusement. "He never cut you any slack." He finished off the glass in front of him, slamming it down with more force than necessary. "Funny how quickly you forget what it was like to work for someone who didn't care a bit about you. I will send you back there a hundred times if it means he pays his dues to society."

Her thumb grazed the rough edge of the paper and the pub's noise faded to a dull roar, its warmth slipping away under the weight of memories best left forgotten.

The scent of warm bread and spiced cider lingered in the air, curling through the bustling marketplace like an invitation. Arden was ten, her hands still soft, her knees scraped from climbing the old elm behind the shop, waiting for Ephraim to take out the trash.

T.S. NICOLE

THE CURSED THIEF

THE CURSED & THE CROWNED BOOK 1

To my husband, my editor, and my favorite chaotic reader—
You read every chapter, flagged every typo, and bravely dove head-first
into a realm of morally questionable fae and emotionally damaged im-
mortals, leaving the best margin notes I could ever ask for.
To everyone reading, try to figure out where he wrote these:
"No kissing the scumbag."
"Don't be a stupid b-word!!"
"Nervous sweating."
"Is it hot in here, or is it me?"
You made this story better with your insight, honesty and unshakable
support. Thank you for believing in me, even when I was spiraling.

Dyer's Wares had been a fixture in Hallow's Reach for years, a modest shop nestled between a blacksmith and a seamstress. Ephraim Dyer, its owner, was a broad-shouldered man with calloused hands and a permanent scowl, which earned him a fearsome reputation around town, especially among the children.

Each day, when Ephraim had brought out the trash, Arden was the first one to get to it. She and the other children dug through it like rats, hoping for a scrap of food to ease the hunger pangs. That day, a boy had shoved her down to get there first, she heard him holler with glee as he found a broken bottle that still contained some juice and envy consumed her as she watched him greedily drink down the last of the bottle's contents. By the time Arden had picked herself up, the bag was empty. She walked away from the torn remnants of the trash bag, her stomach growling and her brain spiralling as she tried to come up with a plan for their dinner.

A small glint caught her eye, and she stooped to uncover it from the muck. As she held it up to the light she realized Ephraim must have dropped a coin, she quickly clutched the copper to her chest knowing that if anyone found out, they would try and take it from her. She ducked around to the front of the shop and snuck inside quickly. As she stood at the counter, rolling the copper coin between her fingers, her stomach was nothing but a hollow knot as she eyed a jar of dried meat sticks.

Ephraim set a crate of goods on the counter with a heavy thud. He glanced at her sunken eyes and the single copper coin she fidgeted with. "Ain't much you can do with that. But for one copper coin, I can offer you a job."

"I can work," Arden blurted as she handed over the only money she had held in months.

Ephraim squinted at her, wiping sweat from his brow. "You're small, but you look like you can hold your own. Stock the shelves, clean the counter, and if you see anyone snooping around where they shouldn't be, tell me."

Arden nodded eagerly, reaching for a basket of dried herbs. The job wasn't much, but it was honest work. Her father had always told her and Callen that honest work reaped the biggest rewards. Hours passed in a steady rhythm of sorting things out onto shelves and cleaning the counters until they shone. She lit up under the pressure, convincing several people to buy more than they had come in for. With each extra sale, she felt her excitement grow as she calculated what Ephraim might give her at the end of the day.

As evening fell a boy, no older than fifteen, sauntered through the door, that's how she had first met Luthan.

"Hey, Dyer!" Luthan called, flashing a sharp grin. "Got any of that spiced cider left?"

Ephraim, oblivious, waved a dismissive hand. "End of the shelf on the left."

Luthan strolled past Arden, his eyes lingering on her just a moment too long. He lowered his voice to a whisper. "The shop's an easy target," he murmured. "No guards, cocky owner. You could come work for me and make enough to feed yourself properly."

Arden stiffened, "I'm not a thief," she whispered, double checking Ephraim hadn't overheard.

Luthan chuckled as his fingers danced over the glass bottles on the shelf seeming genuinely interested. "Then you're just stupid." He picked up one of the bottles and slipped it into his pocket. "Shhh" he whispered, holding a finger to his lips.

Ephraim turned to face them, "You find what you're looking for, boy?"

"Not too interested today, Dyer, but maybe next week when I get paid."

The words slipped from her lips before she could stop them. "He didn't pay for that."

Ephraim's head snapped toward her, then to Luthan. The older boy's expression shifted from confidence to anger, "You little brat."

Ephraim acted first; though he was older, he was quick. He seized Luthan's wrist with an iron grip, wrenching the stolen bottle from his pocket. "Thieving trash," he growled, shoving the boy back.

Luthan stumbled but didn't fall. He met Arden's gaze, his expression a mix of fury and disappointment. "Is this how you want to live?" he sneered. "Begging for scraps from people who don't care about you?"

He scoffed and rolled his shoulders, "you'll learn," he said as he backed toward the door. "One day, you'll have nothing left and there won't be anyone around to help you." The shop's bell jingled as he stormed out, leaving a heavy, suffocating silence in his wake.

Ephraim exhaled, loudly as the door closed and Arden wondered if he had been scared. "Those damned Silver Daggers are going to put me out of business one day," he muttered, replacing the bottle on the shelf. His gaze then flicked to Arden. "You did good, girl" he said with a rough pat on her head.

After closing up shop, Arden anxiously waited as Ephraim counted the coins brought in that day. "Maybe I should bring you on more often, 20 extra silver pieces is no small feat."

She watched as he pulled a key from his pocket and deposited them carefully into the chest he kept tucked under the counter. He turned away from her and locked the small chest before placing it back in its hiding space, offering her nothing that she helped bring in.

Her stomach growled and he plucked a stale loaf of bread from the pile of scraps that still needed to be thrown away. He held it out to her with a small smile, "Thanks for the work today."

That night she and Callen had divided the loaf in half, each slowly savoring the small relief from hunger it gave.

"I'm going back tomorrow," she promised Callen through a mouth full, "even if it means we just get scraps."

She returned the next day eager to work again. Peering around the empty shop she raised her voice a bit, hoping he could hear her. "Ephraim, it's Arden. I'm ready to work again!"

He emerged from a small door that led to his kitchen, "got any copper today?"

"Well, no, but I thought..."

"Then I ain't got a job for you." He said as he turned her away. "Scram kid and don't come back until you've got something to trade."

Not willing to let anyone see her cry, she ran to the end of the alley and sat on the ground, allowing quiet tears to roll down her face as she tried to come up with a new plan. Surely other shops might have work for her, but she didn't have any skills than might benefit them.

Darkness fell around her and she couldn't bring herself to move. She knew that Callen would be waiting at home for her to return with food and she couldn't bear the sight of his face screwed up in hunger again. Luthan and his crew had approached, cursing loudly and throwing bottles at the wall. She shrunk back into the darkness, trying to not make a sound.

"What do we have here?" she heard one of them say as the others began to chuckle.

"Go to the tavern and wait."

"Awe but Luthan we just wanted to..."

His tone changed, "I said go."

Arden heard the sound of footsteps retreating as the group left. She peeked one eye open, seeing the dagger inked on his forearm. "I warned you not to trust him" he said, no malice in his voice. "C'mon, let's get you something to eat."

Arden argued, "but...Callen..."

"We'll get him some too, don't worry." He put a comforting arm around her shoulders as they walked towards the tavern. "How old are you any-way?"

"Ten..." Arden mumbled, feeling like a child for the first time in a long time.

Luthan let out a sigh, "looks like we got our work cut out for us then."

Arden looked up at him, "what do you mean?"

"You're way too young to be going out with the others. But I'll find something for you to do, you'll never have to worry about food again."

That night Luthan had provided her with something no one else had, security. He brought her back to the tavern and introduced her to his crew. Through the years, Luthan had taught her how to pick locks and protect herself against people much bigger than herself. She picked up odd jobs around town and Callen had started working at the docks, both of them reporting back to Luthan what they thought could be useful information.

The memory faded, replaced by the low murmur of voices and the clink of tankards in the dim tavern. Arden turned the paper over and over absentmindedly, her thumb smoothing the crease until the ink threatened to smudge. The edges were damp now, either from rain or sweat, she wasn't sure.

She looked up. "Fine. I'll take the mark."

"Knew you would."

She paused, gathering courage, "I want a larger cut this time."

He raised an eyebrow in surprise, "Oh? What for?"

"I need to hire an alchemist from Aeridor." Her voice tightened. "Callen's getting worse each day."

Luthan scoffed, leaning back with his usual nonchalant arrogance. "You'd have better luck finding the fae than getting those royal snobs to help you."

Her eyes narrowed. "What's that supposed to mean?"

He waved a hand, already regretting his words. "Nothing..." he sighed. "Just the liquor talking. Forget I said anything."

She remained still, her gaze unwavering, "I have to try...I can't lose him."

Luthan's gaze dropped to the table, "I know, listen, you can keep whatever coin you find. All of it this time, just don't get caught."

Arden stared at him in disbelief but unwilling to push him any further she grabbed the paper and fled quickly, before he could change his mind. He shouted after her, "While you're there why don't you grab me some of that spiced cider, we both know Ephraim's got the good stuff."

The tavern door slammed behind her, the noise from within swallowed by the howl of the wind and the pounding of rain. Her breath came in short pants as his words sunk in, *"all of it."* The storm was relentless and water seeped through the seams of Arden's cloak, clinging to her skin. It soaked her hair, trickled down the bridge of her nose, and turned the dirt beneath her boots into thick, sucking mud. Each step towards the shop felt heavier, as if the city itself were trying to drag her down.

Arden maneuvered through the alley, the wet stones slick beneath her boots that were now caked with mud. She could swear she felt every unseen gaze lurking behind the slatted shutters waiting for her to make a mistake. She re-read the paper, Luthan's handwriting smearing as rain soaked it. The instructions were clear, leaving no room for her to mess up, "Door unlocked. Get in, get out."

The door yielded with a soft click beneath her touch and she exhaled quietly. Luthan had been right, again. Ephraim might have counted every coin in and out of his shop, but he hadn't changed his rusty locks in years and even when he used his key it barely latched.

Rain poured in behind her as she slipped inside, the scent of old dust and dried herbs thick in the air. The shop was dim and cramped with shelves crammed full of jars, tools, and crates of things that had yet to be put away. From behind the curtain she could hear the soft snoring of

Ephraim sleeping. She didn't hesitate, her steps were silent and practiced as she avoided creaky floorboards that might reveal her presence. She crouched low, digging beneath the counter until her fingers found the chest she knew was hidden within.

She tucked the chest into her satchel and made her way over to the shelf where she knew Luthan's favorite spiced cider sat. She grabbed a few bottles before retracing her steps to the door. The chest shifted in her satchel, the coins within clinking together and breaking the silence in the shop. Ephraim's snoring stopped and Arden held her breath as she took the remaining steps towards the door, slipping back into the dark.

She lingered outside the shop for a moment, allowing her racing heart to calm. No one called out and no alarms sounded. She ran down the alley, not stopping until she was safely away from the shop. She ducked beneath the overhang of a slanted gutter, shielding herself from the worst of the downpour. Her hands trembled as she withdrew the chest. She removed the small lockpick set Luthan had gifted her and worked by instinct, muscle memory guiding her through the worn grooves.

A gentle jiggle, a twist, and...*Click.*

The lock snapped open and Arden opened the lid. Silver coins lined the interior, not a fortune, but it would hopefully be enough to convince an alchemist to help her. She scanned the narrow street, her body tense. Hallow's Reach dealt swiftly and mercilessly with thieves. Everyone was paranoid and everyone was always watching. With no one in view, she poured the coins into her satchel and discarded the empty chest in a nearby trash pile. With any luck, no one would notice it the next day and even if they did, they wouldn't be able to tie it to her.

The wind howled through the streets, sharp and wild, slicing through her cloak like a knife. Arden pressed on, weaving between crates and puddles, her path instinctive. These alleys were where she had grown up, scraped her knees, bloodied her knuckles, and learned the harsh realities of survival in a city that offered no second chances.

Yet something in the air tugged at her gut. She glanced back, expecting someone to be following her, but nothing was there. Just the pale flicker of a distant lantern swaying in the wind. Still, the unease pressed close, heavy against her spine. Pulling her hood up, she quickened her pace, allowing the noise from the storm to swallow her footsteps.

Her fingers tightened around her satchel as her hovel came into view, a leaning shack wedged between two larger buildings. The door creaked as she pushed it open, revealing a dim interior lit by a sputtering candle. Callen lay on the cot in the corner, his face pale and slick with sweat.

"I'm back," Arden whispered, kneeling beside him. She brushed a damp strand of hair from his forehead. "I got the coins and we'll go to the alchemist in the morning."

She kissed his forehead and Callen's eyes fluttered open, their usual vibrant green dulled by fever. "You shouldn't have gone out," he mumbled. "It's not safe."

"Since when has anything in this city been safe?" Arden forced a smile. "Don't worry about me. Just rest."

Chapter Two

As the night dragged on, the storm raged over the rooftops and alleys, water pouring off sagging eaves. The city lay beneath its weight, the streets drowning in rivulets of filthy rainwater. In the darkness, Aezraen lurked, following the thief until she entered her home.

He was known to the mortals of this realm as only a myth, a whispered warning to children who misbehaved. The monster that hid in children's closets and the one who stole mortals away in the dead of night. But tonight, he found himself standing motionless by the shattered window of a decrepit hovel, his breath condensing into silver mist against the grimy glass. The wind lashed his dark cloak, spattering droplets of rain across his polished boots, now streaked with mud from the mortal streets.

His attention was fixed on the young woman kneeling beside her brother. For weeks he had followed Arden, studying her reactions, her resilience and her breaking points. Each night she descended further into desperation as her brother wasted away.

The taste of her fear and determination mingled in the air like fine wine, almost intoxicating him with its potency. The boy, Callen, shivered beneath threadbare blankets. His skin was damp with fever, his breaths shallow; the sickness clung to him, a hungry thing leeching life from his frame. No mortal medicine would be enough to save him, a fact that Arden had yet to acknowledge.

The cough had started a week ago, no more than a chill picked up from the market's damp air. Arden had worked harder, picked up more jobs from that scumbag she called Luthan, and bartered for remedies that did little but delay the inevitable. Aezraen knew that the mortals had yet to find a cure for Mireblight, a wasting fever that came without warning and left no survivors.

What mortals didn't know was that Mireblight, as they called it, was a curse woven from the depths of fae magic, a sickness that pooled in the lungs like stagnant water, drowning its victims from within. Aezraen didn't make a habit of interfering in mortal lives, but something about Arden had called to him from across the realms. He hoped that his instincts were right and that she would accept his deal without a fight.

He stepped away from the window, shadows shifting around him like living things. The lock on her door surrendered to his shadow magic with a loud snap as the door swung inward on rusty hinges. Arden's head snapped up and her eyes scanned the dim space for the intruder. The floorboard beneath his boot gave a telltale creak, alerting her to his location. She moved quickly; in one practiced motion she snatched the dagger at her hip and positioned herself between the stranger and her brother's cot.

"One more step and you'll find this blade between your ribs," she hissed into the darkness. Despite the exhaustion that plagued her features and the slight tremor in her legs, her hands remained incredibly steady, the blade shimmering in the candlelight.

Aezraen tilted his head slightly, intrigued. "Do not fear, little thief," he said smoothly. "I come bearing an offer."

Arden remained still, her grip tightening around the dagger at her side, its hilt slick with her trembling hand. "Do you have a death wish?" she demanded, forcing the words past the knot forming in her throat as she lifted her dagger.

He chuckled, a low, melodic sound that sent a chill racing up her spine. "Maybe." He stepped closer, his silhouette blurring with the shadows that curled around him like smoke. "Names have power in my realm, Arden." His voice was dark and smooth, a dangerous concoction, "I believe the mortals of this realm call me the Fae Lord. The Lord of Shadows, if you prefer something a bit more dramatic."

Arden stared at him, her breath catching in her chest as she processed his words. "*Fae?* You expect me to believe that?"

"Believe?" He smiled faintly. "No. But I promise, you will." He stepped into the candlelight, allowing her to see the shadows curling around him like serpents.

"What," she spat, taking a cautious step back towards Callen, "could you possibly think I want from you?"

"Ah," he replied, eyes glinting with amusement, "not want, little thief. *Need.*"

She shook her head, attempting to laugh, but the sound came out hollow. "The fae aren't real. They're just stories told to children. Lies made up to keep us from wandering too far from home."

"And yet here I am," he said, willing his shadows to creep closer to her.

She opened her mouth to argue but the way the shadows crept across her floor froze the words on her tongue.

"I know about your brother's sickness."

Her voice was sharper now, edged with panic. "Most people in town do."

A silence enveloped them, broken only by the sound of rain dripping from the leaking roof. "Only magic can cure what he has, just as magic is the cause of his sickness."

"You're insane," she whispered.

"I don't expect much from you, little thief. But I do expect you to be respectful and listen," he said, his voice suddenly sharp. "Because no one else is coming. And if you want him to live, you'll have to decide which is more dangerous. Trusting me or watching your brother waste away and die."

His lips twitched, a ghost of a smile visible for only a second. His gaze wandered to the satchel she had set on the table. "The coins you stole tonight are pitiful, really. The alchemist will fail you, as everyone always has."

She stiffened, "how do you..."

Aezraen raised a languid hand as the stolen coins lifted from the table, floating toward him as though carried by an unseen wind. It settled in his palm, his expression unreadable, "so little," he murmured. "Yet you risked so much to take it." With a flick of his fingers, the money vanished into shadow.

"I had no choice."

Aezraen tilted his head, considering her. "No choice," he repeated softly, as though tasting the words. "You mortals do love that excuse."

"Every hundred years, I choose one mortal. One wish. One chance to claim what they want most." His voice dropped lower, a whisper against the storm outside. "But only the strongest of wills can survive the cost." He stepped closer, shadows curling at his feet, "And you, little thief...you are stronger than most. I should know, I've been watching you for weeks."

Arden's pulse pounded in her ears; the room shrank, the walls pressing inward, stretching, warping, as if the very air had turned against her.

He closed the remaining distance, deliberately pressing his chest against the point of her dagger until a thin trickle of dark liquid seeped into the fabric of his shirt. "I wonder, little thief, what is worth the price of your soul..." His eyes flicked to the boy on the cot, then back to her face, studying her reaction. He leaned down, his mouth brushing against her ear as he whispered, "...and will you still want this life back when I'm done with you?"

She had always survived by instinct, trusting her gut to tell her when to run, when to fight, when to risk everything. In this moment, every fiber of her being screamed at her to flee but something within refused to let her move. "What's the price?" she whispered.

His smile deepened, dark amusement flickering in his eyes. "You, of course."

Her gaze fell and her dagger sagged, falling to the ground. It wasn't the answer that surprised her, but how easily he had spoken it, as though it was the most natural thing in the world. As if her life had already been bartered away, and she was the only one foolish enough to think she still had a choice. Arden forced herself to meet his gaze. "You want my life?"

"No," he corrected smoothly, "I want your service." His voice was unyielding in its weight. "Ten years, bound to me, living in my court and doing my bidding."

Ten years. Her stomach twisted as she glanced at Callen curled beneath the thin blanket, face pale, drenched in sweat, breath shallow and fragile. The fever had stolen the last of his strength, reducing him to trembling bones and fading light. Arden squeezed her eyes shut, trying to will him away. But when she opened her eyes, the man was still watching her, his expression unreadable, his shadow woven into the very air she breathed. "Why me?"

For the first time, something flickered across his face. Something almost thoughtful. "Because I only choose the best."

The weight of those words settled over her like a heavy cloak. She swallowed hard. "And if I say no? Will you kill me?"

"You won't say no."

Arden hated that he was right; if she refused, Callen would likely die. Another nameless boy lost to the mercilessness of the world...and she would be alone the way she had always feared.

Aezraen stepped back, away from her blade and extended his hand, "Well, Arden? Do we have a deal?"

Her name on his lips left a sour taste on her tongue. She hesitated, everything about this felt like a mistake and for a long moment, she did not move. "You'll cure him?" she asked, voice trembling. "He'll be okay?"

"You have my word."

She spared Callen one last glance before reaching out with a shaking hand. Her fingers brushed his palm and his grip closed around hers like a vice. The room shuddered around her, the candle guttered out, plunging her into a sea of writhing shadow. The last thing she saw before the world was swallowed whole was his back as he approached Callen's bed and Arden screamed out against the shadows that covered her brother's body.

Chapter Three

The darkness enveloped her, thick and heavy, like walking through velvet. It pressed against her with an unnatural softness, as though the shadows themselves wished to devour her gently. She had expected cold or pain; instead, the void seemed to welcome her.

Time stretched and unraveled; she couldn't tell if seconds or hours passed as she drifted in the darkness. Direction was meaningless; her body seemed to float and sink within the same breath. Nothing made sense and Arden began to wonder if she was even still alive.

Just as unease began to claw up her spine the darkness around her thinned, parting like silk. She stumbled forward onto solid ground and took in her new surroundings. Her heart pounded against her ribs, panic rising like the tides threatening to consume her. Her pulse roared in her ears and she squeezed her eyes shut, swallowing against the bile rising in her throat.

A voice, smooth and commanding, shattered the silence. "You're in my realm now." The darkness around her shifted, dense shadows melting away as the Fae Lord stepped forward. "Welcome to the Court of Shadows."

Arden pushed down the fear inside her, allowing it to give way to anger. She blinked back hot tears as he held a hand out to help her up. He had taken her from her world, from Callen, from everything she had ever known and now he stood before her, smirking, as if he had done her a favor.

She ignored his hand and stood, "what do you mean 'your realm'" she asked, her voice raw and edged with suspicion.

"Elessian, my realm, where all fae reside." He spoke to her as if everything he said should have been obvious, as though the truths of the fae were common knowledge and she was simply too naive to see them.

Arden's thoughts spun, how much of the childhood stories she had dismissed as nonsense were actually real? A thousand questions pressed against her lips, but the look on his face told her he wasn't in the mood to answer any of them. Frustration and unease warred within her as she forced herself to follow him down the corridor, each step feeling heavier than the last.

The hallway opened into an immense throne room, and Arden stopped short. It was opulent, not in the extravagant manner of kings and queens, but in a way that felt ancient and sacred. Tall pillars stretched toward a ceiling lost to darkness. Silken banners hung from the walls, shifting as if caught in some unseen breeze. At the center of it all stood a throne carved from dark stone, lined with glowing veins that pulsed with magic.

Arden turned to the Fae Lord, who was already watching her with an unreadable expression. He stepped closer, his presence pressing against her skin like an intrusion. "This place... this power..." he said, his voice dropping to a softer, more dangerous tone, "...you belong to it now."

"I belong to nothing," she shot back, spitting the words, stray droplets landing on the Fae Lord's cheek.

He wiped his cheek with the back of his hand and chuckled, low and indulgent. "You made a bargain, little thief... and I fully intend to see it honored." The Fae Lord moved deeper into the chamber, his steps soundless against the stone floor. "Come," he commanded, not looking back to see if she followed.

Her pulse pounded in her throat, each second in this place felt like punishment waited just around the corner. Arden hesitated. "How do I know you actually healed him?"

"You don't."

The words sliced through her like a knife, leaving her feeling foolish for trusting someone she barely knew.

"The only way this works is if you trust me. Do you trust me, little thief?"

Arden shook her head. "No," she admitted. "I don't know anything about any of this. When I was younger, Luthan told us stories about how the fae could grant miracles, but I never listened closely to his stories. I thought they were childish nonsense."

His expression twisted in disgust. "Luthan..." He rolled the name around as if it were bitter on his tongue. "That name means 'guardian of the sun' in the ancient tongue. How ill-fitting for the mortal garbage who preys on the innocent and steals from the weak."

"That's not fair, he..."

"You'll need to learn to trust me, little thief. Otherwise, this is going to be a long ten years."

Arden's face fell as she realized he didn't care about anything she had to say. She was here to serve, nothing else.

"Now, let's continue with the tour," he said, his tone leaving no room for argument.

She hesitated only slightly before trailing behind him, careful to maintain her distance as they ventured closer to the darkness that rimmed the room. The air changed as they approached, it was heavier and more resistant, as if they were pushing upstream rather than walking through an empty space. Ahead of her, the Fae Lord stopped; his hand rose, fingers splayed as he pressed against an invisible barrier. The darkness surrounding the room trembled and vanished revealing windows that lined the space.

Light from a setting sun filtered into the space, illuminating an ancient statue. She stared, unable to move. The figure, carved from obsidian, stood draped in flowing robes, its face hidden beneath the delicate fall of a sculpted veil. In one hand, it held a crescent moon, carved from a stone so white it seemed to glow, the other hand was outstretched, palm open, as if waiting to receive something.

"She's beautiful," Arden whispered, hesitant to break the silence that had fallen over the chamber.

The Fae Lord's gaze flicked toward her, curiosity piquing his features. "Do you recognize her?"

Arden frowned, stepping closer. "Should I?"

Something like disbelief flickered across his face. He studied her for a moment longer before exhaling. "Nythis," he said, his voice low, reverent.

"Goddess of Shadows and Secrets, the unseen, the unknown. Patron of spies, thieves, assassins, those who walk between truth and deception."

"Nythis," Arden let the name settle on her tongue.

"She governs illusions, whispers in the dark, and truths buried by time," he continued. "And she is the one who shaped this court."

Arden's brow furrowed. "Shaped?"

He watched her, something unreadable flickering in his gaze. "I thought all mortals knew of our world. That our legends were passed down, whispered across generations."

Arden crossed her arms, tilting her head. "Like I said, I was too busy trying to survive to worry about bedtime tales of fae Gods I didn't worship" she said, her voice dry.

He laughed softly, shaking his head. "I suppose that's fair." He stepped away from the statue, motioning for her to follow.

At some silent command, servants entered, setting a table on a balcony overlooking the city. Arden hesitated, she wanted answers, but the more she learned, the more tangled she became in something she wasn't sure she wanted to understand.

The Court of Shadows stretched out beneath them, its winding streets bustling under the last light of dusk. It was all strangely normal; merchants packed up their stalls and cloaked figures haggled over goods. For a place of darkness, it pulsed with life.

Arden lowered herself into a seat as a steaming mug of brew was placed before her. She inhaled, the scent reminding her of home and the bitter drinks Luthan used to buy her before missions.

"We don't have cream or sugar here," the Fae Lord mused, watching her reaction. "Hope you like it dark."

She took a tentative sip. It was more bitter than what they had back home and the intensity overwhelmed her but she forced herself to swallow it down, grateful for the heat it provided.

"Elessian wasn't always like this," he said, gesturing to the world beyond them. "It was shaped by the seven Gods. Together, they created Elydris, the First Fae King, who ruled above all the courts. The Gods molded him from their own power, meant to be the perfect king. Centuries later, when Elydris begged the Gods for a child, the courts were separated and the Archfey ruled over them."

Arden blinked. "Did the Gods handpick all the rulers of this realm?"

"No, little thief, they each designed one ruler to be worthy of the powers given to them by the Gods. They were molded by the Gods as Elydris once was."

"And you were one of them?"

His smile faltered, "Nythis actually created Aeshyra." His gaze drifted back to the statue, "she was meant to rule this court," he continued. "She was cunning, elusive, powerful, everything Nythis could have wanted in a ruler."

"Where is she?" Arden asked, narrowing her eyes.

"Dead." His jaw tightened slightly, but his voice remained steady. "When Elydris disappeared and the Caretaker took over Aeshyra was one of the Archfey who dared to stand against her. None of them survived."

A shiver crawled down Arden's spine. "And how did you come to rule?"

He chuckled, low and dark as he swirled the drink in his cup. "Right place, right time, I suppose."

A loud rumbling noise interrupted their conversation as white smoke drifted across the balcony from the throne room. Something within seemed to call to Arden, urging her to brush past the Fae Lord. His face went pale as he grabbed her shoulders, trying desperately to pull her out of her trance. She stood before the statue of the goddess, her eyes glazed over as the statue's veiled face shifted from stone to something ancient and watching.

A voice, smooth and deliberate, curled through the chamber. "He speaks my story so carelessly, as if he were there." Darkness peeled away as the statue transformed into a figure wreathed in living shadow, her eyes gleaming like distant stars. Nythis stood before them, the moon she had been holding was now imprinted upon her skin in black and gold ink, interwoven with vines of stars that crept up her arm.

Her attention focused on Arden, "so," the goddess murmured, a slow, knowing smile curving her lips. "He finally found you."

The Fae Lord tensed, but Nythis did not look away from Arden, nor did she offer him any explanation. "I cannot change fate" she said, her voice weaving through the shadows like silk. "But the prophecy speaks of you, of what you might become...if you survive."

Arden's heart pounded against her ribs so loudly she was sure the goddess could hear. She opened her mouth, a thousand questions trying to claw their way free but she could not get the words to break free.

"I cannot answer what you wish to know but we have waited a long time to bring you home. The others thought you were lost, but I never stopped sending him to find you."

Before Arden could process her words, the goddess was gone, transformed once more from flesh into stone. The silence stretched through the room, heavy and unrelenting. Arden's mind reeled from Nythis' words, the weight of them pressed into her chest, foreign and unwelcome.

Arden swallowed hard, forcing the words past the knot in her throat. "What did she mean? When she said she never stopped sending you to find me?"

"I don't actually know. I have heard that the other Archfey could convene with the Gods of their courts but Nythis..." He studied Arden for a long moment, his eyes unreadable. "...she didn't make me. I figured that was why she never spoke to me."

Memories of her life with Callen flashed through her mind, how things had always been hard for them. The goddess had called Elessian her 'home' but before today she had never stepped foot in this place. Arden wiped away the tears that had escaped, "she must have confused me with someone else."

"I'd be careful, little thief. The Gods rarely take an interest in mortals unless they mean to use them."

The Fae Lord sighed, rising to his feet. He extended a hand toward her; it was a kind gesture, one she hadn't expected. He guided her across the room to a door previously obscured by shadows, a servant stood there waiting to open it. The Fae Lord leaned in, his breath warm against her ear as the door began to open, nothing but darkness ahead of them. "For what it's worth, little thief, I hope you survive too."

Unseen hands shoved her forward, into the darkness of the room, and the fear that Arden had thought was gone crept back in. As the doors slammed shut, leaving her in near darkness only one thought repeated in her mind, this world was about to tear her apart.

Chapter Four

Arden blinked against the dim light, her vision slow to adjust as her heartbeat thundered in her ears. Panic crawled beneath her skin, each breath ragged as she surveyed the unfamiliar stone walls and flickering torchlight. She didn't understand; he had seemed almost kind, his voice low and his touch careful. Then the door had slammed shut behind her, leaving her alone with his final words echoing in her mind: *"For what it's worth, little thief, I hope you survive too."*

When her eyes fully adjusted, she noticed three people standing at the far end of the room, huddled together like a pack assessing an intruder. Their gazes locked onto her but they didn't speak or move. They only watched.

The Fae Lord's voice sliced through the silence like a blade wrapped in silk. "Oh, don't look so lost, little thief." He materialized from the shadows, leaning against the nearest column, his eyes gleaming with amusement. With infuriating laziness, he gestured toward the group. "You see, you're not the first to crawl into my service."

Arden's jaw clenched, *crawl,* the way he said it made her skin prickle with heat. She forced her shoulders back and lifted her chin. "I didn't crawl anywhere."

His chuckle was low and indulgent as he crossed the room, stepping forward with the easy grace of someone who owned the space around him. Every movement was deliberate and controlled. "No? Then tell me, what would you call it?" He tilted his head, mocking her, pretending to ponder. Her fingers twitched, aching for a weapon she didn't have.

"You should be grateful, really." He sighed, as if this conversation bored him already. "Go on, introduce yourself. Let them see the newest stray to land in my collection."

The three figures remained silent and unmoving. They didn't meet her gaze or acknowledge his taunt, but their stillness sent a chill down her spine. They were afraid of him, she could sense it in the way they watched his every movement. Arden clenched her fists, forcing herself to meet his gaze, but the satisfaction in his eyes was unbearable. He enjoyed watching them squirm, relishing the weight of their choices settling like chains around their shoulders.

The Fae Lord shook his head and waved a hand, dismissing them without a second glance. "Fine, sit in silence, but the games will begin shortly now that the final player has arrived."

As he left the room, the door slammed behind him. The four of them stood in the dim light, their faces lined with wariness and exhaustion; he had left them to face whatever came next. Arden took a slow breath, her eyes flicking between the others who now shared her fate. She had been sizing them up since the moment they were abandoned here, and despite her exhaustion, she forced herself to remain sharp. In every mission she had completed for Luthan, information was everything, but right now the Fae Lord held all of it close to his chest.

The broad-shouldered man, Elias, spoke first, breaking the silence. His voice was steady, carrying the weight of someone who had lived too many lives in too short a time. "Might as well get acquainted," he said, offering a nod. "We'll be stuck together for the next decade..." He shrugged. "...or until one of us dies." His smirk was grim, but something flickered behind his eyes.

Arden watched him for a moment before stepping forward and reaching for his outstretched hand. His grip was strong and calloused, as if he had spent his whole life fighting.

"Arden," she said simply.

He nodded. "Elias." He leaned against the nearest wall, arms crossed, as if settling in for a long wait. "So? What did you ask for?"

Arden bit her tongue, reminding herself that anything she said could come back to haunt her. "Nothing worth sharing."

Elias studied her, then shrugged. "Fair enough." He ran a hand through his dark, unkempt hair, his expression unreadable. "I'm here for my daughters. Back home, we don't treat money the way you probably do. You're born into your class, and that's where you stay. Merchants, farmers..." He took a shaky breath. "...and slayers like me."

Arden frowned. "Slayers?"

Elias let out a small, humorless chuckle. "Beasts. Monsters. They carry the only currency that slayers can earn. Kill enough of them, and you can buy a loaf of bread or maybe a week's worth of supplies. Farmers and merchants don't accept charity. There's no bartering allowed." He sighed. "It's a system that keeps men like me hungry and always fighting."

Arden swallowed. She had lived as a thief, a liar, a girl who scraped by on stolen coins, but she had never been forced to spill blood just to eat. The idea of him being dragged into battle over and over again just to keep his family alive filled her with sadness. "Your daughters," she said, her voice softer than intended. "They're lucky to have you."

Elias glanced at her, something flickering in his gaze, an acknowledgment, a silent understanding. "Yeah," he muttered, rubbing the back of his neck. "And I'd like to get back to them in one piece. So, let's hope this fae bastard keeps his end of the deal."

From the corner of the room, the girl, Nia, scoffed. "If he doesn't, I'll tear him apart myself."

Arden turned to her. Nia was striking and poised, her chin tilted upward with the effortless grace that comes from years of privilege. Faint remnants of gold embroidery decorated the tattered sleeves of her dress. Though she had clearly been traveling, she carried herself as if she were still wearing a crown.

"And you are?"

Nia gave a slow, lazy smile, as if the whole situation amused her. "Nia," she said. "Former princess, soon-to-be free woman."

Arden raised an eyebrow. "Former?"

Nia made a show of dusting off her skirts, as if standing in a prison of shadows was beneath her. "Oh, my family is still ruling. Unfortunately." She sighed dramatically, her dark eyes flicking toward the shifting walls of the chamber. "But I am done playing the part. I was raised to be a perfect queen; silent when necessary, obedient, nothing but a symbol to be paraded before suitors." She rolled her shoulders back. "So, I struck a bargain. I wanted freedom, and now, here I am."

Arden studied her, wary. This girl was entitled, spoiled, and blind to the reality of what she had done. Freedom was something people fought for and suffered for; it was not likely to be given freely in the Fae Lord's domain.

"And you think this is freedom?" Arden asked.

Nia smiled, sharp as a dagger. "Not yet. But when my decade is up, I'll walk out of here a free woman."

A soft cough drew their attention. The final boy in the group, Tobin, had been silent until now. He stood slightly apart from them, hands fidgeting and eyes darting between them. Arden could tell he was younger than the rest.

He pushed his glasses up the bridge of his nose. "I'm here for history."

Arden's brows furrowed, but before she could ask, Nia's mocking voice interrupted. "What does that even mean?"

Tobin nodded quickly, as if eager to share his ambitions, unaware of Nia's contempt. "I'm a scribe. A scholar. The fae realm has been a mystery in my world for centuries. No one has ever been allowed to document it properly." His hands twitched at his sides, "the Fae Lord promised me that if I survive, I will be the first to record everything. The first to write it all down. The first to truly understand this world."

Arden didn't know whether to admire his determination or call him an idiot. Yet something in his stance, the way he stood despite trembling limbs, reminded her too much of Callen. She turned away before the ache in her chest grew too sharp. As the conversation continued, Elias spoke of his family, Nia reveled in her rebellion, and Tobin dreamed of the pages he would write, but Arden kept her secrets close.

"I was told that he only chose one mortal, one wish," Arden began. "Were you all told the same?"

The others nodded in agreement.

"Then why are four of us here?" Arden pressed.

"I assumed it was just a technicality since we come from different realms," Tobin replied.

"I don't think so. I believe he meant that only one of us would receive what we asked for," Arden continued.

"If that's true, then how does he decide?" Nia asked.

The Fae Lord stepped from the darkness and the temperature in the room plummeted. He smirked. "Well, well," he mused, his voice like silk wrapping around a blade. "What a delightful line of questioning."

Elias cursed under his breath, but Arden just clenched her jaw, her eyes burning with fury. "Thank you all," he continued smoothly, folding his arms across his chest, "for coming to my favorite part of this whole day."

He let his magic loose and allowed the room to shift, the stone walls melting away to reveal what had been obscured in the darkness. The air hummed with the ancient magic of bargains, suffering, and inevitability. It had a weight that pressed into bones, filling lungs with something thick and suffocating. "Arden is right, I did say *one* mortal, *one* wish."

Doors appeared, each one vastly different than the last, an echo of the soul it called to. The Fae Lord said nothing, letting the weight of reality settle over the mortals. These doors were personal, intimate, and cruel, and he saw the slight widening of their eyes, the way their shoulders tensed, how their breath quickened. The doors did not simply exist; they called to each of them, a trial waiting to be completed.

Elias's door stood tall and unyielding, carved from ancient wood blackened with scorch marks. A sword embedded in its surface pulsed with a dull red glow, as if still smoldering from battle. The scent of blood and dirt curled from the frame, a phantom of past wars and nights spent burying the fallen. A warrior's door for a soldier's regret.

Nia's door was gilded, its surface reflecting not the princess standing before it, but a warped, distorted version of herself. This reflection showed Nia with her face twisted, stretched, and blurred into something grotesque. A heavy crown rested upon the head of this false image, digging into her scalp, its gold flaking off and its jewels melting. She flinched at the sight of herself trapped as the queen, never truly free.

Tobin's door was not solid at all. It oozed like ink spilling into water, with desperate, writhing script scrawled across its frame. Whispers leaked through the cracks, ancient voices speaking languages long since lost. He trembled as he reached for it, his hands twitching as if he longed to copy down the words even as they slipped away from sight.

Then there was Arden. Aezraen knew he should not have been watching her more closely than the others, but he found it impossible to avoid.

Her door was neither the grandest nor the most intricate, yet it seemed to fit her perfectly. It was simple, a worn wooden frame barely standing upright, its surface slightly damaged from use.

Unlike the others, the door did not force its will upon her; it waited for Arden to reach for it first. For the first time since arriving, something close to uncertainty flickered across her face. She reached out, her fingertips ghosted over the handle that was engraved with the same moon she had seen on the statue in the throne room.

"The four of you will enter your trials, and only one of you will make it out," the Fae Lord explained. "If you fail, your bargain is severed; make it out, and your reward will be solidified in stone."

The four of them exchanged glances, sizing each other up. Arden watched as Elias confidently threw open his door and stepped inside, not waiting for permission. Nia followed, leaping across the threshold and into the unknown. Tobin just stood there before glancing at Arden. His expression, so like her brother's, seemed to ask who would go next. After a brief hesitation, she pushed the door open and stepped past the rippling magic within, ready to face whatever lay ahead.

Chapter Five

The shadows didn't merely envelop Arden this time; they seized her. Darkness crashed over her like a violent, cold wave, forcing itself into her lungs until she gasped for breath. Her body spun and twisted through nothingness, leaving her disoriented and lost.

Unlike before, there was no gentle passage or velvet caress. This was an experience of being torn apart and hastily reassembled, her consciousness stretched thin across the void. A silent scream lodged in her throat as vertigo overwhelmed her.

Then, without warning, the shadows convulsed and expelled her. Arden tumbled forward, the impact jolting up her arms, pain shooting through her scraped palms.

The air in this new place felt different. It was sharp and damp, carrying the faint tang of rust. Each desperate breath scraped against her throat, a reminder that she was not welcome here.

She shifted, attempting to rise, but her fingers brushed the slick earth, warmth clinging to her skin. A shiver of unease crawled up her spine. She lifted her hand, straining to see through the dim light. The realization hit her like a blow; it wasn't rust she smelled it was blood. Swallowing back nausea, she forced herself to focus. The cavern stretched around her, jagged stalactites hanging like fangs from the ceiling.

A whisper of movement echoed behind her. She whirled, fists raised. Shadows bled away from the corner of the cavern, shifting like spilled ink. From them emerged a figure, grotesquely elongated, its limbs unnaturally long, fingers tapering to blackened claws. Sickly green eyes gleamed in the darkness, bright and all-knowing.

A slow grin spread across its face, revealing rows of jagged teeth. Fresh blood glistened between them, still wet and crimson against their yellowed surface. "Another thief," it rasped, its voice crawling up her spine. "The Fae Lord sends so many here. Few get the chance to escape."

The creature's unnaturally long tongue slid across its bloodied teeth in a leisurely gesture of satisfaction. As it shifted its weight, the shadows behind it parted just enough for Arden to glimpse what lay beyond and her breath caught in her throat.

In the dim blue glow of the crystals, she could make out a crumpled form huddled against the cavern wall. A bloody heap of torn clothing, mangled limbs, and exposed bone. What she could only imagine had once been a person. Bile rose in her throat as the realization hit her. This wasn't merely a test; it was a feeding ground.

Arden fixed her gaze on the creature in front of her, forcing her voice to remain steady. "What are you?"

"The Keeper of Trials."

She took a measured step back. "What kind of trials?"

The Keeper's grin widened. *"Yours."* With a languid gesture, it summoned a silver dagger at her feet.

Arden stared at the weapon. Its gleaming edge caught the dim light, a cruel reminder of her life among the Silver Daggers. They had taught her to move unseen, to strike first, and to take what she needed without remorse. She had loathed how they glorified crime, dressing desperation as an art. But what choice had she ever had? It was the only way to survive, the only way to keep Callen fed and warm during the winters.

"You took what was not yours," the Keeper murmured, circling her with unnerving fluidity. *"Slipping through shadows. Stealing from your fellow mortals. Let's see if you can survive your sins."*

Arden's pulse thundered in her ears, leaving her no chance to respond. A twisting force surged through the cavern, and suddenly, he was gone. The crystals around her dimmed, their faint glow swallowed by the oppressive darkness.

A whisper brushed against her ear. *"Find the key."* She spun around, but no one was there. *"Take the key."* The Keeper's voice echoed from every direction. *"Escape the labyrinth."* A low, bone-deep chuckle followed. *"Before your shadows catch you."*

A gust of wind swept through the corridor, carrying the sound of something moving in the dark. Arden's breath fogged in front of her.

She turned in a slow circle. The cavern was no longer a single chamber; narrow passageways branched off in all directions, their walls slick and glistening. Each path twisted endlessly, hungry for her. A flicker of movement caught her eye and without waiting to see what it was, she ran.

But the labyrinth deceived her. Passages looped back to where she had started, walls that seemed solid led her in circles, and corridors appeared to shift, though they remained fixed. She thought she was making progress, but she found herself trapped, facing dead end after dead end.

Arden heard a scuttling noise behind her, claws whispering against the stone. She turned a corner, her heart pounding, and froze. A figure loomed ahead in the corridor. The torchlight cast a jagged shadow on the wall, but she didn't need to see his face. The shape alone made her knees buckle, and her breath caught in her throat.

"Callen?"

Her brother's frail frame hovered just beyond the light, his arms limp and head bowed. A whisper of denial curled in her throat, but she forced his name out again. "Callen!" Her voice cracked with desperation as she took a step forward.

His head snapped up.

Her stomach clenched. His eyes were wrong, hollow pits of darkness where vibrant green had once been. His mouth stretched impossibly wide, skin pulled taut over a too-thin face, but no sound came from his lips.

He lunged.

Arden stumbled back, yanking her dagger free and holding it out as a warning. Shadows wrapped around him, living tendrils pulling him forward. This isn't real, she told herself. Just twisted fae magic; a nightmare born from her deepest fears.

She turned and ran.

The corridors twisted around her, shifting and warping. Every turn led her somewhere new, yet somehow back to him. Her breath echoed against the walls, ragged and frantic.

This time, when she rounded the bend, Callen appeared as a six-year-old. He stood trembling in the flickering light, dirt and tears streaking his face. His small fists were curled against his chest. "Arden," he whimpered. "You have to bring Mommy back." His wide, innocent eyes locked onto hers, pleading.

A spear of grief pierced her heart. "Callen," she whispered, reaching for him. The moment her fingers brushed his, a cold wave slammed through her bones, a warning to run.

She bolted, her feet pounding against the uneven stone. Time blurred as she twisted through the maze, corridors folding in on themselves, trapping her in an endless loop.

Turning the next corner, she stopped in her tracks. Before her stood a different version of her brother. He was taller and broader, his squared shoulders radiating rigid fury.

"You ran," he said, his voice thick with betrayal and bitter accusation.

Arden's heart lurched. This was her brother, yet he was no longer the boy she remembered. He had transformed into a man consumed by bitterness and rage, waiting to confront her.

"You ran and left me behind." Callen's dark eyes blazed with resentment. "You swore we'd always stick together."

Arden shook her head. "That's not true... Callen, I left *for* you... I..."

"Liar." His words cut deep as his expression shifted. "You never came back. You let him take you away from me and never looked back." His voice rose, sharp and broken. "You abandoned me. For him. For the fae."

"No." She whispered, shaking her head fiercely.

His expression twisted, growing colder and more cruel. He lunged forward, hands outstretched. "You're just like her."

Arden staggered back as shadows swirled around him, pulling him into the darkness. She reached out, screaming his name, but he was gone.

Her back hit the rough stone wall, and her legs gave way beneath her. A raw, guttural scream tore from her throat, swallowed by the labyrinth's endless corridors. Her breath came in shallow gasps, her pulse roaring in her ears. She rocked forward, then back, desperate to anchor herself to reality. Her mind spiraled deeper, her grip slipping like sand through her fingers. The labyrinth's whispers wrapped around her like a shroud.

None of this is real, she told herself, but the thought felt empty, weightless.

Because if it wasn't real…

Why did it hurt?

Why did her chest ache as if she had already lost?

A memory surfaced, unbidden and unwanted.

She was eleven, standing in a cramped room filled with older boys, their sharp eyes assessing her like prey. The scent of damp wood and stale sweat clung to the air. She had never felt more afraid.

Weakness is death. That was the first lesson Luthan had taught her.

He had leaned in, his voice low, his grip bruising her shoulder.

"Big emotions are ammunition for those stronger than you," he murmured. "Tears won't save you. Fear won't protect you. The second they see you falter, they will pounce."

His fingers tightened on her shoulder and she had cried out.

"So don't let them see you falter. You want to survive? Then get up. Wipe your face. And never let them see you bleed."

Arden had listened. She swallowed her fear, wiped the grime from her cheeks, and met their stares with a glare as hard as steel.

That was the night she learned what it meant to survive.

She forced herself to breathe through the crushing weight in her chest. The labyrinth had gotten to her but she wouldn't let it win. With a sharp inhale, she wiped her face, forcing back tears she refused to let fall.

"Never let them see you bleed." Luthan's voice echoed in her mind, a welcome reminder. She clung to the anger, the heat, the defiance that had carried her through everything life had thrown at her. Her fingers curled around the hilt of her dagger. Did the Fae Lord think he could break her, twist her mind? No. She was done playing his game.

Arden rose, light on her feet, dagger ready. The labyrinth pulsed with magic and menace, but she felt no fear. She had been running blindly, and she knew better now. The corridor stretched endlessly in both directions, its walls shimmering like oil. The weight of the Fae Lord's presence pressed against her, distant yet suffocating. She adjusted her grip on her dagger, the cool metal grounding her.

"If I'm going to survive this, I need to stop running in circles."

Instead of moving forward, she halted at the nearest junction, studying the walls. They were unnaturally smooth, no seams, no cracks. The faint glow emanating from the stone made it impossible to tell whether she had been here before or if every corridor simply looked the same. She exhaled slowly, it was time to start thinking of a plan.

Arden crouched low, pressing the edge of her dagger against the stone. The metal caught the faint glow, flickering like a warning. At first, the dagger slid too easily, leaving no mark. She adjusted the angle, applying more pressure. This time, the dagger bit into the surface, leaving a shallow but visible scratch. The faint screech of metal against stone echoed in the corridor, sending a shiver down her spine.

She straightened and stepped back to inspect her work: a small, diagonal line, clean and deliberate. It wasn't much, but it was a start. At least now she'd know if she doubled back.

Frustration surged within her. Why hadn't she thought of this sooner? She had wasted so much time running aimlessly, panic overriding her common sense. Her chest tightened as the realization struck her: if the Fae Lord had been watching, and she knew he was, he had already seen her at her weakest.

The thought of him smirking in a dark corner, amused by her desperation, filled her with dread. Taking a deep breath, she pushed the thought aside, what mattered now was moving forward. At the next junction, she marked the base of the wall once more. Casting a glance over her shoulder, she half-expected to see something or someone pursuing her. But the corridor behind her remained empty, the shadows still. Yet, she couldn't shake the feeling of being watched.

As she navigated the labyrinth, leaving marks at every turn, a fragile sense of control began to take root. Each scratch on the wall felt like a small act of victory against the chaos surrounding her, and that knowledge steadied her. But the corridors twisted and rippled, revealing the truth: control was an illusion here, like everything else in this cursed place. Her marks might help her move forward, but they wouldn't protect her from what lay ahead.

Twice, she found herself back at the same dead end, staring at a shallow pool of liquid that smelled of sulfur. Her frustration mounted, along with the growing sound of something following her. She caught a glimpse of it once, a shadow skimming along the ground, moving faster than it should have. It had no defined shape, but its presence sent chills down her spine.

"Faster, thief," the Keeper's voice whispered mockingly. *"Your shadows are particularly hungry."* Arden forced herself to move forward, her pulse racing. As she turned the next corner, she encountered a mirror made of impossibly clear glass. It stretched across the corridor, tall and jagged-edged, like a wound carved into the stone.

In it, she saw herself, but distorted. This Arden was different, older. Dressed in black woven with silver filigree, her hair was longer, her shoulders straighter, her eyes colder. Her reflection stood still, unblinking and unbreathing. Arden swallowed hard.

"What..."

In response, the reflection tilted its head and smirked. Arden's blood ran cold.

She hadn't moved.

But her reflection had.

The mirror-Arden's lips parted, revealing teeth too sharp to be human. A biting voice echoed from the glass. "Did you really think you could run forever?"

Arden stumbled backward, her heel catching on the uneven ground. Then, the mirror shattered.

Glass exploded outward, fragments suspended in the air for a brief moment before raining down around her. Arden covered her face as tiny cuts opened across her exposed skin. Instead of hitting the stone floor, the shards transformed into hands, hundreds of pale skeletal hands clawing at her from the floor, the walls, and the shadows that pulled her down.

She kicked, thrashed, and screamed, but it was too much. The hands dragged her into a void deeper than night itself. Cold pressed against her skin, seeping into her bones until she could no longer move.

Then came the whispers.

"You will never leave."

"You are nothing without him."

"No one is coming for you."

They burrowed into her mind, overlapping in a cacophony of cruel truths, or lies, she couldn't tell anymore. Her limbs grew numb, her fingers cold and distant, as if they no longer belonged to her. Was she still moving? Or had she already given up?

Suddenly, she felt a sensation beneath her feet. Faint, barely there, but solid. She focused on it, gritting her teeth, forcing herself to feel her limbs again. But her body resisted. The whispers fought back, louder and angrier, wrapping around her like chains. With a snarl, she clawed her way out of the nothingness, pushing forward one agonizing step at a time.

Her boots struck solid stone, and the shadows hissed, recoiling. The voices faded. Her knees buckled, but she caught herself against the rough surface of a wall. The icy grip of the void released her, and Arden inhaled sharply, her breath shuddering in her aching lungs.

She pressed a hand against the wall beside her, blinking rapidly to clear the haze from her mind. Where...?

The question fractured before it could fully form. The twisting corridors. The suffocating darkness.

The labyrinth.

The trial.

The realization hit her like a blow to the chest.

She hadn't escaped.

She hadn't even moved.

Chapter Six

Arden pressed her forehead against the wall and let the chill ease her pounding head. She fought to steady herself as every muscle in her body screamed at her to give up and rest. The voices had dissolved into wisps, but the burning echoes lingered, curling in the corners of her mind like dying embers refusing to be snuffed out. She squeezed her eyes shut and covered her ears, desperately forcing them away. She shook her head back and forth violently. "Not real... None of this is real."

She slammed her fist against the rough stone and felt blood drip down her knuckles. It would be easier to just stop here; no more running through this place that seemed designed to break her.

As she spiraled, dark thoughts ravaged her mind like an unending storm. Doubt seized her, sharp and suffocating, drowning out any trace of reason. What was she even doing here? This place wasn't meant for someone like her. Everything she had endured felt futile, each step forward a cruel joke played by powers beyond her understanding. The weight of failure pressed heavily on her chest, relentless and suffocating, making it hard to breathe.

A bitter laugh escaped her lips, harsh and hollow. She pressed the heels of her hands against her eyes, trying to block out the world and shut out the fear threatening to consume her. Every step she took felt like trespassing on something sacred, something that would never truly accept her.

Yet the memory of Nythis' gaze lingered like a second skin, piercing and all-seeing as if the goddess had looked straight through her and discovered something within her that she had not even known existed.

Arden could still feel how that gaze had stripped her bare, unraveling her to her core and exposing parts of herself she hadn't dared to acknowledge. Nythis had believed in her but, in this moment, standing in the heart of a place meant to break her, she didn't feel worthy. She felt like a fraud.

Yet every time she imagined giving up, her thoughts drifted back to every fight, every wound she had ever fought through because she hadn't had the luxury of surrender. She had always survived, even when it seemed impossible. She steeled her nerves; she refused to give the Fae Lord the satisfaction of breaking her. She ground her teeth and forced herself to keep moving. "Find the key," she muttered under her breath. "Take the key and then get out."

After what felt like an eternity of navigating the twisting corridors, Arden staggered into an abandoned chamber. The air was thick with an unnatural stillness, as if it had been untouched for centuries. At the center of the room stood a marble pedestal, its surface marred by thick, jagged scars. As Arden approached it, she ran her hand along the deep ridges wondering what type of beast could have possibly left them.

Atop the pedestal sat a small and unremarkable key. The moment Arden's eyes locked onto it, her breath caught. This was it, she was sure, though it bore no markings, something about it radiated significance, a quiet gravity that drew her in. It was perched just out of reach, resting on the pedestal's marred surface like a challenge.

Undeterred, Arden ran her fingers along one of the deep gouges carved into the column's side. She wedged her foot into another, testing the holds with caution. Gritting her teeth, she began to climb, her fingers grasping for leverage against the slick stone. As she shifted her weight, the pedestal groaned beneath her. A low rumble vibrated through the floor, and then the entire structure began to tremble violently.

The sudden motion threw her off balance, and a forceful jolt knocked her backward, sending her sprawling onto the cold stone floor. The air shifted. The shadows that had lingered in the corners of the chamber now writhed to life, stirring with unnatural energy. As the pedestal continued its descent, the key now within reach, chaos erupted around her.

Darkness pooled and surged around the room. From the inky depths, three figures emerged, moving with a wrongness that made Arden's stomach twist. At first glance, they seemed human, but their movements were jerky, like marionettes tugged by unseen strings, their heads tilted at unnatural angles as they took her in.

Arden stumbled away as her body prepared to either fight or run. Their lips pulled back to reveal elongated teeth, sharp and predatory. Arden's adrenaline spiked as they stepped forward, slow and deliberate, they had positioned themselves between her and the key. She rolled her shoulders and shifted her stance, dagger gripped tightly in her hand. She was exhausted and her body begged for rest, but there was no time for that now.

The creatures lunged; Arden barely had time to twist away. She felt the rush of air against her skin as claw-like fingers slashed through the empty space where her head had been moments before.

She didn't hesitate; her dagger lashed out in a quick, practiced motion aimed cleanly at the creature's arm. The blade bit deep, but instead of flesh and bone, her blade revealed a seething core of molten rock and burning embers. The creature did not flinch or recoil; it simply turned to face her again, its movements eerily smooth and deliberate.

A deep, unnatural clicking sound echoed from its throat, almost as if it were summoning the others. "Perfect," she muttered, trying desperately to orient herself back toward the pedestal.

A whisper of something familiar seemed to curl around Arden: "Focus." Her muscles tensed instinctively, and her gaze darted around. The other two figures closed in, their hulking forms blocking her escape routes. Arden darted to the side; her smaller frame slipped between them, the scrape of claws against stone close behind her.

Her eyes scanned the space, looking for something that could give her even a small advantage. When she sprinted, her footsteps barely echoed, her instincts kicking in as she moved erratically, keeping the creatures off balance.

One of them ran forward, claws slicing toward her midsection and Arden dropped low, the swipe barely missing her. She came up quickly, as she tried to sidestep another attack, but this time the creature was too quick, and she felt the burning sting of its claws pierce her right side.

A scream tore from Arden's throat as searing pain exploded across her side. The creature's claws had raked her ribs, and for a moment, she was certain she'd been gutted. Panic flooded her veins as her mind raced with the fear of bleeding out or collapsing here with no one to help her. Her hand flew to the wound, expecting to feel warm blood spilling freely, but instead, her fingers met scorched fabric and blistered skin.

She hissed as she peeled back her hand and stared at the damage. The wound wasn't bleeding, it was burned closed at the edges, as if cauterized. The heat still radiated from it, the pain sharp and relentless, but the wound had sealed.

Chest heaving, Arden's eyes darted to the creature stalking toward her, its body pulsing with glowing veins of heat visible beneath the crust of its skin. Arden's mind raced as she doubled down on her efforts, the searing pain in her side fueling her anger and ambition to escape.

She ducked low beneath a wild swipe, twisted on her heel, and darted sideways, narrowly avoiding the second creature's claws as they sliced through the air where her throat had just been. Her movements were fueled by instinct and desperation, forcing her exhausted limbs to keep pace. Drawing a shaky breath, she pivoted sharply, weaving between them and using her smaller frame to her advantage.

The creatures snarled and lunged again, their coordination faltering in their relentless need to catch her. Arden timed her steps, baiting them into the same line of attack. One creature reached for her with outstretched claws while the other lunged from behind, and in their frenzy, they collided. The impact sent a ripple of heat through the chamber, and in an instant, both figures crumbled into piles of glowing embers, their snarls silenced.

Arden didn't pause. Her heart pounded, and her lungs burned, but there was no time to process what had just happened. Only one creature remained, its molten eyes fixed on her, now standing between her and the pedestal.

Her gaze locked on the key, still within reach if she could make it. Her eyes darted across the floor, landing on a jagged stone. Gritting her teeth, she shifted her stance, ready to move again. Arden reached for the rock, her fingers closing around the sharp edges, and hurled it with all her strength. It struck the creature square in the face and shattered into a spray of fragments. The creature reeled back, its head jerking violently to the side as if momentarily disoriented, but it did not collapse like the others.

Arden surged forward, her injured shoulder clipping the edge of the pedestal as pain flared and blinded her. The creature let out an otherworldly howl, but she didn't stop. She blinked against the pain as her fingers closed around the key, and relief flooded her. She scanned the chamber quickly for the creature but it wasn't facing her anymore; its attention caught by something she couldn't see.

She crept along the edge of the chamber, each step measured and silent, her dagger clenched tightly in case it turned toward her again. The creature snarled into the shadows, poised to strike at whatever unseen threat lingered beyond the darkness. A thunderous growl responded. The noise shook the chamber, deep and resonant, like the earth itself crying out in anger. Arden froze mid-step, the creature's snarls faltering into uneasy whines.

The growling started again, louder this time, and the stone floor beneath her feet trembled. Dust rained down from the ceiling as cracks spread along the walls. The other creature let out a series of guttural screeches as it scrambled to escape. Arden watched it run, her heart pounding as the chamber grew eerily silent.

The oppressive weight in the air only grew heavier until it was almost impossible to take a full breath. Arden clutched the key tightly to her chest, sweat slicking her palms.

The Keeper's voice returned, a cruel, satisfied whisper. *"Well done, thief. But can you make it past the Guardian of the Labyrinth?"*

Arden's pulse raced as she sprinted away from the rumbling footsteps emanating from the hallway on the other side of the cavern. The entire chamber shook, causing her to stumble and fall over newly formed fissures in the ground. From the far side of the chamber, the Guardian emerged from the shadows, and Arden fell, staring up at a massive black lion.

Its body was as large and powerful as a horse, its sleek fur shimmering with an otherworldly sheen. Something about it drew her in, its golden eyes burned with an unnatural fire that called to her. With each step, the ground cracked beneath its enormous paws, sending tremors throughout the cavern. Arden could not force her body to move, staring up at the ancient being; something not meant for the mortal world.

When it spoke, its words resounded in Arden's head. *"You do not belong here."*

The words weren't loud or aggressive, but they rang through her mind, rattling her ribs and sinking into her skin, a voice like thunder, restrained within the throat of a beast. The Guardian's ears flattened; its snarl deepened.

Arden's pulse pounded in her ears as she slowly crawled away, her grip tightening on the key as if it were her only anchor in the crumbling chaos around her. The Guardian stalked forward, its muscles rippling beneath its midnight coat. The Labyrinth groaned and trembled as if the Guardian's wrath had willed it into collapse. Stone walls buckled and cracked, massive chunks of debris crashing down around them.

Arden scrambled to her feet, her body screaming at her to run. Her lungs burned as she sprinted, the sound of the Guardian's thundering paws behind her pushing her forward faster than she thought possible. As she ran, nothing looked familiar, and as the walls crumbled around her, panic overtook her thoughts.

No, no, no,

The walls all looked the same, and Arden had only seconds at each junction to make a decision. There was no room for rational thought anymore, just blind panic once again. The Guardian's roar split the air, and the sheer force of it sent a shockwave through the narrow passages. Arden's footing faltered, the impact sending her sprawling forward.

She rushed to her feet, but the Guardian lunged. Arden twisted, but its claws scraped her arm, tearing through fabric. Pain exploded in her shoulder as blood pooled to the surface. She bit back the screams clawing at her throat and staggered forward.

From the corner of her eye, she saw a flicker of motion. Shadows slithered along the ground, moving with purpose ahead of her like dark rivers carving a path through the chaos. The same voice from earlier echoed in her mind, but this time it was not a whisper; it was a loud, deliberate presence.

"Follow them."

Arden hesitated only a moment before altering her course. She didn't know why she trusted the voice, but she did. Behind her, the Guardian continued its path of destruction, furious and unrelenting.

She refused to look back.

She dodged falling debris, vaulted over deep cracks that threatened to swallow her whole, and kept her eyes locked on the shifting, writhing path of shadows. In the distance, Arden could swear she saw a sliver of light, dim, but real.

They had led her to the exit.

Arden's muscles screamed, exhaustion dragging at her limbs, but she pushed harder, her legs burning as she forced herself to continue running.

The Guardian's pounding footsteps shattered the air, its fury a living, breathing thing. The ground around Arden trembled violently, the chamber caving in.

She leapt forward and felt the light brush of her fingers around the doorknob.

But a horrible, crushing force wrapped around her ankle. The Guardian's jaws clamped down on her boot, and a terrible, unstoppable pull yanked her backward.

The exit had been right there. She could almost taste the air beyond the Labyrinth, almost feel the weight of the nightmare lifting off her shoulders. She closed her eyes, accepting that she had lost.

When her eyes opened, the shadows surged. A tidal wave of inky blackness lashed forward, severing the Guardian's grip and flinging her through the threshold with violent force. She hit the ground hard, rolling onto the cool stone of the passage beyond. Arden watched, unable to move, as the door collapsed in on itself. The Guardian's golden eyes, burning with unquenchable rage as the darkness swallowed it whole.

She lay outside the Labyrinth, seemingly paralyzed and gasping for air. Her entire body trembled, her palms scraped and raw from the mad dash. She lay there for a moment, her chest heaving, the key still clutched tightly in her hand as blood pooled around her from both wounds.

A shadow fell over her, and she forced herself to look up. The Fae Lord stood there, his tall, imposing figure framed by flickering orbs of light.

His expression was unreadable, but the faint smirk on his lips betrayed his amusement.

"You survived," he said, his tone almost bored, though his eyes gleamed with something more sinister. "How... unexpected."

Arden glared up at him, her exhaustion and anger warring with her relief at still being alive. She wanted to say something, to snap back, but she didn't have the strength. Instead, her eyes began to flutter, and everything grew very cold.

The Fae Lord tilted his head, studying her for a moment before kneeling beside her. His pale fingers reached out, plucking the key from her grasp with practiced ease. "You won't need this anymore," he said, his voice dripping with mockery as he held the key up, inspecting it.

He placed his hand over her leg, and at first, Arden braced for pain, pressure, or the cold sting of his magic. But none came. Instead, a strange warmth spread through her body. It enveloped her limbs and sank deep into her skin, reaching areas she hadn't realized were aching. Her breathing evened out as she relaxed into it, the sensation soft and familiar.

Her eyes fluttered as she struggled to focus, noticing darkness creeping across her skin. His shadows danced like smoke, curling around her wounds. She stared in stunned silence, as she watched her bruises fade and blood disappear. The world around her grew distant, softened at the edges, as if wrapped in cotton.

He stood, his cloak billowing around him as he turned away, leaving Arden to pick herself up off the ground. Without so much as an acknowledgement about what he had just done he began walking down the hallway throwing over his shoulder, "are you coming, little thief?"

Chapter Seven

The Fae Lord gave her no time to recover. Pain pulsed through every inch of her body, the healing she'd received doing little to dull it. The adrenaline from the trial still coursed through her veins, draining what little energy she had left.

A few feet away, the Fae Lord toyed with the key she'd nearly died to retrieve, spinning it effortlessly between long fingers like a child's toy. His expression was unreadable. "You seem displeased," he mused, not bothering to look at her. "You should be proud, few mortals survive their trial in one piece."

Arden clenched her fists, forcing herself to swallow the sharp retort rising in her throat. "What was the point of it?" she demanded instead. "The labyrinth, the key, what did any of it mean?"

He tilted his head, studying her with the same amused curiosity he had displayed since they first met. "Your role, Arden, is to serve. To obey."

"If I am to serve, I need to know what…" Her words died in her throat as the Fae Lord raised a hand. Shadows surged to life, coiling around her wrists and ankles like shackles. "What is this?" she stammered, tugging against the unseen restraints.

"A reminder," the Fae Lord said smoothly. "I owe you *nothing*. You are bound to me, body and soul, until your decade of service is complete. Should you attempt to defy me…" He flicked his fingers, and the magical bindings tightened briefly, making her gasp. "You will find it… unpleasant."

He leaned in closer, his voice low and mocking. "Did you think I would trust a thief to keep her word without a little incentive?"

The magic tingled against her skin, "I want proof that you healed him."

The Fae Lord's magic stuttered, allowing her to take a deep breath against the restraints. "I won your trial, I deserve..."

"You deserve nothing." He said sharply. "This world is not your home, Arden. It will take everything from you, it's not my fault that you..."

"Please." Tears pricked her eyes, threatening to spill. "I just want to know he's okay."

He sighed, her tears stirring something deep within him he hadn't felt in ages. From the shadows, he drew a mirror, its surface dark and rippling like still water. "This is a scrying mirror, it allows me to view other realms. It's how I know whom to select, what they need, and what bargain best suits them."

Fascinated, Arden gazed into the black glass as it revealed an image of Callen stretching in the morning rays that filtered into the hovel. She watched as he tentatively placed one shaky foot out of bed, followed by the other, before he finally stood. It had been weeks since he had been able to do that. Suddenly, the image faded, and tears streamed down her face as she longed for it to return.

The Fae Lord turned and continued walking, the pressure on her limbs vanishing as if it had never existed. She shakily stood and rushed to keep up with him.

"Thank you" she mumbled under her breath.

"It won't happen again."

She swallowed hard and quickened her pace, falling into step just behind him. "What happened to the others?" she asked, her voice steadier than she felt.

The Fae Lord didn't break stride. Arden pressed harder. "Elias... Nia... Tobin?" she urged, watching for any flicker of reaction. "They each went through their own doors. Where are they now?"

For a long moment, he remained silent, his face impassive. Then, finally, he stopped and met her gaze. "They failed."

Arden's stomach twisted. "What does that mean?"

His jaw tightened, but his voice remained smooth, cold. "It means they were tested, like you. But they didn't make it through."

"Are they dead?"

He turned away, his body language giving nothing away as he quickened his pace, as if trying to outrun the conversation. Arden refused to let it drop. She stepped in front of him, blocking his path. "Tell me what happened to them," she insisted, searching his face for any hint of an answer.

A flicker of anger passed through his gaze, a tightening at the corners of his mouth, a brief tension in his shoulders. His eyes darkened as he pushed past her. His voice was clipped, "you like to concern yourself with things that don't impact you."

"They matter to me."

The Fae Lord walked faster ahead of her. When he finally spoke, his voice was calm again, "then consider this a lesson. You will see many fall in my service. You would do well not to dwell on them."

The halls of the Fae Lord's domain seemed infinite as they walked the corridors in silence. Arden followed, her thoughts tangled in the fate of the others. *'They failed.'* What did that mean? Were they dead? Trapped? Had they been cast into something worse than the labyrinth?

The Fae Lord stopped suddenly and motioned for her to walk ahead of him into a room guarded by two men clad in black plated armor. The room stretched impossibly far, its towering shelves filled with strange, glittering objects. Weapons, artifacts, delicate trinkets that pulsed faintly with magic. Each item seemed to whisper, humming just at the edge of hearing. Some objects glowed with an eerie light, while others radiated a presence so heavy that Arden felt it in her bones.

"This is my greatest accomplishment, the Vault of Shadows," he said. "Every item in this vault holds a story, a fragment of power," he continued, his voice smooth as ever. Then his lips curled into a smirk. "And now, you will stay here and protect it."

Arden's head snapped up. "Protect it?"

"Mortals like you are always so fascinated by shiny things that don't belong to you. Let's see if your skills as a thief can prevent others from taking what is mine."

She stared at him, incredulous. "You want me to guard your treasure trove? Against whom?"

"Against those who think they can challenge me," he said, amused. "Other fae, foolish mortals, creatures from realms beyond."

His words hung heavy in the air, and Arden's gaze swept the vast space, unease curling in her chest. The Fae Lord's voice sounded distant as she began to walk around the vast space.

"The vault holds many things, little thief. More than you could ever steal, more than you could ever break, and more than you could even begin to understand." His tone was smooth, edged with something unreadable, amusement and warning tangled together.

She turned to find him leaning against one of the shelves. "You won't lack for distractions," he continued, gesturing to the endless corridors branching from the main hall. "Books filled with forgotten knowledge, relics steeped in magic, and puzzles even the wisest have failed to solve." He tilted his head. "But be careful where your curiosity leads you. Some things do not like to be disturbed."

On his way out, he stopped and whispered something to one of the guards. She couldn't quite make it out, but the guard slammed a fist against his chest and responded, "Yes, my lord."

Each day, she awoke in a small chamber carved into the walls, its ceiling too high to see, the darkness pressing at the edges of the space. Every night she tucked herself into a new corner of the vault and every morning, she woke up here. The lack of windows made it hard to sense how time passed, so she had taken to watching the guards come and go as her measure of day and night.

As days turned into weeks and those weeks merged into months, she developed an unexpected friendship with the two guards. She spent time talking to them and listening to the stories they had to share. Kastiel, the commander of the Fae Lord's army, would spend hours regaling her with stories of adventures before the First Fae King disappeared. He spoke about Aeshyra and her adventures exploring the realm with Kastiel by her side. Arden couldn't help but feel a connection to her through him. But whenever Arden pressed for more, both Kastiel and Byron fell silent, as if withholding the truth was an act of mercy.

Byron was vastly different from Kastiel; he spoke in hushed whispers, as if he were afraid that even the walls were listening, waiting for him to slip up. Through months of patient listening Arden had pieced together that he had originally belonged to the Court of Veils, a court that no longer existed on any fae map. The Archfey who ruled over his court,

Kaelar, had started a rebellion that ended in ruin. The Caretaker had destroyed his court, and the remaining residents fled, leaving the Court of Veils nothing but ruins.

Some days, when the guards didn't arrive Arden found herself wandering the shelves, walking the endless corridors of strange, powerful objects. She learned quickly that each of the artifacts wanted something unique. Some wanted to be held, others wanted to be freed, and some yearned to share knowledge; knowledge that Arden craved more than anything.

Whenever she couldn't resist the temptation, she would spend hours poring over ancient fae texts, learning everything she could about the fae realm and the creatures that lived there. While everything she read was fascinating, one book, in particular, drew her in time and time again. *The Creatures Within Shadows*, written by Aeshyra herself. The pages were full of notes that Aeshyra had taken throughout her adventures in the early days of Elessian's creation.

From this text, Arden learned about the creatures that roamed the vault with her. They were constantly hovering just out of view and their whispers threatened to drive Arden completely insane. Aeshyra had named them 'The Watchers'.

"Keepers of Elessian's secrets, these creatures roam between courts and weave whispers between one breath and the next. If you listen closely you may be able to decipher the secrets they hold close. They observe without interfering and guard knowledge against outsiders. Despite trying to talk to them directly, they seem to only speak with each other. I've heard whispers from Kaelar's court that they've spoken directly to him about the prophecy of the Gods, I hope to know more soon when I visit."

The mention of the prophecy of the Gods struck Arden like a blow to the chest. She turned the page, eager to read what Aeshyra had managed to uncover, but the rest of the text was blank. She refused to let it go and with her newfound knowledge, Arden began to take her own notes in the margins of Aeshyra's text.

"The Watchers always flutter just beyond the edge of my vision, shadowy figures that seem to be stitched from darkness given life. Their forms shift like smoke on the wind and their presence is a constant, unsettling hum against the back of my mind, never solid, never fully seen. They gather

in the farthest corners of the Vault, lingering between the towering shelves, watching. I think they've been watching me since the Labyrinth."

They never addressed her directly, but their voices filled the Vault, whispering in tones that slithered through the air like a breeze carrying distant conversation. Whenever she heard them, she found herself writing furiously to capture words that may have any meaning to her later.

"Strange, isn't she?"

"She is like them, but not like them."

"Does she know?"

"Does she understand?"

When the voices faded, she continued exploring. She no longer tried to navigate the vault by memory. Instead, she let it guide her, its corridors shifting like a living maze. There was always something new or unfamiliar for her to investigate. A blade pulsing with cold energy, a crown whispering in a language beyond her understanding, a vial of dark, viscous liquid that sloshed against its glass as if alive. She learned which shelves hummed the loudest, which artifacts glowed in recognition of her presence, and which recoiled, their energy withdrawing as if unwilling to be seen.

After surviving the Labyrinth, Arden had braced herself for constant danger. She expected thieves to slip through unseen cracks, desperate to steal the Vault's treasures. Yet days passed, then weeks, and nothing happened. No intruders, no battles, no threats lurking in the dark. Perhaps the Fae Lord was simply paranoid, as time continued on she became more relaxed.

She moved through the corridors with ease, touching ancient tomes and cradling delicate artifacts. The vault became a sanctuary one that, at times, felt made just for her. She should have known better, life always had a way of disturbing any peace she managed to find.

She awoke as a crash shattered the silence of the vault. Arden's head snapped toward the sound, her body reacting before her mind caught up. A figure darted between towering shelves, swift and practiced. She recognized the movements of someone who had spent their life running from guards, whoever she was chasing was not fae, they were mortal like her.

Arden sprinted faster after the intruder. The woman wore dark leather, a hood pulled low over her face. When she glanced back, she gasped realizing that Arden was closing in. She clutched a small, glowing orb that pulsed faintly in her grasp.

"Stop!" Arden called, but the thief only ran faster.

"A thief."

"A thief chasing a thief."

"Will she do it? Will she make it?"

The woman veered left toward the shelves Arden had instinctively avoided. The artifacts here had made the air colder as magic thickened, dense and heavy. Arden realized that this woman didn't have a clue where she was going. Perfect. Arden lunged, tackling the woman to the ground. They struggled, but Arden pinned her with practiced ease. The thief's hood fell back, revealing sharp features and wild eyes.

The orb tumbled from her grip, rolling across the stone floor before coming to rest against a shelf. Arden pressed a dagger to the woman's throat. "Who are you?" she demanded. "Why are you here?"

The woman's eyes burned with defiance. "You wouldn't understand."

Arden gritted her teeth. "Try me."

Before the thief could answer, a voice cut through the Vault. "Well done, little thief. I knew you could do it."

Arden's blood turned to ice as recognition dawned. She turned her head and found the Fae Lord standing a few feet away, watching with mild amusement. For so long, she had been left alone. She had begun to wonder if he even remembered placing her here.

His presence filled the space, his shadows coiling lazily toward her, almost pleased. His gaze flicked to the orb, then back to the thief beneath Arden. Arden instinctively tightened her grip on the dagger and the woman went still.

The Fae Lord gestured lazily. Shadows moved, lifting the orb from the ground and returning it to its place. The woman's breath quickened, she knew who he was. "Let her up," the Fae Lord commanded. His voice left no room for argument.

Reluctantly, Arden obeyed, stepping back. The thief flung herself to the ground in front of him, "forgive me please I..."

The Fae Lord cut her off, "you've made a grave mistake coming here."

The thief's breath hitched as he raised a hand, "wait."

But he didn't even pause; shadows surged and her scream split the air, sharp and desperate. Darkness wrapped around her, dragging her into nothingness.

Arden stared at the empty space where the woman had been, her heart hammering. Her voice came quieter than she intended. "What did you do to her?"

The Fae Lord turned his gaze on her, calm and cold. "She trespassed," he said smoothly. "Her fate is no concern of yours."

She turned to speak, to ask him something more, but he was already gone.

That night, curled in the corner of the vault, she pulled a stray pelt over her head and wept. Her mind drifted to the first time Callen was caught stealing food down by the docks. He had only been a boy, fourteen at most, trembling as he clutched a bruised apple taken from a shipping crate. But the ship's owner had compassion and offered Callen two apples with a quiet warning not to make a habit of it. Callen had been so frightened he ran home and hid the fruit under his pillow, convinced the guards would come for him in the night. Arden had held him close, letting him cry into her shoulder until he fell asleep.

But now, the ache in her chest wouldn't ease. She should have knocked the orb from the woman's hands or shouted a warning to run. Anything would have been better than letting the Fae Lord take her.

Chapter Eight

Aezraen

Aezraen stood in the Chamber of Whispers, arms folded, watching the woman shiver before him. She knelt on the cold stone floor, her breath ragged, wrists bound by shadow-forged chains. The tendrils coiled around her like living serpents, tightening with each slight movement.

He observed her with detached amusement, though his thoughts churned beneath the surface. He hadn't expected a mortal to breach the Vault, especially not one so recklessly desperate. It was sloppy and ill-conceived, but it was no accident.

Someone had sent her.

His boots crunched against the dust-covered floor as he stepped forward. Crouching, he gripped her face, his nails digging into her cheeks. "I'm losing patience."

She tried to speak, her voice hoarse from wasted screams. No one could hear her here, and even if they could, they wouldn't care. He shoved her, sending her sprawling.

"No. One. Sent. Me." Her cracked, bleeding lips pressed into a thin line. He sensed her fury, admirable yet misplaced.

With a sigh, he drew a single finger through the air. The chains responded instantly, yanking her onto her knees. The shadows twisted, sharpening into razors that bit into her wrists and ankles. Blood trickled down her limbs, pooling beneath her on the slick stone. Held taut, her muscles trembled, and the slickness beneath her knees made it impossible to remain still. Each slip, each involuntary movement drove the blades deeper.

"I won't ask again," he growled. "Who sent you?"

Her knee slipped on the blood-slick stone, jerking her forward. A scream tore from her throat as the razored shadows bit deep into her left wrist, slicing through flesh and scraping against bone. She gasped, frantically trying to shift her weight, desperate for relief from the crushing pressure. Her vision swam, and a strangled sob escaped her lips as she fought to steady herself, her injured wrist trembling under the strain. She couldn't hold this position for long; she was breaking.

Aezraen narrowed his eyes, and with a flick of his hand, the chains shifted. Shadows pooled beneath her, lifting just enough to allow her to regain her balance. The razors loosened slightly, and she collapsed forward, panting, drenched in sweat and blood.

Still shaking, she forced herself to look up. "The..." she choked out between pants "...Caretaker."

Aezraen recalled his shadows at once. Her body slumped forward, wracked with sobs and incoherent ramblings. He said nothing, every muscle in his body tensing. The room darkened with his mood, overhead lights flickering and dying. A familiar ache filled his chest.

Vaelithara.

The first Fae Queen. Ruler of their kind. Keeper of his chains.

His jaw clenched as he straightened and turned away, unwilling to let the mortal witness the fear etched into his face. He had spent centuries avoiding Vaelithara's gaze, ensuring his court remained quiet and unseen. Apparently, he had failed.

To mortals, the Caretaker was a myth, a motherly figure who lost her child to the very beings she had helped create. They saw her akin to a goddess, one willing to grant your heart's desire if you could aid her quest to bring her daughter back from the dead. To the Fae, she was the beginning of time, having breathed life back into their world when Elydris vanished. But for all her power, she was not merciful. She was a queen who demanded obedience from all and punished disloyalty at any cost.

Aezraen exhaled slowly, then turned back to the thief. Her wide, pleading eyes met his. "Tell me," he said, his voice steady. "What did she offer you?"

Her breath trembled. "Immortality."

Of course.

"She said she would help my daughters and me. Give us beauty beyond compare, power beyond mortal means. All I had to do was bring her that orb."

Aezraen arched a brow. "And you never wondered why a queen would send a *mortal* on such an errand?"

Her answer confirmed that Vaelithara was still trying to bring Syliris back. Though the orb had been returned to its shelf, his shadows still felt its faint thrumming, waiting to be unlocked. The Vessel of Elarion predated even the oldest Fae courts. A relic of the First Fae King, it was said to be a key that could control history itself. For centuries, it had sat in his vault. He had tried to undo his mistakes, to free himself. But the orb yielded only painful memories; no matter what magic he tried, it only showed him the past, never a path to change it.

The mortal sniffled, her body sagging from exhaustion. "I didn't even know its name. I didn't know what it did. I just wanted..." She swallowed hard, her voice barely above a whisper. "...I just wanted a better life for my girls."

Aezraen lookedupon her with disgust. "Pitiful."

She had no idea what she'd nearly stolen or the price it carried. The shadows at his feet coiled lazily, eager for his command. He stepped closer. "A better life?" he mused, tilting his head. "You bartered your soul for power you couldn't wield. You didn't understand the game you played. And now..." He let the words trail off.

She knew what came next, tears welled in her eyes, but she didn't beg. He respected that; she was braver than most, but bravery would not save her now. He raised his hand, and the mortal vanished in a breath of darkness. He wasn't foolish enough to think this was over; Vaelithara had marked him the moment he signed his soul away and it was clear now that she would stop at nothing to get what she wanted.

Chapter Nine

Arden's thoughts were restless as she tried to shake the image of the woman's terrified face from her mind as she moved through the Vault. She told herself it didn't matter, if that woman had been foolish enough to enter this place, she should have known the risks.

As she passed the time, she tried not to think about the woman's fate. Digging through drawers and cabinets, she discovered a hidden alcove. Its contents were clearly intended for her: a worn blanket, a crude tin pot, and some ingredients she could use to cook. It was so much more than the scraps she had been given by Kastiel and Byron but her stomach churned knowing what it had cost.

That evening, after the guards had left their post, Arden sat cross-legged in a quiet corner of the Vault, a small fire flickering before her. She had found a small black stone among the artifacts a few days ago. It sat innocuously on the shelf, dull and unassuming compared to the relics that hummed with restrained power but something about it called to her.

As she ate, her mind wandered. The vault was vast, and she hadn't even begun to scratch the surface of what lay inside. She'd tried to map out the paths she'd taken so far, sketching rough layouts on scraps of parchment Kastiel had smuggled her, but the place seemed to stretch endlessly.

The week progressed with no additional intrusions, and Arden settled back into the monotony of her routine. In one section, the shelves were taller and more twisted than those near the entrance, and the artifacts appeared more worn. In another, there were no artifacts at all. The days continued like this, mapping out sections of the vault and documenting the things she encountered.

One morning, Arden stumbled upon a doorway she hadn't noticed before. Intrigued, she sat before it and flipped open Aeshyra's book to sketch its shape and details, intending to ask Kastiel about it later. A soft rustling behind her made her pause. She turned slowly, her hand drifting to the dagger at her waist as her eyes scanned the dim room. Nothing moved, and the silence stretched long enough for her to release a tense breath and return her attention to the door.

It was open.

And something stood within it.

The creature that emerged was flawless, unnervingly perfect. Its body was lithe and unmarred, with skin as smooth as polished marble, glimmering faintly in the low light. Colors shifted across its form like sunlight dancing on water. Wings unfurled from its back, vast and radiant, resembling starlight woven into feathered silk. Each step it took sent ripples of prismatic light spilling outward, the very air around it bending in reverence.

"Another thief?" it asked, its voice carrying an unnatural clarity, as if its words reverberated through time itself.

Arden didn't respond, unsure of the creature's intention or nature. The Seraphyne tilted its head, its too-perfect face devoid of emotion, luminous eyes reflecting Arden's every movement like a mirrored sky.

"No," it pondered aloud. "A captive." It stepped closer, its movements fluid, as though it did not walk but simply shifted through space. "A thread woven back into this realm from long ago." The Seraphyne's voice was a layered, harmonic sound that echoed softly around her.

"I am not a part of this realm," Arden asserted, her dagger poised and ready.

"But you are connected to the others by strings. We can see them all. We know who you are. Do you?" The Seraphyne's gaze did not waver, but something shifted within it, as though the weight of all it had witnessed pressed inward. "You are merely a note in an endless song. One of many forgotten names blowing in the wind. Unless..." It paused, its eyes glazing over as if seeing straight through her.

Her stomach twisted. "Unless what?"

The Seraphyne continued to stare at her. "Nythis did not tell you... Interesting."

Arden bristled at the name of the Goddess. "What are you?"

For the first time, the Seraphyne hesitated; its wings trembled at its back. "Once?" it mused, tilting its head, its voice a breath of something old. "We were peaceful creatures. Keepers of all that has been and will be." Its flawless features remained serene, but something deep within its gaze flickered, an echo of sorrow. "Now, we are what *he* made us. Hungry creatures that yearn for the repair of all that has been broken."

Arden's fingers curled around the hilt of her dagger, her knuckles whitening as tension coiled through her body. "What did the Fae Lord do to you?"

The Seraphyne leaned closer, the faintest shimmer of its breath brushing against her skin. "Like you, he was once a thief. But fate was unkind to him and his faith was betrayed."

Arden opened her mouth, but the creature's luminous eyes dimmed, a quiet resignation settling over its shadowy form. "The council calls me back now. Until we meet again, Arden."

It did not vanish all at once; instead, its edges began to blur, the sharpness of its silhouette softening. Arden's fingers twitched, an instinctive urge to reach out, to anchor the creature to this moment. "Wait," she managed, her voice a fragile thread, but even as the word escaped her, the creature was slipping away. "Not yet," she whispered, her chest tight as both the creature and the door vanished.

Arden stood there, her arm half-raised, fingers splayed toward the emptiness. Her breath came in shallow bursts, and her mind raced, chasing the echoes of a conversation left unfinished. It was as if the creature had never been there at all.

The vault was a puzzle; each artifact, a piece in a game she did not yet understand. Arden had distanced herself from Kastiel and Byron, pouring herself into unraveling the mystery of what Aeshyra had called 'The Prophecy of the Gods'. She wrote down everything she could remember from her interactions with Nythis and the Seraphyne, desperate to find a connection. Every quiet moment became an opportunity to piece together meaning, to decipher riddles left in the wake of ancient voices. Time slipped through her grasp and days blurred, marked only by her need for sleep.

She spent her days exploring, mapping the corridors with rough sketches. She cataloged the ever-changing artifacts, building a ledger of the strange and the dangerous. She learned to avoid a sleek glass pyramid that screamed when she accidentally touched it, a silver chain that burned her palm, leaving a lattice of blisters that healed too slowly. Others, she studied with fascination. A music box that played no song but made the air hum, a shard of glass that reflected flickering shadows she could not see.

The Watchers, ever-present, became more than just background noise. They lingered at the edges of her vision, slipping between the shelves and their incessant whispers curled through the air, soft, insidious things that gnawed at her resolve. As the weeks wore on, she swore that the whispers grew louder until sleep became impossible, and dreams bled into waking nightmares. The walls of the vault seemed to breathe with her, each inhalation drawing the shadows closer, each exhalation pushing them away until she couldn't bear it any longer.

"ENOUGH!" Her scream shattered the stillness, a jagged sound against smooth, unyielding stone. Echoes clawed their way back to her, and the shadows did not retreat. The whispers, however, dulled into a murmur, granting her a fleeting moment of peace.

Then, in the corner of her vision, something else moved. Faint flutters drew her attention as the Seraphyne sought her out. Arden felt their presence like a gentle hum beneath her skin. It wasn't cold, like the Fae Lord's presence, nor suffocating, like the shadows that watched her every move. It was peaceful, a quiet persistence brushing against her mind like a calming breeze. "You came back."

"We've decided to help you on your journey."

"We?"

"Correct." The Seraphyne's voice held no pride, only certainty.

Arden hesitated. "You... don't act alone?"

"No Seraphyne ever does, it would go against nature itself." Their voice was layered, harmonic, like a chord echoing through glass. "We are of many minds, but one purpose. Every path is chosen after deliberation with all."

Arden nodded, trying to wrap her mind around this new information.

"When we choose a path," they continued, "it is because we have measured the cost and agreed to bear it."

Her breath caught. "Why..." she asked carefully, "...have you decided to help me?"

The Seraphyne remained still, as if calculating what to say. "Because the balance is shifting." Their gaze held steady, but something unseen weighed between them, "and you must know what awaits you."

The room trembled as the Seraphyne flapped its wings harder, floating into the air. Its eyes shone bright as hundreds of voices filled the space.

"When fractured blood returns once more,through secret paths and a shadowed door,

A death shall come, that won't unbind,A price once paid, forever etched in time.

And from the ruin, crowned by none, Shall rise the child to mend what's done.

By blood and birth their fate begun,To stand with Gods, when all is won."

"You're speaking in riddles."

"No." The Seraphyne's voice still resonated with the chorus of many. "We are showing you mercy, Arden. We tell you what Nythis and the Gods would not."

Silence stretched between them as the Seraphyne's eyes slowly dulled again and the beating of its wings relaxed into a light flutter bringing it back down to Arden's level. "What comes next is not a question of power, nor of right and wrong." Their gaze lingered. "It is a question of survival."

A shiver traced her spine but Arden forced herself to steady her breath. "Then, please, tell me what you know."

Their gaze held hers, unreadable. "I'm afraid that is all we can say." They lifted their hand, revealing a small, smooth stone, black as midnight, with a faint glow at its center. "This is a fragment of the original power of this realm. Take it, study it. It may lead you to the answers you seek."

Arden hesitated, staring at the stone for a moment before reaching out and closing her fingers around it. The surface was cold and the faint glow pulsed beneath her fingertips like a heartbeat. "How will this help me?"

The Seraphyne tilted their head as if sensing a shift. Before they could answer, they were gone.

Arden sighed. Once again, the Seraphyne offered more questions than answers. She turned the stone over in her hand, hours slipping away as she studied it. No whispers, no visions. Only a steady pulse. Waiting. Frustration gnawed at her as she scribbled everything she could into Aesyhra's book.

The temperature shift in the vault was Arden's only warning that the Fae Lord was coming. She slammed the book shut, shoving it into one of the nearby cases before he emerged from the shadows.

"You've been busy." The Fae Lord's voice drifted through the space, his fingers trailing over her scribbled map.

Arden forced herself to stay calm. She turned, slipping the stone into her pocket, careful to keep her movements unreadable. "You told me to protect the Vault." Her voice remained smooth, controlled. "That's what I've been doing."

He stepped closer, shadows curling at his heels. Amusement flickered in his dark eyes, but beneath it was something sharper. "Yes... and yet," he murmured, studying her, "you seem... *preoccupied* with something else."

Her heartbeat quickened, but she met his gaze. "I need to understand this place," she said carefully. "If I'm to protect it, I must know what I'm dealing with."

The Fae Lord smiled faintly, tilting his head. "You're clever, Arden." Her name rolled off his tongue with quiet mockery, an indulgence rather than praise.

She clenched her jaw. "Ignorance is dangerous."

"Curiosity is worse." His stare pressed against her, heavy and unrelenting, but she refused to shrink beneath it, even as her pulse pounded.

His fingers grazed her cheek, deceptively gentle. "You walk a dangerous line, little thief," he murmured. "One misstep, and the artifacts in this vault could consume you."

"Then show me the right path." She lifted her chin, voice steady. "Or do you want me to fail?"

Something shifted in his gaze. "Desire is a treacherous thing, is it not?" The words hung between them as he stepped back. "But no, failure is not what I desire for you."

Her breath hitched, but she willed herself still. "Then what is it you want?"

He stilled. The question lingered, fragile, volatile. His expression shuttered, vulnerability flickering and gone. His voice came softer, laced with something like regret. "Once upon a time, I knew the answer to that question."

She hesitated. "And now?"

He turned away. "Do you truly wish to know?" There was something raw in his voice, something unexpected.

Arden closed the distance, "I want to know everything."

His shoulders tensed, shadows curling around him. She thought, for a moment, he might vanish into the dark but instead, he exhaled, the sound weary. "Like I told you before, I was not always one of the Arch-fey," he said, his voice a thread pulled from the abyss. "I was not born in this realm, nor created by the Gods like the others."

He crossed to a chair and straddled it, arms draped over the back. Arden perched on a nearby ledge, the Vault's air thick with expectation. "I was once a human soldier," he continued, voice steady now. "A nameless human warrior, serving a king who pulled me from my realm to fight for him in Elessian." His gaze lifted to hers. "My whole world became nothing but steel and blood and I served a king who took everything from me..."

"Did you try to run?"

"At first, yes, but over time I found that each attempt led nowhere and eventually I resigned myself to my role. Every battle I hoped I would be slain and every battle I walked out untouched. Life had no meaning for me here, not until I saw her."

"Who?" Arden asked, sounding a bit like a jealous child.

"Syliris." Her name left his lips like a prayer. "She was everything the fae could be. The future of the realm and I... I was just a mortal fool who dared to dream."

His voice drifted, lost in memory. "We came from different worlds, bound by love but divided by fate. Her mother saw my weakness and preyed upon it. She whispered promises of power and like a fool, I listened."

Arden leaned closer, fully invested in the story, the stone long forgotten.

His jaw tightened, shadows rippling across his skin. "She asked me to steal from the Seraphyne. A single feather from their wing, that's all she needed." His voice dropped, edged with bitterness. "So I did it. But when I gave it to her, she used it to unravel the realm. The first Fae King vanished from existence and with him, his daughter."

"Syliris?"

A muscle ticked in his jaw as he nodded. "Magic always demands a price. But her mother wasn't prepared for that and blamed me. She stripped away my mortality and bound me to this form, an Archfey forged in shadow, cursed to chase what I can never reclaim."

Silence fell, heavy and absolute. Arden felt the weight of his confession, the chains he could never break. Her voice was barely a whisper. "What is this vault?"

"Every attempt to bring her back."

A chill rippled through her as she realized that the vault wasn't just a random collection of relics, it was a monument to his failure. She looked around, at the centuries of artifacts stacked high, guarded by two silent soldiers, and protected by a thief. She thought of those who came before her, bound to his service. Bound to this endless search for redemption.

The truth of it settled over them both like a dark cloud, and Arden bit her tongue, suppressing the secret of the stone in her pocket. If it held answers, it also held power and in this realm, power was survival.

"You must miss her alot to go through all of this."

He rose, the moment between them soured by tainted memories. "Goodnight, little thief, don't go meddling with things you should have left alone." He strode toward the Vault's entrance, pausing only to murmur something to Kastiel before vanishing into the shadows.

Chapter Ten

T he next morning, Arden woke to whispers.

They were soft at first, curling through the darkness like smoke, brushing against her ears in a language she couldn't understand. She lay still, breath shallow, fingers tightening around the dagger hidden beneath her blanket. These weren't the sounds of the Watchers, they were more insistent, more pressing.

The vault remained still, but the air felt charged, as though something had shifted while she slept. Slowly, she sat up, scanning the room, expecting to find something lurking but there was nothing. Her hand went instinctively to the stone, ensuring it was still there. She pulled it from her pocket, holding it up to the dim light and the glow at its center pulsed in rhythm with the voices, strange, overlapping, rising and falling like a chaotic melody. A conversation she was not meant to hear, yet somehow had been invited into.

"What are you?" she whispered, turning it over in her hands, searching for meaning. The whispers swelled, urgent and wild, a desperate roar she couldn't decipher. Frustration burned through her, nerves alight. It was trying to tell her something, but she was blind to it.

Determined, she cleared a space at the nearby table, shoving aside her maps and scattered ink pots. She set the stone at the center and surrounded it with anything that might help: quills, ink, fresh parchment. She focused on the sound, the rhythm, searching for patterns. At first, it was only noise, a flood of shifting syllables and tones with no sense or order. But as she listened closely she noticed that certain cadences repeated, not quite words, but almost.

It was a language all its own.

Grabbing a quill, she began sketching out the sounds she thought she could recognize, turning them into letters based on their sounds. Each attempt felt like grasping at smoke as meaning slipped through her fingers. The moment she thought she had something solid, it unraveled leaving her hopelessly starting over.

Hours passed and her frustration sharpened into desperation. "What do you want from me?" she demanded, slamming her hand against the table, her voice raw with exhaustion. The stone's glow flared, blinding her, and as she squinted against the light something snapped into place and the whispers no longer spoke around her, they spoke to her.

The room tilted. Her vision blurred at the edges, and suddenly she wasn't in the Vault. Her mind was no longer her own. A rush of memory, not her own, poured into her like a flood. The past unfolded behind her eyes, raw and unrelenting, demanding to be seen.

A Fae King sat upon a golden throne, his presence vast, his power woven into the very fabric of the world. Before him stood a woman, her beauty unmistakable, her presence a force all its own. She spoke to him, her words dripping with honey, whispering promises wrapped tightly around a blade. He didn't see it until it was too late and she plunged the blade in.

Arden screamed as the world around her fractured, tearing her in two.

A name, ripped from history, torn from the lips of those who had once sworn loyalty to him. The throne sat empty until she sat upon it. A child caught in the middle, a daughter, and then, a mother's agonized tears. The woman's voice, ripped apart by loss, by something deeper than grief and a new identity born.

A crown placed upon the woman's head. Fae kneeling to The Caretaker, the one who would bring the realm together now that their king had abandoned them. Arden tried to shout, tried to warn them about what she had seen but no one heard her.

Somewhere in the crowd, a familiar voice wept for the loss of his love. "Iris...come back to me, please."

Her body convulsed as the vision ripped through her, and the stone flared, burning its truth into her bones. She succumbed to darkness, and dreams came swiftly, pulling her into a world half-remembered, half-imagined, as if it had been waiting for her return.

She stood in a field of silver grass that shifted without wind. The sky stretched above her in hues of twilight and deep violet, stars blinking in and out of existence like distant echoes. It was eerily still, too delicate, too hollow, as if she walked through a place that no longer existed.

But she was not alone. He was there, the Fae Lord, and he looked at her like she was royalty.

He stood a few paces away, his cloak pooling around him like ink spilled across the earth. His head was bowed, shoulders rigid, as though the weight of a thousand lifetimes pressed down upon him. The air around him trembled, the fabric of the world fraying at the edges. Then, with slow, deliberate grace, he knelt.

His hands trembled. His breath was ragged and uneven, as if bowing before her was unnatural. Arden's heart twisted, an ache blooming in her chest. She didn't know why it hurt so deeply or why his pain settled so heavily inside her. This was a man who had bound her to this realm, yet there was no cruelty in him now. No cold amusement or veiled threats. Only the silent tremor of a man undone by his own choices.

His eyes lifted to hers, shimmering with disbelief. In that moment, he was not the Fae Lord, not the untouchable force that loomed over her. He was simply a man brought down by the agony in his soul. A single tear traced the sharp edge of his cheek, glistening like silver in the endless twilight. His lips parted, but no command followed, no jest, only a whisper, trembling on the edge of ruin.

"Iris?"

She stepped forward, her lips parted to ask why, why he called her that, but the dream fractured.

Arden gasped awake, drenched in sweat, her pulse hammering. She sat up, dragging in sharp breaths, the edges of the dream clinging to her like cobwebs. The field, the sky, the way he had knelt before her, as if she alone held something he had lost. A phantom pressed against her ribs, a weight she could not shake.

Love.

The word surfaced, unbidden, unwanted.

Her stomach turned. No, that wasn't right. It was just a dream. It meant nothing. But as she pressed a trembling hand to her forehead, the truth coiled in the back of her mind, whispering through the hollow spaces left behind. Something within her had changed.

Her limbs trembled as she returned to the table. The parchment was covered in hurried writing, ink smeared across her hands. She had written across the page, the symbols blurred beneath her fingertips.

But one word remained, clear and undeniable, scrawled in her own unsteady hand: *Aeltherion.*

Chapter Eleven

After that, time moved slowly in the vault as Arden processed everything that had happened. Her days were consumed with trying to uncover the secret behind the word. Nothing in the vault gave any indication what it was supposed to mean, and every failed attempt to find answers drove her further into insanity.

She wasn't sure how many days passed before the Fae Lord's invitation arrived. She had grown accustomed to the magic of the vault, but this felt different, intimate. The letter traveled like smoke on the wind. Shadows danced along the edges of her vision, forming shapes that dissolved as quickly as they appeared. She reached out, plucked the parchment from their grasp, and watched as they vanished, as if they had never been there at all.

The letter contained only one word scrawled in elegant print, "*Dinner?*" There were no further details, no hint of his intentions. That lack of clarity gnawed at her, especially after the visions the stone had shown her.

The name Iris lingered in Arden's mind, a phantom echo that refused to fade. The Fae Lord had called her that, a name that belonged to his lost love, and she couldn't help but wonder why. There were infinitely more pressing questions demanding answers, but her thoughts circled back to that name again and again.

Kastiel passed through the vault doors, his presence grounding her, his expression remained neutral, though Arden thought she detected a flicker of curiosity in his eyes. "Shall I show you to your room?" he asked. "Or should I send your regrets?"

She forced a small smile, "I have a room?"

He let out a barking laugh, "normally, no, but we thought you might like to clean up if you're joining us for dinner tonight."

She smiled sheepishly at him and followed him, her boots tapping against the tile floors as she tried to match his pace. As they moved through the corridors, Arden found herself glancing at Kastiel, weighing her options. The urge to confide in someone battled with her instinct to remain guarded. She bit back the impulse to blurt out everything, the stone, the visions, Iris.

"Have you always served here?" she asked, keeping her tone casual, more of a probe than a genuine inquiry.

Kastiel's steps did not falter. His pace remained even, unbothered.

"Yes," he said. "I was brought to the court as a child. My life has always been in service to the ruler of this court." His voice held no bitterness, only a practiced detachment. "I have no family outside these walls, the court is my home."

Her hope of finding an ally dimmed as she realized Kastiel was not the confidant she needed. He was too much a part of this place, and whatever loyalty he held did not belong to her, no matter how close they had gotten. She offered a polite nod and allowed silence to settle between them. Her mind turned inward again, back to the visions, to the way the world had seemed to shift and ripple around her.

They turned a corner, moving deeper into the heart of the Court. Arden noticed servants hurrying through side passages, their arms filled with linens, silverware, and crystal. The air thrummed with preparation, a quiet, bustling energy that set her nerves on edge. "What's going on?" she asked, her voice low.

Kastiel's expression did not change, but he hesitated, the barest hitch in his stride. "Not sure what you talked to him about the other night, but he has requested a formal dinner," he replied. "Formal dinners are a big thing here, so preparations are underway."

His answer did nothing to soothe the unease in her stomach. Arden quickened her pace, she had no desire to be part of whatever spectacle was planned for tonight. The idea of a grand event, of being put on display, made her skin prickle with discomfort.

As they approached the double doors leading to her room, Arden forced her breathing to steady. The door to her room swung open, revealing a world of muted elegance. The space stretched wide, framed by floor-to-ceiling windows veiled in rich, dark purple drapes that shimmered like twilight. The air held a soft scent, a mix of lavender and cedar, that brought comfort to this unfamiliar place. She removed her boots and immediately relaxed as she sank into a plush midnight-blue carpet.

A grand canopy bed dominated the room, its frame wrought from twisted gold and silver strands, mimicking the wild, curling vines of a dark forest. The canopy itself was draped with sheer, smoke-colored veils that whispered against one another when the air stirred. The bedding was layered in deep blues and grays, a mountain of pillows in varying shades promising comfort and an invitation to rest. She ran her hand over the quilted blankets, fingers brushing against embroidery that depicted patterns of stars unknown to her, yet somehow familiar.

Kastiel lingered at the doorway, his expression uncomfortable. "This room was designed specifically for Syliris, but she never got the chance to use it." The words were not meant to hurt, but Arden froze as if he had plunged her into ice water. She looked around the room with new eyes, every piece that had moments ago resonated with her soul, now made her feel out of place.

Charcoal murals stretched across the walls, depicting stories Arden had yet to learn. Shadowy figures danced among curling mist, ancient trees reached for the sky, and rivers of ink seemed to flow along the baseboards. She could have stared for hours, unraveling the tales hidden in the brushstrokes. "Kastiel?" she said over her shoulder. "What can you tell me about her?"

He hesitated, his fingers tightening on the doorknob. He looked as if he wished he could retreat into the shadows themselves. "What do you want to know?" he asked, his voice strained.

Arden turned slowly, her attention drifting from the murals to Kastiel's guarded expression. "Everything," she said, determination in her eyes.

His lips pressed into a thin line, but he did not avoid her gaze. "Syliris was... remarkable. She was introduced to the Elessian courts as a young woman, bright-eyed and fearless." Kastiel's voice carried a reverence, a gentle awe that scraped against Arden's raw nerves. "She had this way of seeing through the masks people wear. She made even the most jaded fae believe in goodness again. She was quite literally a gift from the Gods to Elydris."

Arden walked over to the bed, hopping up as she listened to his story.

"Her relationship with the Fae Lord was controversial. Many dismissed it as a fleeting indulgence, even the King waved it away as youthful curiosity. No one believed she would truly fall for a mortal... It was unthinkable."

"But she did. And he betrayed her." Arden interjected.

Kastiel's expression hardened, a shadow passing over his features. "He did not act alone. Her mother betrayed all of Elessian. To this day, no one fully understands why, whatever poison her mother whispered to him, it was enough to break his will." His gaze wandered to the window, where the Court of Shadows lay under perpetual twilight. "Her mother's betrayal to the King, to Aeltherion, shook us all."

The air in the room chilled, the shadows no longer feeling like companions but silent observers. Arden's pulse thrummed, quick and electric. "What is Aeltherion?" Her voice steadied. "And why do I keep hearing that name?"

Kastiel's eyes narrowed, his wariness resurfacing. "Where have you heard it before? Perhaps we should wait and you can speak with the Fae Lord."

"I'm asking you," she shot back, the strength in her voice surprising even herself. "If you want me to trust you, then be honest. What is Aeltherion?"

Silence stretched between them, thick with unspoken truths. Finally, Kastiel let go of the door and stepped further into the room. "Aeltherion was a crown," he said at last. "Bestowed upon Elydris by the Gods themselves, it was meant to be a vessel of divine power, guiding Elessian's creation. Half of the realm's power rests within it; the other half within Solcryne. When combined, they are said to possess the ability to restore what was lost."

Arden's fingers twitched, itching to grab the stone in her pocket. "So if Aeltherion was his crown, what is Solcryne? And what exactly would the two restore?"

Kastiel's expression softened, "Solcryne was the sister stone to Aelthe-rion. A black gemstone, bestowed upon the Fae Queen. But after she took Elydris' throne and declared herself The Caretaker the Gods stripped her of it."

All the air seemed to leave Arden's lungs. The stone in her pocket grew impossibly heavy.

"Now, what they can revive depends on who wields them. Some say the Fae Lord seeks the pair to restore Syliris, to undo his betrayal. But not everyone believes the crown and the stone would respond to him. Not after what he did."

Arden's mind spun, the truths and half-truths weaving into a tangled web of doubt. "Do you believe he's still searching?"

Kastiel's shoulders lifted in a near-imperceptible shrug. "I don't know. But in the villages near the court, people whisper of his late-night ven-tures beyond the gates and shadows that stretch too far, as if searching for something."

Arden's breath came fast, the weight of Elessian's fate pressing against her. "And what about you, Kastiel? What do you believe?"

"I don't believe he'll ever stop searching if it means he might bring her back one day."

Arden did her best to not allow her emotions to show.

Kastiel, sensing her shift in demeanor, took his opportunity to leave. "If you need anything, I will be just beyond the door." He slipped out silently, the heavy door shutting with little more than a whisper.

Arden remained motionless, her thoughts a whirlwind. The space around her now felt like a waiting room for ghosts and she, a mortal among Fae, stood on the precipice of what was and what could be, the mysteries of Aeltherion and Solcryne swirling below her like a rip tide waiting to pull her under.

With a newfound resolve she stood and strode to the window where the golden hues of dusk filtered in. The view below was breathtaking. The court sprawled before her, winding streets of cobblestone weav-ing through houses built into hillsides, nestled among ancient trees. Lanterns hung from posts and trellises, casting a spectral glow over the paths. Life pulsed below, warm and unexpected. She could just make out children darting between market stalls, their laughter drifting faintly even at this height. Families strolled hand in hand, their faces open, at peace. Her fingers tightened around the windowsill, this world's harmony was not hers.

A wave of longing swept over her, fierce and sudden. Her brother, Callen. She could see him enjoying this place so clearly, the way his dark hair fell into his eyes, the exasperated roll of his gaze when she grew too protective. She wondered how he was doing, he was old enough to care for himself and she knew that. But knowing it did nothing to quiet the ache in her heart.

Thoughts ran through her mind, unbidden. Was he safe? Was he eating enough? Was he still waiting for her to come home? Her reflection in the glass startled her. She looked small against the vastness of the world outside. Her olive skin had paled, her hair was tangled and matted and her eyes were hollow having seen too much.

She turned away from the window, the warmth of the sun lingering on her skin. Arden moved through the room in a daze, each step pulling her further from the ache of reality and deeper into a quiet resolve. She slipped into the adjoining bathroom, the door gliding shut with a soft click.

She stripped off her worn clothes, the layers of dirt and exhaustion pooling at her feet. Solcryne was warm in her palm, a constant hum beneath her skin. Reluctantly, she set it down by the sink, the separation felt wrong, but she needed clarity, and the stone's constant humming muddled her thoughts.

Stepping into the shower, she turned the silver handles. Water cascaded from the showerhead in a steady rhythm, mimicking a downpour. She pressed her forehead against the cool tiles, allowing the warmth to sink into her bones. The scent of rain enveloped her, stirring memories she hadn't thought about in years.

She was nineteen again, soaked to the bone, shivering as the rain caught her and Luthan by complete surprise. "It wasn't supposed to rain until next week!" she said through bouts of laughter.

Luthan's hair spilled over his eyes, shaggy and limp. "All that work and everything is getting soaked. By the time we get home, no one will even want to buy this soggy bread."

"Lighten up," she said, "At least we didn't get caught by the dock guards!"

"I think I see an empty house up ahead, let's see if we can dry off and wait it out." Luthan had found a safe place for them to wait while the rain passed over them.

Once they had gotten inside and Luthan was satisfied that nothing was too far gone to be saved they had huddled close, trying to stay warm. She still remembered how her teasing had finally gotten him to laugh, softening his sharp features.

"You know, one day you're going to do amazing things Arden, and I hope you take me with you. Don't forget me when you rise above us all."

In that quiet space between breaths, she had leaned in and kissed him, her body cold, her heart burning like wildfire.

He pushed her away, his hands gentle but firm. His voice, rough with regret, had cut through her like a blade. "We can't, Arden... You don't even know me, it wouldn't be right."

"What are you talking about? We've been friends for years."

"You only know what I wanted you to know, trust me... You're safer away from me."

Arden stood motionless beneath the spray, steam curling around her like a fog. The warmth sank into her skin, but it no longer eased the chill that had taken root in her chest. She thought of the Fae Lord in her vision, the way he looked at her, the love in his voice when he called her Iris.

She thought of Luthan's voice, and the rejection that had wounded her more deeply than she'd realized until now. She would not make that mistake again, she would not try to sway someone into love by hiding the truth or silencing the past.

She shut off the water and the silence was sudden and heavy, broken only by the soft drip of water echoing in the tiled room. Wrapping herself in a towel, she stepped from the shower grabbing the gemstone and holding it tightly against her chest. "I need to know why you were given to me" she whispered to the stone.

She walked into the bedroom and found a black dress had been laid out. Simple, knee length, with pearl accents that glittered in the rays of the setting sun. She moved through the motions of dressing but her mind was lost in the choices in front of her. Something tugged at her, just beneath her awareness, a tension in the air, subtle but constant.

Crossing the room to the mirror, she hardly recognized herself. The image staring back at her was altogether a different girl that the one who had grown up begging and stealing. As she studied herself in the mirror she felt the stone in her palm warm subtly and she noticed the shadows behind her shifted ever so slightly, curling inward. Then she heard it, a whisper slow and melodic.

"Aeltherion awaits you."

Her gaze snapped toward the stone and she held it closer to her ear. The whisper came again, more urgent now.

"In the vault. It calls to you. It calls to me."

She held the stone in front of her, hands shaking as a glow pulsed from within. Arden stepped cautiously back into the room. Solcryne was speaking to her, it was alive with light, black veins within the gem swirling like storm clouds, a heartbeat made visible. She clutched the stone back to her chest before her thoughts could catch up.

"It is your destiny."

The whisper was inside her head now, no longer soft or passive. It surged like a wave, drowning her thoughts in urgency. Solcryne burned hot against her palm longing to be reunited with its match. A pulse answered from deep within the floor, a vibration that moved through her feet and up her spine, she could feel something calling to her.

The door to her bedroom creaked open and Kastiel stood in the doorway, as if summoned. His eyes dropped to her hand and the faint glow still emanating from Solcryne. "What is...," he said.

Arden didn't move, she couldn't. But as Kastiel approached, "you shouldn't have that. Where did you..."

She took a step toward him, as if she may confess everything. But in that moment, she knew this would be her only chance, she shoved him as hard as she could and ran.

"Arden!" Kastiel's voice cut through the hallway as he scrambled after her. "Stop!"

She didn't look back. The whispers surged around her pushing her forward. The halls blurred as she moved, shadows bowing out of her way, lanterns flickering to life and then dimming behind her. Solcryne pulsed with every step, guiding her.

Toward truth.

Toward memory.

Toward whatever waited for her in the dark.

Chapter Twelve

The hallways blurred around her, a tunnel of flickering torchlight and looming shadows. Her breath came in ragged gasps, sharp and shallow, each pull of air scraping her throat raw. Solcryne burned against her palm, a steady pulse of heat guiding her forward, demanding she move faster.

Behind her, footsteps thundered against the stone floors, relentless. "Guards! Stop her!" Kastiel's voice cut through the air, sharper than steel, no longer calm, no longer distant.

Solcryne had chosen her, had chosen that moment to speak to her. The Seraphyne had placed the stone in her hands not as a burden, but as a key, as a choice and Arden was going to take it. Her heart pounded in her chest, louder than Kastiel's voice, louder than her fear.

Her legs burned, her lungs screamed, but she pushed harder, driven by the fire rising inside her chest. Solcryne's heat spread through her body, into her core, igniting something fierce and alive. The corridors in the vault twisted around her, the walls seeming to shift with her passage, relics watching silently from alcoves and shelves, their dormant power stirring. Solcryne's glow intensified, the pulse aligning with her heartbeat. She followed it, trusted it, the stone wanted to find its other half.

A surge of energy pulled her forward until she was face to face with the door the Seraphyne had emerged from weeks ago. Massive, forged from marbled black and silver stone, its surface shimmering with glowing runes that danced beneath her gaze. The air around it vibrated with unseen power, a hum that reached deep into her bones, setting her teeth on edge.

Arden's steps faltered, as she reached out, her fingers brushing the cool surface. The carvings flared brighter at her touch, ancient symbols awakening. She lifted Solcryne and the stone flared in her outstretched hands, a brilliant light erupting from its core, casting the entire vault in silver and gold. The door responded, opening as if it had been waiting for her, for this exact moment. A tremor rumbled through the ground beneath her feet. The marbled veins of the door blazed with sudden light, the hum rising to a roar.

From somewhere behind her she heard the Fae Lord's voice as he yelled for her to stop.

Beyond the door stretched a cavernous chamber, its end lost to darkness. When she stepped inside, the door slammed shut and all she could hear were fists beating against it as Kastiel and the Fae Lord tried to get inside.

She knelt by the door's seams, "I have to do this, you have to let me" she said, wondering if they could hear her. The pounding on the other side stopped, no voices spoke back.

She stood and walked the corridor, staring at the portraits that lined the walls. They flickered with images of mortals, some wielding weapons, others kneeling before shadowed figures, some fleeing from something unseen. At the corridor's end, moonlight poured through a glass ceiling, illuminating a white stone pedestal. Upon it sat a crown that she assumed was Aeltherion. Silver and gold intertwined, gleaming with an unnatural light, radiating overwhelming power.

The stone in her hand seared white-hot shooting pain through her palm as it tried desperately to break free. She gasped and released it. It shot forward, slicing through the air before embedding itself in the crown.

The whispers in her mind erupted into screams. *"It is your destiny."* repeated over and over in her mind. Arden's pulse thundered as she stepped forward. The power of the crown vibrated in the small space, an unseen force pulling at her, drawing her closer. Her fingers hovered just above its surface and with a final, shaky breath, she grabbed it.

The moment her skin grasped the metal, the world around her shattered. Light and shadow exploded outward as a searing pulse rushed through her veins, tearing through her like wildfire. The cavern trembled, ancient images on the walls shuddering, their faces blurring, flickering like candle flames about to be snuffed out.

The figures surged forward, unraveling from their frames, reforming in midair, their eyes wide with fear. "She is coming!" their voices screamed, overlapping in a cacophony of panic.

Arden gasped, her legs nearly giving out beneath her as the power inside her fought to take shape to consume her. The ancient force crashed over her like a tidal wave, dragging her under. The crown's energy lashed against her very bones, tearing at the fabric of who she was.

It was too much.

"Let go." The Watchers' voices overlapped, some commanding, others pleading. The cavern itself groaned, darkness pressing inward as if the vault rejected her presence.

Arden gritted her teeth, her fingers digging into the crown's cool, twisted metal. This was her choice and no matter what happened in this moment she would not relinquish her hold on the crown. She pulled it closer, allowing herself to feel the weight of magic it held within.

The weight of their judgment bore down on her, but she lifted her chin in defiance. For so long she had allowed herself to be a pawn. To Ephraim, Luthan, The Silver Daggers, even the Fae Lord. For once in her life, Arden wanted to choose something, even if it was selfish. The cavern shuddered and the Watchers stilled, their forms flickering at the edges, shifting like smoke caught in a phantom breeze.

The chamber lurched as something made its way inside. The air twisted, thick with an unseen presence and the Watchers snapped their heads upward as though sensing something vast and ancient pressing against the Vault's walls, testing its limits. She felt it, too, it wasn't just the crown's magic. It wasn't just raw power. This new presence within was searching and now it knew Arden had the crown.

The Watchers shuddered, their screams dissolving into frantic whispers. *"She sees. She knows."*

A blast of unseen rage tore through the chamber. Arden staggered as icy dread coiled through her veins, she clutched the crown tighter and ran towards the now open doorway.

A female voice, laced with amusement and warning, whispered through the Vault, sending chills down her spine. "Run, thief. Run while you still can."

Shadows lunged for her, pulling her forward, forcing her feet to move. The crown's weight pressed against her chest. The vault twisted around her, collapsing in on itself. At the threshold of the Vault, the Fae Lord stood, shadows curling around him. The moment their eyes met, the darkness around him reached for her.

Before she could react before she could fight, plead, or demand his help he was on her. His fingers closed around her wrist, yanking her out of the Vault. A heartbeat later, her back hit stone. His grip pinned a wrist above her head, his presence overwhelming. Arden sucked in a sharp breath, her pulse hammering. Shadows slithered at the edges of his cloak, drawn toward the space between them.

His breath was cool against her skin. His voice, a low growl. "What have you done?" The words scraped against her like the edge of a blade.

Arden clenched her jaw, refusing to be cowed by his presence or the undeniable pull between them, "I did what you asked. I survived."

His scowl deepened. His free hand curled around her throat firm, but not cruel. Arden gasped, her body betraying her as she arched into his touch. His thumb brushed beneath her jaw, lingering where her pulse thundered. His lips parted slightly, as if tasting the tension thick in the air.

His pupils dilated. "Foolish, reckless creature." His voice was softer now, but no less dangerous. "You have no idea what you've done."

"Then tell me." The words were meant to be defiant. They came out breathless instead.

His smirk was slow and wicked as he leaned in, his lips a whisper from hers.

Then the vault exploded. A wave of power tore through the space, dissolving the chamber's interior. The Fae Lord's grip loosened as his gaze snapped to the void where centuries of work had once stood.

His eyes landed on the crown in her hand and his expression darkened. "You stole it."

"It called to me." She willed her voice not to shake.

His gaze burned into her. Before he could move, Arden reacted. With her free hand, she unsheathed her dagger, pressing its tip beneath his jaw. "Don't you dare."

He went still, the air between them crackled charged with something far more dangerous than steel.

"You can't wield it," he said, voice quieter now.

"Apparently, neither can you."

A slow, humorless smirk tugged at his lips. Silence stretched between them, heavy, unyielding. Arden felt the heat of his body, the ghost of his breath against her skin.

"I felt something watching me in there," she admitted, barely audible. A voice telling me to run while I still could.

His gaze held hers. A battle raged in the depths of his eyes. Then, with deliberate slowness, he stepped back, gesturing for her to follow. "The force that sought you out," he said at last, voice low, edged with warning, "the voice you heard?" His speed increased, "It was the Caretaker, Syliris' mother." His expression hardened. "She wants the crown. Maybe even more than I do."

Arden's fingers curled around the artifact. "What makes it so powerful?"

He didn't answer, instead, he turned down a hallway she'd never been through before. "We've got work to do."

Chapter Thirteen

Aezraen knew they had little time to uncover the answers they sought before Vaelithara would descend upon them. Initially, he had planned to let her exhaust herself in the library, hoping to bide his time until he could seize the crown from her. But with the threat of Vaelithara breathing down his neck, he needed Arden's help as much as she needed his.

The door to his private study swung open with a whisper of shadow, revealing a space untouched by mortal feet. It was not a room of lavish excess, his study was built for purpose. Shelves lined the walls, stretching to the ceiling, filled with ancient tomes and relics of lost eras, artifacts of power and consequence.

At the center of the room stood a massive desk, its surface cluttered with parchment, and fragments of forgotten works. Everything in this room had a purpose and everything in this room belonged to him.

Except her.

And, as he had come to realize, the crown.

He stood in the center of it all, arms crossed over his chest, watching Arden's face as she stepped inside. The dim light of the study cast shadows along the curve of her cheekbone, the sharp line of her jaw. There was something cautious in the way she carried herself.

"The vault kept it from me." The words were meant to be cold and indifferent but his tongue came across sharper than he had meant.

Arden turned, her expression unreadable. She knew exactly what he was talking about. Aeltherion. Her grip tightened on the crown, as if he would try and steal it from her.

The Vault, *his* Vault, the one he had spent centuries filling, had hidden the one thing he had ever needed just out of his view. That knowledge unraveled something inside him. For centuries, he had searched, bound mortals to him, sent them into impossible trials, and driven himself to the edge of madness in pursuit of the one thing that could undo the past.

And all this time... it had been right there.

Buried. Waiting. Not for him, but for her.

Aezraen's fingers curled into fists. "Why you?" The words held no kindness.

Arden bristled at his tone. "If I knew, I wouldn't be standing here." She tentatively placed the crown on the desk.

Aezraen studied the crown, his fingers itching to reach out and touch it. "You are not fae."

"No."

"You have no bloodline to claim, no power of your own."

"No."

"You should be dead."

Anger flickered in her eyes. "But I'm not."

Aezraen's jaw tightened. He circled the desk, stepping closer to her and forcing her back to push against it. "Despite all these glaring truths, Aeltherion waited for you like a beast for its master."

She dared not move.

"So tell me, little thief..." He leaned in, shadows curling at his back like a storm ready to break. "What makes you so special?"

She should have been afraid, anyone else would have been. But instead, she tilted her chin higher, meeting him head-on. "I guess that's what we're here to find out."

Her breath was uneven, her chest rising and falling with each slow, measured inhale. She stood firm, chin lifted in that infuriating, intoxicating way that sent a sharp pulse of heat through him, tightening low in his abdomen. His blood roared with the need to break her composure to tear that defiance from her lips and replace it with something raw, something breathless.

Aezraen seized her face, his fingers pressing into her jaw just enough to remind her who held the power between them. Heat licked through his veins, a wicked mix of fury and hunger, both warring for dominance. He leaned in, his breath hot against her ear as he dragged in her scent heady and maddening, fueling the fire beneath his skin. "You are nothing," he whispered, his voice low, dark, dripping with a dangerous promise. "You have no claim to this power."

He pressed her back, forcing her feet off the ground as she slid across the smooth surface. His shadows licked at her skin like a brand. His hand shot out, catching her by the throat firm but not crushing, a silent demand rather than a true punishment.

Her pulse thrummed against his palm, quick but steady. Not afraid. Her eyes met his dark, fierce, full of something too dangerous to name. "Then take it from me."

His body reacted before his mind caught up. Aezraen crushed his mouth to hers, his grip on her throat falling to brace himself. Her lips fought his with every inch of herself, her nails raking against his back as she pressed closer, heat meeting heat. Nothing about her was surrendering. This was war wrapped in temptation. A battle waged with gasps and clenched fists, with every wicked arch of her body against his.

Aezraen growled, a deep, guttural sound as he pressed into her, letting her feel every unrelenting inch of him the heat between them threatening to consume. His restraint snapped like a thread pulled too tight. His other hand found her hip his fingers digging into the soft flesh as if anchoring himself.

His lips found her throat, his teeth scraping over sensitive skin, drinking in the way she shuddered beneath him. Arden moaned against the vibrations, her nails dragging down his chest, sharp enough to sting.

His control unraveled, shredded beneath the weight of her desire the way she pressed against him, unyielding, intoxicating. With a flick of his wrist, his shadows obeyed, slipping beneath the fabric of her clothing like teasing fingers, dragging, pulling, unraveling her piece by piece. He did not rush. He wanted her to feel it, the slow, deliberate way his darkness slid against her skin, leaving her bare beneath his gaze.

"From this point on, little thief, you will call me by my name." His hands followed where the shadows had been, tracing every newly bared curve, claiming each inch as his own. His movements were slow, deliberate. "No more 'Fae Lord.' No more titles. You will call me Aezraen, as you should have from the start."

Her breath hitched, her body arching into him, her pupils blown wide with something wild, something unspoken.

"Beautiful," he murmured, his voice husky, his fingers skimming over heated skin before grasping her throat again, holding her so that she looked up at him with those tantalizing doe eyes.

"I hope you're listening closely, little thief," Aezraen muttered, his lips brushing over hers, just enough to make her chase the kiss he would not yet give. "Because if you forget..." He let the words linger, dark and unspoken. "I will let my shadows devour you."

Aezraen surrendered to instinct, binding himself to her in a way neither could undo. He took his time stripping away every ounce of composure until only need remained, her voice breaking upon his name.

Arden lay entangled with Aezraen, the world creeping back into focus. The flickering candlelight cast elongated shadows along the stone walls, a fragile sanctuary against the looming chaos beyond. But respite was fleeting. As dawn's light filtered through narrow windows, reality pressed in. She disentangled herself, dressing swiftly, the weight of their search settling over her once more.

Each day began at first light, yet progress remained elusive. Arden massaged her temples, exhaustion gnawing at her as she scanned another brittle page filled with looping script. For days, she had been buried in Aezraen's archives, sifting through tomes and scrolls, searching for answers about the crown. Something about it felt... wrong. It pulsed in the recesses of her mind, a presence waiting. For what, she didn't know. But she felt it, an undercurrent of energy threading through her nerves, pushing her to the edge of reason.

Across the table, Aezraen studied a scroll, his usual arrogance replaced by rare intensity. His ink-smudged hands gripped the parchment as he murmured, "If Aeltherion chose you, there must be a reason. A connection we're missing."

Arden sighed, rubbing her tired eyes. "I wish Nythis had just explained the prophecy when I met her."

Aezraen's gaze snapped up, sharp with interest. "What does that have to do with the crown?"

She hesitated. "I wasn't sure it mattered. But now... I don't know. It feels important."

Silence settled between them. Aezraen set the scroll aside, his attention wholly on her. "I left Aesyhra's book in my room but the Seraphyne..." she paused, wondering if what she was about to say would help or hurt. "They visited me in the vault, I wrote everything down."

"Kastiel, retrieve the book." he shouted towards the door. "Tell me everything you remember" he said.

When Kastiel arrived, she read the prophecy aloud. As she spoke, Aezraen paled, "The Prophecy of the Gods...I had forgotten she was looking for that." He trembled whether in fear or fury, Arden couldn't tell. "What parts have you deciphered?"

She opened her mouth to respond, but agony lanced through her skull. A crushing force pulled at her mind and she felt as if she were suffocating. The last thing she heard was the book falling to the floor and Aezraen calling her name before darkness swallowed her whole.

Arden awoke in a world she did not recognize; the air was thick and shimmering, as if dusted with crushed gemstones, and the whole space was consumed by an otherworldly energy. She swallowed hard, stepping forward, her boots making no sound against the unseen ground.

Before her stood a woman of impossible beauty; her gown was woven from strands of midnight and starlight and her hair was cascade of dark silk. There was no malice in her expression, but when the woman smiled, it sent a shiver through Arden's spine. "You search for meaning in places that will give you none," the woman mused, her voice soft and rich.

"Who... who are you?"

The woman tilted her head, as if considering the question. "You do not know me?"

"No." Arden swallowed. "Should I?"

The woman's smile widened, slow and knowing. "Ah. How refreshing." She took a step closer, and the very air seemed to bend around her presence. "I am the Caretaker."

The name rang through Arden's bones but she didn't seem like the villain Aezraen had spoken of. She seemed...kind. She curtsied towards Arden, placing her hand out as if she expected Arden to take it. When Arden just stared, she rose, "you have something that does not belong to you."

Arden stiffened, unsure how to respond.

The woman's expression did not change. "Return it to me, and you may go free. I will handle your bargain."

The weight of those words pressed against Arden's ribs. Walk away. Be free. She could go back to Callen. But despite all of that, something inside her pulled back against the offer.

"If you won't return it then I will have to take it by force, I'm afraid. I cannot let Aezraen keep it."

Arden squared her shoulders, "What do you mean?"

Her expression darkened, as if Arden had asked something profoundly foolish. "Because he will attempt to wield it, and that is a future I simply cannot allow." She took a slow step forward, the weight of her presence suffocating. "You do not know him, Arden. Not truly."

Arden held her ground, "I know enough."

A soft laugh escaped the woman's mouth. "Do you?" Her gaze sharpened, "I wonder how long it will take him to toss you aside when my daughter is brought back."

Her words struck like a physical blow, knocking the breath from Arden's lungs. She continued on, "his true love. The one he lost. The one he swore to tear this world apart to bring back."

Arden's hands clenched at her sides, the weight of the crown pressing against her heart. The Caretaker tilted her head, a slow, deliberate movement. "Did you think he could love a mortal the way he loves Iris?" She sighed, as if bored with Arden's naivety. "Your heartache is really misplaced. You should be more concerned with your brother."

Arden blinked, thrown by the shift in conversation. "Callen?"

A knowing smirk curved her lips as she flicked her fingers. The air between them shimmered and peeled apart like a rip in the very fabric of space. Arden gasped as she glimpsed the streets of Hallow's Reach and Callen.

He was thin, his cheeks hollowed from hunger. His clothes hung loose, tattered and unwashed. He sat slumped against a wall, his fingers trembling as he reached for a crust of bread discarded in the dirt. His eyes dull with exhaustion and suffering.

"No," Arden whispered, stepping toward the vision. "That's not possible. Aezraen...we had a bargain."

She watched Arden with pity in her expression, "I'm showing you the truth, not what he wants you to believe." Her voice was detached, "he is alone, Arden. Because of you."

"No, Luthan wouldn't let that happen...he couldn't" Arden stammered.

The vision shimmered as Callen curled into himself as the chill of night fell over Hallow's Reach, his breath visible with each exhalation. No one stopped to help him, no one even looked at him. "Luthan cast him aside as easily as you cast them all aside to come here."

Arden's throat tightened. "Stop this."

"You need to see the truth." She paused, as if contemplating something, "I could return you to him... all I need is the crown."

Arden shook as sobs wracked her body. The Caretaker sighed, "I'm not heartless, child, you have two days to make your decision. After that, I cannot help you." She snapped her fingers as darkness collapsed inward, and Arden fell into a sleep deeper than she had ever known.

Chapter Fourteen

Aezraen

Aezraen barely had time to react before Arden collapsed, her body crumpling to the ground like a marionette with severed strings.

"Arden!" He screamed as he surged forward, but before he could reach her, something else in the room moved. Shadows stretched unnaturally, thick tendrils of magic unfurling from the air itself. They snapped toward him, winding around his arms, his chest unyielding in their grasp.

He snarled, raw magic flaring around him as he struggled against the unseen force. But the tendrils did not loosen, instead they tightened, forcing him to his knees as a new presence filled the chamber.

A soft hum filled the room followed by a ripple in the air. A pale light, so unlike the inky darkness of the Court of Shadows overtook the room and Aezraen squinted against the harshness of it.

The pressure on his limbs shifted as his captors materialized, the Seraphyne were ethereal beings, neither fully present nor entirely absent, they stood cloaked in veils of shimmering silver mist. Their features were indistinct, save for the piercing glow of their eyes that were all knowing.

"*Aezraen,*" one of them spoke, their voice like wind chimes in a storm.

His jaw clenched, "where did you take her?"

"*The Caretaker has taken her, but she cannot hold her long,*" they corrected. "*We are here to deliver a warning.*"

Aezraen's breath came ragged, fury coiling within him like a storm held at bay. "What warning?"

The tallest stepped forward, the light around them pulsing in time with their voice. *"You must understand what she is."*

The weight of those words settled in his chest like a stone. He had known there was a chance that Arden wasn't as mortal as she seemed. When Aeltherion, a historical fae relic, had claimed her; not everything was as it appeared. "Speak plainly," he bit out, "enough of your riddles."

"She carries the heartspark," another voice answered. *"The tether to the ones who were lost."*

Aezraen's blood ran cold as the Seraphyne's voice faded into background static. Syliris... His Iris... Arden was connected to her. Throughout fae history, two beings sharing a heartspark was incredibly rare, only seen when the magic of the realm deemed it necessary to provide balance. Aezraen only knew of one other in existence, connecting the twins of the Goddess Sylara. His hands balled into fists, "tell me what I must do."

"You do not yet understand the nature of the heartspark," another Seraphyne said. *"It is not merely a connection, it is an origin."*

Aezraen's mind raced, his thoughts running away while the Seraphyne continued. *"What happens next is up to her. Only she carries the key."* The Seraphyne watched him in silence, their eyes unreadable. Then, as quickly as they had come, they were gone. The bindings vanished and the room returned to silence.

Aezraen remained on his knees, breath unsteady, his mind reeling. He turned his gaze toward Arden, still unconscious, her body motionless on the cold stone floor. The love he had felt for her moments ago waning, giving way to his desire to bring Syliris back. He grabbed Aesyhra's book and cast one final look in Arden's direction, watching the soft rise and fall of her chest. "I'm sorry" he whispered as he left.

Chapter Fifteen

As Arden woke, the room was empty around her. She stood, rubbing the last of the fog from her eyes and noticed that her book was now gone. She wandered the halls of the court, desperate to find someone who could explain what was going on but she found them vast and empty. The silence was unnerving, as if everyone had vanished. She called for Aezraen, but only echoes answered.

Her thoughts churned, the Caretaker's words gnawing at her mind. Her boots scuffed softly against the floor as she moved through unfamiliar corridors, past doorways half-hidden behind gauzy curtains and deserted halls draped in tapestries bearing Nythis' crescent moon.

She took her time, exploring each passage as she had in the Vault, yet every path led her back to the throne room. There, the statue of Nythis loomed, a constant reminder of what the Seraphyne had told her, of the prophecy that had driven Aezraen away.

Inexplicably, she was drawn to the throne at the room's center. It faced Nythis, a sign of reverence to the Goddess. Arden sat, staring at the veiled face that had once spoken to her, back when things had been simpler. Beside the throne sat a small table upon which lay a stained book and a goblet tipped on its side. Unlike the pristine texts she and Aezraen had studied, this one was worn, its frayed edges and softened spine bearing the weight of years. The leather cover was unmarked, but as her fingers brushed its surface, a familiar pulse shot up her arm.

Hesitant, she opened it. The ink was faded, the handwriting elegant and precise. Arden held her breath as she read the name once, then again... Aezraen. She turned the page, and the world around her dissolved as she read.

"I met her at twilight, when the sky bled gold and violet over Sylara's gardens. She was more beautiful than any dream I'd dared to have. Her laughter was the sound of rivers over stone, of leaves whispering secrets to the wind. She looked at me like I was more than a soldier, more than a nameless mortal... She looked at me like I was hers."

Arden swallowed hard, flipping through the pages. The words painted in these pages showed Aezraen before the shadows had claimed him, a mortal who dared to love a fae.

"We danced beneath the starlit arches of the Hollow Court, hidden from the Archfey's eyes. She pressed her hands to my chest, and I swore my heart would never belong to another. But she was fae, and I was not... The king would never allow it."

Her fingers trembled as she turned the next page.

"Her mother, Vaelithara, told me she could make us equals. She promised eternity. A future."

The writing grew darker, the strokes heavier, less careful

"The queen said the Seraphyne's feather would grant her the power to rewrite the world, to erase the boundaries between us. To unite the courts, to bring peace to this world."

Arden choked on the bile rising in her throat. Syliris. She wasn't just fae, she was a princess. The Caretaker had betrayed the realm, had destroyed her husband, all for power. Arden's heart pounded, her mind reeling with the weight of revelation. She flipped to the next page, dreading what came next. The entry was scrawled, uneven.

"I have it."

Her stomach dropped but she couldn't stop herself from reading on.

"The Seraphyne's feather is mine. I took it with my own hands. Tomorrow, I will be fae. I will give Syliris the future she deserves. Tomorrow, I will be free..."

Arden exhaled shakily, recalling what Aezraen had told her in the Vault. Vaelithara had paid a price she hadn't been ready to pay. Syliris, and her father, had been erased from history. She turned the page again. The ink was jagged, desperate. Aezraen's once-elegant script now raw and unrecognizable.

"She lied.

She destroyed everything I loved. The feather shattered the timeline. Elydris is gone. Syliris is gone. All that remains is the "Caretaker" and her captives. She calls it balance.

I call it damnation."

The air thinned, as if the room itself held its breath. Arden's hands shook. Every word bled with loss. She turned the page, but there was nothing. Just empty pages, Aezraen had never written again. She closed the book carefully. She didn't know how long she sat there, staring at the leather cover, the final remnants of a past Aezraen longed to reclaim.

Aezraen had loved Syliris, The Caretaker had not lied to her. One question haunted her now, had he ever stopped? In the silence, she swore she heard her heart crack.

Tears fell onto the cover as she allowed herself to grieve a love that was never hers.

A voice rumbled in her mind. *"Princess?"*

She choked on her sobs, trying to listen for the voice she thought she had heard, but only rain struck the glass. At some point, the world outside had begun to mirror her grief. She stood, unwilling to wallow, there were secrets left to uncover.

The journal felt heavier than it should have, its soft leather a fragile comfort. Emotionally numb, her thoughts spiraled. Her lips pressed into a line, swallowing the ache.

Then the voice returned, familiar but distant. *"Princess, is that you?"*

She froze. The words weren't spoken aloud, yet they echoed in her mind.

"You can hear me, I can feel it."

Her heart raced. She turned, scanning the empty corridor. "Who's there?" Her voice was tight.

"I've waited so long for you to return."

Warmth bloomed in her chest, sudden and overwhelming,ancient power, both comforting and disorienting.

"Princess, you must release me. Aezraen has imprisoned us both."

Her throat tightened. "Who are you?"

No answer, only a pull as if unseen hands guided her through the castle. She didn't resist, her feet moved on instinct, carrying her down winding corridors and cold staircases, deeper and deeper. When there were no more stairs, a heavy iron door waited for her.

"Come inside."

Her fingers trembled as she gripped the handle. The door groaned open, revealing a dungeon. In its center stood a cage of shimmering metal. Nothing stirred within, but her heart pounded.

Shadows shifted. Then, within the cage, they moved as a massive form stepped forward, sleek and powerful. Black fur shimmered like twilight laced with stars, golden eyes glowed, not with fury, but something softer. Something ancient. The Guardian of the Labyrinth.

Arden's body trembled. This creature had nearly killed her, now it prowled the edge of its cage, watching her.

"Princess?" The voice was clearer, more familiar. *"Forgive me for before,"* it said. *"I did not know who you were."*

"I don't understand," she whispered.

"You will, if you let me show you."

Warmth pulsed in her chest, a connection to this beast. She gasped as memories, not her own, flickered through her mind. Laughter beneath starlit skies, a jeweled tiara on her brow. A promise whispered: *"Tomorrow we'll be free, Iris."*

She staggered back. "Who are you?" she demanded.

He lowered his head, shame etched into every line of his massive form. *"My name is Noctis."* His name carried the weight of centuries. *"I was Syliris' guardian. Gifted to her by Ortheon before her coronation. I was meant to protect her... and I failed."*

His voice was thick with sorrow. *"I bled for her, but I did not see the betrayal until it was too late."* His golden eyes burned against the darkness. *"Vaelithara was not the only hand in her destruction. Aezraen... he was the blade she never saw coming."*

Arden's lips parted, denial rising, but Noctis pressed on.

"He may have been ignorant, but he stole the feather. In my eyes, he is to blame." His voice dropped, heavy with bitter truth. *"When I felt you, I thought maybe the stars answered her pleas."*

Her chest ached. "Were you there?"

"I was there when she begged the stars to change fate... and when she ceased to exist."

Silence stretched, suffocating.

"For centuries I waited to feel her heartspark again. I thought it was lost, but it lives in you." Noctis lowered his head. *"Forgive me for not recognizing you, Princess."*

Arden's hands trembled. "I'm not Syliris."

"Maybe not," he said. *"But her heartspark lives in you, her heartbreak, her fire. Only through your sorrow could I find my way back to you."*

Her fists clenched. She thought of Aezraen's touch, how he'd looked at her like she was more. But she never had been, if she truly carried this heartspark then it had always been Syliris he had felt within her. Her breath came fast, anger rising. "I don't know what you want from me."

"I want to serve you," Noctis said. *"To make amends for how I failed her."*

"I want out of here," she said. "Take me away from here."

"Then release me."

She stepped forward, fingers brushing the cage. Magic pulsed beneath her touch and she pulled back against it, afraid. The lock shattered at the absence of her touch, her hand trembled as she reached for him. But he didn't flinch and warmth enveloped her.

"If we are leaving, we must go now."

Arden gripped his mane, pulling herself onto his back. "Then let's go."

Noctis surged forward, shadows bursting around them. Together, they vanished into darkness, leaving the Court of Shadows behind as they ran through the main gates, into the freedom beyond.

Chapter Sixteen

The world beyond the Court of Shadows was vast and breathtaking, alive with beauty and vibrant life. Noctis guided Arden through fields of silvergrass, where the delicate stalks swayed gently in the wind, whispering against her fingertips as they passed. Above them, the sky stretched wide and clear, untouched by the dense gloom that shrouded Aezraen's realm. Here, the night felt not oppressive but tranquil, reminiscent of evenings spent with Callen, watching sunsets from rooftops.

Yet even in this peace, Arden sensed a tension that never fully eased. The world shimmered too perfectly, and her instincts prickled with the weight of unseen eyes pressing against her back. Each time she turned, however, there was nothing but the wind.

The trees were unlike any she had ever seen, their trunks threaded with veins of pale light, as if the very roots of the world pulsed with magic. She dismounted and explored freely, with Noctis moving silently beside her, his massive paws barely making a sound.

In the distance, the soothing melody of an unseen river reached her ears, bringing her first moment of calm since entering this strange realm. For the first time in her life, she felt truly free. But beneath that peace, a thread of tension remained, because she knew nothing in this realm was ever truly free. She exhaled, brushing her hand through Noctis's mane. "This place is…" She hesitated, searching for the right word.

Noctis's voice rumbled, almost like laughter. *"Not what you expected?"*

Arden shook her head. "Not at all." She had braced herself for danger, for a world as cold and cruel as the one she had left behind. Instead, she found something magical.

Tilting her head back, Arden let the warmth of the sky wash over her. The endless stretch of blue above seemed to press gently against her shoulders, easing the tension she hadn't realized she carried. For a moment, she allowed herself to breathe. To feel.

But the silence left too much room for thought. She turned toward Noctis, who pawed idly at the grass before settling beside her. The question had lingered in her mind since they left the castle, "why were you locked in the dungeon?"

Noctis didn't answer right away. His gaze drifted across the horizon, ears twitching at some distant sound before he finally stilled. *"When Syliris vanished,"* he began, voice low and even, *"the queen was consumed by grief. I was blamed for failing to protect her daughter... and banished to the darkest corners of this world. It was easier for her to punish me than face her sorrow."*

He exhaled, a deep, weary breath that stirred the grass at his paws. *"When Aezraen found me, I think I reminded him too much of what he'd lost. I refused to take part in his desperate search, refused to give him false hope. For that, he had his guards throw me in the dungeon."*

Arden sat beside him, fingers threading slowly through his fur, grounding herself in the rhythm of his voice. She didn't interrupt.

"He eventually let me out," Noctis continued, *"but only to serve as a predator in the labyrinth. I was a monster to be feared, my hunger honed into a weapon. No one made it out when I entered."* His voice grew quieter with the last words, weighed down by regret.

Arden stared ahead, digesting the truth of it. This new side of Aezraen unsettled her, not because it felt out of place, but because it fit too well. The pieces of him she knew were only fragments, curated glimpses he had allowed her to see. She had been so sure she understood him, but now... she wasn't certain she knew him at all.

Her thoughts drifted as the wind picked up, carrying the scent of wildflowers and sun-warmed stone. The First Court stretched before her, breathtaking in its splendor. Unlike the Court of Shadows, shrouded in gloom and flickering candlelight, this realm pulsed with life. Light seemed to seep from every inch of the land, a gentle glow that spread to everything it touched.

It was radiant, alive. But Arden couldn't ignore the shadow that lingered just behind the light; memories, truths, and a history that refused to stay buried. Ahead, the castle rose majestically, a stunning structure of white marble and pristine glass, its towers reaching skyward like spires of light. After some time, Arden stood and brushed the dirt from her legs. "We should go" she said as Noctis rose beside her.

As they approached the castle, grand doors swung open revealing the Caretaker who stood waiting, her smile radiant. "Welcome home child."

Arden hesitated but followed her inside. "Home?" she queried.

She smiled patronizingly at Arden, "just an expression dear, nothing to take quite so literally."

Arden fidgeted with the crown she had tied to her waist, she was here for Callen. This would never be her home.

Inside, the palace was everything a fairytale promised. Sunlight streamed through stained glass windows, casting rainbow cascades across polished floors. The air was infused with the scents of jasmine and honeysuckle, and crystal-clear fountains danced in the courtyards. When The Caretaker spoke again, Arden almost jumped at the sudden sound, "I'm sure you've heard my story from others..." she trailed off, seeming lost in memory. "But as a queen, I had to do what was best for my people. It's why I started having people call me The Caretaker, but you may call me Vaelithara if you wish, few remember that name I worry."

As they walked, Arden felt her oddly comforted by the woman beside her. "I know this must be overwhelming," she said gently. "I too was overwhelmed when the realm was in endless chaos, but as their queen I knew I had to be strong. Even if it meant banishing my husband...I just never thought I'd lose her too." She put a comforting hand on Arden's shoulder. "But you've done well, Arden. Few mortals would have survived the Labyrinth, let alone had the strength to hold that crown."

Arden's fingers brushed the edge of the circlet, but she remained silent. They entered a garden where night seemed endless. Flowers unfurled under impossible stars, silver leaves shimmered in the moonlight, and tiny, glowing moths flitted between blossoms. A small fountain trickled in the center, its water singing softly. "My daughter used to run through these gardens," she said, her voice wistful. "She loved to chase the moths and splash in that fountain, no matter how many times I told her not to." She chuckled lightly, her gaze distant. "Her laughter used to echo through the halls."

For a brief moment, her smile faltered. She reached out to brush a petal from a nearby flower. "You remind me of her. Stubborn. Fierce. Curious." Turning back to Arden, her eyes softened. "You don't have to be alone, child. Not anymore, you could stay here with me."

The words sank into Arden like stones, heavy and unsettling. She wanted to feel warmth from their kindness, but something in her chest twisted instead. Everything about this place felt artificial, as if it were hiding something darker.

Arden forced a tight smile. "Thank you, I appreciate that. But I'm here for my brother, for Callen."

Vaelithara's gaze lingered on her for a moment, unreadable. Then she nodded. "Of course, and I will return you to him. But first, let me show you the heart of this court."

They continued through the palace, passing grand halls with ceilings carved to resemble constellations. Arden's footsteps echoed, her senses heightened. She couldn't shake the feeling that something was watching from the shadows, even here. When they reached the throne room sunlight poured through glass domes above, illuminating the chamber in golden light. The throne itself loomed on a raised platform, crafted from ivory, its design intricate yet cold.

Noctis stiffened beside her. Arden followed his gaze to the throne, pausing momentarily wondering what he sensed there.

Vaelithara ascended the stairs and paused before sitting, her gaze flicking to the crown on Arden's head. "You've done well, Arden." Her voice was warm, almost convincing, but Arden tensed, a warning curling in her chest. "You made the right choice."

Arden couldn't help but wonder if she had as Vaelithara's smile deepened, the softness fading into something sharp and ravenous. "Come now, child," she coaxed. "Bring me my husband's crown. Let me ease your burden so you can return to your brother."

Arden didn't move immediately and something in the room shifted. Noctis let out a low growl, his body tensing beside her. *Do not trust her, princess,* he warned, his voice tight. *I sense danger.*

Vaelithara descended the stairs slowly, each step deliberate. As she raised a hand, the crown in Arden's grasp thrummed, alive with ancient magic. It sung to her, a melody she felt deep in her bones urging her to wear it.

"The crown will not lead you astray," Noctis said. *"It holds the power of the Gods. It knows where it belongs."*

Arden's fingers trembled as she untied the crown from where it had been secured. She hesitated only a breath and lifted it, quickly placed it upon her head.

Power crashed over her as the crown settled like a second heartbeat against her skull, heavy and electric. Vaelithara's smile fractured. Her hands curled into fists, and the mask she wore moments before shattered. In its place was something cruel.

A surge of raw magic exploded between them, a shock that staggered them both. Arden gasped as her knees buckled. Vaelithara stumbled back, eyes wild. "You stupid girl," she spat, venom coating every word. "Do you have any idea what you've done?"

Noctis leapt forward, placing himself between them. His growl deepened, low and warning. Arden clutched at his fur for balance, her breath coming in short, panicked bursts. Vaelithara stared, her expression warping with fury and disbelief as realization struck.

The crown had chosen Arden.

Arden's chest heaved as the truth settled in. She reached up, fingers trembling as she tried to pull it from her head. "Get off," she urged as she tugged against the power flowing through her. Panic clawed up her throat. She yanked harder, nails biting into her skin. The crown refused to move. It clung to her, as though it had always been hers.

"No," she whispered. "No, no, no "

Another sharp yank. Pain bloomed behind her eyes, the crown resisting her as if it had fused with her skin. "Why won't it come off?" Her voice cracked, eyes wild.

Vaelithara chuckled softly from where she had recovered, smoothing her dress as if nothing had happened. She tilted her head, anger darkening her gaze. "Get it off!" Vaelithara snapped, attempting to wrench it free.

Arden cried out as white-hot pain emanated from the crown, enveloping them both. It stayed fastened to her, as though it had rooted itself beneath her skin. Vaelithara's eyes blazed with fury. Her glamour flickered, the perfect facade cracking to reveal a glimpse of something twisted beneath. "It won't obey me," she hissed. "Why won't it obey me?"

Vaelithara's hands dropped, fists clenched. She stepped back, seething, her breath coming in ragged, furious bursts. "Well," Vaelithara murmured, her voice smooth as glass but no longer pretending warmth. "I'm sorry I have to do this." Her fingers flicked, and power surged through the air. Shadowy figures materialized from the ether, cloaked in dark armor, their faces obscured. Their hands clamped around her arms like iron bands.

"No! Get off me!" Arden kicked, twisting violently trying to get free.

Noctis roared behind her, a sound that shook the walls. He lunged toward her captors, but Vaelithara's magic was faster. A bolt of silver light erupted from her hand, striking him square in the chest. The force sent him crashing into the wall, the air filling with the scent of scorched stone and seared fur.

"NO!" Arden screamed, lunging forward, only to be yanked back.

Silver chains slithered like living serpents from the shadows, coiling around Noctis's limbs. They tightened with every tug of Vaelithara's magic, anchoring him to the floor. His eyes burned with fury, but Arden could feel his pain coursing through their bond like molten lead.

"Stop, please stop!" she cried, tears stinging her eyes.

Vaelithara approached slowly, each step predatory. The mask of calm had fully cracked now, revealing the fury beneath. Her eyes gleamed like cut glass, her smile gone, her voice low and precise. "I had hoped you would come willingly," she said, her gaze flicking toward the crown. "I would have been merciful. Returned you to your pathetic mortal life," her lips curled. "But now we'll have to do this the hard way."

Arden's knees buckled under the weight of her fear. She couldn't breathe. The crown burned. Her limbs trembled. "I didn't ask for this," she choked, "I never wanted it..."

Vaelithara leaned in, her voice a whisper laced with venom. "That doesn't matter now, you have it. Now... you'll die with it. Or you'll figure out how to give it to me. One way or another, girl... I will have it."

Arden struggled as the guards dragged her toward the door. Her screams echoed, clawing at the walls, at reason, at anything that could stop what was happening.

Her heart pounded, and fear rotted in her gut like a sickness. "Noctis!" she cried, reaching for him.

His voice bled into her mind, faint but firm, *"They cannot make me leave you."*

His eyes locked with hers, fierce even through the chains. The last thing she saw was Vaelithara striding toward Noctis, magic pooling like liquid in her palm.

Chapter Seventeen

Aezraen

Aezraen knew something was wrong the moment he stepped back into the Court of Shadows. The air was too still. There were no guards posted at the gates, no servants wandering the halls. It was as if everyone had abandoned the castle.

The Watchers whispered, their voices curling around him, murmuring in fractured, uneasy tones. *"Gone. Gone. Gone."*

Aezraen's jaw clenched. His steps echoed with restrained fury as he moved deeper into the heart of the castle, shadows curling tighter around his frame with every breath.

"My lord," a voice murmured from the darkness. "When we returned, she was already gone." Kastiel knelt before him but did not look up, did not dare to.

Aezraen's chest burned with something he didn't care to name, something he refused to believe. He exhaled slowly, forcing the storm beneath his skin to remain contained. Lifting his chin, his voice was smooth despite the weight pressing on his lungs.

"Where has she gone?" he asked, composure quickly shattering. His shadows lashed out, coiling around the fae's throat, dragging him upward until he dangled above the floor. "I said WHERE!" Aezraen screamed.

Kastiel choked, fingers clawing uselessly at the dark tendrils. "We don't know..." he gasped. "...Noctis missing."

Aezraen dropped him and Kastiel collapsed, gasping, as the shadows slithered away, retreating into the walls. Aezraen was in the dungeons within moments, he had not set foot in here in centuries, but as he stepped into the vast chamber beneath his castle, something ancient settled on his shoulders.

Kastiel had been right, the space had been disturbed. His old journal lay discarded on the cold floor, a rock weighing down a page that now read: "I'm not her." Next to it, the cage where Noctis had been imprisoned stood empty. Aezraen stared at the lock. The magic that once laced the bars had been shattered, a hint of silver magic still crackled across the lock's surface.

The rage within him built to a crescendo, only one person in the realm still possessed silver magic, Vaelithara. The realization landed like a knife, clean and precise, slipping between his ribs. His fingers twitched at his sides before he completely unraveled.

The stone table shattered first. It cracked in an instant, splitting clean through, the force of Aezraen's magic tearing outward. The walls groaned against his magic, the very foundation of the castle threatening to buckle beneath the onslaught of power. The shadows around him swelled, thick and violent, twisting across the dungeon in seething waves.

"She took them..." Aezraen fell to his knees. The words were bitter in his mouth, "she took them from me." That one thought circled again and again, refusing to let go. Tears, angry and hot, spilled down his face. "Not again."

His power lashed out, splitting the pillars that lined the chamber, tearing through them like paper. Darkness flooded the crypt in a storm, choking out all light. "Vaelithara!" The name tore from his chest, reverberating through the halls, carried by shadows that spread through the castle without warning.

Aezraen exhaled, the fury threatening to consume him. Then, slowly, he straightened as a manic smile overtook his face. The storm inside did not settle, but it shifted. He rolled his shoulders, letting the last remnants of his power ripple through his fingers.

Fine. If this was the game they were to play, then he would tear that whole wretched court apart to bring her back. Vaelithara had made her choice, now she would live with the consequences. Aezraen stood in the wreckage of the dungeon, his chest rising and falling in slow, steady breaths.

He made his way back up to the main castle, where Kastiel was still trying to catch his breath. "Send word to the Hollow Court."

Kastiel coughed, trying not to stutter. "Veylis?"

Tell him, "It's time to play war."

Aezraen hated coming to Veylis' domain. It hadn't always been this way, but lately, the Hollow Court had become a kingdom of decadence and ruin.

He stepped through its towering gates, where vines of star-kissed ivy climbed crumbling walls. The scent of spiced wine and sweat clung to the air, mingling with the low hum of music drifting from every corner. The court was coated in skin and silk, the very air thick with indulgence.

The Hollow Court was no longer a place of order, but of delinquency, pleasure, and madness. A place where restraint was forgotten, and those who sought power lost themselves in their own excess. Aezraen despised what it had become, not because he feared what lurked within, but because he understood too well why it had descended into this den of depravity.

He moved through the corridors, shoving masked fae aside as he stepped into the grand hall. It was still a throne room, but barely. The throne itself was worn and broken from misuse. Veylis lounged upon it, one leg draped over the armrest, a half-empty glass of wine dangling from his fingers. He looked every bit the ruler of hedonism, silver-haired and violet-eyed, his silk robes barely concealing the golden skin beneath.

He lifted his gaze lazily as Aezraen entered, lips curling into a slow smirk. "Ah," he murmured, rolling his glass between his fingers. "I was wondering when you'd finally crawl back."

Aezraen did not respond, today was not the day for Veylis' mind games.

Veylis exhaled, his smirk widening as he leaned back against the ruined throne. "Tell me, Aezraen. What brings you here? Have you finally grown tired of lurking in your shadows?"

Aezraen's jaw tightened. "I don't have time, Veylis. Will you stand with me or not?"

Veylis went still, and the entire court seemed to hold its breath. The music stopped, his subjects froze, waiting to see what would unfold. Veylis rose from his throne, setting his glass aside with deliberate care. His movements were unhurried, almost lazy, but Aezraen knew better. This was not a show of indifference, it was absolute restraint.

"The Caretaker," Veylis murmured, testing the word on his tongue. His expression remained unchanged, but Aezraen saw the subtle twitches of anger. Then Veylis laughed, a dark, bitter sound curling around the edges of the room. "She never does know when to stop, does she?"

No one in the room dared speak, Veylis wasn't speaking to them. He was speaking to the ghost that still lived in this place. Veylis lost control, his laughter spilling out manic and unhinged. Aezraen remembered the madness that followed Niko's passing, how Veylis had shattered. After that, he had transformed his court. It became known for its parties, where anyone could be anything and nothing was out of reach.

Veylis had never truly recovered.

He inhaled sharply, shaking his head as if to banish the past. When he turned back to Aezraen, the smirk returned. "Do you really think I'd stand against her again? After everything she did?"

Aezraen didn't hesitate. "I lost everything to her once too." His voice was steady, unyielding. "And I promise you this, Veylis. I will not lose everything again."

Veylis turned, accusation in his voice. "You lost everything because YOU trusted her." For a second, Veylis' smirk faltered. He studied Aezraen for a long moment, and for the first time, there was no amusement in his eyes. "I lost Niko because I couldn't change fate." He looked pointedly at Aezraen, "our stories are NOT the same. Get out of my court."

The music did not resume and he court remained silent as guards escorted Aezraen out. As the doors slammed shut behind him a new plan began to take root.

Vaelithara had wronged many others, he just needed to find them.

Chapter Eighteen

Arden's cell was cold, plagued by a chill that seeped beneath her skin and bones, numbing more than just her body. She paced in tight circles, her thoughts spiraling faster than her footsteps; each step was a futile attempt to quiet her racing mind.

Whenever she brushed her fingertips against the rough stone walls, she felt the ancient magic woven into them. It pulsed like the heartbeat of the prison itself, a constant reminder that this place was alive in its own way, holding her fast within its grasp.

She sank to the floor, pressing her back against the wall, her arms curled tightly around her knees. The silence closed in around her, thick and absolute, swallowing every sound. There were no clinking chains, no footsteps in the corridors, and no muffled voices beyond her cell. Only she and the crown still perched on her head, a weight she could not remove. It teased at the edge of her thoughts, ever-present, like a whisper she could never quite hear.

Her memories kept drifting back to Noctis. It had been days since they had seen each other, and Arden still had not felt him through their bond. Her mind raced with questions she had no answers to. Was he still bound? Hurt?

She had seen Vaelithara move toward him before the doors slammed shut. Had he fought? Had she punished him? The bond between them was too quiet now, even though she knew it wasn't broken. That silence was a blade pressing against her heart.

Silent tears fell as she thought about everything she had lost within these walls. Vaelithara had promised to return her to Callen, luring her in with soft light and honeyed words. Arden had clung to that promise, desperate to believe she could end this and walk away, crownless and free. Now, that hope tasted like ash on her tongue. She pressed her forehead to her knees, fear settling deep in her chest. She had fought for so long, and now she felt farther away than ever.

Her eyes fluttered shut, and in the stillness, a familiar and warm presence stirred, reminding her of home. His voice brushed against her mind, soft and distant, yet undeniably real. *"If we want to escape, you need to listen."*

She reached out along their bond and could feel him once more. He was alive, relief flooded her body as she once again felt her guardian's presence. "Listen to what?" she whispered, her voice raw.

Silence lingered for a beat too long and Arden was almost sure she had imagined his voice. But something shifted within her, like a thread being pulled, a veil lifting as memories unraveled. She closed her eyes and accepted the vision.

When she opened them, she was no longer in her cell but outside the First Court. A palace of white stone stood before her, its walls draped in soft pink blossoms that climbed like living ribbons toward vaulted ceilings. Warm sunlight streamed through high arched windows, catching motes of dust that danced like fireflies. The air was sweet and fragrant with blooming flowers and a fresh spring breeze, filled with gentle magic that felt alive. This was not the First Court as she had known it. Here, life pulsed all around her, in stark contrast to the sterile environment it had since become.

Arden drifted through it like a ghost, her footsteps silent against the marble floors. She passed beneath flowering vines woven into intricate patterns along the walls, their petals glowing faintly in the light. The soft murmur of fountains echoed in the distance, and for a breathless moment, she stood in awe of the beauty, and peace surrounding her.

She stepped into a room bright with sunlight and a child's laughter. In the center stood a young Syliris before a gilded mirror, her face full of wonder. This was surely where the flowers had originated, as Syliris giggled and danced around the room, throwing her magic everywhere without a care in the world.

Flowers grew wild around her; vines with silver-edged leaves swayed as if moved by a breeze only they could feel, while blossoms opened slowly, content in their freedom. The room radiated joy, a place where life flourished without restraint.

Arden stood still, entranced as Syliris lifted her hands toward the crown resting atop a velvet cushion. Sparks of gold and silver flickered between her fingers, wrapping around the crown as if it lived and breathed. She giggled as the crown buzzed in her palms.

A man entered, laughter already in his voice. "Iris... what have I told you about playing with my crown?" His tone was rich and warm, filled with affection.

Vaelithara followed closely, frustration evident on her face. "Syliris," her name sounded like a curse on the woman's tongue. "We have warned you that magic is not a toy you can play with." She picked at the vines encircling the doorway. "The whole castle is covered in chaotic weeds; it will take all day to fix this!"

Syliris turned, grinning as she ran to her father, tugging at his sleeve. "Oh, Daddy, please let me practice a bit more."

He chuckled, brushing her hair back gently. He squatted down next to her, and the pair looked at Vaelithara with pitiful expressions. "How can I say no to that face, my love?"

Vaelithara rolled her eyes at them both as Elydris turned his attention back to Syliris. "Adjust your stance my little moonbeam. Remember to focus, decide your intention, and the magic will flow through you."

Syliris nodded and moved her hands in wide arcs, tracing two circles in the air. "Silver for Mommy. Gold for Daddy. Both for me!"

Tiny bubbles of silver and gold floated around her, shimmering in the light. She giggled, chasing the ones that drifted toward the ground. Elydris lifted her up to pop a few, delight mirrored in his eyes as he held her close.

Arden's chest tightened as she watched them, a strange ache blooming inside her. She had never known such ease, such effortless love. It felt foreign and impossible. She stood like an intruder, locked outside a world she could never touch. Not for the first time, she envied Syliris; the warmth, the magic, the laughter... the life she could never have.

In the corner, Vaelithara lingered, half cloaked in shadow. She did not speak or attempt to move closer. Her gaze followed Syliris and Elydris, arms wrapped loosely around herself. There was love in her eyes, but it was distant and cold, warped by something darker.

Arden could feel it, see how the darkness within corrupted this moment. Behind Vaelithara's eyes lay jealousy. The queen watched them with longing, her expression calm, but Arden sensed the truth. Beneath the stillness lay a hunger for all that Elydris and Syliris shared. They had a bond built of joy and love that she had never truly known with her own daughter.

Arden wanted to look away, but the memory held her in place. The laughter echoed, a sound from a past long lost. Beneath it all, she felt the crown as it waited for her to understand.

Arden gasped, snapping back into the cold cell. Her breath came in short bursts, her heart still pounding from what she had seen. The blossoms, the light, the joy; it was all gone, only the cold remained.

She had witnessed magic before. She had seen Aezraen manipulate shadows and Vaelithara create and move things without a word. But this was something else. This magic had not been forged into a weapon. It had existed to create, to nurture. It had shaped Elessian, not broken it.

Noctis' voice returned, calm and steady. *"You hold that same magic within you."*

Arden shook her head, pressing herself harder against the wall. "No. That's not possible."

"You carry the balance, just as she did. Light and dark, together. That is why Aeltherion chose you. Not because of what you are, but because of what you hold."

Her hands shook. The idea tore at everything she believed about herself. She had stolen, lied, survived. She had never known magic. Never imagined herself capable of shaping anything beyond her own path. "What if I lose myself?" she whispered.

"This power is not a curse. It is a part of you, waiting. Trust it, Princess. Trust yourself."

Her pulse thundered in her ears. She could still see Syliris, spinning with joy, golden sparks dancing from her fingers. Arden had envied her but that piece of Syliris waited within her to be unlocked.

"Try." Noctis urged.

She hesitated, fear twisting in her chest. Her hands trembled as she lifted them, mimicking Syliris' movements. Wide, slow arcs cut through the air. She waited.

Nothing happened.

A sharp breath caught in her throat. She lowered her hands, her pulse pounding in her ears. She was not sure what she had expected, only that something, anything, might answer.

Elydris' voice surfaced in her thoughts, calm and patient. *Decide your intention, and the magic will flow through you.*

She reached for hope. She tried to believe in herself, tried to summon something to help her escape this cell. Still, nothing stirred. Her fingers curled into fists. "Damn it," she muttered.

"Keep trying," Noctis encouraged.

Her jaw clenched. She took a breath, focused again, and reached for it. She thought of Callen. The image of his face came to her, clearer than the stones around her. His voice, his laughter, the way he had always looked to her for strength. The ache of missing him sharpened into something fierce. She needed to get back to him. She needed to protect him. That need burned hotter than anything she had ever felt.

A spark flared at her fingertips.

Gold. Brief. Flickering.

Her eyes widened. It vanished almost as quickly as it appeared, but it had been real. A spark, small and fragile, but it had answered. Deep within her, something shifted. A fire lit where only fear had lived before. It was not just hope; it was purpose.

She closed her eyes again, willing the spark to return. It answered, brighter and stronger. It crackled in the darkness, golden light dancing in her hands. A smile broke across her face, breathless and amazed.

"This is how it begins, Princess." Noctis said, pride clear in every word.

Chapter Nineteen

She continued to practice wielding magic, driven by an unnamed urge. In the quiet of her cell, time blurred, but Arden measured each attempt by the ache in her limbs and the exhaustion that weighed on her body.

Every day, she practiced, and every day, she failed. At first, the spark lasted only a breath. Then, it stretched to three seconds, then ten. Eventually, she could hold it for thirty before it slipped away like smoke.

The magic remained wild and unpredictable, but it no longer frightened her. Even when it lashed out or burned too hot, it reminded her that she was not empty. Not powerless. She had always relied on instinct to survive; now, she leaned into something buried beneath years of doubt.

Hours passed as she sat against the wall, staring at her hands. The power didn't obey her but it responded to her heart and emotions, and that was enough for now. She was beginning to see it as a part of herself.

This realm, with all its beauty and terror, had tried to break her. Vaelithara had promised her freedom only to steal it. Aezraen had cloaked his truths in silence. Everyone wanted something from her. But she was done playing their game. Arden no longer dreamed of mere escape; she fantasized about carving her own path. If she had to burn down every lie and shatter every crown, she would. She would not kneel. She would not wait. She was no longer a piece to be moved across someone else's board.

The spark in her palm was small but glowed with the promise of more. Each time it appeared, it ignited something in her chest, a flame that would not die. She did not yet know how to control it; she barely understood it, but it was hers.

When Aezraen approached the First Court, she felt his magic before he arrived. She was still afraid, but she was no longer hiding. The cell darkened, shadows thickening in the corners. His presence materialized as his bitter words escaped. "You absolute fool."

"Actually, foolish doesn't even begin to cover it," he said coldly. "Do you have any idea what you've done?"

Her jaw clenched. "Spare me the lecture. It means nothing coming from the man who left me alone in an empty court."

His laugh was hollow, humorless. "You ran straight into her hands, and you still want to blame me?"

"What did you expect me to do?" she snapped. "You lied, Aezraen. She showed me Callen. He's still dying; our deal is void."

Aezraen's expression twisted. "You think I would lie about that? You think I would use your brother to manipulate you?"

She didn't answer quickly enough.

His voice dropped, rougher now. "Unbelievable."

She met his gaze, fire in her eyes. "I think you failed me. Just like you failed her." Her words landed like a slap.

His magic pulsed hard enough to rattle the bars between them. "You don't know anything about what you're talking about," he snarled. The air thickened, vibrating with unseen energy. His magic allowing him to step through the bars of her cell. It filled the space, wrapping around Arden like an effort to swallow her whole. Aezraen opened his mouth to speak, but before the words could form, she raised her hand.

Silver power surged from her palm, engulfing him. His shadows fled as Aezraen staggered, his eyes widening for a breath as the darkness around him was torn apart by magic he could not control.

His gaze flicked to her outstretched hand, to the faint silver light still sparking at her fingertips. Arden stared, her breath ragged. The realization hit like ice, "you have her magic." It wasn't a question and Arden noted that the surprise she had felt was not mimicked on his face.

"You knew about the heartspark?" Arden could feel the anger rising within her as gold and silver sparks danced across her skin.

Aezraen's expression softened, but his voice remained firm and commanding. "Arden, breathe."

She was furious at the lies, the manipulation, and the weight of buried truths. It all coiled in her chest, burning too much to contain. The anger crescendoed, and her magic exploded outward.

It tore through the cell like a living storm. The walls shook, cracks splintering like veins of lightning. The air crackled, energy wrapping around her like a second skin. Everything crumbled to dust, and suddenly, she was free.

The dust hadn't even settled before she was moving, ripping herself from the wreckage, chest heaving, magic still humming beneath her skin. Aezraen watched her, his expression unreadable. She didn't wait for him to recover, or wait for the next barbed remark or command.

She ran.

Following the bond to Noctis, she pushed forward. In the distance, she heard the guards' screams as alarms were sounded. Chains snapped, stone crumbled and she saw silver sparks, her magic, still streaking through the castle like wildfire.

There was a brief silence before Noctis' voice echoed through her mind, low and fierce. *"Nothing will keep me from you now."*

She felt him, like a storm crashing into her soul, his rage pouring through their bond, unrelenting. She followed the destruction, the unmistakable sound of Noctis tearing through the fortress. The doors to the lower chambers had been ripped from their hinges, shattered wood and twisted iron strewn across the floor. In the center of the devastation, he stood.

Amid the ruins, his black fur streaked with white dust, Noctis seemed carved from shadow and starlight. Magic clung to him faintly, flickering against his massive frame. In an instant, he was at her side. His head lowered, breath warm against her skin. *"Are you harmed?"*

Arden exhaled shakily, her hand pressing into his mane. "No."

Without hesitation, she climbed onto his back. As he turned, a deep growl rolled from his chest, a final warning that echoed through the halls. No one dared approach.

"If you're finished destroying everything," Aezraen yelled, "perhaps you'd consider not dying."

Arden turned, bracing for a fight. Aezraen stood just beyond the ruins, arms crossed. Noctis snarled.

"Later, kitty."

He looked at Arden. "Now will you let me help you escape, or are we going to fight the whole court without any help?"

She hesitated, then nodded.

"Good girl."

Before she could argue, shadows swallowed them whole.

They reappeared in the silvergrass field where days ago she had felt nothing but freedom. Arden couldn't feel that same freedom now, everything about this place was tainted and she could finally see it.

Aezraen, moved ahead without looking back. His shadows flickered erratically around him, fraying at the edges, as if they could barely hold form. Arden noticed the stagger in his steps, the tightness in his shoulders. She could see how much it had taken to get them out. But he didn't say a word.

Arden's voice cut through the silence. "Why did you come?"

He didn't hesitate. "Because, little thief, I don't like losing what's mine."

The words weren't meant to hurt, but they did. They fed the storm inside her that had been churning since she learned the truth. Her voice trembled. "You didn't have to help me..." She paused, the ache rising in her throat. "...I won't ever be her."

Aezraen stopped. Slowly, he turned, shadows rippling at his heels. His gaze locked onto hers, unreadable, but Arden thought she saw something fracture. The silence stretched between them. Then, his shadows lashed out, sharp and sudden. "Did I ever ask you to be?"

She flinched, not from fear but from everything that trembled beneath those words. "You could've left me."

His eyes burned, exhaustion etched into every line of his face. "Maybe I should have."

The words landed like a blow. Heavy. Unforgiving.

They stood in silence, two people frayed at the edges, barely holding themselves together.

Arden's voice was a whisper now, sharp with the weight of all she didn't understand. "How long have you known I carry her heartspark?"

Aezraen dragged a hand through his hair, slower than usual, the effort weighing him down. He didn't answer right away. "We don't have time for this right now."

Noctis tensed, ears flicking forward. From the treeline, Aezraen's soldiers emerged, clad in dark armor bearing Nythis' crescent moon. The tension in Arden's shoulders bled away, only to be replaced by unease.

Kastiel stepped into the clearing, his white hair gleaming in the moonlight, a familiar smirk tugging at his lips. "Well... that explains the noise."

"You're late," Aezraen snapped.

Kastiel raised an eyebrow. "If you'd waited..."

"Enough." Aezraen's tone cut the air like a blade.

Arden blinked, glancing between them. Aezraen hadn't waited for them, he'd left them behind. He'd come alone... just to get to her faster. Her stomach twisted, her anger faltering for a moment as the weight of that realization settled. He chose to risk everything for her.

Kastiel's smirk faded. His arms crossed over his chest, voice lowering. "We got a report that Veylis' court stirs, it seems your visit caused some unrest."

"Who's Veylis?" Arden asked.

Neither answered.

Kastiel's gaze flicked to her, hesitant, but Aezraen didn't look away. "Niko was well liked by the whole court, I thought they'd want revenge," he muttered. "Maybe I was right."

Kastiel dropped his gaze. "Other courts have heard of your argument with him. They want to know why Vaelithara wants her."

"Melisara will likely already know about the wreckage we just caused," Aezraen said. "So let's give her something else to spread."

Kastiel nodded and summoned one of his men. "What should we say?"

"Tell the Gilded Court that Aeltherion rises with the mortal girl."

The soldier crossed his fist over his chest before vanishing into the night.

Arden blinked, stunned. The words echoed in her mind like a distant roar: Aeltherion rises... with the mortal girl. "Wait... why would we tell people that?"

Aezraen's gaze cut to her, sharp and unrelenting. "If you think Vaelithara is done coming for you, you're ignorant, little thief. We need all the allies we can get and telling Melisara will ensure the whole realm knows you exist."

Arden swallowed hard and glanced at Noctis. *"As much as I despise him, he is right. She will come for you again,"* he murmured through their bond. *"And when she does, you must be ready."*

Her jaw clenched. She was tired of running, tired of feeling powerless. Her gaze returned to Aezraen, her voice steady. "Where do we start?"

Chapter Twenty

When they returned to the castle, Aezraen ordered Kastiel to confine Arden to the study. The room had windows overlooking the courtyard, and Arden alternated between practicing her magic and watching the coming and goings of the court below.

Aezraen had promised not to lock Noctis back in his cage, but few other rooms in the castle were large enough to contain the massive beast. The compromise was that he was allowed to roam the castle's exterior, the first freedom he'd been allowed in centuries.

Aezraen threw the doors open, the force of his entrance shaking the chamber and reverberating through the dimly lit space like the warning of an approaching storm.

His cloak billowed behind him, shadows writhing at his feet, restless and agitated. Arden could tell he had recovered from their fight with Vaelithara, and she hated that it brought her joy to see him well.

She sat on the edge of the windowsill, her spine rigid and her fingers poised to turn the next page of the book she had been reading. Candlelight flickered against her face, highlighting the sharp line of her jaw and the tension coiled tightly beneath her stillness. Her voice cut through the resounding silence like a blade. "You left me."

Aezraen had expected anger; he had braced himself for the fire in her words. But hearing it now, with the undercurrent of hurt, hit differently. His jaw tightened, "you broke Noctis out of my dungeon and ran..." His voice was sharp. "...I have been cleaning up your mess ever since."

Arden closed the book with more force than she intended. "I didn't ask you to."

"You didn't need to."

The shadows in the room stretched toward her, a silent reminder that she was not free, not anymore. He had found her, claimed her. She could be as uncooperative, infuriating, and reckless as she wanted, but it wouldn't change a damned thing. She was his, and he would ensure she stayed exactly where she belonged.

"It's time to go, there are people here to meet you."

Arden looked at him, stunned. She had seen countless groups arrive at the castle's doorstep, but their intentions had been unclear from afar. "Me?"

He held out his hand to her, and she took it tentatively. "They need to know what they're fighting for." He seemed excited and as they walked through the halls, Aezraen reminded her of a child eager to show off a new toy. She just wasn't sure she was ready to be on display.

At the end of the hall he opened a set of double doors to reveal a war room unlike anything Arden could have imagined. It was carved into the heart of the castle, a few floors beneath the throne room. The room was adorned with maps of the realm, paintings of battles fought, and in the center, a heavy wooden table stretched through, its seats fully occupied.

Fae of all kinds filled the table, seated shoulder to shoulder, their voices low with tension and purpose. Some bore the hardened look of mercenaries; others wore the marks of decorated warriors.

Aezraen leaned in close, his voice a murmur meant for her ears alone. "Everyone here has lost something, someone, because of her."

Arden's gaze swept the room. Lords and rogues shared quiet laughter, but beneath it she sensed the cracks, the grief worn like armor. "Are these the other Archfey?"

Aezraen let out a low chuff, "no, they won't involve themselves unless they're threatened." His eyes remained fixed ahead. "These are just some of the people Vaelithara has wronged... just as she has countless others who aren't here, who won't ever be again."

Arden stood frozen, a weight pressing against her chest. This wasn't just a war council. It was a gathering of the broken, the remnants of a world Vaelithara had tried to destroy.

Aezraen motioned for her to join him at the head of the table. As she stepped forward, gold sparks anxiously flickered up and down her arms, her gaze sweeping across the gathered allies. Their faces were unfamiliar, but when they caught sight of her, Aeltherion upon her head, a hush overtook the room.

Arden felt a strange sense of pride settling in her chest. Not long ago, she'd begged for scraps and fought for petty jobs. Now, she stood at the head of a brewing battle, with power at her fingertips and a kingdom in need of saving. The weight of it all pressed against her, but she didn't shrink from it. Not anymore.

A chuckle broke the silence, and every head whipped around to see who dared laugh at the mortal who controlled such immense power. "Look at you."

Arden's eyes drifted over the table, searching for the source, "Elias?"

His smile widened slightly, but there was something different in his gaze now, an intensity she hadn't seen before. "Well, you've done well for yourself. It's good to see you again."

She stepped around the table, still struggling to process what she was seeing. "How? After the trials, I thought..."

"When we failed, we were sent back to our realms," Elias explained, his voice even, though a shadow lingered beneath his words. "Original bargains rescinded but all in one piece."

Arden turned sharply to Aezraen, shock flashing through her.

He let them live.

Aezraen said nothing, simply watching her with the indifferent expression he had perfected.

Elias continued, "About a week ago, he found me again and offered a new deal: to fight beside him and defend you against this 'Caretaker' in exchange for a small fortune, enough to feed my family for years."

Arden placed her hands on either side of his face and placed a kiss upon his forehead. "I will never forget you for this, Elias. Your daughters will have their father back safely."

Aezraen may have been the one to pull Elias into this, but he had also been the one to let him go. She had never considered that Aezraen might possess mercy. As she returned to his side, something inside her shifted, and her hand drifted toward his, seeking him out. He grasped her hand tightly, as if to reassure her that this was real.

As the room settled, voices murmured among the gathered warriors. Arden's gaze drifted over them as they began introducing themselves. Each face carried a story; each had been recruited, convinced, or bound to this war through their own grievances against the First Fae Queen.

The first to swear allegiance to Arden had been the courtless mercenaries, a band of ruthless, battle-worn fae who had once served as soldiers in Elydris' army. Aezraen had sought them out, finding them in a ruined fortress, where their leader, Cairos, agreed to meet.

"What do you offer in return for our services?" Cairos asked, watching Aezraen with calculating eyes.

"I can offer you a prize worth more than coin," Aezraen replied.

Cairos laughed at the absurdity of Aezraen's words.

"Vaelithara stole your title..."

Cairos stopped laughing and gripped his sword tighter.

"You were stripped of your mother's court."

The group of mercenaries, sensing Cairos' tension, gathered around the two.

"I can offer you revenge."

That was enough. The disgraced heir to the Gilded Court locked eyes with Arden. "My mercenaries and I will happily die if it means Vaelithara goes with us."

One by one, the faces around the table shared their stories of heartbreak with Arden. She listened intently, never wavering in her attention. Aezraen had sought them all out and knew exactly what to say to gain their loyalty on the battlefield. She squeezed his hand, reassuring herself that he was still there, feeling a shadow snake around her waist, pulling her closer.

The last to speak was Erelyn, the leader of the Phantom Blades, a brotherhood of assassins from the Court of Veils. Arden knew the story and followed along as it unfolded, a kingdom and their Archfey destroyed by Vaelithara's forces. Byron stood proud amongst them, reunited with those he thought were lost to time.

Erelyn spoke of Kaelar with such reverence that Arden felt a connection to him. He wasn't a distant, forgotten ruler to them; he was beloved and cherished even now, centuries later. They had not required convincing; they needed only to hear Vaelithara's name. When Aezraen had requested their help, Erelyn had agreed without hesitation.

Once everyone had shared, Aezraen looked around the table before releasing Arden's hand. He rose, and the war table came to life, a map formed from his shadows shifting to display the lands of the First Court. The room buzzed with hushed whispers, but Aezraen's voice cut through it all: "She will not expect us to strike so soon."

The room fell silent, everyone hanging on his words. "She has spent centuries untouchable," he continued, "this has made her arrogant; she won't believe we have the strength to challenge her without the other courts." His eyes assessed the room, his smile widening. "She is wrong."

Cairos leaned forward, arms braced against the table. "You have a plan, then?"

Aezraen nodded. "It's a bit unconventional, but we'll take the Hollow Court first."

A ripple of tension moved through the room; never before had an Archfey attacked another outright. Erelyn exhaled sharply. "We agreed to fight Vaelithara, not Veylis."

"There is unrest in his court, we're not there to attack. We're there to gather those who want to fight beside us."

The room erupted into arguments as everyone debated the plan. Suddenly, the doors were thrown open, and a figure with violet eyes sauntered in, tall and imposing.

"Ah, Aezraen," the Archfey said, surveying the group around the table, "it seems your little war is truly beginning."

Arden's gaze flicked to Aezraen, who appeared completely at ease despite the situation. "Veylis," he greeted, "I wasn't sure you would come."

Veylis looked at the battle plans on the table, a wicked grin curling his lips. "I can see that, darling. But tell me one little thing: what was your plan? Invade my home? Or did you finally come to your senses and decide to join in on a little... fun?"

The room fell silent, everyone waiting to see how the two rulers would respond. "I considered staying neutral, but then I thought, well, where's the fun in that?" He turned to Arden, his eyes trailing over her in a slow, deliberate assessment.

"This must be the girl who wields the crown. Fascinating." He took a measured step closer, his expression a mask of amusement and hunger. "My court has been unbearably empty since Vaelithara stole my love," he murmured, his voice a decadent whisper against the tension in the air. "The bed is cold, the nights are long; an Archfey can only deny his appetites for so long."

Aezraen moved then, stepping between them. His voice was low and steady. "She is not yours to take, Veylis."

Veylis chuckled, unbothered. "Imagine it," he continued, his smirk deepening. "All that unchecked power set free; raw and wild. The walls crumbling, your body and magic surrendering to pleasure and ruin alike."

Arden blushed, confusion clouding her mind. Aezraen's anger had been steadily rising, his normally controlled demeanor cracking apart like splintering ice. Shadows coiled at his feet, creeping up the walls like living creatures, responding to his unrest.

Veylis burst into mad, cackling laughter; Arden stiffened, utterly thrown by the sudden change in demeanor. "Forgive me, little queen. I do love pushing his limits. Please, allow me to introduce myself properly. I am Veylis, Archfey of the Hollow Court."

He proceeded to tell her his story as others had, explaining why he would stand against a creature as powerful as Vaelithara. By the time he finished speaking, silent tears were rolling down Arden's face for Niko and all Veylis had endured.

Sparks of silver and gold crackled up her arms and swirled around her fingers. Her heart ached for everything Vaelithara had stolen from the people in the room. The air pulsed with energy spiraling outward as her magic surged in response. Gold and silver sparks showered the chamber like falling stars, the room fell into stunned silence, every gaze fixed on her. Aezraen stared at her as if she were a goddess.

Arden's outburst caused the meeting to break apart, warriors drifting to separate corners of the room, murmuring about strategy and alliances.

Elias moved to stand beside her. "You don't trust him."

She scoffed. "Why should I?"

Elias was quiet for a long moment. "I didn't. At least, not at first." He exhaled, glancing toward Aezraen. "But I'll say this, he's fighting for something. Whether it's for himself or for you... I don't know."

Arden swallowed hard, her gaze lingering on Aezraen's silhouette against the firelight.

The distant sound of war horns shattered the peace in the room, and the walls trembled with the force of magic pressing into the castle. Aezraen and Arden rushed to the hall, peering out of the small windows. Outside the castle walls, soldiers clad in white stood at the ready.

"So much for your surprise," Veylis cackled.

Chapter Twenty-One

Dusk descended upon the court and the haunting chorus of war horns continued to sound as Vaelithara's troops grew closer. Their echoes rolled through the land like thunder, a grim herald of what was to come. Beneath the looming shadow of the castle walls, the city stirred. Warriors and rebels alike rose, rallying beneath banners of defiance against the queen. The clang of steel, the barked orders, the sharp tang of magic in the air. It was the sound of a kingdom bracing for war.

Aezraen stood at the head of the assembled party, his silhouette stark against the horizon, cloak snapping in the wind. His gaze was fixed on the enemy as Vaelithara's forces spilled from the night, their approach silent and methodical, a tide of death cresting the hill.

They moved in perfect unison, their armor catching what little light remained. Upon their chests, the sigil of the First Court burned crimson, a brand of loyalty and madness. Masks shaped like ancient, forgotten skulls obscured their faces, rendering them inhuman and soulless. Behind them, a wall of dark magic shimmered like a storm barely held at bay, thick and suffocating.

Arden stood at Aezraen's side, her heart pounding in time with the earth's tremble. She could not count their numbers, nor did she try. All that mattered was the crown upon her head and the power coiled at her fingertips. Silver sparks crackled wildly, unrestrained, and Aeltherion hummed with anticipation.

Aezraen's hand tightened around the hilt of his sword. "Are you ready?" he asked, low and steady.

Arden did not respond with words. She closed her eyes, drew in a breath, and let her power rise. The ground beneath their feet pulsed in response, ancient magic stirring. A wave of energy surged outward, rippling across the field. The sky itself seemed to shudder, clouds swirling like a great eye opening. The land remembered what it meant to bleed.

Aezraen felt it, a force older than time tightening around them, a promise of reckoning.

Veylis approached with a casual ease, a smile curving his lips as he surveyed the battlefield like a connoisseur admiring a masterpiece. "Shall we begin?" he purred, drawing his blade with a flourish.

Aezraen moved first, his battle cry lost in the roar of chaos. Steel met steel as both armies surged forward, crashing together in a collision of fury and flame. Aezraen's blade sang through the air, biting into flesh and breaking bone. Each strike was precise and brutal. He twisted through the fray, carving a path of ruin.

Beside him, Arden was a tempest of blades. She wove between enemies, her daggers flickering like starlight, slipping through chinks in armor, cutting deep before vanishing. Her movements had changed; she was faster now, sharper. Power coursed through her veins, driving her beyond mortal limits.

To their left, Kastiel was a force of order in the chaos. His commands cut through the din of war, rallying their forces into formation. He struck with calculated efficiency, exploiting every weakness before it could be shielded.

The Phantom Blades, cloaked in shadow, slipped through the battlefield like death's own breath. Their curved daggers found exposed throats and unguarded hearts, their victims collapsing before a cry could escape their lips.

Elias fought at Arden's back, his broadsword a blur of steel and blood. He deflected a blow aimed at her, his blade cleaving through the attacker's chest. "You're welcome," he muttered, grinning, before spinning away to meet another foe.

Then the storm broke as Noctis erupted into the fray with a fury that shook the heavens. He was no longer a beast, no longer bound by flesh, he was the wrath of the Gods. He tore through the enemy ranks, his massive form a blur of shadow and teeth, golden eyes blazing against the darkening sky. His first victim didn't even scream; Noctis crushed him beneath his weight, fangs shearing through steel and bone. Another lunged, but Noctis vanished into shadow and reappeared behind him, tearing through the warrior with a single swipe that sent him flying, armor twisted, body broken.

There was no hesitation. No mercy. This was personal.

Vaelithara's war beasts surged forth. Nightmare creatures of bone and shadow, their eyes glowing with sickly green fire. They roared across the battlefield, maws wide, fangs dripping venom.

Noctis met them head-on.

A beast twice his size lunged, jaws snapping. Noctis crashed into it with enough force to split it into pieces. He locked onto its throat, his fangs tearing through sinew. With a violent jerk, he severed its head, black ichor spilling like oil across the ground. He did not stop; he leapt again, claws raking through another monster, his growl a primal roar that shook the battlefield.

Beyond him, the Hollow Knights had arrived from Veylis' court. They were specters in flickering armor, their eyes empty voids. They moved like ghosts, striking without sound, their blades phasing through armor as if it were smoke. A soldier collapsed, screaming as a shadow blade pierced his chest, his soul ripped from his body before it hit the ground.

Amid the carnage, Veylis laughed. He was the eye of the storm, a shadow spun from silk. His blade danced, slicing through flesh with elegance, each movement an artful mockery of death. To him, this was a game.

Aezraen fought harder, faster, every strike fueled by the fury that had consumed him for centuries. But Vaelithara's soldiers fought with madness in their eyes, driven not by loyalty but by devotion. They did not fear death, they welcomed it. They were her martyrs, and despite losing the upper hand they surged forward, unrelenting.

All at once, the world stilled as Vaelithara's magic swept across the battlefield drawing everyone's attention. It was suffocating and absolute, pressing against the hearts of every soul who stood beneath that darkened sky. The air itself seemed to recoil, shuddering in recognition.

A voice rose above the noise, "Arden!"

The battlefield around them froze as every warrior, every shadow, every breath seemed to move in slow motion. Aezraen turned, his heart slamming against his ribs. From the darkness, Callen was pushed to the ground in front of Vaelithara.

Arden's body went rigid with fear. He was thin, his face gaunt, his skin sickly pale. His clothes hung loose, torn and tattered, wrists bound in glowing shackles. Aezraen's eyes burned with fury, desperation, and something that wasn't entirely his own. His stomach twisted violently because he recognized those shackles and the magic that bound them. He had made a deal with her.

Arden sucked in a breath, stumbling forward, her hands shaking. "Callen..."

His voice came again, cracked, desperate, not entirely his own. "Arden... help me."

The war was no longer about the crown. It was no longer about winning or losing, about thrones or courts. It was about Arden, her power and that she dared to stand against the Queen who had ruled unchallenged for centuries. This war was personal now, and Vaelithara would surely burn the world to ash before she let Arden take it from her.

Arden had never seen anything more terrifying than the smirk that graced Vaelithara's lips. It was a knowing smile, the satisfaction of someone who knew they had a winning hand.

Arden had walked straight into her trap.

Vaelithara lifted a hand, and a thin blade appeared between her fingers. She placed it against Callen's throat with casual precision, as if the mere act of doing so bored her. "Last chance to give me the crown," she purred, her silver eyes locking onto Arden. "Or watch him die."

Callen barely moved, his breath coming in ragged gasps as he tried not to push against the blade. He was too pale, far too thin, his wrists bound by chains that pulsed with Vaelithara's magic. His eyes found Arden, remaining silent, trusting her to fix this as she always had.

Aezraen took a step toward her, his power stirring in the air, but she barely noticed. She felt the shift in the air moments before the dagger bit into Callen's skin. The moment his blood bloomed against his pale skin, something inside her snapped.

The golden sparks climbing her arms ignited. Heat rushed through her veins, scorching, wild, uncontainable. The magic inside her burned, itching to break through her skin.

It was angry.

The crown pulsed in response, its power coiling around her bones, whispering,

More.

More.

More.

It wanted destruction.

It wanted obliteration.

The battlefield warped in her vision, distant figures blurring. The only clarity remaining was Callen and the blood dripping down his throat as Vaelithara continued to press the blade further in.

Aezraen lunged for her, but he was too late.

Arden screamed, and the battlefield shattered into pieces.

A pulse of energy erupted from her, raw power ripping through the battlefield like a living storm. The ground cracked, veins of molten liquid splitting the stone beneath them. Storm clouds swirled above, lightning arcing violently, the wind howling with unseen voices whispering in languages she did not understand.

The force threw soldiers back, their armor splintering like glass. Even Aezraen barely remained standing, shielding his eyes against the blinding light. Arden screamed until there was nothing left. Her body trembled, every breath a battle, her knees threatening to buckle beneath the weight of what she'd unleashed.

Her vision blurred, her heart pounding as she forced herself to look. Through the smoke, past the shattered earth and scorched remains of what had once been a battlefield.

Her gaze found Callen, still in Vaelithara's grasp. She had removed the blade, her eyes full of awe at what Arden had unleashed. His eyes locked onto hers, but there was no relief in his expression, only fear for what she had become.

Arden staggered, air scraping her throat like glass. Her heart beat too loud, too fast. The crown still hummed atop her head, its magic stirring in her veins, but it felt wrong now, like a poison she couldn't purge.

She had done this. She had destroyed everything.

The battlefield was in ruins, bodies unrecognizable in the wake of her magic. The ground was scorched, the sky heavy with ash and silence. A sob clawed at her throat, but she swallowed it down. She couldn't take it back. Couldn't undo the devastation. Couldn't change the way Callen looked at her now. She was supposed to save him.

The queen's shield had held, untouched by Arden's fury, encasing herself and Callen in perfect, unbroken crystal. As the last embers of Arden's magic faded into the ruined air, Vaelithara lowered the barrier, stepping forward with a smile that held only cold, amused pity.

"Fascinating," she murmured, tilting her head, studying Arden like one might admire a rare, dangerous creature. Vaelithara ran a lazy finger along the blade still slick with Callen's blood. Her smirk deepened. "You've barely scratched the surface of what that crown can do." Her eyes gleamed. "But don't worry." Her voice felt like a snare tightening around Arden's throat. "I'll be here when you're ready to embrace it."

Arden wanted to snap back. To tell her that she would never become her. But her magic liked what she had just done; she could feel it curling around her, pleased. The power inside her was still thrumming. She swayed, and the world tilted. Then a pair of strong arms wrapped around her, holding her close.

Aezraen.

"You need to rest." Arden barely heard him as she slipped into a slumber she hoped she'd never wake from.

Chapter Twenty-Two

Arden drifted through each day alive, breathing, but hollowed out. The ache in her chest was constant, not just from her healing wounds but from the knowledge that Vaelithara still had Callen. Her anchor to the mortal world. The reason she had crossed into the fae realm in the first place. She had failed him.

Aezraen had promised they would find him, but in the past few days, he had barely looked at her. Most days, he buried himself in ancient texts and tomes, poring over pages filled with forgotten histories. When he was near her, his mind was elsewhere, lost in thoughts he never shared.

Arden had reached out to him in small ways. She asked questions, lingered in the halls of his court, and watched him when he wasn't watching her. But the wall between them grew thicker, made of silence she didn't know how to breach. She was too weak to fight, too drained to train, too broken to do anything but wait. It was a prison of her own making.

"You're brooding again, little queen," Veylis said, his voice sliding into the chamber. "You know that's terribly unattractive."

Arden didn't flinch as he stepped into view, dressed in embroidered midnight-blue robes, a goblet of something sparkling in his hand. His eyes danced with amusement, but there was no real mockery in his tone.

Veylis had become a constant, a maddening, ever-present distraction from her spiraling thoughts. He taunted, teased, and interrupted at the worst times, but he listened too. When Arden fell into silences that stretched too long, he filled them with laughter, stories, and absurdities only he could conjure.

She looked up from where she sat near the hearth. "Shouldn't you be doing something more important? Like drinking yourself into oblivion?"

"I can multitask." Veylis took a long sip from his goblet and sprawled dramatically onto the chaise across from her. "Besides, you need me. I've decided to train you."

Arden blinked. "Train me?"

His grin widened. "You think I'm going to let Vaelithara keep her claws in your brother forever? No. That woman has already taken too much from me. I won't let her do that to you too." Something in his voice shifted at that.

"Niko?" Arden said softly.

Veylis raised the goblet in a silent toast and then drained it. "I'm not the warrior I used to be. My talents these days lie more in excess than in wielding magic," he admitted. "But I'll teach you everything I can. Magic is unruly, chaotic... like me. You'll fit right in."

That coaxed a breath of laughter from her, light but genuine. It faded quickly. "She pulled her troops back, didn't she?" Arden asked.

Veylis' expression sharpened. "She did. Pretty sure you scared her. That explosion of magic on the battlefield? Complete shock and she's being cautious now. Waiting. Which gives us time."

"And the others?" Arden inquired. "Has anyone else joined us yet?"

Veylis groaned dramatically. "Melisara has likely already whispered half the realm into action. Her spies are everywhere, and her rumors spread faster than plague. With any luck, she'll stir up enough chaos to work in our favor."

Arden's thoughts drifted away from distant alliances and returned to him. She hesitated, then asked the question that had been gnawing at her for days. "You've known Aezraen a long time, haven't you?"

Veylis raised a brow but didn't deflect. "Since before he became Archfey. I remember him as a mortal commander in Elydris' army. A ghost of a man back then, all duty and no joy." He paused, chuckling at his own joke, "Guess not much has changed there."

She gave him a look of disdain.

"No one paid him any mind until Syliris began courting him. It changed his fate overnight." He poured more wine into his cup. "When he ascended, I took him under my wing. I taught him how to live like a fae should. And when Vaelithara took Niko... he stood by me. He watched me crumble and didn't walk away."

Arden took a deep breath, bracing herself. "Do you think he still loves her?" Arden's voice was barely audible.

Veylis didn't answer right away. His eyes lost their humor, and for once, the mask dropped. "I think..." he said slowly, "...he'll spend the rest of his life trying to bring her back."

Arden felt the weight of that truth sink into her chest.

That evening, she found him in the tower study. Aezraen sat hunched over the desk, ink staining his fingers, parchments scattered like fallen leaves around him. Books lay open in chaotic disarray, their pages creased and worn from use. Shadows clung to the corners of the chamber, flickering in the dim candlelight.

He didn't notice her at first, or pretended not to. Arden stepped into the room, each step heavier than the last. Her heart pounded in her chest, louder than it should have. She stopped just behind him, her voice quiet and tentative. "Have you found anything useful?"

His hand stilled over a line of text, but he didn't look up. "Some progress."

She waited, hoping he would continue. Hoping, foolishly, for anything resembling a plan. "On how to take on her remaining troops?"

When he didn't respond her brow furrowed. "Aezraen?"

His finger hesitated over the text, but he still did not answer.

Her voice sharpened, as she peered at the book he was reading, a history of Elessian's relics. "Have you even been researching battle strategies?"

His shoulders tensed.

Arden stepped around the desk, planting herself in front of him. "What, exactly, have you been studying?"

Aezraen finally lifted his head. Shadows lay under his eyes, deep and hollow. His eyes watered, as if revealing what he could not say. "The crown," he finally admitted.

Her voice dropped to a whisper. "Why?"

But he didn't speak. He didn't have to. Her stomach dropped as the pieces fit together with devastating clarity. She took a step back, her voice barely a whisper, raw and cracking. "To bring her back?"

His gaze flicked away from hers. "Yes."

The word lanced through her like a blade. She felt her knees tremble and her hands curl into fists at her sides. But no tears came. Only rage. Only hurt.

She swallowed hard, her voice shaking. "Do you still love her?"

Aezraen didn't hesitate but a single tear rolled down his cheek as he said, "I don't think I ever stopped."

Arden stared at him, searching for anything. She wanted to find remorse or a hint of regret but all she saw was the truth behind his words weighing heavily on him.

She turned on her heel. Her footsteps echoed through the stone hall as she left the study behind. She didn't cry. She didn't scream. Because there was nothing left to say.

She didn't remember how she made it to Veylis' chamber, the winding halls she passed through, or how her legs carried her that far without collapsing. All she recalled was the weight of her heart shattering, drowning her in silence.

When the door opened, Veylis blinked at her, disheveled, his shirt half-buttoned, a glass of something dark in his hand. He took one look at her face, and the smirk vanished. "What's wrong?" His voice was softer than usual, devoid of mockery.

Her lips parted, but no words came. Tears spilled openly, and the room blurred. She collapsed into him before she could stop herself. His glass clattered to the floor, forgotten, as he caught her. She buried her face in his chest, fingers fisting the fabric of his tunic. Her body trembled with grief, and tendrils of silver magic poured from her.

His arms wrapped around her, one hand resting lightly on the back of her head. He didn't ask questions or press for details. He just held her, and in that stillness, in the absence of war, crowns, and betrayals, Arden allowed herself to find comfort in her friend.

The next day, she returned to Veylis, her steps steadier, her eyes no longer clouded by grief but sharpened by resolve. There was no hesitation in her knock, no tremble in her voice when he opened the door. Veylis didn't mention the night before. He only flashed that infuriating grin, twirling a blade between his fingers. "Ready to stop sulking and start doing something useful?" he asked, his eyes gleaming.

Arden couldn't muster a smile. "Let's begin," she said.

Training became her sanctuary. It was a rhythm of repetition and strain, of failure and persistence. Veylis was relentless, pushing her past every breaking point with sharp words and sharper truths.

Arden's magic was volatile, always just one breath away from shattering the world around her. Sparks flared from her fingertips without warning, and flames bloomed and died in her wake. Once, in a burst of anger, she shattered every window in the corridor, the sound of glass raining down like frozen stars.

Veylis didn't flinch. He never raised his voice or backed away. "You are not a weapon," he reminded her. "You are the wielder. Stop letting it control you."

Some days, she felt progress, fleeting moments when the power obeyed her will. But most days, it rebelled: wild and unyielding. Her body was too weak, her spirit too raw.

Aezraen sometimes passed her in the halls, silent and distant, shadows clinging to his heels like ghosts. Their eyes would meet, never for long. He never spoke first, and neither did she. There was a wall between them now, forged by words that could not be unsaid.

Whenever Veylis noticed her losing control he'd put a gentle hand on her shoulder. "Breathe," he'd say, snapping his fingers in front of her face when her concentration slipped, when her thoughts drifted to Aezraen and her control spiraled again.

"I'm trying."

"Try harder."

Days passed like that: silent and fractured. Each moment stretched thin under the weight of things left unsaid. The shift began, subtle at first, then oppressive, a hum in her bones, a pressure in her chest; a feeling that warned of something ancient stirring.

When the Watchers came, Arden knew this peace had only ever been temporary. They moved like ghosts, their forms sweeping over the stone floors of the court with a silence that still made her skin crawl, even after weeks of living among them. Their presence no longer startled her, not like when she had first arrived, but it never stopped unsettling her. She had learned to exist in their company, learned to sleep with their formless figures hovering in her periphery, to eat while their hollow gazes followed her every move. But now, they had come for her.

She stood in the courtyard beneath a sky heavy with clouds, the stone cold beneath her feet. Noctis stood at her side, his massive form a wall of muscle and fur, pressed close as if to shield her from whatever was coming. Aezraen stood to her right, rigid, his shadows flickering in agitation, curling as if they too sensed what approached. Veylis lingered on her left, arms crossed, a rare frown marring his face. His usual levity had vanished, replaced by something sharper.

Their movements formed a slow, deliberate procession, culminating in a perfect, unnatural line before her. The air was heavy with expectation as they waited for what was coming. The Watchers had never spoken directly to her, only whispered in the darkness, observing, waiting. Now, for the first time, they stood as messengers, not merely observers.

A voice emerged from within the darkness. "You stir what should have remained sleeping."

Arden's heart pounded, but she didn't flinch. She felt the power humming beneath her skin, the crown thrumming against her skull. Something ancient began to wake within her, something that both thrilled and terrified her in equal measure.

Another Watcher stepped forward, its movement inhuman and unnaturally smooth. "The Crown was silent for centuries. But now it stirs, as do the remnants of what was lost."

Beside her, Aezraen tensed, the darkness around him trembling, shadows coiling in defiance. "Quit speaking in riddles," he growled, his voice sharp.

They ignored him. Their focus never wavered from Arden. "It is no mere coincidence that your power awakens now."

Her voice was steady, but only barely. "What do you mean?"

"For centuries," the Watcher continued, "Vaelithara sought to undo the past. She twisted the fabric of time, shredding the names of those who once shaped this realm. But even she could not erase them fully."

A pause rang out across the land, a silence that seemed to stretch across lifetimes.

"The king is not gone," the Watcher said.

Aezraen's voice sliced through the air like a blade. "You lie."

The Watchers did not move. "Did you ever wonder why there was no tomb? No bones? No relic that could bring him back?"

Aezraen's shadows writhed wildly now, lashing at the stone floor, rage curling off him in waves. "Enough with your lies."

Arden snapped at him. "Be quiet, Aezraen."

"The whole realm was deceived," the Watcher said, tilting its head in that eerie, slow motion that made her skin crawl. "The Gods hid them, they knew one day Aeltherion would find someone to wield its power again."

Arden's mind reeled, she was the key, "why now?"

"Your blood woke it," the Watcher answered. "Now, the magic calls, and only you can answer."

Another stepped forward, and this time, Arden felt the words echoing inside her mind, ancient and familiar. "The crown chose you because you carry his blood," the Watcher said. "Elydris sleeps, but you can wake him."

Noctis growled, stepping closer, eyes burning,a protective force, but Arden felt numb.

"This is impossible," Aezraen snarled.

"I said ENOUGH," Arden snapped, her magic surging from her hands toward Aezraen. His power surged in response but she didn't care. The truth was unraveling everything she thought she knew. Her voice trembled. "Where do I need to go?"

The Watchers turned in unison as a portal opened, creating a space between moments. Arden turned toward Aezraen. His jaw was tight, his fists clenched.

Noctis pressed against her side. *Be wary, princess.* Arden nodded and gave him a quick pat before walking with him into the portal.

Chapter Twenty-Three

Aezraen

Her boots met soft earth. Before her stood the ruins of an old fae temple, its skeletal remains half-buried in creeping ivy and silver-threaded moss. Moonlight glowed faintly on the weathered stone; the intricate carvings that once adorned its towering pillars now cracked and worn by time.

Arden had never been here before, she was sure of it. Yet something within her recognized this place; it felt safe. Noctis stalked forward, his paws silent on the damp ground. He sniffed the air, his eyes narrowing. Arden watched as the muscles beneath his mane tensed. Noctis turned toward her, his gaze heavy. *"You may not like what you find inside."*

Aezraen took a slow breath beside her, his gaze flicking over the temple's entrance. He knew this place, remembered it in the marrow of his bones, in the ghost of forgotten laughter that whispered through the ruins, and in the way the air itself carried the scent of memories long buried.

This was where he and Syliris had run when the walls of her father's court became suffocating. Where they had stolen moments between duty and rebellion, breathless in their escape, losing themselves in the sanctuary of these stones. The weight of those memories clawed at him, had she really been this close all this time?

Arden walked beside him, and he could sense her unease. He noticed how her fingers hovered near the crown she had tied to her hip and how she kept casting glances his way. Aezraen should have felt grateful;

Aeltherion was the key, the very thing he'd spent centuries chasing. The crown could bring Syliris back. But as he looked at it now, all he felt was anger for the pain it had carved between them. If it had only revealed itself to him centuries ago, Arden would have been spared the suffering he had inflicted upon her, but that was no longer an option.

The deeper they moved into the temple, the more the air changed. It wasn't just stagnant with dust and forgotten magic; it had been waiting. The walls were engraved with sigils that pulsed like dying embers against the night. Shadows clung thickly to the corners, but they did not belong to him. The entire chamber was alive with something ancient, something lingering.

The collective hush that overtook the group ahead signaled to Aezraen that something lay beyond the next doorway. When he stepped through, he saw them. Two stone coffins lay at the center of the chamber, bathed in the glow of ancient runes. Aezraen's steps faltered. His breath caught in his throat.

The first bore the mark of the First Fae King but he barely spared it a glance; it was the second coffin that caused his heart to stop entirely. The name carved into the lid burned itself into his vision.

Syliris...His Iris. The sound that escaped him was raw, a choked exhale mingled with a broken whisper. "No." His feet carried him forward before he realized he had moved, his legs unsteady, the weight of centuries pressing down on him all at once. The air turned thick and suffocating, the chamber spinning around him. "No, no, no."

It wasn't possible. It couldn't be possible.

But it was. She had been right here all along, he just hadn't known where to look.

His hands trembled as they found the cool surface of the stone. It was solid beneath his touch, unyielding. Real. He traced the letters of her name, his breath coming too fast, too ragged. It felt as if someone had reached into his chest and torn something loose.

His voice was barely a whisper. "It can't be."

A sound tore from his throat, raw and guttural. His forehead pressed against the stone casket, his body shaking under the crushing weight of grief, agony, and a love that had never been allowed to die.

The golden runes flickered, their light bending around him as if the magic itself felt his sorrow, as if it, too, mourned. He did not hear Arden step closer, did not feel her presence at his side, did not care. All that mattered now was the casket beneath his hands and the one who lay inside.

"I failed you," he rasped. The words felt like shards of glass in his throat. He had searched for her, torn through time and memory, clawed at the past with bloodied hands, chasing shadows that had never led him here.

The past surged in his mind like a wound reopening: the sound of her laughter, soft against his ear; the way she tilted her head when amused, her lips curving into that secretive smile meant only for him. He had loved her. He had lost her. Now, he would bring her home.

Arden's voice was hesitant and quiet. "She's still here."

Aezraen choked on a sob. He had spent centuries trying to bring her back, sacrificing his name, his mortality, his soul, on the chance that he could undo what had been done. He couldn't help but let the fear creep into his mind. What if he was too late? What if she woke and looked at him with nothing but hatred in her eyes? Could he really survive losing her a second time?

He couldn't breathe, couldn't think clearly. The weight of grief and unbearable hope warred within him. A warm hand brushed his shoulder, hesitant and grounding. But he didn't look at her; he couldn't bring himself to, because this moment did not belong to her.

Despite everything, his heart had never left the woman in this tomb. As he knelt there, his forehead pressed to the stone, Aezraen mourned. For what was lost, for what had been stolen from them, for the love he promised never to break.

Arden's hand rested lightly on Aezraen's shoulder, yet it felt as though she were reaching across a chasm. His body shook beneath her fingers, burdened by grief that belonged to another time, one which she had no part.

Her chest tightened, the ache in her heart spreading until it hollowed her out. She blinked, and tears slipped silently down her cheeks, falling not for the woman in the tomb, but for herself. She had foolishly hoped and dared to believe she could be enough, that she could ever be more than a fleeting comfort in the shadow of his love for Syliris.

He had chosen Arden in the quiet moments shared in the castle. But now she understood, it was never because he had let Syliris go; it was because he thought he could never reach her. Her lips trembled, her throat raw with unspoken words.

The Watchers stepped forward, their voices slicing through the charged silence. "You must call to him," they intoned, each word reverberating through the stone and her bones. "Your blood will awaken the power."

Arden wiped her tears and turned toward the altar. With shaking hands, she placed the crown upon her head. Its weight pressed against her scalp like an unyielding hand. The crown had always felt too heavy, its presence foreign. But now, with its power thrumming in her blood and the magic of this place calling to it, it felt alive.

Arden swallowed hard, tightening her grip on the blade in her palm. Her fingers trembled, but she forced them to steady. The Watchers stood around her, faceless and eternal, their dark forms melding into the stone of the cavern.

She had not asked for this, but this world did not care for the desires of mortals. Before she could second-guess herself, she raised the blade and sliced. Her blood met the altar, and the world around her shook with the changing fates.

A surge of power burst through the chamber, emanating from the crown. The sigils around the room ignited, flares of light racing along the walls, filling every crack and carving with searing energy. The force of it knocked the breath from her lungs.

Arden gasped as golden vines spread outward from the spot where her blood had fallen, spiraling like roots across the stone floor. The runes on Elydris' tomb cracked, splitting open like shattered glass. Magic unraveled from within, power unbound. Dust billowed into the air, curling like smoke, filling Arden's lungs with the scent of earth and time. Her heart raced against her ribs.

When Elydris breathed, a deep, terrible inhalation filled the air, as if the world itself had just drawn its first breath. The sigils flickered and faded, their purpose fulfilled. The cavern lurched in recognition, its very foundation acknowledging its king.

Golden light exploded outward, searing through the darkness like the dawn of a new age. The air crackled with unrestrained power, the force of it sending Arden staggering back as Elydris stood. His body was wreathed in golden energy, power radiating from him in waves so intense that the cavern trembled beneath his fury. He was impossibly tall, his form untouched by time, his presence suffocating in its intensity.

His eyes blazed with molten gold, burning with a fury that locked onto Arden. Then his gaze shifted to Syliris' coffin. The silence that followed was lethal. A pulse of rage radiated from him, shaking the very foundation of the chamber. His body trembled as fury rolled off him in waves, a storm barely contained. The world had moved on without him, but time had not softened the betrayal carved into his soul. His magic ignited, golden fire licking at his fingertips.

"Aezraen," Arden whispered in an attempt to warn him but he did not move. He remained gripping Syliris' coffin, lost in his own torment, blind to the chaos unfolding around him.

Elydris took a single step forward, and the weight of his power was crushing. His eyes burned with recognition and hatred. "You." The word was low and furious, the sound of a man wronged.

Aezraen barely lifted his head, his fingers still curled against the stone of Syliris' coffin. "Elydris, please, bring her back," he rasped, his voice hollow.

The cavern shook as the First King stepped forward, magic crackling at his fingertips, his voice low and vengeful. "You stole my daughter from me."

A maelstrom of power raged through the chamber as Elydris approached Aezraen. His body shimmered with uncontained energy, golden light rippling from his skin as if the sun itself had taken form. Each step he took carried the weight of centuries, a storm long held at bay, until now.

Aezraen had spent centuries preparing for this moment, envisioning every outcome, every possible confrontation, every plea he might have to make. But not this, not the unrelenting fury in the First King's eyes.

Not the raw power rolling off him in waves, suffocating and absolute and certainly not the words that left his mouth. "I know what you did."

The words were razor-sharp, causing Aezraen to freeze, his breath uneven, his hands clenched into fists. Shadows writhed at his feet, responding to the turmoil surging within him.

"You were a soldier in my army," Elydris continued, stepping forward, his presence overwhelming. "A traitor who helped my wife steal the Seraphyne's feather."

Aezraen did not try to deny it, he could not.

Elydris' golden gaze bore into him, heavy with accusation. "You do not belong here."

A wave of golden energy erupted from the First King, a wall of power so forceful it sent Aezraen sprawling against the stone. Syliris' casket opened, revealing the princess who had been lost to time. Aezraen's shadows lashed out in protest, surging forward like a living storm, but they were no match for Elydris. They withered, shrinking back into the void from which they came.

As the last remnants of magic shattered into dust, a soft gasp echoed through the chamber; Syliris awoke. The moment her breath returned to the world, Aezraen reached for her. But Elydris moved first, a father ready to defend.

Syliris blinked slowly, her breath uneven, her fingers trembling as they pressed against the stone of her tomb. Confusion rippled across her features, as if her mind could not reconcile what she was seeing. Her gaze flicked between her father, the golden light spilling from his form, and Aezraen, who lay breathless on the cold ground, his eyes filled with something deeper than grief.

"What is happening?" she whispered, her voice hoarse from centuries of silence. Her delicate fingers touched her temples, wincing as though the weight of the world pressed down on her mind. Her gaze finally settled on Aezraen, and something shifted. The haze of confusion gave way to recognition, and a name left her lips, soft and disbelieving. "Aez?"

He crawled forward, heedless of the dust and broken stone biting into his hands. His trembling fingers found hers, grasping them as if they were the only thing anchoring him to this world. He pressed her knuckles to his cheek, his breath shaky and unsteady, his eyes wet with unshed tears. "Iris," he whispered, his voice barely a breath. "I'm so sorry."

"Forgive me," he murmured, pressing apology after apology into the warmth of her skin. "I failed you. I tried. I swear, I tried for so long."

Syliris' chest rose and fell in shallow, uneven breaths. Her fingers curled faintly around his, the barest movement, but it shattered the last of his restraint. A single sob escaped him, his head bowing against her hand, as if the sheer act of holding her was too much to bear.

She reached for him, her hand lifting slowly and unsteadily, brushing against his hair. Aezraen stilled every muscle in his body, locked in place and trembling.

A low growl rumbled through the chamber, reverberating off the ancient stone. Elydris' expression darkened, his golden eyes burning with raw fury. "No matter what good you remember of him," he thundered, "he is a traitor. He helped your mother doom us both."

Aezraen did not react; he did not argue or try to defend himself. His shaking hands remained locked around Syliris', his forehead still pressed against her palm. Shadows curled around him like a dying thing.

Syliris turned toward her father, fear flickering in her eyes. "What happened? Why can't I remember?"

Elydris' expression softened as he looked upon his daughter, the fury in his golden gaze dimming to sorrow. He stepped toward her, his hand rising as if to reach for her, then falling to his side, helpless in the face of her confusion.

"It was your coronation day," he said, his voice roughened with memory. "The day you were to take your place among the Archfey and help govern Elessian as you were born to do. All the courts had gathered in the First Court's courtyard, at your demand, of course." He let out a breath, almost a chuckle, though it carried the brittle edge of grief. "You always hated the throne room. Too cold, too formal. You said the sky should bear witness when you were crowned."

A shadow flickered across his face, and his tone darkened. "I saw one of my guards slip away before the ceremony began. I didn't think much of it until I recognized him, Aezraen. Clad in our colors, loyal... or so I believed." His jaw clenched. "He met with your mother in secret, voices raised. He argued with her. I couldn't hear their words, but the look on her face... I should have stopped them. I meant to confront them after the ceremony."

Elydris' hand closed into a fist, his knuckles white with strain. "You wore a gown of gold and silver, meant to reflect the balance we had fought so hard to preserve. Silver for your mother, gold for me. A symbol of harmony. A promise of peace." He looked away, pain tightening his voice. "But then she struck."

Syliris gasped softly, but Elydris continued, his tone like stone breaking. "Your mother spoke a spell laced with the power of the Seraphyne's feather. The sky broke apart and the ground split open. I tried to reach you, but you were already gone. She erased you before my eyes, and I saw something in her that I had never seen before." He swallowed hard, his voice breaking. "Fear. Panic. She hadn't meant for you to vanish, not like that. She wanted to reshape history, not lose you to it."

He paused, the weight of the past bearing down on him like a storm. "The world shattered around me. I tried to fight it, to reach her, to stop everything from breaking apart, but the magic was too strong. The Gods whispered to me before the dark claimed me. They said the balance would return and that all would be made right."

Elydris barely hesitated, but Aezraen seized the moment. "I did not come here to fight you, Elydris," he said, his voice low and heavy with emotion. "I came to undo what was done and to right what I wronged."

Elydris' golden energy crackled, his power still simmering beneath his skin. "You cannot erase your betrayal, mortal."

Aezraen lifted his chin. "I am no longer mortal."

A heavy pause hung in the air, and Elydris' fingers twitched, poised to unleash centuries of anger.

"Do you think I do not carry the weight of my actions?" Aezraen's voice cracked, his control slipping. "Do you think I have not relived that moment every day, every year, every damn century?" He took a shaky breath. "I did what I thought was right, and I have paid for it a thousand times over."

Syliris looked between them, her brows furrowing as she observed her father and Aezraen, the war evident in their faces.

Elydris' gaze flicked to Syliris, noticing how she touched Aezraen's hair and regarded him not with hatred, but with pity. His fury intensified, "you have no right to kneel before her."

Aezraen remained silent, regaining the composure he had lost. When he spoke again, his voice was a whisper. "I have no right to ask for forgiveness," he murmured. "But I will never stop trying to reconcile for all I have done."

Chapter Twenty-Four

The silence in the chamber was no longer just silence; it was the echo of history reclaiming its place. Aezraen knelt before Syliris, his forehead pressed to her hand, shadows coiling tightly around him like chains. Whatever love he had buried, whatever pain he had swallowed, erupted in this moment, raw and unrelenting. Arden could only watch.

Her gaze shifted to Elydris, noting how his golden light seemed to warp the air itself and how his magic filled every crack in the stone as if it had never left. He had his daughter again. The First King had returned. Arden stood at the edge of it all, the outsider who had undone the seal, the mortal meant only to wear the crown, not shape the fate that followed.

The weight of Aeltherion upon her head reminded her of the power she had awakened and what it had cost. She should have felt triumph. Instead, she felt hollow.

Syliris' fingers twitched beneath Aezraen's, her chest rising slowly with breath. Her eyes opened, bright with a life that hadn't touched them in centuries. They found Arden through the fading shimmer of magic. "You woke us," she said softly, as if revealing a long-awaited truth.

Arden didn't answer right away. Her throat was tight, her thoughts spiraling. She had stood at the heart of a storm, watching the impossible unfold around her, and still, she didn't know where she fit within the wreckage. "I did."

Syliris studied her, her gaze flickering from the crown to the faint silver and gold sparks lingering on Arden's skin, then back to her face. Her brow furrowed slightly, her fingers pressing against her chest as if searching for something unseen. "You... feel different," she murmured, almost to herself. "There is something in you that is not wholly mortal."

Arden shook her head. "I am mortal."

But Syliris was unmoved. She tilted her head, watching her with an intensity that sent a shiver down Arden's spine. "If you were fully mortal, the crown would not be yours," she countered.

Arden clenched her jaw. "And yet, here I stand with the crown. Mortal."

Syliris' lips curled into the faintest of smiles. "Yes. Here you stand..."

Elydris stepped forward, his golden aura flaring as he cut through the strange tension that had begun to weave between them. His fury simmered beneath the surface, barely restrained. "We don't have time for this," he snapped, his voice low and commanding.

His eyes locked onto Aeltherion. Slowly, deliberately, he extended a hand. "Give me the crown," he commanded.

Arden froze. Her fingers hovered near the base of the crown, heat prickling at her palms. The air in the chamber shifted, thickening as if it recognized what was about to happen. "It chose me...," she said quietly.

Elydris' jaw clenched. "Why would it do that?"

"I carry your blood, I carry her heartspark."

His expression darkened. "That's impossible," he whispered. Without another word, his hand moved to grasp the crown. The moment his fingers brushed against the metal, the air crackled with energy. A pulse of golden light surged outward from Aeltherion, not hostile, not cruel, simply... firm.

Elydris was pushed back. He stumbled several steps, his own energy flaring around him in shock as he steadied himself, eyes wide with disbelief. The crown's magic settled back against Arden, quiet once more.

The room fell silent. Every fae in the chamber stared, stunned. Arden didn't move.

Aezraen's voice broke the silence, low and distant. "It wouldn't let me take it either." His gaze flicked to Elydris, his face unreadable. "Or Vaelithara." The words settled over the room like a storm breaking open.

The Watchers, silent until now, finally spoke. Their voices, layered and ancient, reverberated through the chamber. "She must reunite the fae courts and bring together those scattered in the wake of Vaelithara's rule.

When all of the courts stand together, only then can you declare victory over the realm."

The words rang in Arden's skull, reverberating like a chime struck too hard. A war against something that had helped shape this world before she had even drawn her first breath.

"The courts must rise as one," the Watchers continued. "Or this war will consume everything."

Aezraen exhaled sharply, his expression dark. "How much time do we have?"

The Watchers ignored him, addressing Arden instead. "Time always moves against us. It races forward if we are ready or not."

Syliris' fingers slipped from Aezraen's as she turned toward them. "Then we must be ready."

Arden barely had time to catch her breath before Elydris turned toward her, the golden fire in his eyes dimmed, but not extinguished. He moved with the same gravity, the same pressure of magic clinging to the air, but now his steps were slower, measured.

"You claim to carry my blood," he said, his voice low, controlled. "The power inside you... it should never have awakened in mortal hands."

Arden held his gaze. "I didn't ask for any of this."

Elydris nodded once, sharply. "No one asks for the Gods to choose them." His voice tightened. "We cannot change what has already happened. But we can decide what happens next."

A pause. His golden gaze sharpened, the weight of centuries pressing into each word. "You will help us, Arden. You must. The realm cannot face Vaelithara without you, without that power."

Arden's throat tightened. "I don't even know how to use it," she admitted, her voice low. "I don't know if I ever will."

Elydris stepped closer, his presence towering but not threatening, absolute. "Then I will teach you," he said, each word a vow. "You are tied to me through that crown. That power is yours now, and you will not waste it."

Arden clenched her jaw mentally preparing for what was to come.

The journey back to the Court of Shadows was steeped in tense silence, broken only by the occasional murmur of conversation between

Syliris and her father. Arden trailed behind them, her mind a storm of conflicting thoughts.

Aezraen kept to himself, his shadows writhing as if feeding off his turbulent emotions. He had barely spoken since they departed the ruins. If he felt the weight of Syliris' confusion, if her misplaced memories sent him spiraling deeper into whatever madness gnawed at his soul, he gave no sign of it. But Arden saw the way his hands trembled, the way his shadows recoiled whenever Syliris so much as glanced in his direction.

The moment they passed through the shifting veil of shadow that marked the entrance to Aezraen's court, Elydris faced the gathered group. His presence radiated absolute authority, and when he spoke, his voice was cold and commanding. "You will not set foot in this court again."

Aezraen froze. The air between them thickened, tension crackling like the space before a storm. "Excuse me?" His voice was dangerously low, his posture rigid. "This is *my* court."

Elydris did not waver. "You are not welcome here." His gaze flicked briefly to Syliris, who stood between them, confusion flickering behind her golden eyes. "Not while her mind is still clouded."

Syliris' gaze darted between them, her brows knitting together in unease. "Father..." she hesitated.

Elydris' expression hardened, his golden aura flaring. "She is my daughter. You are a traitor." The words were like blades, each one driving deeper than the last. "You are not to speak to her. You are not to look at her. Do not test me, Aezraen."

The shadows surged violently before retracting just as quickly. Aezraen's lips parted, his breath uneven, but for once, he said nothing.

Syliris took a tentative step forward, her voice uncertain. "Why?"

Elydris' expression did not soften. "Because you do not remember the truth, and I will not have him filling the gaps with his own delusions."

Aezraen flinched as if struck. Arden felt something sharp twist in her gut as she watched the way his entire body tensed as if barely restraining the storm inside him. He turned, his jaw tight, shadows pulling away from Syliris like severed threads. His voice, when he finally spoke, was eerily calm. "As you wish, *Your Majesty*."

As Aezraen walked away, Noctis let out a low, guttural growl that rumbled through the courtyard like distant thunder. Elydris watched the massive lion prowl in slow, deliberate circles, an embodiment of raw magic and ancient power. Once, he had been Syliris' protector. A guardian gifted to her by the Court of Beasts, standing between her and the world's dangers with unwavering loyalty. Now, he stood by Arden's side.

Unease stirred in Elydris' chest. Aezraen was reckless, dangerous. The exile had already lost everything, and a man with nothing left was the most volatile of all. Desperation bred chaos, and Elydris would not allow that chaos near his daughter.

Noctis huffed, his massive form tense, muscles coiling beneath a twilight-streaked hide. Elydris reached out, brushing his hand along the lion's dark coat. Golden magic flickered at his fingertips, subtle but present. "You were hers once," he said, his voice low. "I ask you now to protect her again."

The lion rumbled, deep and resonant, his tail flicking behind him in clear displeasure. The sound echoed like a warning.

"I do not trust Aezraen," he continued, his voice sharpened by cold certainty. "If he returns to these halls, Syliris will allow him in. She has always been merciful, even to those who do not deserve it."

He stepped back, eyes burning with quiet intensity. "I will not lose her again. Not to him. Not to fate. Not to anyone." Elydris' magic pulsed faintly against his palm, but he did not press. The lion was bound to Arden now, and no force could sever that bond.

He let his hand fall, regal composure settling over him like armor. "Your loyalty is to her now. I do not question that." His gaze lingered on the lion's steady eyes. "But you love Syliris, as do I. Should she be in danger, I will act. And I trust you will do the same."

Noctis growled again, a sound filled with understanding. He would not abandon Arden, he could not. But Syliris was still part of him and always would be.

Arden's voice cut across the courtyard. "Noctis, go with her." Every syllable was clear, steady, undeniable.

Elydris turned. Arden approached them both, her expression composed, her steps unwavering. The firelight caught on her skin, flickering across her face. She stopped beside Noctis, laying a hand gently against his broad side, her voice soft but firm. "You're hers, too. You always have been."

Noctis's eyes locked onto hers, searching. The question came not in words but through the silent thread of their bond. *"Are you certain?"* Her heart twisted, but she nodded. The loss cut deep, yet she did not waver. The great lion exhaled a slow breath and lowered his head in acknowledgment.

Elydris inclined his head in return. "Then it is settled."

Noctis turned and followed Syliris as she was led toward the castle. Arden watched him go, her chest tight, the ache of parting mirrored in the bond that still faintly tethered them.

Chapter Twenty-Five

As Noctis vanished into the shadowed halls beside Syliris, silence settled over the courtyard. In that moment, Arden lost more than just a guardian, she lost a piece of certainty. Before she could speak or gather her thoughts, Elydris turned to her, his eyes sharp and unreadable. The tension that had lingered between them shifted, tempered by necessity.

"Come," he said. "There are things you must understand, truths no one else can tell you." Elydris gestured for her to follow him inside. For the first time since his awakening, he allowed himself to look beyond anger and grief, turning instead to the past. As they walked through the silent halls, he seemed like a relic from another age, shaped by a time older than memory.

"This world," he murmured, his voice distant, "was not always as it is."

"I keep hearing that," Arden mused.

She followed cautiously, watching as memories overtook him. Elydris' gaze drifted beyond the chamber, beyond the present, as though he were staring into echoes of a time long buried. When his voice returned, it was low and reverent, edged with something unreadable. "The Gods did not shape this world. They tasked me with forging it."

His fingers trailed across the ancient stone walls, golden sigils pulsing faintly beneath his touch, marks left by a power that once ruled unchallenged. "They placed the weight of creation in my hands, gifted me Aeltherion to mold the land, shape its magic, and carve balance into the bones of existence. I built the courts, crafted their purpose, and ensured each had a place in the eternal cycle of power." A slow breath escaped him, measured and deliberate. "I believed I had succeeded."

"But the Gods knew better. They saw what I could not. The sun cannot exist without the moon. Light, left unchecked, casts shadows too deep to ever be contained." His jaw clenched, golden energy sparking across his knuckles. "So they sent me Vaelithara."

Arden stiffened, even the air seemed to recoil at her name.

Elydris let the silence stretch between them, heavy and charged. When he finally spoke again, his voice was softer, more thoughtful. "She was brilliant." He exhaled, and for a moment, something like fondness flickered in his eyes before grief swept it away. "A force unlike any I had known. She was meant to balance me, to temper creation with change. If Aeltherion was my gift, hers was Solcryne, a stone born from the same divine thread." He lifted his gaze to Arden. "Individually, they were powerful. Together, they were unstoppable."

He took a deep breath. "We were never meant to rule apart," Elydris said. "We were designed as a single force. Light and dark, order and chaos." He ran his hand across his chin. "We built this world side by side. For a time, she was everything the Gods had promised. Cunning, ambitious, always looking ahead. I..." He exhaled sharply. "I thought I loved her."

Arden swallowed hard. She had seen the aftermath of Vaelithara's ambition, history twisted, lives torn apart, the truth buried. "What changed?" she asked.

Elydris' expression darkened. "She did." He turned to face her fully, his golden aura pulsing with the fury tightening his jaw. "Vaelithara was never satisfied. She always wanted more. And when she discovered she could rewrite reality, she did not hesitate."

His voice was iron, cold and certain. "By the time I saw her for what she truly was, she had already set her sights on corrupting Syliris." His golden eyes burned as he stepped closer. "She will do the same to you if you are not strong enough to resist her."

Arden squared her shoulders, feeling the weight of the realm settle on her.

The next morning, Arden stood in ill-fitting garments that Kastiel had retrieved from the armory. The guard only housed men and it showed.

The fabric hung loosely on her frame, sleeves too long and boots too wide. The crisp morning air bit at her skin, stiffening her muscles and slowing her movements more than she cared to admit.

Elydris studied her for a long moment. "Brace yourself."

The first blast of energy struck her square in the chest, sending her sprawling into the dirt. She gasped and rolled onto her hands and knees, her body trembling from the force.

"What the hell," she began, but before she could finish, another pulse of golden magic surged toward her. She barely raised a hand in time. Silver sparks flickered against her skin, the energy inside her surging but remaining untrained and chaotic.

Elydris circled her like a predator, his expression unreadable. "Do not defend. Control."

Arden gritted her teeth and pushed herself upright. The golden and silver light crackled in her veins, just out of reach. She could feel it slip through her fingers each time she tried to grasp it.

Elydris lifted a hand again, energy pulsing at his fingertips. "Again."

The attack came swift and sharp. Arden twisted to dodge it, but another followed immediately. This time, she did not try to block it.

The magic responded. Golden and silver sparks burst from her fingertips, colliding with Elydris' strike in a blinding explosion of light.

For the first time, his expression shifted, just slightly. "Better."

Arden exhaled, her body shaking. She had barely scratched the surface of her power, yet it felt as if she had pulled the sun from the sky. "Let's go again."

Arden quickly learned that Elydris did not train her to prepare her; he trained her to survive. He left no room for hesitation, no space for weakness. Every morning before the sun rose, before the world stirred to life, he pulled her from her chambers and marched her to the training grounds. The air was crisp in the early hours, mist clinging to the damp stone, curling around her ankles like living things.

It began with the simplest demand. "Call the light."

Arden scoffed at first, half-expecting some grand summoning ritual. But Elydris merely stared at her, his gaze unwavering. "You think power comes from nothing? That it obeys your will without question? You are the conduit, Arden. Until you understand that, you are useless."

The first week was agony. Elydris dismantled every remaining piece of her. He refused to let her rely on instinct or reactive emotion. "That is not control. That is survival. Power will always come when you are cornered. But to master it, you must call it by choice."

He forced her into stillness each evening, sitting for hours in the chamber of the Watchers, where ancient magic pressed down like a weight. She felt every shift in the air and every current of power.

Some days, the magic answered. Most days, it did not. But without fail, whenever she faltered, Elydris struck. Golden energy flared through the air before she could brace herself, crashing into her like waves of blistering heat. The first time, she barely stumbled aside. The second time, she raised her hands instinctively, silver and gold sparks erupting in a chaotic burst. She learned to anticipate, to breathe, to endure.

The first time she called the light of her own volition, it was a flicker, no brighter than a candle flame. The moment she lost focus, it vanished. Elydris was relentless. "Again."

She summoned it again and again. Until her fingers trembled and her breath came in ragged gasps, her body and mind drained from the effort. But the light came easier the next day.

During another evaluation, Elydris declared her body weak and her mind untrained. So she ran miles through the twisting corridors of the Court of Shadows. She learned to fight blindfolded, to trust magic oversight. She sparred with Elydris himself, his strikes swift as fire. He showed no mercy, and she grew strong. "You rely too much on your eyes. Listen to the world around you."

So she listened.

Training to surrender to her power was the hardest thing Arden had ever done. Elydris threw her into the deep lake beyond the training grounds and told her to find her way out, without swimming.

She hit the water hard. Breath stolen, she sank, dragged down by the weight of her own body. Darkness closed around her, the surface a distant shimmer. Her limbs flailed, but the water offered no hold. She struggled, kicked, fought, but she only sank faster. Panic clawed at her chest. Her heartbeat thundered. Pressure built against her ribs. She was going to drown.

She squeezed her eyes shut and forced her mind to still. Panic, desperation, and fear threatened to consume her. They would kill her if she could not control them. She recited her mantra like a prayer and let go of the fight.

She stopped struggling and opened herself to the silence. The water was not her enemy; it moved and flowed around her. The power stirred, flickering softly beneath her ribs, a whisper. As she surrendered to the ebb and flow of the water, her magic responded. Warmth spread through her chest, light blooming from her skin.

Currents bent and swirled not against her, but with her. They carried her like a breath released. The lake parted, lifting her toward the surface with effortless grace. She broke through with a gasp, air flooding her lungs.

Elydris stood waiting on the shore. "Better," he said. "But not good enough."

Every spare hour that Arden had, she trained. She held fire in her palms, letting it burn her fingers until she could shape it without pain. She wielded light in the darkness, forcing the shadows back and bending them to her will. She destroyed illusions and twisted them into her own. Weeks bled into months, and Arden lost herself in the endless cycle of breaking and reforging. Her magic no longer flickered like an untamed storm; it surged at her command.

The first time she held the energy steady in both hands, a stream of silver and gold flowing from her palms, Elydris nodded in approval. Then he threw her into battle; no warning, no hesitation. One moment, she stood before Elydris, breath stilled in her chest, and the next, the world erupted into chaos.

The sky darkened, the air crackled, and the ground beneath her feet splintered as raw power surged from his outstretched hands. A storm of magic swallowed the training grounds, twisting the air into howling winds thick with lightning and shadow.

The first bolt of power struck with the force of a collapsing star, tearing through the space between them. She barely twisted away in time, feeling the heat graze her cheek and tasting the singed air filling her mouth. Another strike followed, and another. There was no pattern, no rhythm, just unrelenting force. She fought back, not with brute strength or reckless fury, but with precision and control. Her blade danced through the storm, carving light through the abyss. She met his attacks with the sharpness of steel and the weight of her own will. For every torrent of power he unleashed, she found a way through, slipping between the fractures and stepping into spaces where the storm had yet to touch.

Golden fire erupted from his fingertips, a storm of power meant to break her. Arden lifted her hands, and the silver and gold light flared to life, meeting his power in a brilliant, blinding clash of magic. This time, the energy did not consume her. It did not slip through her fingers or buckle beneath Elydris' force; she held firm. The First King lowered his hands, a slow smile curving his lips. "Now, you are ready."

Chapter Twenty-Six

Aezraen

Aezraen stumbled through the threshold of Veylis' castle, his shadows trailing behind him like smoke, frayed and restless. Each breath was a struggle, the weight of something unspoken pressing against his ribs.

Veylis looked up from his position on a velvet settee, his eyes gleaming with curiosity. A half-empty glass dangled from his fingers, the scent of spiced wine and incense curling in the air between them.

"Well..." Veylis drawled, setting the glass aside, "you look like death."

Aezraen didn't respond. He could barely stand, one hand braced against the doorframe, as if remaining upright was a battle he was losing.

Veylis rose, a flicker of genuine concern breaking through his amusement as he waved the others out of the room. "What happened after you left the courtyard?" His voice lowered, less sharp now, edged with wariness.

Aezraen let out a ragged breath. His throat was dry, and his voice nearly broken. "Elydris has returned."

The words hung heavily in the chamber, their weight overwhelming. The First Fae King. Veylis stepped closer, studying the ruin etched into Aezraen's features. "What else?"

Aezraen's voice cracked. "Syliris doesn't remember me." The admission hollowed him. His hands clenched at his sides, nails biting into flesh. "She knew me, but it was like I was a stranger, not someone she loved." He shook his head, as if trying to dislodge the memory. "Elydris... he doesn't care what I have to say. He cast me out like I was nothing. Barred me from my court, from seeing her."

Aezraen's legs gave out, and he sank to his knees, shadows coiling around him like wounded things. His breath hitched, sharp and broken. "I tried. I tried for so long to bring her back...I guess I hoped there was still a place for me in her life."

Veylis crouched beside him, the sharpness in his gaze softening.

Aezraen stared at the floor, his voice barely a whisper. "I don't know who I am without her."

"What use is a broken man in a broken kingdom?" Veylis mused. "Come, Aezraen. Let us see how deeply you can drown in this misery."

Aezraen became little more than a specter in the Hollow Court, a shadow among the lost souls seeking solace in its endless distractions. He drifted through its halls like a man untethered, aimless in a place perfectly built for forgetting.

Syliris had been his anchor, the last thread tying him to a world that made sense. He had lived for the hope of her return. But now that she was back, she was little more than a ghost. When he could no longer bear the weight of her absence, he did the only thing he could. He stood at the edge of the Court of Shadows, his power reaching toward the walls that had once felt like home. But the air repelled him, a silent and absolute decree.

So he watched from the darkness.

Hidden in shadow, he tracked Elydris' movements, the way Arden followed him into the night. He saw her stumble beneath the weight of power she did not yet understand. He saw her rise again, silver and gold sparks flickering to life at her fingertips, bending but never breaking under Elydris' relentless will. The thief he had once known, the girl who had stood defiant against him, was becoming something more without him.

Time blurred. Nights bled into bitter dawns, each morning colder than the last. Weeks stretched into months. Arden no longer needed him, Syliris barely remembered who he was, and in the quiet of his exile, Aezraen feared he was becoming nothing at all.

The Hollow Court suffocated him with incense and indulgence, its air thick with spiced wine, smoke, and desire. Shadows moved unnaturally along silk-draped walls, dancing to the rhythm of forgotten sins and whispered regrets. They offered oblivion here, wrapped in satin and gold. Aezraen, stripped of everything that once defined him, stood at the threshold of that darkness, wondering how long he could resist.

He sat in one of Veylis' opulent chambers, a glass of dark liquid in his grasp. Its burn did little to numb the ache in his chest. Across from him, Veylis lounged like a serpent at rest, his eyes gleaming with dark amusement.

"You're brooding again," Veylis purred. "Tell me, does self-loathing pair well with wine? Or would something more bitter suit your taste?"

Aezraen said nothing, taking another slow sip.

Veylis sighed, ever the dramatist. "Tragic. A man of your reputation, reduced to sulking in corners like a wounded beast."

Aezraen tightened his grip on the glass. "What do you want, Veylis?"

Veylis tilted his head, considering. "I want you to wake up my dear, miserable friend." He gestured lazily to the chamber, to the revelers drifting through smoke and candlelight, their eyes glazed and laughter infectious. "You act as though you've been forgotten. But here? Here, you can be anything."

Aezraen looked away, his jaw tight.

Veylis' voice dropped, tinged with something darker. "You are wasting away in grief, Aezraen. Stop clutching the ashes of a life that is no longer yours."

Aezraen exhaled sharply, a flicker of anger sparking beneath his skin.

"I've seen men fall apart for far less in this court," Veylis continued, his voice soft, almost coaxing. "And you? You are already falling. At least have the spine to decide how far you're willing to let yourself go."

Aezraen rose, the glass slipping from his hand to shatter against the floor. He walked into the endless corridors of the Hollow Court, his shadows writhing restlessly around him.

Veylis' laughter followed him, low and knowing. "We'll see how long you last, old friend."

Chapter Twenty-Seven

Arden stood outside Syliris' door, her hand hovering just above the intricately carved wood. Her pulse thudded beneath her skin, the weight of uncertainty pressing against her ribs. She had lingered too long, staring at the wood grain as if it might reveal something if she waited just a moment longer. She urged herself to knock, but the will to act had slipped away.

With a quiet sigh, Arden turned on her heel, ready to retreat. Then came the sound of footsteps. Steady. Unhurried. Panic flared in her chest. She froze as Syliris rounded the corner, gliding toward her chambers with a grace that made her seem almost untouchable, as though she drifted outside the bounds of time.

Syliris' eyes locked onto Arden's and she realized with a sinking certainty that it was too late to run. "Arden?" Syliris' brow furrowed as she stopped in front of her door, studying her with mild curiosity. "Were you looking for me?"

Arden shifted awkwardly. "Uh, no... Well, yes. Sort of?"

Syliris arched an elegant brow. "That was an impressively vague answer."

"I wanted to give you something." Syliris tilted her head slightly and watched as Arden pulled a small, leather-bound book from her satchel. The moment Syliris laid eyes on it, her expression flickered with something unreadable. Arden swallowed. "It belonged to Aezraen, when he was mortal."

Syliris stilled, her gaze darting back to Arden's face, searching for something she couldn't seem to find.

Arden forced herself to continue. "He wrote about his time in your father's court. About... you. A lot about you, in fact." She wet her lips, feeling ridiculous for how nervous she was. "I thought it might help you remember."

Syliris stared at the book for a long moment before finally reaching out to take it from Arden's grasp. Her fingers traced the edges of the worn leather cover, her thumb brushing over the embossed design. "Thank you." The words were quiet but sincere.

Arden nodded and took a step back. "I'll, uh, leave you to it."

She turned, ready to walk away before embarrassing herself further, but Syliris' voice stopped her. "Arden."

Arden turned back, half-expecting Syliris to hand the book back, to say it was too much, too soon. Instead, Syliris tightened her grip on the journal, her expression thoughtful. "I appreciate this," she murmured. "Truly." With a small nod, she retreated to her chambers, the door clicking shut behind her.

The firelight danced against the stone walls, casting long, twisting shadows as Syliris crossed the room and sat on the edge of her bed, turning the journal over in her hands. It felt strange to hold something so personal, something that should have felt familiar, yet didn't.

Taking a steadying breath, she unfastened the strap and opened the book. The scent of aged parchment rose to meet her, earthy and brittle, as if the pages themselves were holding the memories she sought to find. She scanned the inked words, eyes tracing the lines with growing unease.

Each passage felt distant, like hearing a lullaby in a language she almost knew. Close, but wrong. The words blurred at the edges of her thoughts, familiar in shape but hollow in meaning. Confusion crept in, quiet and cold. It began as a whisper, curling through her mind like a lie in the dark. Familiarity twisted into strangeness, and the book, this piece of someone she might have been, felt suddenly like it told someone else's story.

Initially, it was easy to dismiss. Her memories were fractured, shattered pieces of a past stolen from her by time and magic. Some resurfaced effortlessly, fitting back into place like missing puzzle pieces, while others remained elusive, buried beneath layers of fog.

His journal overflowed with pages of devotion. She traced her fingertips along the inked lines, sensing the desperation in each carefully penned word. His grief resonated in the unsteady flow of his writing, heartbreak woven into every stroke.

"We danced beneath the starlit arches of the Hollow Court, hidden from the Archfey's gaze. She pressed her hands to my chest, and I swore my heart would never belong to another. But she was fae, and I was not... The king would never allow it.

We were both heartbroken as we realized that this love could never be more than a secret in the dark of night. I comforted her as she cried against my shoulder. But when she looked into my eyes, I knew I would do anything to make the king change his mind. I would rewrite history to be with her. When we kissed, the whole world around us shifted. Suddenly, everything made sense. In the morning, I will seek out the king, ask for his blessing, and beg the Gods to change my fate."

Syliris' vision blurred as the inked words on the page wavered, as if the journal itself recoiled from her touch. She blinked hard, striving to focus, but her mind was already spiraling. Her hands trembled, and the room felt unnervingly still and quiet, as if it held its breath alongside her.

She read the lines again, this time more slowly, hoping for a spark of familiarity, but nothing came. No warmth blossomed in her chest. No starlit arches appeared. No whispered vows echoed. Just cold ink on yellowing pages and a suffocating sense tightening around her lungs.

Her throat constricted, and the room tilted slightly. She grasped the edge of the bed with her free hand to ground herself, but it didn't help. The memory Aezraen described was vivid and emotional, overflowing with devotion, yet to her, it felt like a void. There was no hint of truth resonating in her mind.

A weight pressed against her chest, heavy and unrelenting. Her pulse roared in her ears, and her breaths came too fast and too shallow. She curled forward, eyes squeezed shut, trying to push the memory into place. She begged her mind to uncover something even if it was just a flicker of that night, the softness of his touch, a whisper of some truth.

But there was nothing.

Only the certainty that she had never kissed Aezraen, never danced beneath those arches, never whispered promises to him in secret. Page after page of false memories, carefully crafted yet deeply felt. He remembered loving her, but she had never loved him.

She didn't know which was worse, that he believed these memories were true or that he might have helped someone implant them in her mind. Her hands flew to her head, pressing hard against her temples. Her skin crawled, and her body ached. The words had embedded themselves beneath her skin like splinters and she wanted them out.

The journal thudded against the floor, prompting her to back away, staggering as if it might leap up and pull her back into the web of lies. Panic gripped her chest, heaving and causing her knees to buckle. Her memories twisted like charred paper, fragile and useless, unable to withstand the weight of the falsehoods threatening to replace them.

She collapsed onto the floor, gasping for air. The journal lay a few feet away, its pages fluttering in the draft. Vivid images of the past flooded her mind. Aezraen standing loyally by her father's side, walking the halls, sharing smiles and laughter with her.

The realization crashed over her like a tidal wave, leaving her breathless. Syliris struggled to breathe as her mind unraveled, the carefully woven illusion fraying at the edges. Desperately, she sought to regain her composure as memories surged back, undeniable and relentless.

It wasn't Aezraen's voice that echoed in her past; it was deep and rich with laughter, filled with heat and hunger. It belonged to someone who didn't whisper empty promises but growled them into her skin, branding them as marks of ownership. The scent of wild earth, storm-laden air, smoke, sweat, and something untamed enveloped her senses. Her world flipped upside down as memories resurfaced, unstoppable and flooding through her like a torrent unleashed after centuries of suppression.

She recalled his rough hands, calloused from battle, tracing the contours of her body. Syliris surrendered to the memories, embracing them as they overwhelmed her. The firelight in her chambers flickered and dimmed, drawing her deeper into the past.

The forest air was thick and warm, rich with the scent of pine, damp earth, and the promise of an approaching storm. Her laughter echoed through the trees as she darted among them, her skirt hitched up, feet barely grazing the ground.

Behind her, a familiar sound rumbled through the woods, a low, playful growl that sent her heart racing. "Run all you want," Ortheon called, his voice rich with amusement. "I always catch you."

Syliris laughed, breathless with excitement, dodging around a thick tree trunk. "Maybe I'm just letting you think that."

"Oh? Brave words for someone already cornered."

Before she could take another step, strong arms enveloped her waist and lifted her off the ground. She squealed, laughter bubbling up from her chest as Ortheon spun her in a circle, the momentum stealing her breath.

"You're mine," he declared, his eyes gleaming as he set her down gently, pressing her back against a nearby tree. His wide, unrestrained grin made her feel like the only person in his world.

Syliris arched an eyebrow, her cheeks flushed. "I let you win."

Ortheon grinned. "Is that what we're calling it now?" His forehead rested against hers, their breaths mingling. The tension between them was warm and steady, like a low crackling fire. He brushed a stray leaf from her hair, lingering at her temple before trailing down her cheek.

"Say it," he murmured softly but insistently.

Syliris smiled and brushed her lips against his. "Yours."

A low sound escaped him as he wrapped his arms around her and pulled her close. She melted against him, her fingers threading through his hair, her heart thudding not from fear or anticipation, but from pure joy.

He pressed gentle kisses along her jaw, the bridge of her nose, and her forehead, before finally claiming her lips. The kiss was playful and sweet, yet beneath it lay a promise, a connection deeper than words. She giggled as he kissed her again, nipping lightly at her lower lip. His smile widened when she playfully swatted his chest.

"Mine," he whispered again, pressing a kiss to the sensitive spot just below her ear.

Syliris rolled her eyes. "You keep saying that like I'll forget."

Ortheon pulled back, his eyes glowing. "I just like hearing it."

She sighed with mock exasperation and kissed him once more, slowly. "Always."

With a contented hum, he lifted her off the ground, her legs instinctively wrapping around his waist as he carried her deeper into the clearing. The forest hushed around them, with only the distant rumble of thunder and rustling leaves as witnesses.

They lay together in the soft grass, his arms wrapped around her while her head rested against his chest. His thumb traced lazy circles over her hip as they watched the clouds roll overhead, the storm still far away.

"Do you think we'll always have this?" she asked quietly.

Ortheon looked down at her, gently tucking a strand of hair behind her ear. "As long as I have breath, you'll have me."

Syliris smiled, her eyes fluttering closed, content in the warmth of his arms and the steady rhythm of his heartbeat. The afternoon sun filtered through the trees, casting dappled light across their skin as the forest lulled them into a slow, blissful sleep.

They lay intertwined in the grass, the world beyond the clearing forgotten, until a sound stirred them awake. At first, it was subtle, a rustling in the underbrush, too measured to be the wind, too deliberate to belong to any passing animal.

Ortheon was already moving. His body tensed beneath her as he sat up, every line sharpened by alertness. The lazy warmth they had shared vanished in an instant, replaced by a tension that buzzed through the air like a drawn blade. Syliris followed his gaze, her pulse quickening; the shift in atmosphere was undeniable. The clearing no longer felt like a sanctuary but rather exposed.

Then the voice came, slipping through the trees like smoke.

Low. Sweet. Poisoned with familiarity. "How terribly disappointing."

Vaelithara stepped into the clearing, seemingly untouched by the wilderness. Her pristine gown trailed behind her like liquid shadow, and not a single strand of her raven-black hair was out of place.

Syliris' breath hitched, dread coiling tightly in her stomach. Ortheon moved instinctively, shielding her with his body, his eyes narrowing. "You shouldn't be here." His voice was steady, but an underlying warning lingered.

Vaelithara smiled, slow and sharp, her gaze sweeping over the two of them, taking in their disheveled state. "Neither should you," she murmured, tilting her head. "But I imagine Elydris would be far more interested in knowing where our daughter has been."

Syliris stiffened, her heart racing. "You wouldn't."

"Wouldn't I?" Vaelithara's gaze shifted to Ortheon, her expression unreadable. "What would your precious father say if he knew his beloved daughter had been ruined by a beast?"

A snarl tore from Ortheon's throat as he tightened his grip on Syliris, his body coiled with restrained violence. "Watch your tongue, Vaelithara."

Her eyes gleamed with dark amusement. "Or what? Will you tear me apart?" She stepped closer, her voice soft yet laced with venom. "I am the Fae Queen. You will remember your place when you speak to me."

She locked eyes with her daughter. "We both know your father would rather imprison you than allow you to be with an Archfey who refuses to bow to him."

Syliris' stomach twisted. She knew her father loved her, but deep down, she understood her mother was right. He would never approve of their love. Vaelithara smiled, as if she could read Syliris' thoughts. "He would never let this stand." Her voice took on a pitying tone. "You know that, don't you, little princess?"

Syliris' skin grew hot at her mother's patronizing words, and she dug her nails into her palms. "You have no right to interfere; I am an adult now."

Vaelithara sighed, shaking her head. "Oh, Syliris. Your coronation isn't for another three months. Until then, your father won't care about your opinions. Do you think this is about what's right?" Her gaze flicked back to Ortheon. "Do you think this is about love?"

Ortheon stepped forward, muscles taut with fury, but Syliris grabbed his arm. "Don't," she whispered, barely audible.

Vaelithara's lips curled into a smile. "In this world, we make our own way, darling." She lifted her hands and began to chant. The words were foreign and twisted, laced with something that made the air crackle with wrongness. Syliris' heart sank; this was not fae magic.

Putrid green smoke coiled from Vaelithara's fingertips, slithering across the forest floor like a living thing, creeping toward Syliris with unnatural speed. Ortheon lunged for her, but he was too late.

The magic slammed into Syliris, knocking the breath from her lungs and seeping into her very bones. A scream tore from her throat, swallowed by the haze as her vision darkened and the world tilted.

She heard Ortheon roaring her name, felt his hands grasping for her, the world splitting at the seams, and then silence engulfed her.

Warm fingers brushed her cheek, prompting her to smile and rub her face against the soft pressure.

"Syliris," a voice breathed, smooth and familiar.

Her eyes fluttered open. Everything felt slow, as if she were waking from a dream she couldn't quite grasp. Her body felt heavy, her limbs reluctant to move. But the moment her gaze found him, all the tension melted away.

Aezraen.

His face was inches from hers, his eyes soft and shining with relief, as if he had been waiting forever. He cradled the side of her face, his thumb reverently stroking her cheek.

Syliris smiled slowly, her heart fluttering with warmth. Everything in her yearned to be closer to him. "You're here," she murmured.

He leaned in, his forehead pressing against hers, their breaths mingling. "Of course I am. I never left your side." His voice was gentle, though a tremor lay beneath it. "I told your mother I would do anything. She said she would make me an Archfey. Soon, we won't have to worry about your father, and we won't have to hide anymore."

His other hand slipped into hers, holding it just a little too tightly. "You'll never be alone again," he whispered.

Syliris closed her eyes, content in the safety of his embrace, unaware of how intently he watched her, how still he sat, like a man clinging to a dream he refused to wake from.

Chapter Twenty-Eight

The firelight flickered weakly against the walls, offering no comfort. The warmth in the room felt deceptive as she paced back and forth trying to make sense of everything. Syliris stared ahead, her gaze unfocused, her chest rising and falling with shallow, ragged breaths. Her pulse throbbed in her ears, each beat echoing the truth that blossomed within her. Her chest ached from the loss of a love that was not imagined or abstract, but painfully real.

She remembered Ortheon, every stolen moment they had shared in his court. His voice, his touch, his laughter. The way he had drawn her close without hesitation, how he had accepted her love without apology. She had chosen him, only for her mother to take it all away.

A low sob escaped her as her fingers clutched her chest. Syliris had been forced to love within a narrative that was never hers, while the truth of her own heart lay buried beneath her mother's lies. The sense of violation ran deeper than mere manipulation; it felt like theft.

Her legs buckled, and she sank to the floor, heaving sobs wracking her body as she grappled with the realization that Vaelithara had rewritten her story, carved out her heart, and filled it with someone else's fantasy. She pressed her hands to her face, striving to ground herself, desperately trying to halt the unraveling within. But the grief surged, raw and furious, awakened from centuries of slumber.

She wondered if Aezraen had known. The thought twisted in her gut. He had believed so completely, spoken with such devotion. Had he been a pawn in her mother's game? Or had he played a role in it knowingly?

The uncertainty left her hollow, and she had no room left for anger, only sorrow.

The journal lay open beside her, its inked words mocking her with their sincerity. Pages filled with longing and tenderness, yet none of it truly belonged to her. She hated that it almost did, that a part of her had once dared to believe it could.

She pushed herself up from the floor, her knees stiff and limbs trembling, but she moved anyway. This was not the time to mourn the love she had only just recalled. Right now, she needed answers. She needed the truth.

Turning toward the door, she didn't bother to wipe her tears. Let them see, let the entire court witness what had been taken from her. Syliris did not look back at the journal as she stepped into the hall, fire ignited in her chest and fury fueling her steps.

She dashed through the halls of a court she despised, not stopping until the guards opened the grand doors to her father's chamber. Her breath came in uneven gasps, but she ignored it. Her footsteps echoed across the polished stone floor as she entered, the memory of betrayal still burning within her.

Elydris watched her in silence, his expression carved from stone. Only his eyes moved, tracking her as she paced. Unsure of where to begin, her words spilled out in a flood of truth, a story that had been stolen from her and was finally being reclaimed.

She spoke of Ortheon, the forest, the laughter, and the love. She recounted how Vaelithara had ripped those moments away and filled the void with falsehoods. She continued until her throat ached and every tear that needed to fall had been shed.

When her voice fell silent, the room felt heavier, as if the walls themselves struggled to bear the weight of everything she had shared. Elydris closed his eyes and exhaled slowly, his fingers relaxing as the crackle of magic dissipated into the still air.

When he opened his eyes again, they were darker. "You are certain of this?" he asked, his voice devoid of challenge, filled only with quiet pain.

Syliris nodded, her hands clenched tightly at her sides. "I remember him. Not as a vision or a dream. It was real. I remember how he made me laugh and how safe I felt with him. I remember wanting him more than anything. I would have burned Elessian to the ground to be with him."

Elydris looked away for a moment. When he spoke again, his voice was soft but laced with regret. "Ortheon was always defiant, always beyond the reach of courtly rule, even as an Archfey. He never bowed to anyone...not even to me. I could see how Vaelithara would see him as a threat."

Syliris hesitated, her voice now quiet. "Do you think Aezraen was involved?"

The question hung in the air between them. She hated asking it, hated that she had to. Yet it had lingered at the edge of her thoughts since the memory returned. Aezraen's tenderness, his loyalty, the journal filled with love that wasn't his. Could someone fake all of that?

Elydris turned back to her slowly. "No."

She blinked. "But how can you be sure?"

"No man who willingly conspired with your mother would lay down in the tomb and beg for your forgiveness, or mine, not like he did. He was broken when we found him, ruined. You cannot fake that kind of desperation."

Syliris dropped her gaze, struggling to process that truth. If Aezraen had truly believed they were in love, then he was a victim too. Her mother had not only stolen her love but had also twisted another's perception of it. A heavy ache settled deep in her chest, filled with fury for what had been done.

Elydris moved closer, resting a gentle hand on her shoulder. "You are not alone in this. We will face it together. Your mother will answer for every mind she corrupted on her path to tainting Elessian."

Syliris bit her lip, her thoughts racing. "We have to tell Aezraen; he deserves the truth."

Elydris nodded slowly, his expression grave. "Yes. But you must be prepared. He will not accept it easily. What you have remembered will shatter everything he believes."

She turned her gaze to the chamber doors, her breath catching in her throat. The truth had already taken so much from them all. But letting it fester would only take more. She could not allow that to happen. "Then we bring him here," she said quietly. "Now. Before my mother buries this any deeper."

Elydris observed her for a long moment, as if seeing her with fresh eyes. "Are you certain you're ready to confront what he will become when he hears it?"

Syliris nodded, though her voice trembled. "Yes. I know how it feels to have your truth taken away, I can't allow him to live within someone else's lie."

Elydris summoned one of his guards. "Find Aezraen and bring him to the war chamber. No delays, no distractions." The guard bowed and swiftly exited into the hall.

Syliris moved closer to her father, fear still lingering in her heart but no longer controlling her. "He needs to know who I truly am, even if it hurts."

Elydris placed a reassuring hand on her shoulder, his voice calm yet firm. "Then let's hope this truth can be his anchor and not his undoing."

The air in the Court of Shadows was thick with an unnamed tension that weighed heavily on all present. The war chamber had been stripped of distractions leaving only the essentials and those closest to Aezraen.

Arden stood near the edge of the room, arms crossed, her eyes darting between the others. She hadn't been informed why she was summoned, only that it was urgent. Syliris paced slowly near the table, her steps deliberate yet restless. The storm in her eyes was unmistakable. She had barely spoken since her arrival; her silence spoke volumes. Her hand occasionally traced the etched lines on the table, her fingers trembling as she sought to ground herself in something real.

Veylis lounged at the far end of the table, exuding casual grace. However, the way he watched the door and the slight twitch of his fingers against the armrest revealed the unease beneath his calm exterior. His customary smirk had vanished the moment he entered the chamber, leaving him devoid of the usual amusement.

With a groan, the doors opened, breaking the heavy silence.

Two guards entered, dragging Aezraen between them. He slumped heavily, barely upright, his shirt rumpled and open, shadows flickering weakly at his heels. The sharp, sour stench of liquor clung to him, mingling with perfume and remnants of smoke. His hair hung damp with sweat, obscuring his eyes.

"Let go of me," he muttered, his voice low and cracked. He attempted to shake off the guards, but it was more a suggestion than a real effort. "I can walk. Gods, I said I can walk."

They released him, and he stumbled briefly before catching himself on the edge of the table. Squinting into the torchlight, he surveyed the room. "This better be good," he muttered. "I was in the middle of something." His gaze landed on Arden, then Syliris, and finally Elydris. A flicker of emotion crossed his face but vanished before it could take shape. He wiped his mouth with his sleeve and pushed himself into a slouched stance. Aezraen looked between them, "what's going on?" he asked slowly.

Leaning heavily against the table, his grip unsteady, Aezraen's lips curled into a semblance of a smirk, though it felt hollow. "Why are all of you looking at me like that?"

Syliris glanced at her father and he responded with a single, steady nod. The weight of the moment pressed down on her, but she straightened her posture. Her eyes shifted back to Aezraen. He looked ragged and unsteady, a mere shell of the man she once knew. Yet none of that changed what needed to be said. "My memories have returned," she said, her voice quiet but clear.

The words fell into the stillness like stones into deep water, their echoes rippling through the chamber and affecting everyone present. Aezraen's smirk faded, and he tightened his grip on the edge of the table until his knuckles turned white. His jaw clenched. "And?" he asked, the humor stripped from his voice, which now sounded low and brittle, held together by frayed threads. "What is it you remember?"

Syliris hesitated before answering. She reached into the folds of her cloak and retrieved the worn journal that Arden had given her, the one that contained a stranger's love disguised under her name. She placed it on the table between them, her hand lingering on the cover for a moment before she withdrew it. "Read it," she instructed.

Aezraen stared at the leather-bound book as if it were a weapon. Slowly, he extended his hand, trembling slightly, and opened the cover. Familiar script greeted him, the words in his own handwriting. He flipped through the pages slowly, each entry a reminder of his path to self-destruction and the love he lost. He slammed the book shut, "I don't want to read it, I know what it says."

"I do not remember this love," Syliris said softly, her voice barely louder than the crackling fire behind them. "Because it was never real."

Aezraen laughed, broken and bitter. What began as a choked noise in his throat erupted into wild, shaking laughter. His entire body trembled as it came in jagged bursts, filled with disbelief and madness, everything he could not articulate. The laughter echoed too loudly in the quiet room, bouncing off stone and steel as if it were alive.

He clutched the journal in both hands, his fingers shaking as the leather creased under the pressure. His mouth moved, but no words escaped. Shadows writhed at his feet, crawling up the walls as if trying to escape him. When his eyes met Syliris', he looked like a man watching the sun go dark. Suddenly, the laughter ceased. Disbelief washed over his features, and his breath hitched. "No," he murmured, his voice cracking on the word.

Syliris hesitated, her expression pained as she stepped closer to him. "She used us, Aezraen," she said quietly. "She planted memories in our minds, shadows of something that never existed. A love that wasn't ours. She needed you devoted, willing to do anything for the illusion of what you thought we shared. And I... I was easier to control when I believed someone truly loved me." Her voice faltered. "We were never given a choice. Not in that."

"You don't understand," he said, his voice rising. "You cannot *possibly* understand."

She opened her mouth to respond, but he slammed the journal onto the table with a force that rattled the floor.

"I waited for you. I abandoned my mortal life for you. I carved myself hollow and filled that emptiness with you. Every breath I took, every blade I bled on, every God I cursed; it was all for you." He backed away from the table, his shoulders rising and falling with each shuddering breath. "I became a shadow and I let her strip away everything that made me human because I thought that if I suffered enough, if I gave enough, I could somehow deserve you back."

"You may say it was never real," he rasped. "But I felt it. I feel it now. I remember how your name tasted in my mouth. I remember every night I spent screaming for you in my dreams. You were mine, Syliris. You were mine, and that feather took you from me."

Syliris trembled, tears streaming down her cheeks. "I am sorry. I am so sorry. But what you remember... it is not the truth. That love, whatever it became, was twisted. You were used. None of it should have been placed on your shoulders."

Aezraen looked at her as if he could no longer recognize her. His hands fell to his sides. Shadows twisted violently around him, lashing at the walls and cracking the stone. "I have loved you for centuries!" he shouted, his voice raw and thick with pain. Aezraen's hands trembled, "this was supposed to be my redemption. This was supposed to prove that I mattered, that I had something in me worth saving."

He took another staggering step back. "I killed for her. I bled for her. I gave up everything I ever was for her. But she was never mine at all?"

Arden stepped forward, tears streaming silently down her face, but he couldn't see her. His gaze was distant, staring through the past and into a future that no longer existed.

"Your death left me in the dark..." he whispered. "...and I built a life out of shadows."

Without another word, he turned and walked out of the chamber. His shadows trailed him like grieving hounds, snarling at the room's edges as if mourning the love that had just died.

Veylis exhaled slowly and leaned both hands on the edge of the table, staring at the door through which Aezraen had vanished. His shoulders were tense, his jaw tight; the easy charm that usually graced his lips was absent. He straightened, ran a hand through his hair, and glanced around the room. Elydris and Syliris remained silent. No one moved. The weight of the moment hung in the air, settling like dust, with no one knowing how to disperse it.

Then Veylis turned to Arden and studied her for a long moment. Her cheeks were streaked with tears, her hands clutched in front of her as if she couldn't decide whether to chase after Aezraen or collapse where she stood. "Well," Veylis muttered, pushing off the table. His voice was low and dry, as if even speaking felt burdensome. "Looks like I'll have to chase him down before he drowns himself in some hellhole."

Arden didn't respond. She simply nodded numbly and wiped at her eyes again, but the tears continued to flow. Veylis stepped closer, near enough that his words wouldn't carry to the others. His tone softened just enough to breach her defenses. "I'm going to find him," he said quietly. "I'll do whatever it takes, drag him out of whatever pit he throws himself into. Slap some sense into him if that's what it takes."

Arden looked up at him, her lip trembling. "And then what?"

"Then," Veylis said, fixing her with a serious gaze, "I need you to be there when he emerges from it. I can mend what's broken, but I can't explain to him why it's worth it."

Arden's breath caught in her throat, and she looked away.

"I know you're hurting," Veylis continued, his tone softening. "I understand this hasn't been easy for you. But he is broken, Arden. If there's anything left of him worth saving, it's because you reminded him he wasn't alone in that darkness. So if you still care, even a little, I need you to gather your strength."

"I don't know how," she whispered.

"You don't have to know how," he replied. "You just need to want to, that's enough. That's where it begins."

Arden swallowed hard, her throat constricting. Her hands relaxed slightly.

Veylis placed a brief but steady hand on her shoulder. "Figure out what you want, Arden. If he comes back from this and you aren't there, it will break him all over again." He stepped back before she could respond, his shadows already curling at the edges of the room, reaching for the path ahead. "And this time," he added, glancing back, "I don't know if he'll survive it."

Chapter Twenty-Nine

Aezraen

Aezraen left the war room, wandering aimlessly. His feet carried him far from the heavy stone walls and the judgmental stares, but the truth clung to him. When Syliris had spoken, when her memories returned and shattered everything he believed, something within him had cracked open. The pieces returned in sharp, vivid, disjointed fragments that cut through his mind with every breath.

Vaelithara's voice came back first, wrapping around him like velvet. He could still feel her breath against his skin, the way her fingers curled around his shoulder with the softness of a mother and the calculation of a snake. She whispered promises that sounded like salvation, painting a future where Syliris would be his, where the Gods themselves would kneel, and where love would triumph, rewriting the past in their favor. But what she truly offered were chains.

As a mortal, Aezraen had always believed in order, protocol, and the weight of oaths. So when the queen approached him unannounced, alone, and without a formal escort, something felt immediately wrong.

She glided through the courtyard like a shadow, her presence commanding yet strangely soft. Her voice was sweet and warm as she asked for a favor, a simple escort to retrieve an artifact. The Seraphyne's feather, a relic older than most living fae, powerful enough to record history in its truest form. Vaelithara claimed it had been lost for too long and needed to be returned. Aezraen stood stiffly, unsure how to respond. It seemed like a mission for the king's elite, one requiring approval through official channels.

"His Majesty is aware," she said, her smile not reaching her eyes. "All will be arranged."

But it didn't sit right with him.

After he was dismissed for the day, Aezraen made his way to the king's quarters, seeking clarity and assurance. As he approached the throne room, he paused, hearing raised voices through the thick wooden doors. Vaelithara's words rang clear; she was furious, scolding Elydris for Syliris' rebellious behavior. She spoke of disobedience, of sneaking away, and of failing to honor her future as heir. Elydris, ever calm, responded gently, suggesting that Syliris needed a bit of freedom before her coronation bound her in expectation.

Aezraen turned to leave, but his timing failed him. The doors opened just as he stepped away, and Vaelithara's gaze locked onto him. For a moment, they exchanged silence until Elydris' voice broke it. "Aezraen. Escort the queen back to her chambers."

He obeyed, as he always did.

Inside her chambers, the queen softened, almost maternal. She poured him wine, smiled, and asked for his thoughts. She spoke of Syliris again, weaving a new story about finding the princess sneaking into the Court of Beasts. She claimed Syliris was making poor choices, led astray by Ortheon's wild nature. Her tone turned sorrowful, her eyes glassy with concern. Aezraen, uncomfortable and uncertain, drank deeply.

She continued pouring, coaxing words from him. He had always admired Syliris, everyone did. He admitted, his voice slightly slurred from the drink, that he cared for her and had once considered courting her. Yet he knew it was foolish because he was mortal and she was not. But it didn't matter; he had never expected anything.

Vaelithara smiled.

Then came the smoke, faint green tendrils curling from her lips as she whispered encouragement in his ears. He felt lightheaded, his thoughts swirling. Memories began to form that he had never lived: Syliris laughing in the moonlight, kissing his brow, reaching for him with eyes full of love. It felt real. He could see it, feel it.

She handed him a journal and told him to write down her words. He did, pouring every word onto paper as if he had lived it. His fingers moved as if possessed, the words flowing faster than he could process. The room filled with sickly sweet smoke, and her voice wove through it, coaxing and praising. He wrote until he could no longer hold the quill. Then her hands cradled his face, and she whispered, "Sleep."

The next day, she visited him again, informing him that the Seraphyne would hold a conclave in the morning. He needed to strike then, retrieve the feather; for the future of his love, for Syliris. Blinded by ambition, he agreed, eager to be with her forever.

Later that day, guards carried Syliris into the castle, unconscious and pale. Aezraen rushed forward, demanding to know what had happened. Vaelithara met him in the hall, tears streaming down her cheeks. She told him Syliris had been found on the border of Ortheon's court. Her grief was so convincing that Aezraen never questioned it. He stayed by Syliris' side that night, guilt and rage knotting inside him like iron chains.

When she awoke, dazed and scared, he whispered the words that would bind him to her fate: "Soon, I'll be fae. We won't have to hide anymore... You'll never be alone again."

Now, in the silence of his own mind, Aezraen remembered everything. He saw every string Vaelithara had tied around him, every moment she had reshaped. She had used his loyalty and love, twisting him into a weapon and making him forget he had ever been one.

He had been a victim.

Just like Syliris.

The worst part was not that he had lost himself or betrayed Arden in the process. It was that, in all the lies, he had never questioned who was pulling the strings. Every move he had made, every sacrifice, every quiet ache in his chest had been for a lie. He had not been a man in love; he had been nothing more than a puppet.

The truth struck him with the weight of every century he had been cursed to be fae.

Aezraen found himself back at the Hollow Court, the name a bitter echo of his feelings. Every step through the winding paths felt heavier, as if he were dragging centuries of regret behind him. The torches lining the halls cast long shadows across the walls.

The memory of Arden surfaced, sharp and uninvited. He saw her in that chamber, her eyes wide with hope, confusion creeping in as he turned away. Then came the hurt he had seen bloom on her face. She had uncovered Aeltherion, pieced together the shattered past, and brought Syliris back into the world, fully aware of the cost; yet he had cast her aside the moment Syliris opened her eyes. Not because he truly loved Syliris, but because his mind had been twisted to believe he did.

His heart had never truly belonged to Syliris; Arden had taken that part of him without him realizing it. She had simply seen him. All the pieces, all the darkness, and still she had wanted him.

He stumbled into his chambers, shadows curling low around his boots. The place reeked of old incense and wine, and broken glass crunched beneath his feet from scattered bottles. He dropped into a chair, hands dragging down his face, trembling and unable to breathe past the weight in his chest.

No peace awaited him in this silence. His mind wandered to every mortal friend he had watched die, every face blurred by time, every funeral he had endured in silence. The weight of it all crushed him. A roar built in his throat, but he swallowed it. He didn't deserve release.

He reached for the bottle on the table and drank deeply. The burn did nothing to fill the emptiness he felt inside. He had loved Syliris because the spell told him to. But he had chosen Arden, without magic, without manipulation, and he had broken her.

The need to destroy something overtook him, but his magic refused him. It coiled tight, distant and cold. Once it had answered his every command; now it echoed the truth he had only just begun to face. He wasn't whole anymore. He was cracked and lost. Whatever power he had clung to had abandoned him, leaving only a man sitting in a ruined room.

Veylis entered the room, watching from the corner, silent and amused. He lounged with lazy ease, legs crossed, swirling a goblet of blood-red wine in his fingers. "What will you do, Aezraen?" he mused, his voice rich with indulgence.

Aezraen said nothing.

Veylis tilted his head, eyes sharp despite his smirk. "Such a waste. A once-feared warrior, now nothing more than a man drowning in his own misery."

Aezraen exhaled sharply, rolling the glass between his fingers. "I was never great."

Veylis chuckled, stretching out lazily, curls falling over his forehead. "At least you were interesting once."

He leaned forward, lips curving into something wicked and knowing. "Tell me," he purred, "if you are so determined to wallow, would you mind if I entertained your little thief?"

Aezraen froze.

"She is quite the fascinating thing, isn't she?" Veylis continued, tapping a ringed finger against his wine goblet. "All that fire. All that fight. I imagine she'd look breathtaking beneath me, all fury and surrender."

Aezraen snapped as his shadows lashed out, slamming into Veylis and sending him crashing against the far wall. The glass table between them shattered, shards scattering across the floor. In an instant, Aezraen was on him, his hand wrapped around Veylis' throat, squeezing enough to bruise.

"Ah," Veylis murmured, his voice lilting despite the pressure against his windpipe. "So, you do care."

Aezraen's grip tightened. "Stay away from her."

Veylis' smirk widened. "And why is that, Aezraen? What right do you have to keep her from me?"

Aezraen shoved him back, stepping away, hands trembling.

Veylis was right; he had no claim over Arden. But the thought of her with anyone else sent a pulse of fury so visceral he could hardly breathe. He sighed as he sank into the seat again, dropping his head into his hands, the world spinning around him.

Chapter Thirty

The war room fell silent after everyone had left. Syliris stood at the far end of the table, her hands lightly resting on its carved edge, her gaze unfocused.

Nearby, Elydris remained seated, watching his daughter with a steady, silent presence. Finally, he broke the silence, his voice hesitant. "How are you holding up?"

Syliris swallowed hard, having anticipated the question. "I feel like I should be doing more for him," she said softly. "She used me... I hurt everyone who ever cared about me." Looking down at the floor, guilt tightened her throat. "I couldn't stop her."

Elydris stood and approached her with quiet steps. "This is not a burden you must carry alone. Your mother's choices were her own. Manipulation, magic, lies; those were her means of rule. But you are not her, nor did you choose to be her pawn."

Syliris met his gaze, her eyes glistening. "It still feels like my fault."

He placed a reassuring hand on her shoulder. "I know. But we cannot dwell on this; we must move forward. There is work to be done."

Before she could respond, the chamber doors swung open. Guards entered first, parting to reveal Arden, who followed behind. Her cheeks were streaked with tears, her hair disheveled, and her eyes red from crying. She appeared exhausted, the weight of the evening's events evident on her face.

Syliris rushed across the room and enveloped her in an embrace. "I'm so sorry," she whispered. "For everything. For what she did to Aezraen, to all of us. I promise you, Arden, she will answer for this."

Arden stiffened briefly before returning the hug. Elydris cleared his throat, drawing their attention.

"We have little time to reunite the courts. We will travel to each one with a small convoy of soldiers and trusted allies. Most of the Archfey should join us, but we cannot underestimate Vaelithara's influence."

He turned to Arden, his gaze firm. "You are the key. A mortal bearing the weight of Aeltherion, chosen by the Gods. You embody what our realm has forgotten, hope. They need to see that."

Syliris glanced at her father. "How do we move without her seeing us? The ley lines are fractured, and the magic is unstable."

Elydris nodded. "I know. I've been studying the fault lines in the magic, and I believe I can create a temporary tether between the courts. It won't be as safe or swift, but it might be enough to keep us ahead of her." He walked toward the door, his nerves getting the better of him. "Be ready to leave with the morning light. We can no longer afford to wait."

When the doors closed behind him, Syliris approached the guards stationed in the room. "Send word to Veylis," she ordered, her voice steady despite the weight in her chest. "Aezraen's exile is lifted. He must return before sunrise." The guards exchanged wary glances before bowing in acknowledgment. "See to it personally. I want no mistakes."

She hated the idea of forcing him back against his will, but left to his own devices, he would waste away in the Hollow Court. She had witnessed how Veylis enabled Aezraen's downward spiral instead of stopping it. If Aezraen hoped to recover, to become himself again, he needed to be here. He needed to face it.

"Come take a walk with me," Syliris said softly. "Before we leave for the courts, we need to talk."

Arden hesitated but eventually nodded. They walked in silence at first, the sounds of the court fading behind them, replaced by the rustling of leaves and the distant murmurs of night creatures.

"I need you to understand something," Syliris said quietly, her voice nearly lost in the wind. "Aezraen was never mine. Not in the way that matters."

Arden's pace slowed, her eyes flicking toward Syliris.

"I cared about him," Syliris continued. "He was good to me, loyal to my father, and kind in ways most fae never bother to be. But my heart belonged to someone else. It always did."

A faint smile touched her lips, soft and sad. "Ortheon," she whispered, almost like a prayer. "He was wild and stubborn. He hated court rituals, refused to wear a crown, and insisted his subjects call him the 'primal lord.' He fought for everything he believed in and never apologized for being exactly who he was."

Arden blinked, caught off guard. "You were in love with another Archfey?"

Syliris nodded, her gaze distant. "Madly. We were always trying to outdo each other. He once gifted me Noctis when he was just a tiny thing, no bigger than my forearm. He said I needed a proper guardian, something with teeth. But I coddled him, which drove him crazy. I fed him from my hands and tucked him into my silk robes. Ortheon said I was spoiling the most dangerous beast he had ever bred." She laughed softly. "But he never stopped me."

Arden's brow furrowed. "Then why didn't anyone know?"

"My mother," Syliris said simply, the warmth fading from her voice. "She saw what Ortheon and I had and despised it. He was too free, too wild. She wanted me quiet, obedient, and easy to manipulate. So when she confirmed our 'affair,' she took him from me. She erased him from my memories, burying our love so deep inside me that I forgot he ever existed. She rewrote my story, filling the gaps with Aezraen and crafting a romance that was never real."

Arden didn't know what to say.

"But I won't let her steal anything else from those I care about," Syliris said, her voice steady. "You still have a chance, Arden. He's hurting and lost, but his love for you is not a spell. It's real. So if you want him, fight for him. You can't let him slip away just because it got hard."

Arden didn't answer, but her jaw tightened as she processed the new information. They walked in silence back toward the court, neither wanting to break the tentative friendship they had begun to form. As they stepped into the hall, the sound of raised voices echoed throughout the court.

Aezraen was back.

Syliris spotted him near the hearth, surrounded by guards who had clearly been ordered to keep him from another drink. His clothes were wrinkled, his hair a mess, and he looked on the brink of losing whatever patience he had left.

Syliris' smile was thin. "Perfect timing." She marched toward him, folding her arms as his glare settled on her. "You look awful," she observed.

Aezraen scowled. "You dragged me back here against my will for the second time tonight, so forgive me, *princess*, if I don't look my best."

"You're forgiven," she said sweetly, brushing aside his sarcasm. But then her expression hardened. "Now listen to me, because I'm only going to say this once."

He clenched his jaw, yet she continued, unwavering.

"Your past does not define you. You were used and manipulated, but you still have a choice. If you want to drink yourself into an early grave, then fine, but not here. Not with us."

Aezraen tensed, shadows curling around his feet. Syliris tilted her head, her voice sharp as a blade. "You will dry yourself out, or I will tell my father to leave you behind. He'll cut you loose, and you can waste away in whatever pit you so choose." She stepped closer, her eyes blazing. "Right now, you are more of a liability than an ally. If you don't start acting like the man I remember, then you have no place here."

Syliris straightened, linking her arm with Arden's as they walked toward the dining room. The space buzzed with the hum of final preparations. The gathered soldiers stood ready, each one bracing for the journey ahead. Arden lingered near the edge of the gathering. Aeltherion throbbed with an awareness that sent shivers down her spine. It sensed what lay ahead, the weight of destiny pressing on it as much as on her. She exhaled slowly to steady herself.

To her left, Elydris stood in quiet command, scanning the assembled group with practiced precision. His mere presence was enough to keep the gathered fae in check, his posture unwavering, the sunlit energy of his power a constant reminder of who he was.

Arden's gaze searched for Aezraen. He stood apart from the others, clad in dark leathers and a loose tunic, his hair tousled as if he had run a hand through it too many times. He looked better than the last time he had been at court, though that wasn't saying much. The remnants of his indulgences in the Hollow Court still lingered, shadows clinging too tightly to him, bruises fading along his throat, and the faint scent of liquor woven into his clothes.

When their eyes met, something unreadable passed between them. Arden wasn't sure what it was, but whatever it was, it didn't matter now. There was no more time for what-ifs.

The air shifted as Veylis sauntered into the clearing, his familiar smirk resting lazily on his lips. "Well, well," he drawled, his violet eyes sparkling with amusement. "It seems we are all playing nicely after all. How... delightful." Elydris shot him a glare, which only made Veylis chuckle.

"We leave within the hour," Elydris announced, his voice slicing through the noise of the gathering. "Ortheon's court will be our first stop. We need his support and his warriors. Given recent events, we must ensure that no surprises await us once we enter his territory."

He scanned the group to confirm everyone had arrived before continuing. "The ley lines were never just roads," he explained. "They were veins, carrying not only people but also energy and intent across the lands. I can mimic that, but the spell requires us to stay together. If anyone strays too far from the group, they will be left behind, and I won't be able to retrieve them."

Elydris' tone softened. "Once we reach the Court of Beasts, the path ahead should become clearer. The northern courts have always maintained their portals. Lysara wanted the twins to visit each other easily, so the travel channels should be more intact than those in the southern courts. If we reach Ortheon's court safely, we can reestablish a more stable route from there."

"I wouldn't count on that being easy," Veylis mused, flicking imaginary dust from his sleeve. "The Primal Lord does not take kindly to unannounced visitors, even those bearing old lovers." His gaze flicked toward Syliris, smirking as her cheeks flushed. She straightened her spine.

"He will listen to me," she said firmly.

The group dispersed to finalize their preparations. Arden busied herself checking supplies, ensuring her weapons were secured and her mind focused. Yet, despite her efforts, she found herself drawn back to Aezraen, watching him linger near the edge of the conversation, his hands flexing into fists and then relaxing as though he was grounding himself.

A soft rustle behind her pulled her from her thoughts. She turned just as Noctis padded up from the treeline, his fur dusted with dew, eyes sharp and unblinking. The breath caught in her throat. For a moment, Arden couldn't move or speak.

He nudged his broad head against her shoulder, his warmth melting away the cold that had settled deep in her chest.

"I missed you too," she whispered, her fingers curling into his fur. He leaned into her touch, a low rumble of comfort vibrating beneath her hand.

Noctis didn't speak; he didn't need to, his presence was enough.

An hour passed quickly. The group gathered at the crossroads just outside the Court of Shadows. The ley lines shimmered beneath their feet, pulsing with potential, a thread of ancient power called back to life.

Syliris stood near the front of the group, her shoulders tense as she gazed toward the horizon, where the trees thinned into the wilds hundreds of miles away. She had imagined this reunion countless times, but now that it was imminent, fear crept into her chest. What if he had moved on? What if he didn't remember her the way she remembered him?

Arden joined her, with Noctis at her heels. The three of them stood together, quiet and still. Syliris exhaled slowly, her fingers twitching at her sides.

"This is it," she whispered, more to herself than to anyone else. "I'm going to see him again."

She didn't pray aloud, but in her heart, she hoped he still wanted her. That after everything her mother had done, after all the silence and lost years, Ortheon still carried a flame for her as she had for him.

The ley lines brightened in response to Elydris' power, and the portal opened like a breath being drawn.

Chapter Thirty-One

The enchanted crossroads twisted and turned as the group advanced, the air thick with the hum of raw magic. These were not the ley lines the fae typically traversed, they were broken remnants of a world shattered by Vaelithara's influence. Each step felt precarious, as if the very fabric of reality might shift beneath them.

Arden sensed the distortions pulsing through her veins like an erratic heartbeat. Noctis padded beside her, his massive form silent, yet his presence anchored her amidst the chaos. "You are safe here, princess," the great beast communicated through their bond. "This was my home once."

As they crossed into the border of the Court of Beasts, it felt as though the realm exhaled around them. The group departed from the magical pathways, and Elydris sighed with relief. Towering forests merged into violent plains where grass shimmered and bent without the influence of wind. In the distance, mist-shrouded mountains held secrets within their jagged peaks.

They were being watched. Eyes gleamed in the darkness between the trees, low and unblinking. No growls echoed and no challenges were issued, but the air was thick with unspoken judgment. The beasts assessed them.

The Primal Lord emerged from the trees like a storm made flesh. Raw, untamed power rippled off him. His skin gleamed bronzed by sunlight and battle, his hair swept back by the wind. He wore no crown or jewels, only leather and fur, embodying the weight of something eternal. His blue eyes crackled like distant thunderclouds as he approached. Without warning, he drew his blade. His advance was silent and swift, and Aezraen barely raised his arm in time to block the first strike. Steel met shadow, the force of the impact rattling the air. Ortheon pressed forward, relentless, moving like a predator as if this fight had been foretold the day Aezraen was made fae.

"Ortheon!" Syliris shouted, her voice sharp with command.

He halted, blade still raised, muscles tense, and turned toward her, his gaze piercing.

"Enough," Syliris said, cutting through his fury like a knife.

"Syliris." Her name escaped him in a whisper, reopening a wound. He approached her with slow, deliberate steps, circling once and inhaling deeply, his fingers twitching as if resisting the urge to touch her.He stopped, blade drawn, and pressed it carefully against her throat. "Why," he growled in a low voice meant only for her, "would you bring your lover here? Do you want to watch him die?"

Elydris stepped forward, golden energy flickering around him. "Watch yourself, Primal Lord," he warned, the tension of magic crackling between them. "I do not take kindly to threats against my blood."

Syliris shot her father a sharp glare. "Stay out of this."

She neither flinched from the blade nor retreated. Instead, she tilted her head, allowing the knife's edge to brush her skin. "He was never my lover." Her voice was steady and unwavering as she placed her hand on his chest, "*yours*." The word hung in the air between them, electric. Syliris leaned in, her breath warm against his lips, a challenge and a promise.

Ortheon growled low in his throat, a primal sound that sent shivers down her spine. He leaned closer, his lips brushing against her ear. "Mine."

His fingers tightened around the hilt, the blade trembling slightly under the strain of his grip. For a moment, he held it there, a breath away from drawing blood not as a threat, but as a long-overdue sentence. Then, with a shuddering breath through flared nostrils, he pulled it back in a slow, deliberate motion.

He did not retreat.

His gaze remained fixed on Syliris, sharp and furious, as if daring her to break first. The silence between them was thick with tension, an ancient storm waiting to be unleashed.

"You have much to answer for," he said, his voice low and rough, like stone grinding against steel.

Syliris held his gaze. "I will tell you everything. But first, we need your help."

His expression twisted. Ortheon turned away from her with a sharp movement, sheathing the blade with a hiss. He stalked toward the trees, his steps heavy, fingers raking through his hair in frustration. The calm he usually wore like a second skin was slipping, cracked open by her presence. He had never been a patient man, especially when it came to the things he claimed.

He halted just before the shadows, the boundary between his realm and Vaelithara's. "I noticed the change in you before you disappeared. I saw the way you looked at him. I convinced myself you were happy, that if you needed me, you would come back. So I did nothing. I let you go."

He shook his head, his jaw clenched. "And for that, I lost you."

Syliris stepped closer, her hand outstretched but not yet touching him. Her voice softened, losing its edge. "You didn't lose me because you did nothing. I was lost to time."

He turned his head slightly, but not completely.

"I didn't stay away," she continued. "I wasn't hiding. I wasn't with someone else. I was gone, Ortheon. Torn from the realm by her hands."

Ortheon's expression morphed into one of outrage.

"I never chose to leave you," Syliris whispered. "I am only alive now because of Arden."

For a long moment, he remained silent. The air grew heavy with grief, mistaken for betrayal. When he finally faced her, his eyes still burned with intensity, but something deeper lay beneath the fury. "Then know this," he said, his voice quieter yet still menacing. "I have no more patience for silence. No more tolerance for stolen time. I demand the truth. All of it. And if war is the only way to set things right, then I will burn the world to achieve it."

When he spoke again, his voice was raw.

"I've heard whispers," he said, glancing at Arden. "From Melisara. From spies. A mortal who claimed Aeltherion, who swayed the wildest of my guardians to her side. I wondered if the stories were true."

Arden lifted her chin, unsettled by the weight of his gaze. "I did what I had to."

"You brought her back to me," he said, nodding toward Syliris. "For that, I owe you more than I can express. But gratitude alone won't suffice for war."

Elydris stepped forward, golden magic pulsing at his palms. "We come seeking an alliance, not challenges."

Ortheon's gaze remained fixed. "The mortal is your answer. If she cannot stand before me, if she cannot confront what lives in these woods, she will not stand before Vaelithara. I will not send my beasts to die for someone who cannot command them."

Arden stepped forward slowly, Noctis by her side. "What do you want me to prove?" she asked, her voice quiet but resolute.

A wild, wicked smile curved Ortheon's mouth, something fierce dancing behind his eyes. "That you are not merely wearing the crown. That it truly belongs to you." He turned, raising a hand and gesturing for them to follow. "You will show me," he said, his voice low and final. "Or you walk away alone."

Arden stood at the center of the clearing, her breath steady despite the rapid pounding of her pulse. The Court of Beasts had formed a loose circle around them, their eyes glinting in the twilight, waiting. Ortheon stood before her, a figure of untamed power, his presence as unyielding as the wilds themselves. He lifted his chin, his voice ringing out with an authority that allowed no dissent. "Arden must prove she can control Noctis without relying on their bond. Only then will the Court of Beasts stand with her."

The weight of his words pressed down on her. Her bond? A flicker of uncertainty ignited in her chest, but she kept it at bay. What did he mean? She had spent months strengthening her connection with Noctis, learning the intricate balance of magic and will between them. He had fought by her side, bled for her, and protected her even before she fully grasped the significance of their bond. But now, Ortheon was demanding she forgo that?

"What does that mean?" she asked sharply.

Ortheon's lips curled into a challenge, revealing sharp fangs. "It means I sever it, temporarily. You will have to tame him as a beast, as those in my court do." His eyes gleamed with something inscrutable, something ancient, as if he had witnessed this trial unfold countless times before.

Beside her, Noctis emitted a deep, warning growl, his muscles tensing beneath his sleek black fur. His golden eyes were fixed on Ortheon, barely containing his fury. He did not like this. "Arden, I do not wish to fight you," Noctis's voice resonated in her mind, a tether of warmth amid the growing unease.

She inhaled deeply, steadying herself. "And you won't have to," she replied, locking her gaze onto his with unwavering resolve. "I will win."

Ortheon brushed past her, his fingers grazing her shoulder as he moved. The air crackled with raw magic, thick and biting as it swirled through the clearing. Arden barely had time to brace herself before the magic snapped, sending a sharp, severing pulse through her that left her reeling. Her vision blurred, her breath caught in her throat, and an unbearable emptiness settled into her chest.

The bond was gone.

Noctis let out a fierce snarl, shaking himself violently as if shedding an unseen weight. His golden eyes met hers, but the warmth, familiarity, and silent understanding they had once shared were lost. This was not the same creature who had fought beside her, who had followed her into the depths of battle. This was something wilder, something untamed. This was the beast that lay within him.

Before she could react, he vanished into the woods.

Ortheon's grin widened, the air still vibrating with his lingering magic. "Find him," he commanded, folding his arms over his broad chest. "Tame him. If you can."

As soon as Ortheon released her, Arden sprinted after her beast, her boots barely making a sound against the moss-covered ground. The night enveloped her, the thick canopy overhead casting twisted shadows through the forest. Every instinct urged her to call out for him, to reach through their bond, but it was gone. It felt like running blind, like losing a part of herself, and the weight of that emptiness clawed at her ribs.

She slowed to listen. The woods were alive, not just with the rustling of wind or the distant hoot of an owl, but with something older, something watching. These were the hunting grounds of the Court of Beasts, a place where only the strongest survived. Arden had no illusions about what lay ahead. Ortheon had told her to tame Noctis, but she knew the truth: this was a hunt, and she was the prey.

A low growl rolled through the trees, deep and guttural, vibrating through the earth. Arden turned sharply, her heart pounding as she scanned the darkness. The forest was dense, the trees intertwined like skeletal fingers, their roots curling along the damp soil in tangled webs. A flicker of movement caught her eye, a shadow slipping silently between the trunks, too quick to grasp. He was circling her. Toying with her.

She crouched low, gathering her strength, her hands brushing the dirt as she sensed the space around her. No magic. No connection to him. But she knew Noctis; she understood how he moved and how he thought. He was a predator, and having spent enough time at his side, she had learned the rhythm of his hunt.

A blur of black fur erupted from the shadows. Arden barely had time to twist away before massive claws slashed through the air where she had just stood. She hit the ground hard, rolling to the side as dirt bit into her skin. Noctis landed just feet away, his eyes ablaze with primal intensity.

Arden gritted her teeth, pivoting at the last moment to narrowly avoid the full force of his attack. He was faster than she had ever seen him. His muscles coiled with raw power as he lunged, and this time, she didn't dodge.

Instead, she confronted him head-on. At the last moment, she ducked beneath his strike, twisting her body to the side and wrapping her arms around the thick muscles of his neck. He snarled, twisting violently in an attempt to throw her off, but she held on, gripping his fur tightly. This was not a battle of brute force; it was about proving her resolve.

Noctis snapped his jaws, but she did not flinch. His body writhed beneath her grip, muscles tense with the promise of destruction, yet she held firm.

"Enough," she whispered, her voice steady despite the fire coursing through her limbs. "I am not your enemy."

His eyes flashed, and his body went rigid beneath her hands. She sensed the hesitation, the internal conflict, as raw instinct battled against recognition.

Slowly, his snarl faded. His heaving breaths steadied, and Noctis lowered his head.

Arden exhaled, relief washing over her as she pressed her forehead against his. He was still there, beneath the wildness, beneath the magic that sought to strip him of his essence. Together, they emerged from the woods, stepping back into the clearing.

When Ortheon saw her, his expression flickered for just a moment before he announced to the waiting crowd, "The Court of Beasts will ride with Arden!" The crowd cheered, eager for the thrill of battle.

Syliris turned to Ortheon, her heart racing as she extended the invitation. "Come with us," she urged, her voice steady yet soft. "To the Gilded Court. Stand with us." She searched his face, waiting and hoping. For a moment, Ortheon merely studied her, his expression unreadable. Then, without warning, he closed the distance between them, tangling his hand in her hair as he crushed his lips against hers. The kiss was fierce and claiming, a silent vow that even time could not erase.

When he pulled away, his grip on her waist lingered, his breath warm against her lips. "I will rejoin you in time," he murmured, his voice rough with promise. "But first, I must prepare my warriors. They need to understand what they fight for, that they protect their future queen, or they will die by my hand." His gaze darkened, sharp as the wild lands he ruled, sending a shiver of anticipation and desire through Syliris.

He traced his fingers along her jaw, his touch lingering as if he were memorizing her. "For now, we train. When I return to you, there will be no separating us ever again." The weight of his words settled between them, an unspoken certainty pulsing through the air. His loyalty was absolute, his love fierce and consuming.

Syliris swallowed and nodded once. "Then I'll be waiting." After centuries of being trapped, her fate dictated by another, she was finally free. Now, the choice was hers. When Ortheon returned, she would meet him as his equal, not as someone stolen from him, but as someone who had fought to find her way back.

Without a word, Ortheon turned and strode purposefully toward the edge of the clearing. The air shifted as the surrounding beasts stirred, parting in silent respect for their lord.

He guided them along a narrow path winding through ancient trees, where wild magic hummed thickly in the roots. At the base of a jagged stone outcrop, shrouded in mist and shadow, a rift shimmered. It was neither a doorway nor a gate, but something older, a threshold shaped by the Gods themselves.

Ortheon halted before it, extending his hand as golden magic flared to life across his skin. The portal pulsed once before opening fully, revealing a spiral of distorted air and soft, echoing whispers emanating from the other side.

"This will take you to the Gilded Court," he said without looking back. "Melisara already likely knows you're coming."

Ortheon stood at the edge of the clearing, the ancient portal pulsing with divine energy behind him. The stone archway shimmered, glowing faintly with the touch of the Gods.

The group gathered in silence, the weight of what lay ahead pressing heavily on their shoulders. One by one, they approached the portal, its light washing over their faces with each step.

Ortheon remained quiet at first, his sharp, unreadable gaze sweeping over the group until it settled on Syliris. For a heartbeat, he didn't move. His eyes softened, and his jaw tightened as if he were holding back unspoken words. "You have your path," he said, his voice low but steady. "Now walk it."

Arden stepped through first, followed by the others, but Syliris lingered at the edge, her fingers brushing the stone. She turned to him one last time, their eyes locking.

Ortheon did not move, yet his expression held an ache as if a part of him would forever remain in this moment. As Syliris vanished into the light, his gaze remained fixed on the spot where she had stood.

Then the portal shimmered once more, and the clearing fell silent.

Chapter Thirty-Two

The sun dipped low on the horizon, bathing the Gilded Court in a warm glow as the group moved along the edge of Melisara's domain. Syliris walked in silence, her thoughts spiraling despite the strength she had displayed just hours earlier. Ortheon's words echoed in her mind; his accusations, his longing, his pain. They had parted on good terms but beneath the surface doubt gnawed at her.

Elydris called for a halt as the first stars appeared in the darkening sky. "We'll make camp here," he said, his voice low yet firm. "Melisara's court lies ahead, but I won't lead us into her realm uninvited and exhausted. This area is neutral, safe enough for us to rest."

Veylis let out a soft snort, but no one dared to argue with the king. The weight of the day's tension hung heavily on their shoulders, and rest was a mercy none would refuse. They unpacked their bags, checked their weapons, and staked their tents to the ground. Magic flickered softly between hands as they wove wards into the soil. Noctis prowled the edges of the camp, silent and alert, his eyes glowing with quiet purpose.

Syliris did not linger long. She scanned the group until she spotted Arden loosening the straps on one of the tent packs. "Come with me?" she asked, tilting her chin toward the woods. "We need more firewood."

They moved into the trees, the hush of dusk settling around them. Branches swayed above, and the wind carried the faint scents of moss and dying leaves. Syliris remained silent at first, waiting until they were far from the camp's noise before stopping beneath a twisted willow.

Kneeling to gather some kindling, her fingers trembled slightly as they brushed against the dry bark. "I've been thinking about what Ortheon said," she began, her voice quiet and uncertain. "About how he thought I left him."

Arden stilled beside her, straightening slowly. "I'm not sure any of us can predict the havoc Vaelithara's magic would have wreaked on his memories."

Syliris looked up, her eyes shadowed. "I think... I think he believed it to be the truth. But I can't help wondering, if Ortheon thinks I ran, what do the other Archfey recall? What really happened when she attempted to rewrite everything?"

She rose, arms laden with dried wood, her mind elsewhere. "Has Veylis ever mentioned anything about my coronation day?" Syliris avoided Arden's gaze, focusing intently on the edge of a branch as if it might hold the answer.

Arden frowned, her brows knitting together. "No. We've discussed the old courts, the fall of Elydris, and Vaelithara's rise, but he never specifically mentioned that day." She tilted her head. "Why do you ask?"

Syliris chewed her cheek, contemplating. "The Seraphyne's feather is a powerful artifact. If my mother had used it correctly, none of them would remember us at all. But they do, and Ortheon recalled a reason though not the truth why I was gone." Uncertainty flickered in her eyes as she looked at Arden. "I remember preparing for my coronation: the colors of the banners, the scent of the blossoms woven into my hair. But when the doors opened, everything just... ends."

Arden remained silent for a moment, processing Syliris' words. "And you want to know what happened next."

Syliris nodded slowly. A quiet tension hung between them, broken only by the wind rustling through the trees. Arden crouched to gather another bundle of twigs. "If he remembers you leaving, maybe the others do too," she said softly. "Perhaps Vaelithara planted different truths in each of them, rewriting the story to fit whatever narrative kept them obedient."

Syliris inhaled shakily. "That's what frightens me. Once this is over, I need to bring the Archfey together to ask what they remember. I need to know how much of my life was erased."

They stood in silence for a moment, the weight of Syliris' words settling around them like dust. Then, Arden lightly touched her shoulder.

"Whatever you discover, you won't be alone," she reassured her. "We'll piece it all back together."

"You should ask him yourself," Arden suggested, tucking her bundle of twigs under her arm. "Veylis, I mean. If anyone knows what really happened at your coronation, it's him."

Syliris halted, disbelief washing over her. "You're joking, right?" she laughed, though the sound was hollow. "I barely recognize the man he's become. That's not the Veylis I knew."

Arden raised her brows, intrigued.

"He used to smile," Syliris continued quietly. "Even in the Hollow Court, surrounded by bones and smoke, he found joy in the smallest things. He and Niko often visited the palace for dinners, parties, and festivals. He was charming, but he was also kind always kind."

Arden observed Syliris for a long moment before speaking, her voice low. "You truly don't know, do you?"

Syliris blinked, her brow furrowing. "About what?"

"Your mother... when she lost you," Arden said, her words heavy with weight. "She destroyed everyone around her. When Veylis wouldn't submit..."

Syliris covered her mouth, a small sob escaping before she could stop it. "She wouldn't." Her eyes filled with sudden, unspoken grief.

Arden's tone softened, yet the truth remained sharp. "She killed Niko and made Veylis carry her to the Gods."

Syliris turned away, her shoulders trembling. For a while, she said nothing, letting the silence envelop them like a shroud. Then, her voice thin and cracked, she spoke. "I don't know how to lead them. After missing so much... how can I ask anyone to follow me?"

Arden stepped closer. "You start by not pretending to know everything. You ask. You listen. And when the time comes, you fight for what's right, not what's easy."

They returned to camp in silence, discovering a fire already crackling in the center of the clearing. The scent of roasting meat wafted on the breeze, and Noctis lay curled near the flames, eyes half-lidded but alert.

As they approached, Aezraen stepped forward, reaching out to take the extra firewood from Arden's arms. His fingers brushed hers, lingering just a moment too long. "Thank you," he said, his voice low.

Arden nodded, her cheeks warming. "You're welcome." She quickly pulled her hand back, stuffing it into her cloak pocket as if the gesture hadn't just sent her heart racing.

As night gently enveloped the camp, stars began to twinkle above a quiet canopy of shifting leaves. The fire crackled at the center, casting flickering shadows across tired faces and worn boots. The group sat in a loose circle, sharing a simple yet warm meal of roasted meat and thick bread passed from hand to hand.

Without a word, Aezraen settled beside Arden. He avoided looking at her, yet his presence felt solid and intentional. Arden stole a glance, pretending not to notice how her heart fluttered at his nearness. His shoulder brushed against hers lightly, and though he remained silent, his stillness felt almost like companionship.

Syliris cleared her throat, capturing the group's attention. "Veylis," she said softly, "would you tell us a story?"

Veylis raised an eyebrow, smirking over the rim of his wine goblet. "A bedtime story, princess? How quaint. Shall I recount the tale of the maiden and the rogue prince? Or perhaps the stag who stole the moon?"

The others chuckled uneasily, but Syliris remained undeterred. "My coronation day," she stated, her voice steady. Laughter faded instantly, leaving only the sound of the fire popping in the ensuing silence.

Veylis' smile sharpened rather than waned. "Ah," he said, swirling his wine. "So that's what Ortheon got under your skin with." He leaned forward, his eyes glimmering with something unreadable. "I wondered when you'd bring it up."

As the firelight danced across his features, he leaned back and stretched his legs out in front of him. "Well then, settle in, and let me tell you what I remember from the day our little star was meant to rise."

Bodies shifted, cloaks tightened, and all eyes turned toward Veylis. His smile widened, and the shadows seemed to draw closer as he began. "It was an outdoor affair, of course. You insisted on it, something sentimental about being one with nature." He tilted his head toward her with mock fondness. "I suppose now we understand why you felt that way."

Syliris offered no response. She simply sat up straighter, her hands resting in her lap, waiting.

"You wore silver and gold," Veylis said, swirling his wine. "Perhaps a bit too much of both, if you ask me. The entire outfit seemed like something Vaelithara had chosen, but Niko was obsessed with it. She wouldn't stop gushing, claiming it made you look like the moon come to life."

Arden glanced at Syliris, who gave the faintest nod of agreement. "She helped me pick it," Syliris murmured quietly.

For a brief moment, Veylis' mask slipped. At the mention of Niko, a raw, broken grief flickered in his eyes grief so profound it had never healed, only scarred. "The ceremony took place in the courtyard, near the old fountain," he continued, his voice trembling slightly. "The entire First Court and the Archfey from the other courts were present."

He paused to sip his wine. "Elydris was in rare form; his pride was evident in the way he carried himself. He announced that you had chosen and named your crown, Lunethil. You addressed the crowd, explaining that the name came to you one evening as you watched the moon reflect off the water at the edge of our lands. At the time, I thought it was silly. Now..." He trailed off, shaking his head.

Noctis growled softly from Arden's side, prompting her to place a calming hand on his thick fur.

"The king stepped forward and raised the crown. Just before it touched your brow," Veylis snapped his fingers, "it was as if the Gods were lashing out. Lightning split the sky and the ground trembled beneath us as if the realm itself cried out. In that moment, something shifted, as if the stars themselves had turned away. Chaos erupted, magic flared, and then you and your father vanished."

The fire popped violently, causing Syliris to jump despite herself.

Veylis lowered his voice. "Vaelithara intervened before anyone could regain their composure. She claimed the Gods were displeased, stating that the realm had fallen into imbalance and needed a new order."

"Did no one question where we had gone?" Elydris murmured, his voice tense.

"She said you had both been cast out by divine judgment," Veylis replied with a shrug. "Some believed her; others did not."

"But hope means little when the entire realm is drowning in fear," Veylis continued. "And Vaelithara? She thrived on that fear and made herself indispensable. Her magic... I still don't understand what she did, but something changed. People forgot. Details blurred. There were whispers, yet no one acted. No one could challenge her without risking their court. Kaelar tried and lost half his court to plague within a month."

A heavy silence followed.

"She didn't rewrite the past," Syliris finally said. "She just made sure no one could question it."

Veylis nodded, his eyes darker than usual. "You disappeared, and she convinced us it was your fault."

Arden glanced at Syliris, whose knuckles had turned white. Elydris' jaw was clenched, his gaze fixed on the fire as if trying to burn the memory away, but no one spoke.

As the night wore on, the group began to disperse one by one, the air thick with unspoken words. The fire crackled softly, its light dimming under the weight of the truth they had just heard.

Elydris offered a quiet goodnight and slipped into his tent, his cloak trailing behind him like the last shadow of a fallen crown. Veylis finished his wine and vanished into the darkness without a word. Even Syliris retreated, her expression unreadable as she passed Arden and Aezraen without meeting their eyes.

Aezraen stood slowly, brushing his hands over his pants. He looked toward Arden, uncertain. "Would you mind if I walked you to your tent?"

Arden blinked, surprised, then nodded. "That would be nice."

They moved through the camp in silence. The night was cool, and the stars shimmered faintly above, distant and cold. Aezraen kept a few paces behind her, his presence more comforting than she wanted to admit. When they reached her tent, she paused at the flap but didn't enter.

Instead, she turned to him. "I don't know if I'm ready for what's coming."

Aezraen looked at her, his expression softer than it had been all day. "I'm not sure any of us are."

Her voice dropped to a whisper. "I keep thinking about Callen. What she's doing to him. Is he scared? Hurt? Alone?"

"You raised him to be strong," Aezraen said gently. "If he's anything like you, Arden... he's fighting, even now."

Her throat tightened. "I wish I could believe that."

"I do," he said, stepping closer. "With every part of me."

They lingered in silence, the night heavy with unspoken thoughts.

"Goodnight," she finally said, her voice barely steady.

"Goodnight, Arden." He turned away first, heading back to his tent.

Arden slipped into her cot and sat on the edge, her hands trembling as she pressed her palms together. Tomorrow, she would face another court, another ruler, and more questions she didn't know how to answer. Would they look at her the way Ortheon had, waiting for her to fail?

She exhaled slowly, trying to steady her breathing, but her heart wouldn't cooperate. She had come so far and survived so much, yet doubt still lingered. What if she wasn't enough?

Looking down at her hands the same hands that had picked locks and wielded daggers she felt a disconnect. They didn't feel like the hands of a leader. But they were all she had. She couldn't break. Not now.

Chapter Thirty-Three

The morning air was crisp, laced with dew and the faint scent of wildflowers, yet the group moved through it in silence. No one spoke as they dismantled the camp, each person lost in their own thoughts. Veylis' tale from the night before lingered, its echoes remaining long after the fire had died.

As they walked, the scenery began to transform. The stark beauty of the Gilded Court unfolded around them like a vivid dream. Trees shimmered with golden-tipped leaves, and the grass sparkled underfoot as if dusted with diamonds. Petals drifted lazily on the breeze, infusing the air with a scent so rich it bordered on overwhelming. Yet beneath this beautiful façade lay an undercurrent of chaos. The terrain shifted unexpectedly, as if the land itself were indecisive. Paths curved without warning, and shadows pooled where sunlight should have been.

It was undeniably beautiful, yet untamed in a way that whispered of danger. Arden kept her gaze moving, absorbing the sights while remaining alert. They were entering a court where even beauty could be a weapon, and with each step closer to Melisara, the tension escalated.

The Gilded Court dazzled in molten gold and deep maroon. As they approached the gates, it became clear they were expected. The guards stepped aside without question, their white armor glinting in the sun. Ortheon had been correct; Melisara knew they were coming.

Polished marble floors mirrored the sky, grand pillars displayed intricate carvings of fae history, and walls draped with silken cloth seemed to breathe. Here, beauty was an illusion, a flawless façade that threatened to consume those who gazed too long. Every smile concealed sharp edges, every movement was choreographed, and every word was a hidden blade waiting to strike.

At the center of it all, seated on a throne woven from golden silk, was Melisara. She was just another Archfey, like the others, but she demanded her subjects call her the Gilded Queen. Those who refused had not lived long enough to make that mistake twice.

She was a vision of elegance and excess, her gown an intricate lattice of lace, velvet, and metal chains. Her fingers sparkled with rings that resembled stolen stars. Her beauty was unnaturally perfect, every feature symmetrical, and every movement deliberate.The

Gilded Queen's court was a realm of extravagance and deceit, a delicate interplay of wealth and influence where debts extended beyond mere coins. Melisara was not one to give freely, nor did she partake in straight-forward transactions. Every deal made in this throne room left one party in debt, and it was never Melisara.

As Arden stepped forward, she felt the weight of Melisara's gaze upon her. With a graceful raise of her hand, Melisara commanded silence. The courtiers, murmuring behind their golden masks, fell silent, their painted smiles freezing in place. A thick hush enveloped the room, heavy with anticipation. Then, Melisara smiled a slow, practiced gesture that hinted at impending ruin.

"I was beginning to wonder when you'd arrive," Melisara purred, her voice laced with amusement, as if this meeting was a performance she had choreographed from the beginning. Leaning forward on her throne, golden chains clinked softly with her movement, each reflecting the flickering candlelight. "Desperation suits you, Arden."

Arden blinked, taken aback. "Excuse me?"

Melisara chuckled, as if Arden had just shared the world's funni-est joke. The golden-masked courtiers echoed her laughter, sharp and mocking.

With a flick of her wrist, Melisara silenced them. The room quieted, her gaze shifting to Aezraen, glimmering with cruel delight. "Did you not inform your little thief about Mireblight?"

Arden furrowed her brows. "Mireblight?"

"You're from Solmyr, aren't you?" Melisara asked sweetly, tilting her head as if discussing the weather. "Hallow's Reach, if I recall correctly?"

Arden nodded slowly. "Yes, but... I don't understand."

"Stop," Aezraen interjected, his voice low and controlled, yet tinged with anger. "That's enough, Melisara."

Ignoring him, she continued, "Your brother was ill," feigning sympathy. "The people of your realm call it Mireblight. But it's merely chaos magic born from my court."

Arden turned to Aezraen, searching his face for answers. "Why is she telling me this?"

Aezraen stepped closer, his expression tense. "Arden, please. Let me explain."

"Explain what?" Melisara interrupted smoothly, her tone suddenly sharp. "How you came crawling to my court, speaking of a girl from Solmyr whom you wanted for this century's trial? How you needed her desperate enough to accept a bargain from you?"

Arden recoiled as though struck. Her mouth opened, but no words emerged. She looked at Aezraen as if she no longer recognized him.

"And so you watched her," Melisara continued, her tone laced with venom. "For months, you tracked her movements, identified her brother as the weakness in her armor, and came to me. You sought something that would not kill the boy outright, but something slow something that would fester and instill fear, leaving her vulnerable to a deal with you."

Fury ignited in Arden's chest, too intense and sudden to contain. Her hands clenched at her sides, her jaw locked. She redirected her rage toward Melisara, refusing to allow the Archfey to witness her unraveling.

"We need your army," she said, her voice low yet steady. "Will you stand with us against Vaelithara, or will you squander more of our time on theatrics?"

Melisara smirked, clearly entertained. "Bold," she remarked. "I see why he favored you."

She stood and began to pace in front of her throne. "Ah, war. Such a dreadful, messy affair." Her fingers trailed along the arm of her throne, her eyes gleaming with an inscrutable light. "And yet you ask me to spill blood, to risk my court and my people... for what, exactly?"

Elydris stepped forward, his presence commanding as flickers of golden energy crackled at his fingertips. "For balance," he declared, his voice steady and resolute. "For the future of the realm. Vaelithara has twisted things for long enough, and eventually, she will come for you too."

Melisara's expression remained unchanged, her smile deepening like a cat toying with a cornered mouse. "Will she?" she mused, tilting her head. "Or will she keep me exactly where I thrive whispering poison and allowing gossip to rot the court from within while she reaps the benefits?"

Her gaze flicked back to Arden, appraising. "Tell me, dear, why should I involve myself in a war I do not need to fight?"

Arden's jaw tightened, her voice steady despite the fury simmering within. "Vaelithara tried to rewrite history, but she failed. Now she rules through fear, for it is all she has left. You believe you are safe in the chaos she creates, but that safety is an illusion. Sooner or later, she will turn on you too, and when she does, your entire court will unravel, one thread at a time."

For the first time, something flickered in the Gilded Queen's gaze. A hum escaped her lips as she settled back into her throne, studying Arden like an exquisite piece of art. Finally, she nodded slowly. "A valid argument," she conceded, "but not a particularly compelling one."

Melisara paused, as if weighing her options. "I will grant you my army, but not without payment. War is costly, my dear, and you must share the burden."

Leaning forward, Melisara drummed her fingers lazily against the carved silk of her armrest, her smile promising devastation. "Three paths, three choices," she purred. "Each will provide what you need, but each comes with a cost only you can bear." Her eyes sparkled as she gestured toward the crown.

"The first option is simple," she said. "Destroy Aeltherion."

The room fell silent.

Arden's heart skipped a beat, the words taking a moment to register. "What?" she breathed.

"Burn it. Bury it. Shatter it into a thousand pieces and cast them to the winds," Melisara continued, her voice lilting and wicked. "That crown has made you a target. It ties you to the old world, and look what it has brought you nothing but pain."

Elydris' magic surged in warning, but Melisara merely chuckled.

"I don't want to rule," she said, "but I do want freedom. That crown is a leash, one the Gods placed long ago. If you truly wish to change things, you must let it go. Prove you are something new."

Arden instinctively raised her hand to the weight resting against her brow. She felt the pulse of the artifact beneath her skin, quiet and steady. It had become a part of her. "No," she said firmly. "I won't destroy it."

Melisara sighed, feigning disappointment but remaining unbothered. "Very well," she murmured. "Let us move on to another option." She snapped her fingers, and a servant appeared from behind her throne, presenting a golden tray with a crystal decanter and matching goblet. She took her time selecting the glass as if choosing a weapon, then poured the deep red wine with deliberate grace.

She swirled the wine lazily, watching the light catch the liquid, then turned her gaze to Arden, her smile dripping with false sweetness. "Give me a name, and I will have them killed right here. Someone of value. Someone close to you. A death that will mark the turning of fate itself."

Arden's voice was low, edged with darkness. "Vaelithara," she said. "Take her."

Melisara's laughter echoed through the hall like shattering glass. "You misunderstand; this must be personal. Someone you care about. Someone whose death will hold significance."

A cold chill raced down Arden's spine. "I can't," she whispered.

Melisara sighed again, though her frustration never reached her eyes. "Then there is only one last offer, my dear," she said, satisfaction dripping from her words. Rising, she stepped toward Arden, her gown trailing behind her like waves.

"You are wasted in the shadows," she whispered. "I offer you a throne beside mine. A position of untouchable power. Become my consort, and the Gilded Court will bow to you."

The words coiled through the air like a spell, suffocating Arden with their implications. She would never be weak or threatened again. She would want for nothing, because she would be the one making the rules.

Melisara reached out, brushing a single finger down Arden's arm, the touch featherlight yet disarming. "I will make you powerful beyond measure," she murmured, tilting her head. "All you must do is kneel before me."

Arden stepped back, rage and disgust churning in her stomach. "Absolutely not."

Melisara's expression remained unchanged. If anything, the glint in her eye deepened. "I expected as much," she mused, amused. "You are strong-willed. I like that."

Aezraen stepped forward. "Take me instead," he said, his voice low and firm. "I will pay the price."

Melisara turned toward him, her golden gaze flickering with interest. "Oh? And what do you have to offer?"

Aezraen met her gaze without flinching. "Whatever you want."

For the first time, Melisara's expression hardened. She clicked her tongue, disappointed. "No, no, my dear. That is not how this works." Her gaze returned to Arden, sharp and unyielding. "I want her, not you."

The room felt smaller and heavier, as if the walls were closing in. Arden's heart raced, the weight of the decision pressing down on her.

Melisara sighed, her amusement evident in the exaggerated sound. "What a shame," she said lightly, stepping away from both of them.

As Arden turned to leave, Melisara's voice wrapped around her like both silk and a blade. "You're playing a dangerous game," she murmured, stepping closer, her presence brushing against Arden's skin like a whisper of temptation. "Make sure it's one you can afford to lose."

Melisara slipped a delicate gold chain into Arden's hand, the metal gliding over her skin. The links were warm from the Archfey's touch, and the charm at its center glinted like a promise made in secret a token, a key, a way back.

"My offer stands," the Gilded Queen purred, her breath grazing Arden's ear. "When the war turns against you, when the shadows you trust begin to crack, return to me. Bring this with you, and I will know you are ready to pay the price."

With a soft laugh, Melisara stepped back and waved a graceful, dismissive hand. Her voice echoed through the throne room. "Run along now, go play your war games."

She turned her gaze to Syliris, her lips curling with a mix of amusement and condescension. "And do wish my dear sister, Sylara, the best, won't you?" A smile tugged at the corners of her lips. "I do love a good spectacle," she mused, flicking her wrist. In an instant, the air shimmered with magic, and they vanished, torn from the golden decadence of her court.

The path from Melisara's court shimmered behind them, fading into the distance like remnants of a dream. Silence enveloped them as they approached the portal nestled within a grove of vibrant blossoms. Vines wound around the ancient archway, their petals unfurling in colors too vivid for the natural world. The air was sweet with perfume and magic, clinging to their skin and catching their breath.

Arden stood closest to the portal, her fingers still curled around the chain Melisara had pressed into her palm. It felt heavier than it should have, the weight of temptation and choices yet to be made. Behind her, Aezraen remained silent, shadows coiling tightly around his boots, restless.

Elydris was the last to arrive, his expression calm yet weary. He glanced at the tangled, bloom-covered structure before them and then toward the horizon, where the afternoon sunlight bathed the trees in soft gold. "I suppose we should see Sylara next," he said quietly.

No one replied; the weight of their failure hung heavily in the air. The path ahead felt more burdensome now, the stakes higher and more personal. Together, they stepped into the Court of Blooms.

Chapter Thirty-Four

When Arden stepped through the portal, she immediately sensed a shift in atmosphere. The air was thick with floral perfume, the wind soft and steady, and magic hummed beneath her skin like a lullaby. This court was alive in a way none of the others had been. The Court of Bloom breathed. Sylara's presence was subtle yet pervasive, woven into everything like sunlight filtering through leaves or the whisper of vines curling along the stones.

Arden glanced around, her fingers brushing against the petals of a nearby blossom. The tension in her shoulders eased, but it didn't fully dissipate. "It's beautiful," she admitted. "But I don't see any warriors here. What exactly do you hope to gain from Sylara?"

Elydris stood beside her, arms folded, scanning the endless stretch of blossoms. "In Elessian, things are rarely as they appear. What looks like one thing could be another, and Sylara, despite her appearance, is not gentle." He turned his head slightly. "Tell me, Arden. What do you see?"

Arden hesitated, glancing around once more. "I see... a garden. Dozens of flower beds, twisting vines, rose-covered trellises. Orchids, marigolds, lilies. Everything is perfectly tended. It looks untouched by violence."

Elydris exhaled through his nose. "Each of those flowers was once a fae who crossed Sylara." He watched her face carefully as she stiffened. "Sylara does not tolerate betrayal. Those who cross her are turned into flowers and added to her garden."

Arden instinctively stepped back, her eyes scanning the blossoms with newfound understanding. What had seemed beautiful now felt wrong, eerie in its stillness. "She... turns people into plants?"

Elydris nodded. "Sylara's magic comes from the same goddess who empowered Melisara. They are twin spirits, created by Lysara. One draws strength from wild chaos and desire; the other, from the still and silent power of growth and life. Don't underestimate either; they are both dangerous."

Arden swallowed hard. The garden rustled around them, vines shifting toward the sunlight as if listening. She straightened her spine and took another look at the blooms. They were delicate, yes, but also a warning a thousand silent screams trapped forever within the garden.

The group moved through the garden with silent footsteps, each aware of how easily the peace could be shattered. Flowers brushed against their ankles, vines stretched lazily across their path, and overhead, the canopy filtered the light into shifting hues of green. Every petal seemed to carry a warning, as if the garden were watching them.

No one spoke, not even Veylis. Arden walked ahead of Aezraen, her steps careful but determined. She felt him move closer behind her, his presence heavy, his breath catching as though he wanted to say something. "Arden," he finally whispered.

She didn't look back. "Not now," she said, her voice firm but low. "I can't do this right now."

He hesitated, then fell silent. His footsteps remained close, but he didn't try again. Arden's heart twisted with guilt, but she forced herself forward. There was no space for his apologies or empty words at that moment.

Branches arched overhead into a natural gateway, and the scent of blooming roses and lilacs thickened as they neared a wide clearing. Butterflies flitted lazily through the air, and the hum of bees created a constant chorus.

They emerged into a sun-dappled glade where a long, root-bound table awaited them. Plates of fruit and pastries captured the group's attention. Goblets rested beside them, filled with nectar that glowed faintly in the light. Flowers grew directly from the table's wood, their petals shifting colors with strange precision as they took in the scene.

Her lips curled into a slow, knowing smile as she gestured for them to join her. The clearing was bathed in soft, dappled light, a feast laid out on a table seemingly woven from living roots. Sylara stood at the head of the table, radiant in a gown crafted from pale green silk and moss. Her long, auburn hair curled like vines around her shoulders, adorned with delicate blossoms in a crown. She looked ethereal, but a sharpness lurked behind her eyes that made Arden's skin prickle.

"I've been expecting you," Sylara said, her voice melodic, touched with wind and rain. "The birds told me you were traveling the northern courts. I had hoped you would stop here."

Elydris inclined his head politely. "Your hospitality is appreciated, Sylara."

She gestured to the seats with a graceful wave. "Come, eat. You've traveled far, and the next part of your journey will not be gentle."

As they approached the table, the group exchanged wary glances, but none dared to refuse. Sylara's voice was as rich as honey as she spoke, "This is a place of life, not war. But I am curious, what brings you to my garden?"

Arden hesitated only a moment before explaining their purpose. She spoke of Vaelithara's growing threat, of the courts that had already chosen sides, and of the war looming on the horizon. Sylara listened, her expression never wavering from polite amusement.

"The First Court has never tread on my gardens," she mused, running a delicate finger over the petals of a violet bloom, watching as it curled toward her touch. "Life and death are both inevitable. What happens beyond my borders does not concern me."

The group sat in uneasy silence around Sylara's table, the last of the sunlight spilling through the trees. The tension felt thicker here, as if even the air were listening, like the flowers themselves were holding their breath. Sylara tilted her head, unconcerned. "Who stands with you?" she asked, plucking a berry from the vine at her side and rolling it between her fingers.

Veylis raised his chin, his usual smirk gone. "The Hollow Court stands with Arden."

Aezraen's voice followed, steady despite everything. "The Court of Shadows as well."

"Ortheon has pledged his beasts and warriors," Elydris added.

Sylara nodded slowly. "What about my sister? The Gilded Queen? Does she stand with you?"

Arden's throat tightened. She had known the question would come, but hearing it aloud still made her stomach twist. "She refused," Arden said. "She offered challenges I could not accept."

At that, Sylara's hand froze. The berry in her fingers burst, dark juice trailing down her palm. The garden shuddered. The whispering flowers stilled, their colors fading. Then, one by one, the petals began to shrivel, blackening at the edges, curling inward.

Sylara focused her gaze on Arden. "What did she ask of you?" Her voice was quiet but cold, like a blade being drawn from its sheath.

"Three challenges, of which I could choose any." Her voice did not waver, though her fingers curled tightly into her cloak. "The first was to destroy Aeltherion."

Sylara showed no emotion.

"The second," she continued, her voice low, "was to name someone close to me, anyone, for her to kill."

At that, Sylara's face changed. Her expression crumpled into something like grief, something ancient and heavy. Her eyes glistened, though no tears fell. She exhaled slowly, her hands trembling before bringing them to rest in her lap.

"I am sorry," she said quietly, looking at Arden. "If anyone in all of Elessian understands what it is to suffer from Melisara's cruelty, it is I." She looked down at the dying flowers, and new blossoms sprouted in their place, their petals soft and pale, like a whispered apology.

"We were born of the same spirit," Sylara continued, her voice gentler now, as if telling a story no one else was meant to hear. "Twins, given life by Lysara. Life and chaos. Growth and desire. From the beginning, she devoured what I loved; she could not bear to share. As we grew older, she tore away the one thing that brought me happiness, and I have never forgiven her."

The group remained silent, unsure whether to speak. Arden watched Sylara closely, seeing the rawness in her that had not been there before.

"If you refused her temptations," Sylara said, finally meeting Arden's gaze again, "then I believe you are stronger than most who stand before me." She straightened in her seat, her voice firm. "The Court of Bloom will not take up arms. But we will stand with you in the only way we can. My healers will travel with your soldiers. We will protect the wounded. We will ensure your people survive."

Arden's shoulders dropped slightly as the weight of disappointment gave way to cautious relief. It was not what she had hoped for, but it was not nothing. Sylara would not march, but she would shelter. She would heal.

Elydris bowed his head. "Your support means more than you know."

Sylara's gaze softened, just enough to be seen. "You may not think it, but this is how I fight."

The flowers surrounding the table brightened, their colors returning in gentle waves of light and life. The vines stilled. The garden breathed again.

As the last of the meal vanished from the table, and the flowers at its edges dimmed to soft, sleepy hues, Sylara turned her gaze toward the fading light beyond the trees. Her expression was serene, but Arden saw something thoughtful behind her eyes.

"Where will you go next?" Sylara asked.

Elydris stepped forward, brushing his fingers across one of the glowing blossoms. "The portals have taken us as far as they can. The Court of Echoes is our next destination."

At the mention of that place, a flicker of unease crossed Sylara's calm demeanor. "Be careful," she warned, her voice softer now. "Sierath plays with minds; not all who enter return with their sanity intact."

"We'll be careful," Arden said, though the knot tightening in her stomach made her words feel hollow.

Sylara rose from her seat, the petals of the garden responding to her movement. She approached Arden, her hands light as she gently touched her shoulder. "You are stronger than you believe," she said. "Hold onto that. Especially in his court."

Elydris raised his hand, golden magic curling around his fingers as he turned to the rest of the group. "We must stay close. Remember, these ley lines are unstable, and my spell will not hold if we are separated. The sun is setting. If we are not through the border before nightfall, we may not find the way again. Night in the Court of Echoes is... unforgiving."

The air began to shimmer as Elydris pulled the magic taut, drawing the broken threads of the ley lines into a glowing doorway. The flowers bent gently toward the portal as if offering a silent farewell.

One by one, the group stepped through, leaving behind the warm, fragrant air of the Court of Bloom. The moment they passed through the doorway, the colors dulled, and the broken ley lines stretched out before them once more twisting, uncertain, and waiting.

Chapter Thirty-Five

As the group entered the Court of Echoes, a strange sensation enveloped them. It prickled against Arden's skin and coiled in her chest like a half-remembered echo. The landscape existed in a perpetual loop, shifting in ways that defied logic. Cautiously, she stepped forward, only to find her own footprint already pressed into the dust, as if she had walked this path before. Elydris murmured something under his breath, but before the sound fully formed, it stretched ahead of them, as if time itself had unraveled at the seams. Noctis shifted with the realm's will, one moment a towering grey beast with eyes dulled by age, and the next, a tiny kitten padding beside Arden, his oversized paws stumbling with innocent clumsiness.

They approached the castle slowly, unsure if they were truly moving or if the world was adjusting around them. The terrain beneath their feet twisted like a living thing, stone turning to sand, grass vanishing into ash, then reforming again. Every step felt both familiar and foreign, as if they had traversed this path a thousand times in dreams they couldn't remember. The air hummed with layered voices, too numerous to separate; their whispers brushed against Arden's skin like invisible threads pulling her forward.

As they neared the castle, its form shimmered and shifted. One moment it appeared ancient and ruined, its towers broken and swallowed by ivy; the next, it gleamed with impossible symmetry, freshly built and untouched by time. The front gates stood open, but there were no guards, no doors, only a yawning darkness pulsing with quiet power.

Silence enveloped them. Even Elydris, usually composed, looked uneasy as they stepped inside.

The corridor within was long and narrow, illuminated by hanging lanterns that flickered between different moments in time. The walls were lined with glass mirrors that did not reflect the travelers but offered glimpses of the past and future as they walked. Arden caught sight of herself once, younger, alone in a shadowed alley. In the next pane, she saw herself cloaked in gold, a crown on her brow and blood on her hands.

By the time they reached the throne room, Arden's heart was pounding. The transition had been seamless, as if time had folded inward and carried them here without crossing distance. The chamber pulsed with temporal energy, its mirrored walls rippling like the surface of a disturbed lake and the very air seemed to hum with layered realities.

Sierath stood in the center of the hall, or at least a version of him did. His form flickered like a candle in the wind, never quite solid, existing in a space between moments. His robes shifted in deep shades of dusk and shadow, shimmering like liquid time. His face was a blur, features never settling, yet his presence was unmistakable. He had been expecting them.

"Welcome," Sierath's voice resonated through the hall, layered and fractured, as if spoken by a thousand versions of himself at once. "Or perhaps I should say... welcome back." The way he said it sent a sharp bolt of unease through Arden's chest. Had they been here before?

Elydris stepped forward, his aura flickering in protest against the shifting reality of the court. "You knew we were coming," he stated, his tone unreadable. It was not a question.

Sierath tilted his head, his body blurring before solidifying again. "Of course," he mused. "Every possibility has already played itself out. You have already won. You have already lost. You are simply walking the path that has been tread before."

Aezraen's jaw clenched. "Enough riddles," he snapped. "We came for your aid." Shadows lashed out, curling around his feet, yet even they seemed uncertain here, their tendrils flickering between past and present.

Sierath smiled, and though it was not unkind, it carried the weight of something far older than time itself. "Then I suppose the only question that remains," he murmured, "is whether this time you will make a different choice."

Sierath turned his gaze upon Arden. "You must decide," he told her, his tone calm and knowing. "But not now... before." The weight of his words pressed against her, and she swallowed hard, the hairs on her arms rising.

"What does that mean?" Arden asked, her voice steady despite the unease coiling in her gut.

Sierath's lips curved slightly. "You are about to enter my hall of mirrors. You've faced this test before; you are merely walking through it again." He stepped closer, his robes shifting through time, their colors changing as if caught in an endless dusk. "This place is not bound by linear existence, Arden. The concepts of past and future are mortal constructs. Here, you must ask yourself: Is your mind strong enough to choose the same path twice?"

Before she could reply, the world around her blurred. The grand mirrored hall of the Court of Echoes twisted and folded like a reflection rippling across broken glass.

Her name echoed faintly in her mind, but it felt wrong, as if it belonged to someone else. "Why am I here?" she thought as a corridor formed ahead, its walls composed of mirrored glass so clear it seemed unreal.

Sierath gestured toward it, his voice a distant echo. "Step inside. Face yourself."

Arden moved forward, her legs heavy as if trudging through memory. As she crossed the threshold, the corridor sealed behind her with a soft, final hush. She was alone, except she wasn't. The walls shimmered with possibilities.

To her left, a version of herself stepped forward from the glass. She appeared... peaceful. Sunlight haloed her hair, her hands calloused from farmwork rather than battle. No crown. No burden of prophecy. She stood in a field of golden wheat, the faint echoes of a child's laughter behind her.

"You were never meant for this," the reflection said gently, her smile tinged with quiet judgment. "You could still walk away. Be free. Live your life."

"But...I made my choice," Arden whispered.

The woman laughed softly. "No. You believed salvation could be stolen. Some things aren't taken; they're chosen. It's not too late to make that choice."

Before Arden could respond, the glass rippled.

Another version of her stepped forward, this one draped in shadow, Aezraen at her side. His arm wrapped around her waist, his expression fierce and full of love, untouched by war. Their gazes locked, filled with desperate pleading.

"Throw away Solcryne," this version urged, her voice cracking with emotion. "Choose *us* this time. End this madness before it costs you everything. Aeltherion isn't worth it."

Arden's heart twisted as she felt the truth in the woman's voice like a blade. But she couldn't, *wouldn't*, look away from what lay ahead.

The mirror rippled again, causing Arden to shrink back. This reflection of herself crawled from the glass, her hands cracked and bleeding, her body translucent and flickering like a dying star. Her eyes were hollow, her lips sealed shut. Her presence chilled the air. This version had died before becoming anything more than a thief no crown, no purpose, no name remembered.

Though she remained silent, her presence thundered with unspoken words.

Other reflections surrounded Arden, their voices overlapping.

"You're going to get them all killed."

"You think you matter because you wear a crown? You're just a shadow draped in gold."

"He's going to die for you."

"You're still just a girl who stole something she didn't understand."

Arden's pulse pounded in her ears, and her breath came shallow and uneven. The corridor twisted around her, warping into a dozen fractured versions of her life, each shaped by someone else's hand. Luthan's corruption, Aezraen's bargains, Vaelithara's manipulations, Melisara's taunts each had used her, molded her, pushed her to become what they wanted.

Never what she wanted.

Her throat tightened as she surveyed the versions of herself that had surrendered and bent for the sake of others. Each reflection stared back with empty expressions, and for the first time, she despised a world that thought it could keep making her small.

Her fingers curled into fists, her spine straightened. A deep breath steadied the quake in her chest. "No," she declared, her voice ringing like steel in a silent battlefield. "I am not your weapon. I am not your pawn. I choose my path. I choose *me*."

The reflections screamed, and the corridor shuddered as glass cracked from every wall, splintering the illusions that had confined her. Shards of herself exploded into light, dissolving into nothingness.

When Arden emerged from the hall, Sierath awaited her. His form appeared more solid now, though his features still refused to settle. His expression was unreadable, but something in his gaze felt different. "You are not the first to make this choice," he said. "But you are the first to make it twice."

As Sierath guided her back toward the throne room where the others waited, he finally spoke, his voice low and hurried. "The Court of Echoes will stand by your side. I will use my magic to shape the threads of fate in support of your cause. But understand this: nothing is ever freely given."

Arden's shoulders stiffened, her alertness returning. "What is it that you want?"

Sierath stepped in front of her, cutting her off. "When the moment comes," he said, his voice barely above a whisper, "I will come to you with knowledge of a future, a truth. All I ask is that you embrace it and do not run from it."

Arden frowned, confusion tightening in her chest. "What kind of truth?"

He offered no answer, only that same unreadable smile. "You may not understand it now, but you will. When that time comes, I ask that you face it without fear. Let it unfold."

Silence stretched between them.

Arden glanced around the empty hall. She didn't know what Sierath would reveal, but she had come this far and would not back down now. "I accept," she said quietly. Sierath nodded, and the air around them shifted, as if time itself had taken a breath.

The throne room shimmered with the quiet pulse of Sierath's magic, time bending at the edges of perception as Arden and the Lord of Echoes stepped through the archway to rejoin the others.

Syliris was the first to approach, crossing the room in an instant with quick, urgent steps. "Arden," she breathed, "are you alright?"

Aezraen followed closely behind, his hand half-extended toward Arden. She flinched and took a subtle step back, her expression shuttered.

"Don't," she said, her voice low and firm. "Just... don't."

Aezraen hesitated, pain flickering across his features, but he did not press her.

Syliris tried again, her hand brushing Arden's arm. "Are you sure you're okay? You were gone longer than we expected, and we heard..."

"I said I'm fine," Arden replied quickly. Then, softer, "I just need time, please."

The room fell silent once more as Sierath stepped forward, his presence effortlessly commanding. His gaze swept over everyone before resting on Elydris. "I have given my answer," he announced, his voice deep and smooth. "The Court of Echoes will stand with you. However, the future remains uncertain. There is still something looming that will determine the direction of the war."

He fixed his gaze directly on Arden as he continued, "I believe you may already know what it is."

All eyes shifted to her. Arden opened her mouth to respond, but no words came immediately. Her fingers slipped into her pocket, closing tightly around the hidden necklace. When she finally spoke, her voice was unnaturally calm. "I don't know what he means."

Sierath didn't dispute her claim; he merely nodded faintly, as if her denial was anticipated. "The night here is too perilous for travel," he said, turning toward the curved staircase at the far end of the chamber. "You will not leave tonight. The mists are thick, and time slips away quickly after sunset in this realm. You may rest here under my roof."

He guided them up the winding stairs to their rooms. At the top, he paused beside a heavy, carved door and opened it with a flick of his fingers. "This is yours for the night," he said to Arden and Syliris. "Sleep while you can; time is not on your side."

Inside, the room was quiet and still. Two beds stood beneath a tall arched window, their frames crafted from bone-white wood and dressed in dark silk and thick comforters. The door clicked softly shut behind them, enveloping them in a heavy silence. Outside, the Court of Echoes buzzed with its strange, shifting magic, but within these walls, all was tranquil.

Arden walked to one of the beds and sat down slowly, the silk sheets whispering beneath her. She rubbed her palms along her thighs, seeking grounding. Syliris lingered by the window, her gaze fixed on the thick mists curling against the glass. Neither spoke at first; the silence between them was heavy with the weight of what had transpired and the uncertainties still ahead.

Syliris finally turned from the window and crossed the room, lowering herself onto the edge of the second bed. Her gaze flicked toward Arden, who had been carefully observed since they left the throne room. Now that they were alone, Syliris wanted to uncover the truth. "What did you choose?" she asked softly.

Arden looked up, her throat tightening. "What do you mean?"

"I've heard whispers about Sierath's hall of mirrors," Syliris replied. "All those versions of yourself, the ability to choose a different life. Very few emerge without losing their sanity... Then we all heard the glass shatter and grew concerned." Her voice was gentle, yet it carried a strange tension, as if she already knew the answer but needed to hear it spoken. "What did you choose to change?"

Arden exhaled slowly and glanced down at her hands. She had seen so many possible versions of herself in that place, but each required sacrifices she wasn't willing to make. "I didn't choose any of them," she finally said. "I chose this version of myself, with no changes."

Syliris tilted her head. "You chose to change nothing?"

"Yes," Arden replied, her conviction growing. "Every version of me was chasing something regret, power, love, revenge. But none felt real... None of them were me. I've spent so long being shaped by others, and for once, I didn't want to play someone else's version of myself."

There was a pause, then Syliris smiled slowly, a soft pride blooming on her face. "You are wiser than I expected," she said quietly. "Many come here to beg for another life."

Arden let out a small, humorless laugh. "I'm tired of chasing a fate someone else wrote for me."

Syliris leaned back on her hands, the tension in her frame easing slightly. "Then stop chasing. Start becoming. That is the only thing any of us can do."

They fell into silence again, but this time it felt lighter. Arden leaned back into the pillows, the ache in her bones finally beginning to ease. Sleep overtook her quickly as she allowed herself to truly relax for the first time in a while.

Chapter Thirty-Six

The group gathered in the grand foyer of Sierath's castle, morning light streaming through the high windows. They appeared more rested, the tension from the previous day eased by a few hours of sleep. Arden stood near the back, arms folded, her gaze sweeping over the others.

Elydris stepped into the center of the group, his expression unreadable. "Our next destination is the Court of Embers," he announced, his voice low yet firm. "We leave within the hour."

Before anyone could respond, Aezraen moved to stand beside him. "Before we go, I think you should all know... Seraphis's court is not what it once was." His tone carried a weight that silenced the room. "All the courts have felt Vaelithara's influence, but some have suffered more than others."

"What do you mean?" Syliris asked quietly, her brow furrowing.

"He resisted her longer than most," Aezraen explained. "He held her off until she threatened the one thing he couldn't risk: his people. Everything he built, she twisted. His forges were destroyed, and his people were transformed into warriors forced to train and fight for a queen who doesn't even know their names."

"Do you think he'll listen?" Elydris asked. "After everything she threatened? Would Seraphis abandon Vaelithara now?"

Aezraen's jaw tightened. "I don't know," he admitted. "There was a time he would have, but she took that choice from him."

Elydris nodded slowly, his face unreadable as he looked toward the doors. "Then we prepare for both outcomes," he said. "If Seraphis still remembers who he was, we might find an ally. If not..." His voice trailed off.

Elydris raised his hand, golden light curling from his fingertips as the broken ley lines shimmered into view. Cracks of energy pulsed through the air like veins, flickering with unstable magic. He pressed his palm against the fractured space between realms, and the path snapped open, jagged and bright. Without hesitation, the group stepped through. The air changed instantly; the weight of Sierath's magic faded behind them, replaced by a clinging heat and the scent of smoke that filled their lungs.

They moved swiftly, their boots striking the cracked stone that shimmered with embers beneath the surface. The wind howled through the blackened ridges and scorched hills, carrying the scent of melted metal and the faint, haunting sound of clashing steel. Ash drifted through the air like falling snow, coating their cloaks in a layer of gray dust.

Arden pressed on, her steps quick and her jaw clenched. The Court of Embers loomed ahead, and she could already sense the fury of the land, the restless energy of something ancient and wounded. As they stepped out of the portal into Seraphis's territory, Elydris was the first to speak. "The land remembers," he said in a low voice as they crested a ridge, "and it is angry."

They descended into the valley, the gates of the Court of Embers just visible through the haze of smoke. Whatever peace this place once held had long since burned away. As the group approached the gates, the ground beneath them trembled with distant thunder. Flames flickered along fissures in the earth, and the heat surrounded them like a living force. The great gates swung open with a low groan, revealing a wide courtyard lined with soldiers in iron armor, each standing rigidly at attention.

At the center stood Seraphis.

Clad in crimson armor, he embodied the image of a warlord. His broad shoulders were squared, and his hands rested lightly on the hilt of a massive sword strapped across his back. His expression was hard and unreadable until his gaze landed on Elydris.

When he spotted the First Fae King, Seraphis's eyes widened, and his stoic demeanor shattered. Without a word, he strode forward, his heavy boots echoing against the stone. He dropped to one knee before the returned king, bowing his head in reverence. "I never gave up hope that you would return."

"Rise," Elydris said gently, placing a hand on his old friend's shoulder.

Seraphis stood, and in the next moment, the two men embraced. The tension in Seraphis's posture melted away, and for a brief time, there was no war, no kingdom, only two friends reunited after far too long apart.

"I prayed for your return," Seraphis said, pulling back just enough to meet Elydris' gaze. "I knew you would make things right. That you would fix what she broke."

Elydris' gaze was steady. "Then stand with us. Help me restore balance to Elessian."

Seraphis glanced past Elydris to the others, his gaze landing on Arden, filled with curiosity. "Is that the mortal girl? The one who carries your crown?"

Elydris turned, placing a hand on Arden's back to guide her forward. "This is Arden," he said. "The one chosen by the Gods to bear Aeltherion."

Seraphis studied her in silence, the flames around them flickering in the reflection of his armor. His jaw twitched, revealing nothing, before he nodded in acknowledgment. "Then we have much to discuss."

He addressed Elydris first, his voice steady and low. "You know I would follow you into any war or storm. But this decision is not mine alone. To defy Vaelithara outright, to risk my people and territory, I must be certain. I need to know her heart is true."

Elydris' brows furrowed, his expression turning colder.

"This isn't just about loyalty. You know what Vaelithara is capable of. If I act against her without cause, my court will be the first she burns... I must be sure."

Seraphis then focused on Arden, his gaze intense. "Come with me. There is something I must see for myself."

Elydris stepped forward. "She does not go alone."

"I give you my word, old friend. No harm will come to her. But this must be done alone."

Tension filled the silence that followed. Elydris held Seraphis's gaze, while Arden gently touched his arm to draw his attention. "I'll go," she said quietly. "I don't sense any malice from him. Let me do this."

Elydris hesitated, his jaw tight. After a long breath, he finally nodded.

Seraphis gestured to one of his guards. "Take the rest of the group to the castle. Prepare a meal and provide them rest. I will join you shortly."

Without another word, he turned and began walking, trusting that Arden would follow. She did.

As Seraphis led Arden through the scorched edges of his territory, waves of heat rose from the blackened ground. At the base of a jagged cliff awaited two magnificent beasts, their bodies formed from flame and molten rock, their eyes glowing like coals in the dark. When Arden approached, one dipped its head in recognition. Seraphis gestured for her to climb on.

"They are called Brimfire Steeds," he said, resting a hand on the creature's neck. "Born from the heart of a dying volcano."

Arden swung onto the creature's back, surprised by how solid it felt despite its appearance. They rode along the outskirts of the Court of Embers, passing war camps and battle-scarred training grounds.

"This land did not always look like this," Seraphis said as they rode. "It used to be alive with fire, yes, but it was controlled. The forges never slept, and the sound of steel singing through flame was our heartbeat. My people were craftsmen. Artisans of battle, not mere soldiers."

Arden listened in silence as they passed the ruins of a court crushed by Vaelithara.

"When the Court of Veils rose against Vaelithara," Seraphis continued, his voice laced with bitterness, "I made a grave mistake. Kaelar was like a brother to me. We stood side by side through centuries of change and chaos. So when he called for aid, I answered."

His knuckles tightened on the reins. "But Kaelar underestimated her; we all did. His rebellion was crushed in less than a week, and for my part in it, she came for me."

Arden turned to look at him, but Seraphis kept his gaze fixed on the path ahead.

"She gave me a choice: serve her or watch my people burn, one by one, until there was nothing left but ash. So I surrendered. I let the forges grow cold, turned smiths into soldiers, and built her an army to ensure our survival."

Seraphis slowed near a cliffside, overlooking a once-great city now reduced to shattered stone and flickering torches. He dismounted and motioned for Arden to do the same. "This is what loyalty to the wrong person cost me," he said quietly. "I will not make that mistake again."

He turned his head slightly, his voice dropping to a cautious tone. "I cannot risk my court again," he said. "Not without knowing the heart of the one I would stake everything on." He paused before continuing. "There is someone you must meet, an elder blacksmith. She has served my court longer than most can remember. If you allow her, she will look into your soul."

"I'll do it."

Seraphis nodded solemnly. They mounted their steeds and ascended a narrow, winding path leading to the rim of a smoking volcano. The air grew hotter with each turn, and the wind howled in strange, mournful patterns. At the summit stood a stone forge carved into the mountainside, glowing with steady embers. A woman with ash-streaked skin and sharp eyes awaited them, a hammer resting against her hip. She seemed to know their purpose without being told.

"We will need time," the woman said. "I will summon you when we're done."

Seraphis gave Arden a lingering look before turning and disappearing down the path they had come. The blacksmith led Arden into the forge, where the heat enveloped her like a living thing, pressing against her skin and sinking into her bones.

"You seek our help," the blacksmith said without looking at her. "But first, we must understand the fire you bring with you."

Arden swallowed her instinct to respond; words would mean nothing here. This was not a place for persuasion; she needed to demonstrate her intentions. The heat from the forge was thick and relentless. She nodded and stepped forward.

The woman spoke little at first, working in silence as her hammer struck the metal in a steady, unhurried rhythm. When she finally spoke, her voice carried a quiet strength. "My name is Maeryn," she said, still focused on the blade she was shaping. "I was one of the original blacksmiths of this court, before it became what it is now."

Arden nodded, unsure if she should reply.

"I am here," Maeryn continued, "because I was entrusted with more than just steel. I do not give my loyalty freely. Not to Seraphis, not to Vaelithara, and not to you."

Arden stepped closer. "Then why am I here?"

Maeryn turned to face her, her features partially obscured by a streak of soot. Her eyes, the color of smoke, were calm yet unreadable. "Because Seraphis believes in you, and belief alone is not enough." She paused before adding, "I will judge your soul; not through magic or spells, but through your work, your hands, your choices."

"What if you don't like what you see?" Arden asked.

"Then you are no different than Kaelar," Maeryn replied. "Trusting you would only bring this court down again."

From that moment on, their days became a quiet test. Maeryn assigned Arden tasks without explanation. She directed her to gather ore from deep within the mountain caverns, carry buckets of water from the base of the slope, cut wood, stoke fires, and maintain a forge that never cooled. The work was brutal; her arms trembled, her feet bled, but she refused to complain.

As hours turned into days, the silence between them began to shift. Maeryn asked questions with intent. Her words often came while Arden's hands were full and her body too tired to guard her thoughts.

"You said you raised your brother alone," Maeryn remarked one evening as they shoveled coal into the forge. "How old were you?"

"Ten," Arden replied, sweat dripping into her eyes. "Callen was six."

Maeryn's hammer rang once, then again. "No one helped?"

Arden shook her head. "Not in the ways that counted. Ephraim gave me odd jobs when he had them, but he barely paid enough to keep us fed. It wasn't until Luthan brought me into the Silver Daggers that anything actually changed. That was the first time someone really helped."

Maeryn looked at her, not with pity, but with understanding.

Setting a heavy iron basin on the workbench, Maeryn wiped her hands with a cloth and fixed her gaze on Arden. "When your brother was ill," she asked quietly, "what did you feel?"

Arden stilled, tightening her grip on the tongs. For a long moment, she said nothing. "Helpless," she finally admitted. "He was slipping through my fingers, and there wasn't a single thing I could do to stop it."

Maeryn watched her closely but remained silent.

Arden's voice grew sharper. "But now? Knowing Aezraen was the one who cursed him? That he watched us suffer just to set up a deal... I feel furious. I wish he had never looked our way. He had three others. He didn't need me too."

Maeryn tilted her head slightly. "Then why do you think he chose you?"

Arden blinked at the question, her mouth opening and closing as she struggled to find an answer. Finally, she sighed and muttered, "I don't know. I wasn't anything special back home. Just another girl trying to survive."

Maeryn stepped closer, her voice now softer. "Maybe you were more than that. Perhaps he saw something in you that no one else noticed. Elessian has a way of revealing what Solmyr hides. Your magic may have always been there, just waiting to be discovered."

On the third morning, Arden found herself alone at the forge, stoking the flames as the sun rose behind the smoky peaks. She wiped the sweat from her brow and looked up when she heard footsteps echoing down the stone corridor.

Maeryn approached silently, her hair pulled back in a loose braid and soot smudged on her cheek. She studied the glowing coals and gave a small approving nod. "Keep it steady," she instructed, then gestured for Arden to follow her to the worktable.

Together, they began the final steps of their task. Maeryn guided Arden through each movement, her hands layered over Arden's as they aligned the metal pieces. "Precision is more important than force," she said softly. "Feel it breathe. Let it tell you where it wants to bend."

They started with the gauntlet, working in silence as the heat enveloped them, the only sounds being the rhythmic hammering and the hiss of quenched metal. Arden's arms ached and her shoulders throbbed, but she pressed on. Each strike infused the metal with pieces of herself: her rage, her loss, her hope.

Next came the dagger. At first glance, the design appeared simple, but the carving was delicate and intricate. Maeryn handed Arden a fine engraving tool, demonstrating how to etch meaning into every curve of the blade's spine. "Not everything powerful needs to be loud," Maeryn murmured. "Sometimes the quietest things are the most enduring."

They shaped the hilt together, using woven leather from a beast native to the volcanic slopes, its hide resistant to flame. Maeryn whispered a charm in a language Arden did not understand, a magic that hummed through the steel. When the metal cooled, Maeryn dipped the blade into a basin of water drawn from the mountain's deepest spring. Steam curled into the air as the enchantment settled.

When the final piece was shaped, cooled, and polished, Maeryn placed it in Arden's hands. "The gauntlet is forged with the strength you have built through every hardship," the blacksmith said.

Arden traced her fingers along the dagger's edge. "And this?"

The blacksmith met her gaze. "That depends on you. The magic within will grow from your actions, and how you wield it will determine what it becomes."

Arden stared at the items for a long moment, her throat tight. "Thank you," she whispered.

Maeryn looked at her, calm and assured. "These are not gifts," she said. "They are pieces of who you are. You created them; I merely guided you."

The sound of hooves approached as Seraphis appeared, seemingly summoned by thought alone. He dismounted, his broad form cast in shadow by the early light. Clad in a dark tunic and gloves, he wore no armor now. His hair was tied back, and the tension that had clung to him on their first day seemed to have softened. Maeryn stepped up behind him, her expression as unreadable as ever, until she drew close enough to press a soft kiss to his cheek.

It was a small gesture, but Arden froze, noticing how his hand brushed briefly against Maeryn's waist and how she tilted her head toward him as if it were instinct. "You're his wife," Arden said aloud before she could stop herself.

Maeryn didn't deny it; she simply turned to her workbench and picked up a piece of glowing metal. "I needed you to speak freely and see clearly. Not telling you was the only way."

Seraphis gave Arden a faint, knowing smile. "She sees what I cannot, and she is rarely wrong."

The blacksmith turned to Seraphis, her expression calm but resolute. "Her heart is true. She may not have every answer yet, but she carries purpose with every step. I will allow our people to fight alongside her."

Seraphis nodded, his expression flickering with what seemed like relief. "Then so be it. We will stand with you."

Maeryn smiled and returned to her forge. "Go," she said. "The others are waiting."

Chapter Thirty-Seven

He and Arden mounted their steeds again, riding in silence for a time, the air filled only with the steady sound of hooves striking the hardened earth. "Why didn't you make the decision yourself? You are the Archfey of this court. Shouldn't you be the one to rule it?"

Seraphis laughed. "I once thought that power alone was enough to lead." His tone turned somber. "But look where that led us. Vaelithara was created to rule, shaped by the Gods themselves, yet she has become a poison to this realm."

He gazed thoughtfully ahead. "When I met my wife, I realized something important. She wasn't born of divine power, but she understands people in ways I never could. She sees into their souls. Because of that, I trust her judgment more than my own."

Arden frowned slightly. "Even if you desire something different?"

"Especially then," Seraphis replied with a grin. "Desire can blind us all. Her clarity keeps this court from descending into chaos. She has earned the right to make these decisions, even when they contradict my instincts."

Arden nodded slowly, the weight of his words settling deep in her chest as they approached Seraphis's castle. The rest of the group was gathered in the war chamber, maps and notes strewn across the long stone table. Arden paused at the threshold, narrowing her eyes. "Didn't you need Maeryn to decide whether you would help us?"

Seraphis chuckled, a deep and warm sound. "She made her decision the moment she met you," he said. "Everything that followed was simply to confirm what she already knew."

At the head of the gathering, Elydris stood tall, his golden gaze scanning the assembled faces. He wasted no time, his voice carrying authority. "We've made progress, but we are far from ready." He met each of their eyes before laying out the truth about their alliances.

"The Court of Beasts stands with us. Ortheon's forces are strong, but they are wild. They fight as predators, not as a disciplined army."

Veylis chuckled darkly from his position against a column. "A fitting description, wouldn't you agree?" His smirk held amusement, yet something unreadable lingered in his violet eyes. "They'll tear through the First Court's ranks easily enough, provided you don't try to control them."

Elydris ignored him and continued, "The Hollow Court is committed, though we all know Veylis is as much a liability as he is an asset." He shot a pointed look at the Archfey, who merely grinned in response. "That said, his court will fight alongside us."

"The Court of Embers stands with us," Elydris announced, his gaze sweeping across the room before settling on Seraphis.

Seraphis stepped forward, his voice rumbling like distant thunder. "You have my word, Elydris. My court will carve a path to Vaelithara's gate if necessary."

"The Court of Bloom refuses to fight," Elydris continued, his tone clipped with frustration. "However, Sylara will assist our injured."

Arden exhaled slowly, her fingers slipping into her pocket. She felt the cool curve of the necklace Melisara had given her, the delicate chain biting into her hand. "The Watchers said the courts must stand united," she said quietly, uncertainty thick in her voice. "Not most. Not some. All. What if this isn't enough?"

Elydris met her gaze, his expression unreadable. For a moment, he remained silent. Then, with a calm certainty that felt more rehearsed than genuine, he shook his head. "We will make this enough," he declared.

A hush fell over the room. The absence of the Gilded Court loomed over them like a blade poised to strike. They were close, but without the full strength of the courts, they would remain outnumbered. The First Court was waiting, and Vaelithara had already shown she would not hesitate to act first. The missing Gilded Court left a gaping void where an army should have stood.

The air itself seemed to still, as if waiting for someone to acknowledge the reality they faced. Without Melisara's forces, their war effort was incomplete. Her court represented power, wealth, and deception, and whether they liked it or not, its absence left them vulnerable.

Veylis, never one to let a moment of tension go to waste, laughed softly, the sound curling like smoke through the room. He pushed away from the column he had been leaning against, a wicked grin splitting his face. "You know," he mused, "Melisara did make you quite the offer, Arden. You could have had an army draped in gold and silk." He took a slow step forward, amusement dancing in his violet eyes.

"Really, darling, why did you refuse?" His voice dripped with mockery, the smirk on his face widening as he tilted his head. "You would have probably been her bedroom plaything, but at least you would have had a pretty collar for agreeing to be Melisara's newest bitch." The words hung in the air, sharp and deliberately cruel.

They lingered like an unsheathed blade, glinting with the harsh edge of truth and venom. For a moment, no one moved. The heat in the war room, already heavy with the lingering fire magic of the Court of Embers, seemed to intensify.

Arden's jaw tightened, but she remained silent. Turning away, she did so not in defeat but in quiet dismissal, refusing to give him the satisfaction of a reaction. Yet the damage was done. Whatever momentum had been building and camaraderie forged now cracked.

Syliris shifted uncomfortably, her gaze darting toward Elydris. Aezraen's shadows twitched at his feet, but he held his ground, silent and unreadable. The silence deepened, heavy with unspoken words.

Elydris cleared his throat, breaking the tension. "We need to return to the Court of Shadows," he said sharply. "Every day we delay gives Vaelithara more time."

No one argued or even nodded. One by one, the group began to move, the earlier fire in their steps replaced by a weight none dared to voice.

Seraphis followed them to the gates of his court, his expression solemn with understanding. Elydris stepped forward and clasped Seraphis's arm. "You've given more than I hoped for. Thank you."

The group exchanged final farewells, none lingering longer than necessary. The excitement of gaining a new court had faded, overshadowed by the burdens of what lay ahead. As they walked, Arden remained quiet, her fingers brushing against the hidden necklace in her pocket.

Ahead, Elydris snapped open the doorway, and they all stepped through. Arden lingered behind, her thoughts louder than before. She felt the weight of inevitability pressing upon her. The Watchers had not spoken in riddles; their meaning was clear: the courts must stand as one, and right now, they did not. Melisara was the missing piece.

As their feet touched the familiar stone of the Court of Shadows, the magic behind them hissed and sealed shut. The cool, dark air enveloped them instantly, a stark contrast to the smoldering heat they had just left behind. Shadows shifted along the ancient walls, as if acknowledging their return, curling lazily through the corridors with a welcome that was both eerie and intimate. Noctis padded ahead in silence, his ears twitching at every whisper.

Arden passed Aezraen in the hallway. He seemed to want to say something, but the words didn't come. She didn't stop; she couldn't.

"Syliris called her name as she neared the main gates of Aezraen's castle. "Where are you going?"

Arden hesitated before answering. She placed her hand on the iron bars, feeling the cold of the night beyond. When her voice came, it was quiet but resolute. "To ensure this war isn't over before it begins."

Syliris paused, then stepped closer. "You're going back to her?"

Arden nodded.

"She'll take something from you."

"I know."

Syliris searched her face but chose not to argue. "Don't let her take more than you're willing to lose."

"I don't think I have that choice."

Noctis nudged her hand, silent and steady at her side. Arden reached into her pocket and curled her fingers around the necklace. With a breath, she slipped the chain over her head. A portal shimmered ahead, rippling faintly with gold-tinted magic.

She glanced back once, just long enough to see Syliris still standing there, watching her. Then she stepped through. She was running toward something she had buried long ago; toward her past, toward her debt, and toward the cost she now chose to pay.

The Gilded Court rose in the distance like a dream made of gold and lies. Its towers glittered beneath the night sky, casting a glow that looked warm from afar. Arden knew better; beneath its beauty, the rot ran deep. Every golden spire, every polished marble stair, every sweet scent that clung to its perfumed halls was a mask hiding power, manipulation, and cruelty.

She didn't slow when she reached the gates, and the guards didn't stop her. Courtiers stepped back, parting like silk as she passed. Their whispers coiled around her, veiled in laughter and laced with venom. She didn't meet their eyes.

The doors to the throne room loomed ahead, tall and gilded with etched roses and coiled serpents. Arden didn't knock. She pushed them open with both hands, the gold creaking under the force, and stormed inside.

Melisara was waiting.

The Gilded Queen reclined on her throne, draped in silk and diamonds. Her hair fell in soft waves, perfect and dangerous, framing a face carved from beauty and cruelty alike. She didn't rise; she just smiled.

"You came back," she purred, her voice sweet as spun sugar and just as sharp. "What a desperate little thing you are."

Arden did not flinch; she didn't look away. She had not come for Melisara's games; she had come to make a deal, and she knew exactly what the price would be.

"I have chosen a challenge." Her voice was steady as she spoke. "I will give you a name."

Her smile faltered slightly, and Arden could tell this was not the path she thought Arden would choose. The playful gleam in her eyes narrowed into something cooler. She leaned forward, resting one elbow on the gilded arm of her throne. Her nails tapped once. Twice.

"Lillian Varnell."

The name lingered in the air like smoke.

"And why, pray tell," Melisara asked, her voice dropping to a velvet purr, "should that woman be the price?"

"She is my mother."

Chapter Thirty-Eight

Arden stood before Melisara's throne, the weight of her past pressing against her ribs like a vice. The Gilded Queen's gaze was sharp and expectant, demanding more than just a name; Melisara sought the story, the suffering, the wound laid bare, nothing less would suffice.

"Explain," Melisara purred, her eyes fixed on Arden's face.

Arden swallowed, her throat dry. She hadn't spoken this story aloud in years, nor had she allowed herself to linger in the memories. But now, she had to. "She left us," Arden began, her voice low yet steady.

Melisara raised an unimpressed brow. "You'll need to be more specific, darling. Parents leave their children all the time. What makes your story so special?"

Arden's fingers curled into fists at her sides. She could feel the weight of Callen's small hand in hers, the sticky warmth of summer air clinging to her skin, the ache in her feet from standing too long. "We lived within the walls of Aeridor, a kingdom by the sea. We had a small cottage, and Mother worked for a local woman, repairing dresses," she continued, forcing herself back to that day the sun-soaked cobbled streets and the scent of fresh bread from the marketplace. "She told us we were going to a different town to get food. We walked for hours, with Callen complaining the whole time. When we reached Hallow's Reach, Mother guided us to the market stalls."

She could still see her mother's eyes darting around, the way she pulled her shawl tighter around her shoulders, as if bracing against something unseen.

"She told us to go play with the other kids while she went into the shops, assuring us she wouldn't be long."

Melisara tilted her head. "So what did you do?"

Arden's nails dug into her palms. "We waited for as long as we could." The words tasted bitter on her tongue. "Until it started getting dark and Callen got cold. We went searching for her."

She could still hear the sounds of the market the merchants haggling, the clatter of hooves against stone. She remembered how Callen tugged at her sleeve, asking when their mother would return. Back then, she believed their mother was simply delayed, that something had held her up, and that she would step out of one of the shops any second, smiling, arms full of food.

"Other children went home," Arden said, her voice quieter now. "The vendors began packing up their stalls."

"She did not return?"

Arden exhaled slowly. "No."

That was when doubt first crept in, the initial shiver of fear. Callen had been six, too young to understand why Arden scanned the crowds, why her grip on his hand had tightened. He still believed, but Arden had known. They wandered the streets until their legs ached, searching for a face that would never reappear.

"She was just gone," Arden said, her voice clipped and emotionless. "I took Callen and we returned to Aeridor, to the cottage. It had been completely emptied."

Arden straightened her shoulders, her jaw tight. "I had to become Callen's mother before I had even stopped being a child."

A beat of silence passed, then Melisara smiled, slow and knowing, a glimmer of satisfaction in her eyes. "How tragic," she murmured, tilting her head. Melisara's lips curled into a slow, satisfied smile as she leaned forward, resting her chin on her fingers while regarding Arden.

"So you want closure," she mused, savoring the words. After a deliberate pause, she added, "or do you want revenge?"

Arden met Melisara's gaze directly, her voice unwavering. "Both."

The Gilded Queen let out a soft chuckle and rose gracefully from her throne. "How predictable," she murmured, her tone lacking real mockery. "Very well. Let's see what we can find, shall we?" With a flick of her wrist, the chamber plunged into darkness. The gilded walls faded as a heavy mist rolled across the floor, curling around Arden's ankles like living tendrils. At the far end of the room, a massive mirror shimmered, its golden frame twisting like vines frozen in time.

"Come now, Arden," Melisara purred, beckoning her forward. "Look upon the past you were never meant to see."

Arden hesitated for a moment before stepping toward the mirror. The surface rippled, colors shifting like spilled ink, pulling her deeper into the past. She braced herself, jaw clenched, but nothing could prepare her for what she was about to witness.

In the dimly lit shop, Arden's mother stood before a merchant, her hands trembling as she reached into the folds of her cloak. She withdrew a simple, well-worn gold band that Arden recognized as her father's. The merchant took it, weighed it in his palm, then nodded and handed her a small pouch of coins.

Arden's stomach twisted. The scene shifted, following Lillian as she exited the shop, clutching the coins to her chest. Without hesitation, she ran, not looking back for her children. Arden watched her mother navigate the crowded streets, her shawl pulled tight over her shoulders. It wasn't fear that propelled her; it was purpose. She wove through alleyways, past familiar storefronts, until she reached a small courtyard.

A man stood waiting.

Arden barely registered Melisara's quiet hum of intrigue behind her. Her ears rang as the stranger stepped forward, arms open, and Lillian collapsed into him. He embraced her, pressing his lips into her hair, whispering words Arden could not hear.

The mirror surged forward, years spilling across its surface like ink spreading through water. Arden watched as her mother settled into a new life, a new home. She grew older with this man, and together they built a quiet existence in a village far from Aeridor, where no one would recognize her or ask about the children she left behind.

The mirror jumped again, revealing the woman who had abandoned her now standing in a sun-dappled garden, laughter rising in the warm afternoon air. Beside her was her husband, the man she had chosen, who gently brushed a graying lock of hair from her face.

Two children ran toward them. "Mama! Papa!" they cried, their voices brimming with untainted joy.

Lillian knelt, arms outstretched, beaming as she pulled them close and kissed their heads. Arden could no longer breathe. Her mother had a new family. A whole family. She had moved on, and she had done it so easily.

Flashes of Arden's own childhood surged behind her eyes; Callen's small, trembling hands clutching hers as they huddled together on cold nights, the empty ache of hunger, and the desperate, humiliating pleas for help from strangers who turned them away.

She had done that to them.

Something inside Arden snapped. Throughout her life, she had searched for answers, begged for understanding, and prayed for an explanation that would bring clarity. But none came.

Arden's nails dug into her palms as a sharp, bitter laugh escaped her lips.

"Well then, darling," Melisara purred, wrapping an arm around Arden. "Shall we?"

With a slow, deliberate motion, power surged through the air, golden and intoxicating, as threads of shimmering magic wove around Arden's form. The fighter clad in worn leathers and practical armor vanished, replaced by something far more befitting royalty. The colors of the Gilded Court, deep crimson and gold, draped over her like liquid wealth. The bodice cinched ruthlessly, emphasizing power over comfort, while gold chains layered her throat, each one heavier than the last.

Melisara tilted her head, surveying her handiwork. Dark kohl lined Arden's eyes, enhancing her piercing gaze, and her lips were painted a deep, unforgiving red. The transformation was complete. "You can't meet your mother looking like a brute," Melisara said, stepping back to admire her creation. "No, this..." she gestured at Arden, at the striking elegance she had crafted, "...this is much more sophisticated."

Arden remained silent, filled only with hatred.

Melisara smiled knowingly and turned toward the mirror. With a flick of her fingers, the image of Arden's mother vanished from view. Arden watched as a man stumbled forward, grasping desperately at nothing. Children screamed and cried, their faces streaked with panic, their little voices hoarse as they called for someone, anyone, to help.

Arden observed with a cold expression. She hoped no one came for them, so they could understand what she felt.

Lillian appeared in the center of the throne room, her frail, aging form trembling as she realized where she was. Arden looked down upon her, her golden-draped figure perched high above like a goddess of vengeance. She let the silence stretch between them, allowing her mother's confusion to curdle into fear before she finally spoke.

"Well, hello, Lillian," she said, her voice no longer her own. "Or would you still prefer I call you mother?"

"Arden?" Lillian whispered, her voice barely audible. She instinctively leaned toward her daughter, as if she had any right to seek comfort from the very child she had abandoned. Fear flickered across her face, and her hands trembled at her sides.

At first, Arden remained silent. She simply lifted Aeltherion to her brow and withdrew the dagger that Maeryn had forged for her.

Melisara clapped her hands once, the sharp sound echoing through the grand, gilded hall. The elite of her court entered, surrounding Lillian. Draped in silks and adorned with gold and precious stones, each of them hid behind a golden mask.

"Come now, my lovelies," Melisara cooed, her voice laced with amusement and cruel anticipation. "We have a trial to attend to."

They descended in waves, their laughter lilting yet dangerous. They took their places in the growing crowd, eyes gleaming with eager anticipation for the unfolding entertainment. In the center stood Lillian, trembling, her confusion deepening into something darker as her wide eyes darted across the unfamiliar masks.

Arden turned, her voice slicing through the rising chatter of the court. "This woman," she announced, her tone cool and lethal, "is a traitor to her own blood. A coward. A liar. A woman who discarded her own children like unwanted scraps."

The crowd stirred, murmurs transforming into sharp laughter and mocking whispers. Some jeered, while others leaned forward, eager for the spectacle to begin.

Melisara sighed in delight, practically glowing with amusement as she ran her fingers through her golden curls. "What a delicious scandal," she purred. "A mother who abandoned her own daughter, only to find herself at the mercy of the child she cast aside."

Lillian gasped for breath, sharp and shallow. "Arden, please," she whispered, stepping closer. "There is so much you don't understand "

"I understand perfectly," Arden interrupted, her voice cutting like a blade. "You left. You *chose* to leave. You sold the last piece of my father you had left to crawl into another man's arms."

The murmurs in the crowd grew louder, shifting closer, their eyes filled with ravenous anticipation for the chaos about to erupt. Melisara's laughter echoed through the hall, her delight unmistakable. "It is time for the fun to begin!" she declared, throwing her arms wide as if blessing the savagery to come.

The court descended upon Lillian.

Screams erupted in the hall as hands reached out, golden rings glinting, and sharp nails tearing into fabric and flesh. Lillian stumbled, clawing at unseen hands, gasping and pleading, but her cries were drowned by merciless laughter and the deafening roar of bloodlust.

Arden watched, unwilling to intervene. Blood splattered across her face, ruining the pristine makeup Melisara had applied, yet she could not look away. A tear rolled down her cheek and landed on her chest, jolting her out of her trance.

When the screams finally ceased and the frenzy ended, only the tattered remnants of a woman who had once called herself a mother remained. Melisara sighed in satisfaction, reclining on her throne, her eyes fixed on Arden with lazy amusement. With a graceful tilt of her head, she lifted a goblet of deep, ruby wine to her lips and took a slow sip, savoring the moment. "A pleasure doing business, my dear."

Arden stood silent in the flickering candlelight, unchanged yet entirely transformed. The royal ensemble Melisara had conjured for her remained; both a gift and a reminder of the power she had claimed. She did not shed it, nor did she attempt to.

She had expected to feel something, but she felt nothing. She was completely numb to the horror that had just unfolded.

Melisara rose. "My army will await your command," she said, smooth and unhurried, as if war were merely another game she intended to win.

Arden pivoted sharply on her heel, striding toward the towering gilded doors of the throne room. She offered no thanks and made no acknowledgment of the blood-soaked bargain she had struck. Instead, she simply walked away.

Melisara's voice followed her like a whispering serpent in the dark. "You and I are not so different, you know."

Arden refused to look back. She would not grant those words any power or allow them to seep into her bones as Melisara intended. Instead, she stepped into the cool, crisp night, where the air did little to quell the fire raging within her.

Her fingers curled around Aeltherion as she removed the crown. As the portal opened before her, she knew one thing: the courts were now united, and they were ready for war.

Chapter Thirty-Nine

The first rays of dawn barely illuminated the dark spires of the Court of Shadows as Arden stepped through its gates. The air was crisp and heavy with mist, sharply contrasting the warm night she had just left behind in the Gilded Court. Though she returned to familiar ground, she felt like an intruder. The maroon silk of her gown clung to her, stark against the muted grays and blacks of the court she had once called home. The intricate embroidery shimmered in the dim torchlight, ornate and regal, a testament to Melisara's influence.

When the first guard spotted her, the castle stirred to life in a blur.

Syliris was the first to arrive, her eyes widening in shock at Arden's appearance. "What did she do to you?" she whispered, desperately trying to wipe the blood from Arden's face.

Her hands shook as she searched for any light behind Arden's eyes. What she found must have frightened her; one hand clutched her chest while the other covered her mouth to muffle her sobs.

Veylis approached next, his gaze sweeping over her slowly, taking in the blood spattered across her clothes, the tremble in her hands, and the distant glaze in her eyes. "Did I miss the coronation, little queen?"

When she didn't answer, his teasing faded completely. Concern etched itself into every line of his face. He stepped closer, his voice low and careful. "What happened?" He examined her again, this time more slowly, and then his voice turned sharp. "Arden, whose blood is that?"

"Guards!" he called, snapping his fingers without breaking eye contact. "Find Aezraen. Now." Turning back to Arden, his tone softened, lined with steel. "Talk to me. I know that look. I know what it's like to come back different, to carry pain that isn't yours. But you don't have to carry it alone."

She flinched, just once, just enough. Her breath hitched, and her knees buckled slightly before she steadied herself. She couldn't look him in the eye. She couldn't face any of them.

The words barely registered. The weight of their stares and probing questions became too much to bear. More bodies crowded around her, relentless inquiries swelling like a tide. Hands reached out, fingers brushing against her gown, as if confirming she was real.

The world tilted, walls closing in and suffocating her with pressure. Too many voices, too many hands, too many questions. Her breath quickened, her chest tightening. Melisara's perfume lingered in the air, the memory of her actions burning behind her eyes.

She began to hyperventilate, struggling to draw enough air. Concerned voices rose around her, desperately trying to ground her. Through the chaos, only one voice rang out across the courtyard, "Enough."

The voice was sharp and commanding, and instantly, the crowd stilled. He stepped toward her without hesitation, wrapping his arms around her and lifting her effortlessly off the ground. The world narrowed; there were no more questions, no more prying hands, just the solid warmth of him as he carried her inside.

As Aezraen moved, the noise and chaos quieted, and Arden's breaths came more easily. His presence sliced through the suffocating pressure like a blade. Shadows coiled around them both, blocking out the rest of the world. He didn't ask what had happened or why she had returned this way; he simply accepted it.

As he pushed open the door to his chambers, her exhaustion settled in. The space was just as she remembered: dark and warm, illuminated by the soft glow of the hearth. It felt like a sanctuary, untouched by the war raging outside.

Aezraen moved with careful precision, lowering her onto the bed. She noticed how his hands lingered for a moment too long, as if reassuring himself that this was real. She didn't resist or move; instead, she stared at the flickering firelight, her thoughts tangled in a web of choices and a mother who had never returned who never would now.

Melisara's challenge had completely gutted whatever spirit remained inside her. She felt empty, devoid of anything that made her whole. Aezraen removed her gauntlet carefully and laid it on the table beside the bed. When he took the blade Maeryn had crafted, he tried to hide the shock on his face but failed. The silver blade now looked tarnished, completely blackened by the choices she had made. Aezraen knelt before her with quiet reverence, allowing them both to sit in silence for a while.

"Let's get you cleaned up," he said, his fingers deftly unfastening the intricate clasps of her attire. The finery of the Gilded Court unraveled beneath his touch, slipping from her shoulders like the weight of the night itself. He didn't ask questions or demand answers; he simply helped her shed the remnants of a world that no longer belonged to her.

Each golden chain, each delicate fastening, felt like a shackle being removed. Arden barely moved, allowing him to undress her in silence, her skin prickling as cool air met her flesh.

Aezraen stepped toward her, his expression unreadable but his movements careful. "Come on," he said softly, leading her to the bathroom. He moved ahead of her, turning the faucet until warm water began to fill the deep, sunken tub. Steam curled into the air, carrying the calming notes of lavender and cedarwood from the oils he added.

Without a word, he returned to her side and steadied her at the edge of the tub, guiding her as she stepped in. The warmth of the water wrapped around her limbs like a balm, coaxing out the pain within.

Aezraen knelt beside the basin, reaching for a cloth. "Just breathe," he murmured. "You're safe."

Arden sank into the comforting warmth. The water swirled around her, the surface rippling as Aezraen dipped a cloth and gently wiped away the remnants of Melisara's world from her skin.

At first, she barely noticed the reddish tint seeping into the water. But then it spread, tendrils unfurling in slow, haunting spirals. Her mother's blood. She could still hear the children's screams, their father shouting for help, for mercy. The reality of what she had done pressed against her chest, and she began to cry softly.

Callen's face flashed in her mind; she had sworn to protect him. But now she didn't even recognize herself. She had become the very thing she once hated.

Aezraen lifted her from the bath, water cascading off her skin in rivulets. His grip was steady and strong as he wrapped her in a thick towel, shielding her from the cold and the burden of her thoughts. She did not resist, leaning into the warmth of the fabric, allowing him to guide her away from the cooling water and the memories it held.

He led her to the bed and pulled the towel from her shoulders. He slipped a loose shirt over her head, the fabric pooling over her frame oversized and warm, smelling of cedar, fire, and a faint trace of something uniquely his. He guided her arms through the sleeves, the material whispering against her skin as he adjusted the fit, his fingers lingering at her wrists before stepping back.

Arden felt small in his clothing, weak. The shirt draped over her, acting as a shield and offering a comfort she hadn't realized she needed.

Neither of them spoke.

He sat beside her, his warmth a steady presence in the dim room. He reached for her, his fingers barely brushing her hand. "What do you need?"

Arden lay down and rolled onto her side, turning away from him. She didn't have an answer. What did she need? To undo what she had done? To go back to before? To feel something other than this gnawing, hollow ache?

She didn't know.

Aezraen exhaled heavily and pushed himself up from the bed. His movements were slow and careful as he crossed the room, putting space between them.

The distance should have made it easier to breathe, but it didn't. Aezraen's voice was gentle yet insistent. "Arden, please, just talk to me."

She squeezed her eyes shut, fingers curling into the fabric of the sheets. She tried to speak, to force the words out, but her voice barely rose above a whisper. "I killed my mother."

Aezraen stilled, the air around him shifting and darkening. He did not move toward her or speak. Instead, he let the words settle, allowing her to feel and own them. The silence was unbearable. Arden felt herself sinking beneath its weight, drowning in something she could not name. She closed her eyes, waiting for the world to shatter.

Without hesitation, Aezraen slid into the bed beside her, the mattress shifting under his weight. He didn't ask for permission or offer words that would do nothing to mend her fractures. Instead, he pulled her against his chest, his arms caging her as if he could physically hold her together.

Arden didn't resist; she lacked the strength to fight him or anything else. She folded into him, pressing her forehead against his collarbone, her breath uneven and shaky.

His shadows stretched out, curling around them like protective tendrils, creating a barrier against the world beyond his chamber walls. The weight of them settled over her like a second blanket, a tangible force pressing down on the chaos inside her, urging it to be still.

Aezraen said nothing. He simply held her. His grip was steady and unrelenting, his warmth sinking into her, reminding her that she was not alone not in this moment. That realization made her truly come undone.

A sob tore through her throat, silent but violent. Her fingers dug into his shirt, clutching the fabric in a desperate attempt to anchor herself, to keep from unraveling completely. Aezraen tightened his arms around her, pressing his lips to the top of her head not in demand or expectation just there, a steady presence against the storm inside her.

She broke down in the safety of his arms, her body trembling with the intensity of everything she had been holding back: the weight of her mother's death, the blood she had spilled, and the past she had desperately tried to escape. Aezraen held her through it all, enveloped in shadows and silence, offering a sense of solace.

In the quiet between heartbeats, she wondered if she could ever be whole again, or if the cost of unity was the breaking of herself.

Chapter Forty

Two days had passed since Arden's return, and she had barely stirred from Aezraen's chamber. Silence enveloped the room, and Aezraen allowed no one past his threshold. The door remained closed to the world, a barrier between her shattered quiet and the storm brewing outside.

Outside the room, the Court of Shadows held its breath, waiting for the bloodstained girl to rise. Whispers began to creep through the halls as allies arrived, ready to fight under her command.

Aezraen stood vigil, his fury simmering just beneath the surface, holding the world back for as long as he could.

When Elydris summoned them, it felt as if the inevitable had finally emerged from the shadows. Both he and Arden had known this moment was coming; no amount of darkness could stave off the weight of war forever.

Aezraen knelt beside her one last time, gently brushing his hand through her hair. "Rest," he murmured. "No one expects you to face the world today." But even as he spoke, he knew his words weren't entirely true. Understanding had its limits, and patience wore thin with every court that arrived for battle.

As he stepped into the hall, his boots echoed softly against the stone. Though this was his court, his home, and the place where his magic had been bound for centuries, he felt no connection to its walls. The shadows trailed obediently at his heels, but they no longer offered any comfort; instead, they served as a brutal reminder of his chains.

He loathed what they had both become. His transformation had stemmed from greed, his soul twisted by Vaelithara's hands. Arden's fate was no less cruel, chosen by Gods who saw her as a solution to their problems; a weapon to be wielded.

The bitter taste lingered in his throat as he reached the war room.

He opened the doors without hesitation, silencing the ongoing discussions with nothing more than his presence. "She needs more time," he declared, his voice hard and cold.

Elydris' gaze was unwavering. "We have no more." The First King's voice carried the weight of authority and responsibility, devoid of cruelty, but Aezraen bristled as if the words were a blade at his throat.

"She just..." Aezraen stopped himself, raking a hand through his disheveled hair. He struggled to explain to him how Arden had collapsed against him, how she had clung to him, trembling yet silent. She was not ready to face them, not ready for any of this.

Syliris stepped forward cautiously, her voice soft. "If there were even a few more minutes, I would grant them to her." She met Aezraen's gaze, sympathy in her expression. "But there isn't. The other courts have all arrived; they expect her to appear."

Aezraen gritted his teeth as Syliris' words sunk in, the sharp sting of truth embedding itself beneath his skin. She wasn't wrong, but that didn't make it feel right. The thought of forcing Arden into a room filled with those who expected her to lead them in battle when she had only just begun to breathe again twisted something in his chest.

A few days of solitude in his chambers could not restore the girl who had entered the Gilded Court and torn herself apart for them.

Over the last two days he had witnessed the tremor in her fingers and the emptiness in her eyes. That kind of pain didn't just vanish, it lingered.

He turned away from them, pacing the length of the chamber as his shadows surged with agitation, thick and suffocating. His fists clenched and his jaw tightened as grief and fury bloomed within him.

Syliris looked at Aezraen, understanding softening her gaze. "We don't have the luxury of waiting," she said. "The courts are restless, and without Arden's voice at the table, they will begin to question everything we've worked for."

Elydris nodded solemnly. "The realm is in turmoil, and each day Vaelithara creates more troops. War is coming, Aezraen, and Arden has to stand beside us or all of this will have been for nothing."

His jaw clenched, breath shuddering through his teeth as he glared at them both, challenging either to press him further. The silence felt suffocating, like a noose tightening around him. But he knew they were right, this war would not wait for her to piece herself back together.

He closed his eyes, swallowed his pride and fury, and when he finally spoke, his words were heavy with resignation. "If there's no other way," he said, "then I will retrieve her."

Arden sat motionless on the bed, leaning against the headboard with her arms wrapped around her knees, her gaze fixed far beyond the stone walls of Aezraen's chamber. The hearth crackled softly, but its warmth eluded her. Her thoughts were drowned by echoes of her mother's screams, mingling with the laughter of golden-masked partygoers as they tore her apart. Each heartbeat carved the memory deeper. Blood. Laughter. Firelight flickering across cruel smiles as blood splattered across their masks.

Her vision darkened around the edges, like ink spilling across parchment but she didn't resist; she allowed the darkness to claim her. As the shadows enveloped her completely, the room shifted. A hush fell over the space, so complete it felt unnatural. The crackling flames faded to silence, and the air grew still. From the void, Nythis stepped forward.

The Goddess stopped in front of the bed, her presence silent yet undeniable. Cloaked in darkness, her movements were graceful and weightless, as if she were made of smoke. Arden remained silent, drawing her knees tighter to her chest, her chin resting on them, too weary to run, too worn to hide.

Nythis crawled onto the bed silently, the mattress sinking beneath her, though she hardly seemed to touch it. She approached like a mother tending to a wounded child, folding her legs beneath her as she knelt before Arden. One hand reached out, gently brushing tangled strands of hair from Arden's face.

"Shh," the goddess whispered, her voice a soothing lullaby, a breath of wind. "You are safe."

Arden's expression twisted as she jerked back, as if burned, fury breaking through her numbness. "Safe?" Her voice cracked, harsh and broken. "You call this safe?"

Nythis did not flinch at her outburst.

"You let this happen," Arden continued, trembling now. "You made me your pawn. You threw me into the jaws of every court, every monster that calls this realm home. For what? To destroy something *you* helped create?"

The goddess remained silent.

"I've lost everything," Arden whispered. "Callen, my past, myself. You chose me for this... this prophecy, but you never told me what I'd have to become."

Nythis tilted her head, her shadowy form shimmering slightly. "I know," she said finally. "Your anger is understandable, but there is more to the story." Nythis' voice remained low and steady, wrapping around the space like a binding spell. "More than you have seen. More than I am permitted to reveal."

"In time," Nythis continued, brushing her hand lightly over Arden's temple, "you will understand. What you've endured serves a purpose. It is a path that leads to something brighter than you can imagine."

Suddenly, a sound broke the stillness as the door to the chamber creaked open. Arden blinked, and Nythis was gone. The noises of the room returned the fire crackling once again. She gasped softly, breath flooding back into her lungs.

Aezraen stood in the doorway, watching her closely, his eyes burning with unspoken emotion. "It's time," he said, his voice quiet but firm.

For a moment, Arden didn't move. Slowly, she unfolded herself, allowing her feet to touch the ground for the first time in days. The ache in her limbs remained, and grief clung to her like a second skin. Yet the fire that had nearly gone out inside her sparked again.

Even if she was shattered, even if the world had tried to break her apart piece by piece, she would not let Vaelithara win. She would not allow her brother to become another forgotten soul in the God's war.

"I'm ready," Arden whispered. "Whatever she takes from me... I'm ready." She stepped toward the clothes Aezraen had laid out for her, determination ringing in her voice. "This is for Callen."

Chapter Forty-One

The meeting of the court leaders sent a ripple of unease through the already tense halls of the Court of Shadows. Their presence reminded everyone of the fragile alliances they had forged and the centuries of bitterness simmering beneath the surface. The atmosphere was heavy, laden with the weight of impending conflict and long-standing grudges that had festered too long.

At the far end of the room, Ortheon's gaze remained fixed on Syliris. He tracked her every movement, his body coiled tightly, as if anticipating a reason to close the distance between them.

Elydris stood at the head of the large table, his presence unwavering. "The time to act is now," he said, his voice steady and firm. "Vaelithara is forming her army." A murmur swept through the gathered leaders, but Elydris pressed on. "Melisara's spies have confirmed what we suspected. Vaelithara knows of our plans. She knows I am alive."

A hush fell over the chamber; there was no longer room for secrecy. Melisara stepped forward, her voice clear and cold, echoing against the stone walls with undeniable truth. "My spies in the First Court report that Vaelithara still holds the Seraphyne's feather."

She let the silence stretch, allowing unease to settle into their bones. "Even now, she is learning to wield it properly," Melisara continued, her gaze sweeping across the gathered courts. "If we fail, we may not only lose our thrones; we may cease to exist."

Ortheon broke the silence first. "Then what are we waiting for?" He leaned forward, knuckles pressed into the table, his restless energy barely contained. "We march now, or we lose whatever advantage we have left."

Seraphis scanned the room before raising his voice. "Where is the mortal?" he asked, his tone sharp and unyielding. "Where is Arden?"

A murmur rippled through the chamber. Heads turned. The realization spread like wildfire: she was not among them.

"The one chosen by the Gods should be here," growled one of Ortheon's lieutenants. "Has she fled?"

Voices rose in anger, discord swelling like a storm about to break. The gathered leaders argued, accusations flying. Some questioned her loyalty; others doubted her strength, chaos taking root.

From her seat at the table, Melisara began to cackle. Sylara's head snapped toward her, fury igniting in her eyes. "What did you do to her?" she demanded, slamming her hands on the table as she rose.

Elydris raised a hand, his magic pulsing outward like a wave of calm. "Enough," he commanded, steady but forceful. "She is coming. Give her a moment more."

Arden paused as she stood before the doors. Every bargain, scar, and scream echoed through her bones. Her limbs ached, and her spirit felt worn, yet this was the moment she had been preparing for. Taking a slow, deep breath, she recognized that she was not fully ready. The arguments from within reached her ears, and she sensed the tension beyond the doors. But with Aezraen at her back, she knew she had to act for Callen. It was time.

As Arden entered the room, her presence elicited a ripple of whispers among the gathered. She knew her appearance was startling. Dark circles marred the skin beneath her eyes, and although she stood tall, the weight pressing down on her shoulders made her seem on the verge of shattering.

As soon as Sylara laid eyes on her, she gasped, hands flying to her lips. Her magic stirred instinctively, reaching for Arden, curling around her in soft tendrils to provide comfort. The warmth of Sylara's power enveloped Arden's chest, urging her wounds to close, her body to heal, and her soul to find solace.

Arden scoffed, shaking her head slowly, almost in resignation. "There's nothing your magic can fix," she said, her voice strained with exhaustion. It was not her body that was broken; it was something deeper, something beyond Sylara's gifts.

Sylara's hands clenched into fists, her eyes flashing with anger. She turned on Melisara, her delicate features contorted in rage and disbelief. "You've gone too far!" she snapped, her voice trembling with barely contained fury.

Unfazed, Melisara tilted her head, studying Sylara as if amused. "Have I?" she mused, reclining in her chair, a faint smirk gracing her lips. "I seem to recall Arden approaching me. She made her choice."

"You manipulated her!" Sylara accused, stepping forward, her power flaring as the very flowers embroidered into her gown wilted under her distress. "She was desperate, and you exploited that. You always do."

Melisara's eyes narrowed. "Do not confuse desperation with weakness." She flicked her wrist, dismissing Sylara's anger as if brushing dust from her sleeve. "Arden understood the cost when she came to me, and she bears it well."

Arden remained silent during their exchange, refraining from argument. She stood with an unreadable expression, as though she were not entirely present. The weight of her decisions felt like iron chains, and she could still feel the blood on her hands, despite it long being washed away.

Elydris moved to stand behind her, placing a reassuring hand on her shoulder. "This is not the time for petty disputes," he said, his gaze sweeping across the room. "We did not gather here to fight amongst ourselves."

Before he could continue, Arden spoke. "I didn't do all of this for us to fall apart now."

The room turned toward her. Her gaze hovered near the table, not quite ready to meet theirs. "I broke myself for this alliance. I bargained with those who sought to break me just to bring us all here." Her hands trembled slightly at her sides, but she didn't try to hide it. "I did it... because I believed we could stand together."

She lifted her head then, her voice soft but resolute. "You don't have to trust each other. But you need to trust me. Because if we face her divided, we lose. Which would mean everything I've sacrificed... will mean nothing."

Elydris nodded, his expression grim yet approving. One by one, the leaders nodded in agreement.

Ortheon revealed a grin. "The Court of Beasts does not shy away from a confrontation. We march with Arden."

Seraphis smirked, rolling his shoulders as if already anticipating the forthcoming battle. "It has been some time since I encountered a war worth engaging in."

Elydris exhaled slowly, then nodded once. It was settled. "At dawn, we ride."

Chapter Forty-Two

On the eve of battle, the Court of Shadows was shrouded in an uneasy stillness. The familiar darkness felt more oppressive, as if the walls were holding their breath, bracing for the impending dawn. Arden sat by the window in Aezraen's chambers, tracing the swirling patterns of condensation on the glass. Outside, the moon hung low, casting everything in shades of silver and black.

Aezraen sat across from her, perched on the edge of the table. He looked exhausted, not just from the war or the burden of caring for her, but from everything. Centuries spent as Vaelithara's pawn, fighting for memories that were never his, and failed attempts to reshape his destiny weighed heavily on him. His shadows curled around him listlessly, devoid of their usual sharpness.

"You've been unusually quiet since the meeting," he remarked, studying her intently.

Arden exhaled, pressing her forehead against the cool glass. "I'm just processing everything."

Aezraen offered a faint smirk that lacked genuine humor. "That dire, is it?"

She turned to him, noting the dark circles beneath his eyes and the fatigue that clung to him. "Tomorrow," she said quietly. "We either die at the hands of a murderous queen who wants complete control of this world..." She looked toward the floor, "...or we survive. Whatever that means for Elessian."

"I assume Elydris will claim his throne again," he replied quietly, swirling the amber liquid in his glass. "Syliris as his heir, training to be the future queen."

Silence enveloped them, heavy with unspoken words. Arden glanced at her hands, noting the faint golden marks left by Aeltherion's magic. She felt caught between worlds, neither of which seemed to want her.

Aezraen's gaze swept over her. "You did it, you know?"

She tilted her head, a questioning look on her face. "Did what?"

He leaned forward, resting his elbows on his knees. "You survived."

"Did I?" she asked softly, more to herself than to him. "Sometimes I question that."

"When this is over..." she paused. "...is our bargain still binding?"

She stammered, trying to convey her thoughts. "I just mean..."

"With Vaelithara no longer controlling my actions, does our bargain dissolve?" There was no anger in his voice, only understanding.

She had bled for the courts and broken herself to unify them, but when the war was over, none of it would matter if Callen remained in danger, whether mortal or fae.

"I'm not sure. I've wondered myself...if I would still be fae. Or if the Gods would strip me of a title that was never meant to be mine."

She met his gaze, and for the first time in a long while, she saw something raw beneath his carefully crafted facade. "Melisara shattered a big part of me," Arden admitted, her voice hollow. "I know Vaelithara did the same to you. We are ghosts of ourselves now."

He chuckled darkly. "So poetic, that we continue to haunt each other."

She tilted her head. "Do you regret any of it?"

Aezraen considered this for a moment. "Regret? No." His voice was quiet yet resolute. "However, I do pity our fates."

Arden laughed softly, shaking her head. "Pity? That's even worse."

His lips curled into a semblance of a smile that vanished all too quickly. "I'm sorry I used Callen against you...to force your hand."

Arden sighed. "I don't think the Gods would have let you choose. If it wasn't you, something else would have brought me here by force."

Aezraen then stood and crossed the space between them. He knelt before her, reaching for her hands; his touch was cool yet grounding. "Regardless..."

Arden swallowed hard, squeezing his hands. Both were profoundly broken and lost, yet in this moment, they felt almost whole. They sat together in silence, the weight of the impending dawn pressing down upon them. No words remained to be spoken, no further wounds to inflict. Only the night, the darkness, and each other lingered at the precipice of the war that would determine their fates.

The Court of Shadows stirred before the first light of dawn. The air was thick with tension, a hushed anticipation woven into the stillness of the halls. Arden sat at the window, her fingers pressed against the cool metal of Aeltherion. Its weight had never felt heavier. Beyond the windows, the sky remained cloaked in darkness, yet the world was awakening, preparing for what was to come.

Elydris stood on his balcony, surveying the assembled army. His eyes burned with determination, though he said nothing. There was no need for words; they all understood the stakes. At his side, Syliris adjusted the leather straps of her armor, her expression inscrutable. Yet, when she gazed toward the horizon, toward the court she had once called home, her jaw tightened.

When Kastiel and Byron sounded the horns, Arden watched as Syliris and Elydris withdrew inside. Arden made her own way down to the courtyard, the halls empty around her. Outside, the camps buzzed with murmurs and final preparations. Soldiers checked their weapons, tightened their armor, and whispered quiet prayers to the Gods. The distant clang of metal against metal echoed through the fortress as warriors tested their blades one last time. This was not merely another battle; this was the reckoning.

Aezraen remained silent as he secured his sword to his hip, his movements precise and methodical. He had spent lifetimes chasing after ghosts, searching for meaning amid the chaos left by Vaelithara. Today, he would finally confront the one who had bound him to this fate. His fingers tightened around the hilt of his blade, his breath steady despite the fire igniting in his chest.

Veylis leaned against a courtyard wall, observing as those around him prepared for battle. A rare stillness accompanied his gaze, a seriousness that felt foreign to his features. "I suppose this is it," he murmured, tilting his head toward Arden as she approached. "All our little war games coming together in a single, final act." He grinned, but there was no warmth in it. "What a shame we won't all make it out alive."

Arden ignored him and stepped forward, addressing the crowd of gathered leaders and soldiers. The weight of their gazes pressed against her, yet she stood firm. "This is our last chance," she stated, her voice steady. "If anyone wishes to withdraw, now is the time."

No one moved.

Elydris stepped into the courtyard, his golden armor gleaming in the candlelight. Syliris was right behind him, wearing an outfit resembling the leathers Ortheon and his soldiers wore.

"The plan remains unchanged. We will strike as one, forcing Vaelithara to divide her forces. The Court of Beasts and the Court of Embers will lead the charge." His gaze swept across the assembly. "Today is a day that will be written about for centuries to come..." Elydris paused and looked around.

"Make it count."

Arden turned her gaze toward the horizon as the first sliver of light began to pierce the darkness. The dawn of battle had arrived. Whatever lay ahead, there was no turning back.

Chapter Forty-Three

The army advanced silently toward the First Court, tension palpable as they approached an empty field where soldiers should have awaited them.

"My spies are never wrong," Melisara broke the stillness. "She knew we were coming."

"So where is her army?" Elydris inquired.

Arden's unease deepened as their footsteps stirred only dust. The wide, open path to the First Court felt too easy, too still. Aezraen's shadows slithered beneath their boots, curling like warnings. Arden focused on her task: seeking illusions.

The air was taut, the silence sharp. Even the youngest soldiers sensed it; this was not the calm before a storm, but a trap lying in wait.

Arden signaled for Noctis to move to the front line, her posture tense. Every breath felt too loud, every heartbeat a countdown. She exchanged glances with Elydris and Aezraen, both wearing the same grim expression.

Ortheon sat atop a massive brown bear, his beasts running and flying ahead. A low growl echoed unnaturally through the field, a warning. He raised a fist. "Stop," he commanded, his voice slicing through the tension.

Aezraen appeared at his side moments later. "Why are we stopping?"

"They're unsettled," Ortheon replied, nodding toward the massive predators. "Their hackles are raised. Something isn't right."

Aezraen closed his eyes and pressed his palm to the earth. Shadows surged around him, dancing across the terrain like ink on parchment. He whispered ancient words, the language of darkness and secrets, allowing the shadows to reveal what he could not see. The ground pulsed with hidden magic that mirrored his own.

His eyes snapped open. "We're not in the First Court," he declared. "It's a veil. This entire field is cloaked in shadow illusion. I can overpower it, but it will take time."

"Stay vigilant," Ortheon muttered, drawing his blade.

"You too," Aezraen replied, summoning Kastiel for assistance.

"Arden..."

The whisper was barely audible, yet it rang in her ears like a scream.

"Arden... help me..."

"Callen?" she breathed. Noctis shifted beneath her, sensing her rising panic. Her vision blurred, the edges swimming as the voice echoed again, frantic and desperate. She spun in place, scanning the field, but no one else reacted. No one else seemed to care.

"Please..."

She urged Noctis into motion.

"Arden, stop!" Aezraen shouted, his voice cutting through the stillness like a blade.

But she was already gone.

Noctis leaped forward, the world blurring around them. All she could hear was her brother's voice; frantic, terrified, but alive.

"Hurry up!" Ortheon yelled, commanding his beasts to follow.

Aezraen and Kastiel worked to dispel the illusions cloaking the area. The ground beneath Arden shimmered as magic twisted in the air and reality rippled. Noctis stumbled as they broke through the illusion, skidding to a halt. They were no longer in an empty field.

Arden's heart raced as she surveyed the transformed space. The sky above was split and bleeding silver, and the trees stood frozen, blackened and twisted. At the center of it all stood the queen herself.

Vaelithara smiled. "Welcome home, child."

In one hand, she held the Seraphyne's feather, pulsing with light and shimmering in blue and silver hues as it bled time into the air.

Behind Arden, the ground erupted with a roar, silver light splitting the earth. A wall of power surged upward, a tidal wave of magic that severed her from the army. Noctis vanished, as if he had never been there at all.

Arden fell, hitting the ground with a jolting pain as she saw hundreds of soldiers materialize from the haze. Armor clanged as they approached her army behind the barrier, and battle broke out in full force.

Arden drew her blade as she rose from the ground, breath ragged. She was in this alone.

Vaelithara was relentless. Each clash sent sparks into the air, but Arden's blackened dagger never landed true. Every time she found an opening, Vaelithara slipped away. The queen moved through time like smoke, repositioning mid-swing and reappearing behind Arden with a cruel laugh and a glint in her eyes that said: *You are nothing.*

"You've come far," Vaelithara murmured between strikes, circling like a predator. "But you were never meant to win this war, girl."

She raised the Seraphyne's feather, and the sky pulsed with a burst of shimmering blue magic. It erupted from her hand and spiraled across the battlefield as the world stuttered.

Time fractured around them.

Arden screamed as the army that had marched behind her began to fall in impossible ways. Some collapsed before blades reached them. Others moved too slowly, their weapons frozen in the air while enemies sliced through them like shadows. Some vanished entirely, blinked out of the timeline as if they had never existed.

Arden turned, horrified.

"No, no, no, stop!" she shouted, running from Vaelithara, Aeltherion humming with power that she fought to control. The queen did not follow, but her magic did. It chased Arden in twisting ribbons of light, dragging at her limbs, trying to pull her back.

"SIERATH!" Arden screamed. "I need you! Please..."

Another burst of blue light tore through the ground beside her. She watched as a soldier disintegrated mid-step, his sword dropping to the dirt before his body even hit the ground.

The feather's power ripped holes through time, turning the battlefield into a graveyard of paradoxes. She stumbled to her knees, gasping, and the magic caught her again. It coiled around her ankle like a tether, dragging her back toward the queen.

"SIERATH!" she howled, the name tearing from her throat.

She clawed at the ground, trying to resist the queen's magic. Desperately, she fought to control her emotions so she could use Aeltherion as Elydris had taught her.

Suddenly, everything around her froze. A voice spoke softly, sorrowfully, as if it had always existed within the new silence. "You call, and I answer."

Sierath materialized before her like a dream, garbed in robes that shimmered like ripples across still water. His expression was grave, his eyes ancient and endlessly sad.

"Will you bear my burden?" he asked. "To mend what she has broken, your soul must stretch across the cracks."

"I'll do whatever it takes," Arden said without hesitation. "Just... just stop this."

The sky above them splintered like glass, thin veins of white light cutting across the dark. Soldiers stood frozen mid-strike, magic stalled in half-bloom. Nothing moved but them.

Sierath's fingers brushed hers. "You will need to give me access to your power."

Arden closed her eyes and reached inward. She found the well of her power, the threads of Aeltherion humming in her blood, and she gave it freely.

Sierath's eyes glowed as his hands lifted, and with their combined magic, he turned to the sky. Threads of silver and gold extended from his fingers like stitches across a wound. He wove them into the broken tapestry of time, pulling the fractured pieces back together.

The Seraphyne's feather pulsed before igniting into flame, curling in on itself until only ash remained. Reality shuddered. The blue magic disintegrated, and slowly, time began to resume.

"I hope you know what you're doing," he said before disappearing.

Arden took a steadying breath as the wall separating her from her army disintegrated. Soldiers inhaled and the ground shifted. The ripple of motion returned like a wave washing over the battlefield.

Vaelithara's expression twisted. She stared at her empty hand, the place where the feather had been. Her eyes met Arden's and rage, pure and unfiltered, bled through her expression.

As time resumed its flow, Vaelithara's shriek pierced the air, echoing across the battlefield with raw fury, shaking the ground beneath their feet. She clenched her fists, silver light flaring around her in a violent storm.

"No!" she roared, unleashing a surge of magic that pulsed outward like wildfire. Wherever it touched, soldiers were flung back, trees splintered, and the earth cracked open.

Yet Arden's army did not waver; they surged forward.

Ortheon's beasts were the first to regain their momentum, howling as they crashed into the front lines of Vaelithara's army. Their fangs found weak points in the twisted armor of her soldiers, tearing through steel with ease. Ortheon himself fought like a storm made flesh, blazing with primal magic, leading the charge with unrelenting fury.

Behind him, Seraphis's warriors moved in disciplined formation, flanking the chaos with precise, brutal strikes. Their battle-forged blades sang through the air, cutting down enemies in rhythm with war-drums. Flames danced at their heels, igniting the ground where Vaelithara's magic had tried to take root.

Sierath's influence lingered, scattering her foresight and distorting the future she clung to. Her soldiers stumbled through broken visions, unable to predict their enemies' attacks, and in that confusion, the Hollow Court pressed forward, soldiers collapsing in their wake like shattered glass.

Amidst the chaos, Sylara's magic wove through the bloodshed, knitting wounds together. Vines erupted from the ground at her command, shielding the fallen as she attempted to repair what she could. With a wave of her hand, golden blossoms burst into the air, releasing clouds of healing magic that swept over the wounded. Where her light touched, breath returned to stilled lungs, gashes sealed, and bones mended.

But not all could be saved.

Aezraen stumbled over the crumpled form of Kastiel. Blood pooled beneath him, soaking into the cracked earth, and his skin had already turned cold. "No..." Aezraen knelt beside him, gripping his shoulders. "Kastiel, wake up. Get up!"

There was no answer.

For a moment, the battle around him faded away. There was only the scent of iron, the crackle of fading shadows, and the knowledge that Vaelithara had stolen one more thing from him.

Rage surged within him.

Aezraen rose, and the shadows rose with him.

He tore through the battlefield, his magic lashing out in sharp, brutal arcs. Every enemy he struck fell without a sound. He didn't stop to breathe or mourn; he fought for vengeance.

At the center of it all, Arden faced Vaelithara. She moved with purpose now, her strikes no longer wild. Every blow was measured, every dodge a memory of training with Elydris. The battlefield faded around her; it was just them the First Fae Queen and a mortal, two paths twisted into inevitable collision.

Aeltherion's magic blazed in her hands, the crown reacting to her fury, pain, and purpose. For the first time, Vaelithara seemed afraid. Arden landed a blow of gold and silver magic that knocked Vaelithara to the ground. Anger burned in her heart as she prepared to end the battle once and for all, but she paused when she saw Elydris step in behind her.

His hand tangled in her hair, yanking her backward. She stumbled, her magic faltering, unsure of his intentions. In his other hand was a blade she had never seen him wield before. His face was twisted in grief, his eyes brimming with unshed tears.

"We were supposed to rule together," he whispered, pressing the blade to her throat. "Day and Night. Two parts of the same whole. But the realm has Syliris now. The best of both of us. It doesn't need us anymore."

Vaelithara choked on a laugh, her eyes wild. "You were never strong enough."

"I loved you, Vaelithara... I *truly* loved you."

Tears slid down his cheeks. "And that's why I have to let you go."

With one clean motion, he sliced through her throat.

The light in her eyes flickered as her body crumpled to the ground.

The world shuddered as her magic began to seep from the realm, bleeding into the soil, the sky, and the veins of power she once controlled.

For a moment, the battlefield stood still in disbelief. Vaelithara's body lay crumpled at Elydris' feet, her lifeblood seeping into the cracked earth, her magic unraveling into the sky like smoke fleeing a fire. The corruption that had once gripped the land began to fade. Trees exhaled. The skies lightened. The pressure choking the realm began to ease.

Vaelithara's reign was truly over.

Chapter Forty-Four

The battlefield trembled, dust and magic hanging in the air, but Arden didn't care. As soon as Vaelithara's presence vanished, she took off running.

Her breath came in ragged gasps, her heart pounding as she raced across the field, scanning the bodies, the wounded, the fallen. "Callen!" she screamed, desperation hoarsening her voice. She stumbled over shattered armor, pushing past healers and soldiers, panic clawing at her throat.

Frantically, she searched, tearing aside corpses and examining every person who even remotely resembled her brother. But he was nowhere to be found.

"Callen!" she shouted again, her voice raw and her throat burning. Her trembling hands were smeared with blood and dirt, and her vision began to blur. Where was he? He should be here. He had to be here.

A firm grip caught her around the waist, halting her frantic search.

Aezraen's arm wrapped securely around her, anchoring her to the present. "He's not here," he said, his voice steady yet gentle. "Arden, stop. He's not on the battlefield."

She twisted in his grasp, wild-eyed. "Then where? Where is he?"

Aezraen's jaw tightened as he gazed toward the ruined remnants of the First Court's castle. "The lower cells," he murmured. "Vaelithara would have kept him close. If he's still alive, he'll be down there."

Before Arden could respond, shadows enveloped them.

The battlefield vanished, replaced by the cold, damp stone of the First Court's dungeon. The air was thick with mildew and despair, the scent of rot clinging to every surface. Flickering torches cast weak, trembling light along the corridor of cells, each one filled with forgotten prisoners.

This place was nothing like the cell Vaelithara had kept Arden in. While she had torches to keep shadows at bay and windows to let in air, there was no comfort here no attempt to soften the suffering. The darkness pressed in from all sides, suffocating and absolute, broken only by the occasional groan of stone or a cough that echoed like a death rattle. The rot wasn't just in the walls; it seeped into Arden's skin.

Aezraen led her forward, his footsteps eerily silent against the stone. In the farthest corner of a cell, huddled in tattered, filthy rags, was her brother. "Callen," Arden whispered, her breath catching.

The sight stole the breath from her lungs. His frame had withered, his skin a sickly pale, and his wrists were bruised from whatever restraints had held him. But when she stepped forward, his head snapped up, and the fear in his eyes shattered her.

"Callen," she tried again, reaching for the bars.

His entire body flinched, pressing deeper into the corner as if trying to disappear into the stone itself. His hands curled tightly into his tattered clothing, and his breath came in ragged gasps. "Go away," he rasped, bitterness lacing his voice. "Just go away."

She recoiled as if struck. "It's me," she pleaded. "It's Arden. Callen, please, you're safe now..."

"NO!" he screamed, his voice raw and broken. "Go away! I don't want you here!"

Arden staggered back, the force of his rejection knocking the breath from her lungs.

Aezraen was at her side instantly, watching Callen with a guarded expression. "It's been a lot for him," he said quietly. "I know how he feels; Vaelithara ripped him from his world and..." he trailed off, leaving the rest unspoken.

Arden swallowed hard. "I...I have to..."

"We don't know exactly what she did to him," Aezraen continued, his voice steady. "He needs time. He needs space." He turned to her, shadows curling protectively around them both. "I'll take care of him," he promised. "But you should go."

Arden stared at her brother, trembling in the darkness, his eyes filled with fear.

She had fought for him. Bled for him. Killed for him. A hollow ache spread through her chest, but she nodded, her voice barely a whisper. "Take care of him."

Aezraen inclined his head, already stepping into the shadows, beyond the bars.

Arden turned away, forcing herself up the damp stone steps and emerging into the ruined remnants of the First Court's throne room, where Elydris and the others waited.

Aezraen sighed, kneeling beside the shattered man on the floor. "Callen?"

Callen shook but didn't answer. "You don't have to see her if you don't want to," Aezraen continued, leaning against the door. "But you should know, she never stopped thinking of you. She fought through hell for you."

Silence stretched between them before Callen replied, "She shouldn't have."

Aezraen sighed. "That's not how it works." He hesitated, choosing his words carefully. "I know this has all been a lot, but you're not alone in this. You don't have to understand any of it right now. But at least… come upstairs. See her."

The silence lingered. Then the door creaked open just enough for Aezraen to glimpse Callen's wary expression. His hands trembled at his sides, yet he stepped forward. "Fine," he said, his voice hoarse and weary. "But I'm not promising anything."

When Aezraen stepped through the cell bars, Veylis was waiting. His violet eyes caught on the figure uncurling from the corner. There was something in the way Callen held himself shoulders tight, hands clenched in his lap, gaze flickering between shadows that pulled at something long-buried in Veylis' chest. He recognized that look: the quiet panic, the guarded silence, the ache of not knowing where you belonged anymore.

It felt too familiar, too much like someone he had once watched fade away, piece by piece.

Aezraen held out a hand to Callen, using his magic to allow him to pass through the bars like a shadow. Veylis exhaled slowly and stepped closer, his usual smirk softened into something quieter, more honest.

"I hear you're without a proper place to stay," he said, voice low but steady. "I'd like to offer you one."

Callen looked skeptical. "Why would you do that?"

"I see something in you I recognize, and I don't think you should have to figure all of this out alone."

"Where would I go?"

"The Hollow Court," Veylis replied simply. "My private wing. No courtesans. No prying eyes. Just... quiet. So you can recuperate." He tilted his head. "I lost someone once, someone I would have done anything to bring back. I don't know what you need right now, but I'd be honored to provide you a space to figure that out."

Callen hesitated, studying him carefully. Finally, he nodded, though he said nothing.

Veylis smiled as he wrapped an arm around Callen and helped him up the stairs.

Callen winced at the sunlight, and something in Arden's chest broke apart. She spared him a small smile. "I can't wait..."

"Stop." He cut her off, not allowing her to finish. "I haven't come to terms with any of this yet, Arden... I need time. You're... different now."

Arden was taken aback, pain in her gaze as her brother appraised what she had become.

"I don't know when I'll be ready... but I'll let you know."

Arden was still processing Callen's words when he turned away, his shoulders trembling. "I'm leaving."

Veylis was already waiting, and Callen walked toward him without hesitation. Arden stood frozen, numb, as Callen disappeared through the front doors, leaving her by choice this time.

Aezraen watched them go, then turned back to Arden, concern etched on his face. "He just needs time "

"Go with them," Arden whispered.

Aezraen hesitated. "Arden..."

"I never want to see you again." Her voice was hollow, lifeless. "Go."

Aezraen didn't argue. He stepped back, shadows curling around him, and then he was gone too.

Leaving Arden alone with the ruin she had created.

Chapter Forty-Five

E lydris approached Arden, his presence steady as he placed a reassuring hand on her shoulder. "I know this is hard for you, but..."

"Please don't try to convince me that this is somehow going to be okay."

"Then I won't. But you are strong, Arden. Never forget that."

With slow, deliberate steps, Elydris ascended the shattered stairs to the throne. He knelt before the throne of bone that Vaelithara had created and, using his magic, restored it to its former glory. He sat down, feeling the weight of duty settle upon him.

The crown on Arden's head hummed with magic, calling to him in a way she could not ignore. She approached Elydris, removing Aeltherion and handing it to him. When he rested Aeltherion upon his head, the world seemed to breathe a sigh of relief.

The First Court had a ruler once more.

The grand hall felt heavy with the weight of victory; the air was charged with lingering magic and the silent echoes of a world reborn. Yet, amidst the shifting tides of power, one farewell remained unspoken.

At the foot of the throne, Syliris took a deep breath before stepping forward. Her gaze, reminiscent of her father's, shimmered with something softer; not duty or obligation, but the quiet certainty of a decision long made. She curtsied before her father, the ruler who had fought and bled to reclaim his throne.

When she straightened, Ortheon stood beside her.

The Primal Lord was not a man of courtly elegance. He had never bowed or yielded; he was an untamed storm, a relentless hunter, living by the laws of the wild, where strength triumphed and submission was seen as weakness. But Syliris reached for his hand, squeezing gently. No words passed between them, only a silent plea.

His jaw tightened, muscles tensing as his body resisted even as his heart softened. With a quiet exhale, Ortheon knelt before the king. Elydris' eyes flickered with understanding; he had known Ortheon long before the war and had fought beside him. Yet for Syliris, the wildest of men bent his knee.

Syliris turned back to her father, her voice steady but tinged with emotion. "I do not wish to rule," she said, her truth pouring out. "I never have. My place is not here, bound to a duty my heart despises. My place is with Ortheon, among the untamed lands of the Court of Beasts."

A heavy stillness enveloped the hall.

Then Elydris stood and descended the steps of his throne with measured grace, the weight of centuries pressing upon him. He halted before them, gazing at the daughter who had finally found her true home. One hand rested on Syliris' shoulder while the other grasped Ortheon's arm, strong and steady.

He then pulled them both into an embrace.

There were no grand speeches, no formalities; only the quiet weight of a father's love, a warrior's acceptance, and the final farewell of a king.

When he released them, his golden eyes met Ortheon's, heavy with meaning. "Treat her well."

Ortheon's lips curved into a grin. "With my life."

Satisfied, Elydris stepped back, lifting his hand in silent blessing.

With one last glance at the court they were leaving behind, Syliris and Ortheon turned and walked together toward the massive doors, stepping beyond the stone walls and the heavy legacy of the First Court.

"What will you do now?" Elydris asked Arden.

Arden barely heard the murmurs of the remaining court leaders or felt the presence of those surrounding her, waiting and watching. They all awaited her decision.

"I want to return home."

She had fought for this. She had bled for it, sacrificed, lost, and given up more than she ever thought possible. The war was over, yet her personal battle continued.

Aezraen was gone.

Callen had left her.

She was alone.

Her throat tightened as the weight of reality settled in. She felt too numb to mourn, too hollow to grasp the full impact of her losses. The absence of them was suffocating; she had fought fiercely and held on tightly, only for both to slip from her grasp.

She had always imagined this moment would feel different, that it would bring relief and clarity to guide her forward. But standing there, asking the fae king for freedom, Arden felt nothing but exhaustion.

Sierath's voice echoed through the room. "That is no longer an option."

Everyone turned to him, and questions murmured throughout the hall.

"Speak your peace, Sierath."

"When you lent me your power to heal the realm, I warned you there was a cost."

Arden nodded slowly, remembering his words.

"Your soul is now a piece of Elessian. You may be free from Aezraen's bargain, but you cannot leave."

The room erupted into a haze of voices, all talking over each other. Elydris' voice cut through the noise. "You have a place here," he said, his tone measured and careful. "If you choose it."

Arden swallowed and shifted her gaze to him. She had spent so much time following, reacting, and surviving. But what was she supposed to do now? The weight of expectation pressed down on her. The eyes of the courts, of Elydris, of the realm itself, all awaited her answer.

But she hesitated.

"You have fae magic within you. I need an heir to my throne. Without Vaelithara, I do not know how much longer the Gods will let me rule."

The First Court was hers if she wanted it. She could take the throne, guide the realm toward balance, and forge a new era from the ashes of destruction. She could lead. But was that the life she truly wanted?

Aezraen had once asked her long ago what she truly wanted; not what duty required, not what fate had predetermined, but what she desired for herself.

She had never found the answer.

It would be easy to step forward, to take the seat beside Elydris, and let the courts mold her into the queen they desired. But she had never wanted to be a queen. She had never wanted to be tied to anything.

She glanced at the empty space where Aezraen might have stood.

Her heart clenched, but she pushed the thought aside.

She had made her choice.

Finally, she lifted her chin and met Elydris' gaze. "Then teach me to rule." She had no answers yet, no certainty. But she could learn.

Elydris inclined his head, understanding passing between them without a word.

Chapter Forty-Six

The months that followed were filled with activity as Arden wandered the realm she had nearly sacrificed herself to save. The land felt different now. Vaelithara's corruption had dissipated, but the scars remained. Forests gradually regrew, rivers carved new paths, and the fractured, weary courts began to rebuild.

As she passed through small villages on the outskirts of the courts, people whispered her name. Soldiers bowed, children stared, yet she felt like a ghost in her own body, caught between the mortal girl who had once stolen bread to survive and the future queen destined to bear the weight of Elessian's crown.

She and Elydris never discussed Vaelithara's final moments, and Arden kept silent about how the shadows of Melisara's court still haunted her in her dreams.

But on some nights, when the wind grew still and the stars stitched their way across the sky like ancient threads, she would lie back and listen, trying to unravel the strands of the prophecy that loomed over her.

It was during one of those nights, with the scent of moss and ash clinging to the air, that the wind shifted. The stillness bent. The sky trembled, and Sierath appeared.

At first, she thought it was a dream. He emerged at the edge of the clearing like a ripple of forgotten time, his form glimmering between solid and spectral. His robes sparkled like broken glass, refracting the moonlight around him. He was not still, but had never been. He shifted with each breath, a being composed of moments suspended in time.

Arden sat up, heart pounding, breath caught halfway between fear and reverence.

He said nothing at first, only gazed at her with eyes that held a thousand futures. When he finally spoke, his voice was as soft as the wind through the trees. "It's time, Arden."

She swallowed, her pulse quickening. "Time for what?"

Sierath tilted his head, his expression unreadable. "Come see what fate has woven for you."

Arden hesitated. Every part of her ached with fatigue, but deep down, she knew this was the moment she had been moving toward. Slowly, she stood, her bare feet pressing into the soft grass as she stepped toward him. The world shifted and blurred, and when the fog lifted, everything changed.

The first image hit her like lightning. It was so vivid it left her breathless.

She and Aezraen lay together in a sun-drenched room, wrapped in tangled sheets. There was no grief on their faces, no war in their hearts. Only peace. He was beside her, tracing lazy circles along her ribs, placing soft kisses along her throat as she laughed, the sound so light and free that it didn't feel like her own voice. This was joy in its purest form.

Aezraen smiled like a man who had finally come home. There was no darkness behind his eyes, only warmth. No weight pressing on his shoulders. Just the two of them, alive and whole.

The vision shifted.

She stood beside him in a bustling market square in the First Court. The streets were once again vibrant, vendors cheerfully calling out as spices, bread, and flowers filled the air with their scents. Callen walked just ahead, animatedly pointing at something in a nearby stall. Arden held Aezraen's hand, their fingers intertwined. He plucked an apple from a basket and handed it to her with a soft grin, brushing a kiss across her forehead.

Children raced past, their laughter echoing through the square. One of them dashed straight into Aezraen's path. He caught her easily, spinning her in a circle, his shadows flaring gently in play. The little girl shrieked with delight, and Arden found herself laughing too, watching him in wonder. She saw Callen nearby, talking to a vendor, healthy and safe, his eyes bright and full of life.

Then another shift.

The sun dipped low over a quiet field. It was peaceful, golden light turning the grass into a sea of amber. Aezraen stepped behind her, sliding his arms around her waist, his touch grounding and steady. The breeze stirred her hair as he pressed closer.

His hand moved to her stomach, resting there gently.

"I can't wait," he whispered.

Her breath caught as time stilled.

The vision shattered. Arden gasped and stumbled as it broke apart around her, slipping away like sand through her fingers, vanishing into darkness. She returned to herself with a jolt, her chest heaving, the memory of warmth fading too quickly to hold onto.

Her hands flew to her stomach, trembling fingers pressed against her abdomen, yearning to feel the life that had yet to come into being.

Her mind reeled. The warmth of Aezraen's touch, the soft, golden morning light, the laughter had felt so real. More than a glimpse of fate, it had been a promise of what was to come. She turned wildly, searching for the presence that had guided her here. Sierath stood at the edge of her vision, his form flickering, shifting in and out of time. His knowing gaze met hers, a faint smile curving his lips.

"You will name him after your father," he murmured, his voice echoing with certainty. "You will have a happy life."

Arden's breath hitched. She opened her mouth to question, to demand more, but before she could form the words, Sierath faded, dissolving into the wind, leaving only silence.

Her heart pounded as she grounded herself in reality once more. She knew she needed to find him, to apologize for sending him away. Her feet barely touched the ground as she sprinted through the narrow passages of the ley lines, her vision blurring. She didn't care who saw her or who tried to stop her.

She would find him.

Arden's power surged around her, raw and unrestrained, warping the space between her and the Court of Shadows as she propelled herself forward. The familiar darkness loomed in the distance, but she couldn't reach it fast enough. Her heart raced, and her breaths came in sharp, frantic gasps.

The ley lines spat her out into the market square of the main court. The streets were flooded with people trying to finish their shopping before closing. They stepped aside, startled by her presence, but Arden hardly noticed them. She searched frantically, her eyes darting from face to face, shadow to shadow, a gnawing fear creeping into her thoughts. What if she was too late? What if he didn't want her now?

She spotted him just beyond a bakery, his back to her, shadows curling around his feet like restless ghosts. Even from a distance, she could see he had changed. He seemed lighter, more at ease, like a man who had finally stopped running.

Arden calmed her frayed emotions as she approached him, contemplating what to say. He turned just as she reached him, surprise flickering across his face before quickly shifting to shock. She threw herself into his arms, the breath knocked from her lungs as she wrapped her arms around his waist, holding on as if she might vanish if she let go. The feel and scent of him hit her all at once, familiar and overwhelming.

Aezraen staggered slightly, caught between disbelief and instinct. Then, slowly, his arms enveloped her, pulling her tightly against his chest. He buried his face in the crook of her neck, his breath ragged and uneven, filled with disbelief and something more fragile.

There were no words, not yet. Just the fierce press of bodies, a desperate, silent confirmation that neither was dreaming. His grip was bruising, as if he feared that letting go would mean losing her all over again. Arden clung to him just as fiercely, her fingers twisting into his shirt, holding on as if the world might end. She felt his heart thunder beneath his ribs, matching her own frantic rhythm. It wasn't enough; it would never be enough, but it was real.

Aezraen pulled back just enough to see her, cradling her face with his hands, his thumbs brushing over her cheekbones. His gaze swept over her, searching, trying to memorize every detail.

Her lips parted as if to speak, but he interrupted. "You came back," he breathed, his voice raw and hoarse, filled with disbelief.

Arden couldn't respond; words failed her. Instead, she surged forward, pressing her lips to his.

The kiss was desperate and raw, infused with every moment they had lost, every promise left unspoken. It was fire and fury, love and sorrow; the taste of the past mingled with a demand for a future.

Time blurred, and nothing else mattered. The press of his body, the warmth of his touch, and the way he kissed her as if she were the only thing that ever mattered consumed them.

When they finally pulled away, they didn't let go. Their foreheads pressed together, breaths mingling, bodies entwined in desperation. For the first time in a long time, neither of them had to be alone.

Chapter Forty-Seven

The mirrored throne room of the Court of Echoes existed in a constant state of motion, its surfaces reflecting and shifting, whispering fragments of both past and future.

Sierath lounged on his throne, his form wavering between solidity and shadow, never fully present nor entirely absent. The room pulsed with power, as if the walls breathed in sync with his thoughts. He sensed the disturbance without needing to turn his head; he was no longer alone.

The mirrors around him trembled as reality bent and twisted with the arrival of an unfamiliar force. Kairon, the God of Time, emerged from the breach, his presence so commanding that even the chaotic echoes stilled in his wake. Where Sierath was fluid and unpredictable, Kairon was rigid and unyielding; a keeper of destiny's threads. Sierath could feel his anger in the air.

"You meddled."

Sierath merely tilted his head, his expression a lazy mask of amusement. He had anticipated this; predictability was one of Kairon's defining traits.

"You showed her what she was never meant to see," Kairon continued, his voice resonating with the weight of millennia. The air crackled around him, time itself shifting uneasily in response to his anger. "Do you have any idea what you've done?"

A slow smile spread across Sierath's lips. "Of course I do. I see every thing... Even when I don't want to."

Kairon advanced, his footsteps fracturing the mirrored floor, shattering futures before they could materialize. "Then you knowingly disrupted fate. You altered the course of what was meant to be."

Sierath stretched, unfazed. "Altered? No, no. I simply provided a glimpse. A small mercy to a child you all have been playing with for years."

"Mercy?" Kairon spat the word like poison. "You call disrupting the balance of destiny mercy? You allowed her to see a life that will never be."

Sierath exhaled slowly and rose, his form remaining insubstantial; a flicker of a being caught between present and past. "But it's the future I wanted her to have."

Kairon stiffened. The weight of those words settled between them like a stone dropped into an endless void. He had suspected Sierath of manipulating fate for his amusement, but this...

This was intentional.

"What are you playing at, Sierath?" Kairon's voice dropped, quieter yet more dangerous. It resonated with finality, the slow ticking of a thousand clocks winding down. "What have you done?"

Sierath's laugh was soft, but it echoed with layered meaning, like the distant tolling of a bell heard across lifetimes. He drifted past the God with no reverence, his form blurred at the edges as if even time refused to pin him in place. "You worry too much."

Kairon didn't move. His eyes followed Sierath with a stillness that could freeze centuries. "What are you playing at, Sierath?" he asked again, this time quieter, sharper. The weight of his words pressed down like gravity. "What have you done?"

Sierath paused as if listening to something only he could hear, a whisper from the strings of fate, a secret in the pulse of time. "I didn't write the prophecy," he replied calmly. "I only interpret the knots it leaves behind."

Kairon's gaze narrowed. "Don't play coy with me. You saw how this ends."

"I did," Sierath said with a nod. "And yet... every time the dice roll, they fall a little differently. Fate shifts. People make choices. But there is one constant, no matter the version. No matter how Arden bleeds or how she breaks, she always finds her way."

His voice dropped, the amusement fading. "Kaelar may have chosen a selfish, wretched wife who left their children to die in the street like vermin, but he gave them both more power than he knew. More than the realm was ever meant to hold. And yet...they're both here."

Kairon's silence deepened, but the tension in his posture gave him away.

Sierath's eyes gleamed with the sheen of inevitability. "Callen or Arden. The prophecy doesn't say who. So the question isn't whether she will claim her father's legacy." He smiled, but it did not reach his eyes. "The question is whether she will be the last to claim it."

"You wouldn't interfere unless you had something to gain."

Sierath hummed knowingly, trailing his fingers along a mirrored wall. On its surface, images danced: Arden, standing strong, Aezraen at her side, a life yet to unfold. Then the reflection wavered, shattering into countless fragmented possibilities, each more uncertain than the last.

"You shouldn't concern yourself," Sierath murmured, his gaze distant. "The future I showed her won't come to pass anyway."

Kairon's breath caught. Despite his vast knowledge and dominion over time, there was something in Sierath's certainty that unsettled him.

"Why?" Kairon pressed, stepping closer. "What have you done?"

Sierath turned, his golden eyes glinting with amusement. "Let's just say... I simply nudged something along."

Kairon studied him for a long, tense moment. Then, without another word, he vanished, the threads of time pulling him back into his domain.

Sierath sat alone once more in his throne room, the echoes swirling around him, shifting and reshaping.

He let out a breath and leaned back, smirking at the fractured reflections of fate.

"Well," he murmured to himself, "let's see how this plays out."

www.ingramcontent.com/pod-product-compliance
Lightning Source LLC
Chambersburg PA
CBHW071544110726
47908CB00007B/1994